World of Silence

»»»»»»»»»»»

DON COLDSMITH

BANTAM BOOKS

NEW YORK • TORONTO • LONDON • SYDNEY • AUCKLAND

WORLD OF SILENCE

A Bantam Domain Book / March 1992

ISBN 0-553-28945-4

Published simultaneously in the United States and Canada

*Bantam Books are published by Bantam Books, a division of Bantam
Doubleday Dell Publishing Group, Inc. Its trademark, consisting of the
words "Bantam Books" and the portrayal of a rooster, is Registered in U.S.
Patent and Trademark Office and in other countries. Marca Registrada.
Bantam Books, 1540 Broadway, New York, New York 10036.*

PRINTED IN THE UNITED STATES OF AMERICA

OPM   0 9 8 7 6 5 4 3 2

He paused to water his horse. Something white caught his eye on the other shore, and he waded across the riffle to investigate. It was a buffalo skull, bleached white by the sun and wind and water. There were other bones, too, moldering in the sod of the narrow strip along the bank.

He looked up, nearly straight up the cliff's face. Dark, forbidding gray stone, pocked with crevices and holes and small caves. Its spirit could be felt. He felt drawn, however, like bees to flowers in spring.

But wait . . . was there not something else to the story? Why had the People passed at a distance instead of along the river? Thinking back, he could remember his mother's dread of the place. *I do not like its spirit*, she had said.

Standing there on the grassy bank and looking up, Speaks-Not could feel the power of the place's spirit, but little of the dread. Of the legends about this place, were not all favorable to the People? Maybe it was all in one's attitude, how one related to such spirits.

Well, not today. But someday, he would return and explore this Medicine Rock.

Bantam Books by Don Coldsmith
Ask your bookseller for the books you have missed

Part I

Speaks-Not

1

» » »

As a child, Possum never doubted that he was loved. It is strange, perhaps, even to question the amount or intensity of such a nebulous thing as love. It is a thing that cannot be weighed or measured, only felt. It is a thing of the spirit, as real as the spirit of a budding tree, or new grass in the Moon of Greening. Or a sunset, a distant storm over the plain, or the laughter of clear water over white gravel shoals in a prairie river. All of these are things of the spirit, like . . . like love. Not only seen or heard or tasted or touched, but *felt*, in the fullness of spirit that is known to those who love and are loved.

Though one cannot measure the extent of love, it was apparent that there had never been a child among the People whose parents loved him more. This was an idyllic union, admired, sometimes envied by others of the Eastern band. Possum's mother, Otter Woman, had been a Warrior Sister, sworn to chastity until she chose to resign her high position to marry.

She could have continued for several more years if she chose. The honor of this office was great, and she performed it well. The dance steps, the ceremonies, the elaborate costuming, all seemed designed with this young woman in mind. Her tall form and graceful movements were greatly admired by all, both members of the warrior society and the spectators. There had never been a Warrior Sister so skilled, so well suited to the position. Or so beautiful, it was said.

Any one of many young warriors would have gladly died for her, both those in the Elk-dog Society and in the other warrior societies, the Bow-strings and the Bloods. It was no great surprise, however, when she chose Walking Horse, a young man of the Elk-dogs. He came from a prominent family, that of Red Feather, an important chief of the band back in the days of the Blue Paints War. Horse was surely destined for greatness, but remained as humble and friendly as if he did not even know about it.

These two young people had been friends since their childhood together in the Rabbit Society. They learned to swim, run, wrestle, to use weapons, and to ride with skill. When, at puberty, they graduated into the diverse worlds of men and women, these two remained good friends. Others of their age paired off and established their own lodges, but these two seemed in no hurry. Such a friendship needs no proof, but stands by itself.

This one had lasted so long, however, that the entire band was relieved when it came to fruition. Otter Woman resigned her position as Warrior Sister to marry Walking Horse, and the People rejoiced with them and for them. A union based solidly on a friendship that already exists is a good one, the old women told each other. And it seemed true. The love between these two handsome young people shone in their eyes and in their actions. The People laughed and made jokes, but they were pleased, and sometimes envious of this happy couple.

A child of such love will also be loved, and it was so with Possum, who was born the following season. It was not that he was such a beautiful child, for he was not. But he was born with the wide-eyed, knowing stare that some infants have, already old and wise, yet inquisitive about new surroundings. Beyond that, his face was narrow and long, and carried a droll expression of underlying amusement at the strangeness of all things. The first thing that anyone noticed about the child, however, was his hair. Many infants are bald, some have hair that lies close to the head like a fur cap. This hair, nearly three finger-breadths long, stood erect, bristling in all directions. In addition, it was not quite the jet-black color that was familiar to the People. An occasional infant was born with hair of a lighter shade from the influx of blood from outsiders. There had been intermittent contact with Spanish, French, and with other tribes through the generations. Usually the baby hair gave way to a color that was uniformly dark. At least, not noticeably different. It would undoubtedly occur in this case, and the color was no detriment. Many of the People, in fact, proudly traced their family back to Heads-Off, an outsider who brought the First Elk-dog to the Southern band, and became a subchief.

The child would probably be a handsome man, too. Both parents were quite attractive. But that was in the future. Just now his appearance was amusing. Nearly everyone who saw the infant was made to smile. The wide-eyed, solemn, yet amused expression, the bristling hair that stood erect like . . .

"His hair is like that of a porcupine," chuckled Walking Horse.

"No, no," said Otter Woman in mock rebuke. "It does not bristle with quills! It is soft fur, like that of a possum."

So, the child became Possum. It was a baby name, one that would be discarded soon anyway. But it was bestowed with love, which was apparent to all, and especially to Possum.

Such a child, loved by his parents and amusing to all, responds well to the actions of others. Possum smiled early. As others smiled, chuckled, or laughed, he began to do so in response. He regarded everyone as his friend, and related to all with delight. He grew chubby and happy, nourished not only by the breasts of his mother but by the extra nutrition of the spirit . . . the love of all who knew him. He returned that affection with a love of his own, a love for everyone he met. That in itself was ironic, in light of later events in his life.

It was in the Moon of Awakening that he became ill. That, too, was ironic. A small infant, one might suppose, would be most subject to illness in the dark moons of winter. Possum, of course, was sheltered and protected and well cared for, and prospered through that period, even the Moon of Hunger.

It had grown quite warm on several sunny days before the end of the Moon of Awakening. But Cold Maker, saving one last sally for the end, swept down once more, coating the prairie with ice and blowing his chilling breath. It was a chill that seemed to penetrate through and through, clear to the bone. The People hovered over their lodge-fires and waited for Sun Boy to return and drive Cold Maker back to the Northern Mountains and his caves of ice.

And it happened, of course. It has always been so. But the People were weary of winter's cold, and their spirits were vulnerable. The changes, from cold to warm, then cold and warm yet again was too much for mere human flesh to bear. A sickness raced through the camp, striking down old and young alike. A sudden cough, a rapid warming of the skin, and increasing difficulty in breathing. There were those who insisted that two different spirits were involved. One attacked the elders, filling their lungs and choking their ability to move air in and out. The other was limited to the young. It was a particularly severe form of an illness that sometimes struck the children. It, too, was accompanied by a cough, fever, and difficulty in breathing. Some died from this, too, their skins reddened and blotchy, hot to the touch in their last days.

The holy men did not attempt to explain the differences, but only assisted as best they could. Dances, prayers, and chants of supplication. Plant powders in the lodge-fires to produce pungent smoke. Sweat-lodge ceremonies, which seemed to help some with the lung congestion. There were also potions and teas to help the cough and reduce fever.

Despite all these efforts, the Song of Mourning was heard almost constantly. The very old and the very young were hard hit, of course.

One old warrior, half blind and infirm, challenged the spirits that had claimed his grandson. He arrayed himself for battle, painted his face, and walked out into the chill of the night, singing. It was not the Mourning Song that floated back to the ears of the distant listeners, but the Death Song:

> The Grass and the Sun go on forever,
> But today is a good day to die.

It was a statement of intention, a declaration that he intended to die fighting this thing that was killing the People. Perhaps his death would appease whatever spirits were claiming the old and the young.

Finally he was heard no more. His body was found later, where he had fallen facedown, apparently in midstride, fighting for breath as his own lungs failed.

Who is to say what turned the course of the battle? The chants and potions of the holy men, or the Death Song of old Red Snake? Maybe the combined prayers of all the families whose old and young had fallen ill. At any rate, the battle had turned. There were fewer new cases. With the warming days, those still ailing were brought out into the sunlight, and this, too, seemed to hasten their recovery.

But it was too late for Possum. One of the last to be struck down, the infant hovered between life and death. Otter Woman slept little, and then only fitfully and for short periods. Mostly she held the baby, rocking and crooning to him, and praying.

The holy man performed his rituals and prescribed a syrup of plant teas and honey, but he was not encouraging. He said very little, but it was apparent that he was exhausted. It must have been many days since he had been able to rest. Otter Woman felt sorry for him as he finished the ceremonies and shuffled away. But she feared that he had said little because he held little hope for the infant Possum.

The child lay near death for four days and nights, while his mother hovered, rocked, fanned, crooned, and bathed the fevered face. The blotchy roughness of hot dry skin persisted, and it was difficult not to despair. Possum no longer took the nipple well, and her breasts became engorged and tender. She knew that when he began to improve, he must have nourishment, so her breasts must continue to produce. To keep the flow coming, she milked it out with her fingers, catching the flow in a small gourd. She managed to feed a little to the sick infant from the gourd each time, sacrificing the rest to the fire. Maybe that would appease the hungry spirits that were devouring the children. Anyway, it could do no harm.

Of most concern to her was the look on the infant Possum's face. Where he had always worn a look of amused understanding, now his facial expression was one of worry. Of *terror*, almost. He no longer smiled. Day after day, his fever and labored breathing were accompanied by the pained, anxious expression. It was as if the child *knew* of his desperate battle for life, and was uncertain whether anyone could help him. Otter Woman sometimes had the strange feeling that *he* knew what to do but was unable to communicate it to her.

"*Tell me, my child,*" she whispered when they were alone. "*What must I do?*"

The infant would stare into her face with burning dark eyes and whimper softly, nothing more. Then she would fall into an exhausted sleep, and wake again with no answers.

At last came a morning when she awoke, frantic that she had slept too long. There was no sound from the child. His eyes were closed. *He is dead!* she thought, reaching to touch the tiny face. But it was not cold. Cool, yes. The fever had broken. The big dark eyes opened now, and the infant looked straight into her face. There was a new look. The frantic, terror-filled stare that was so frightening had changed. The old look, of amusement and understanding, flickered there. Weakly, but it was there.

Then, that most beautiful of all sights . . . the infant smiled. He had not done so for days. Weeping, she gathered him into her arms and cradled him, rocking gently. Eagerly, he turned toward her and she opened the front of her mothering-shirt to put him to breast. He sucked hungrily, draining the life-giving fluid. Her body responded, and she smiled when the other breast began to leak in unison.

"Your time will come," she whispered softly as she wiped the spill from her shirt. "Our man-child eats again now!"

Walking Horse entered the lodge, and she called to him excitedly.

"Look! The fever is gone . . . he feeds!"

Horse dropped to his knees beside her, and the two clung to each other, their tears of joy mingling while the tiny Possum continued to feed noisily.

"We must give thanks," she murmured.

"Yes. At the Sun Dance . . . we will make a good sacrifice."

"What?"

"I do not know. We must consider. A horse, maybe?"

Otter Woman smiled. "I do not know. We will speak of it later. For now, our joy is enough."

And it was good.

2

» » »

The Sun Dance was especially meaningful that year. The family of the Real-chief had procured a magnificent bull for the ceremonial effigy. Its fur was dark and thick, especially fine for this late in the season. The head had been propped facing the east, and the effigy of logs and brush, with the skin stretched over it, was so lifelike that there was much comment.

That was good, for this must be a special Sun Dance. Everyone had been affected by the illness that had swept through the winter camps of the People, three moons before. The Eastern band had been hardest hit, with nearly every family either in mourning or rejoicing that they had been spared. There were many bittersweet reunions with relatives from other bands, people clinging together and weeping in the sharing of their grief.

Those whose loved ones had been spared, like Otter Woman and Walking Horse, offered gifts and prayers of thanksgiving. Three fine furs they had chosen to sacrifice in appreciation for the survival of their son. An otter, dark and shiny, a thick soft beaver, and a beautifully colored foxskin were offered. Ceremonially, the couple walked to the west end of the brush-roofed medicine lodge where the buffalo effigy stood. Slowly, with great emotion, Walking

Horse tied each skin in turn to the poles of the open-sided lodge. As Otter Woman handed each symbol of their gratitude to her husband, there was a hushed murmur among the onlookers. The People were impressed by the value and the beauty of the gifts. These sacrifices were of the best, befitting the status of this couple, as well as the depth of their gratitude.

Many other sacrifices were made that season. There were beautifully carved and decorated prayer sticks, garments, footwear, a blanket. One warrior gave up his favorite bow to fulfill a vow. He had promised this to atone for the survival of his beloved young wife. Another promised a horse, to be left behind at the end of the last day of ceremonies. Surely the prayers that accompanied such lavish sacrifices reached appropriate deities. It was a time of thanksgiving.

There were, of course, prayers of entreaty also, and vows of penitence if only this would be a better year than the one just past. And above all, there was the basic theme of the Sun Dance: joyous celebration for the return of the Sun, the grass, and in turn, the buffalo.

This was Possum's first Sun Dance, of course. Not yet a full year old, much of his understanding had yet to come. Still, the toddler was impressed by the whole scene. He had never seen so many people before. And, since this was a child who had always loved people and the communication with other human beings, the youngster was in his glory. He wore a broad smile during the entire five days of the celebration.

Of course, he received much attention, as a pleasant child does. His friendly smile, his droll expressions, all attracted more attention. In addition, the story of his having been spared from near death by the fever was well known. Friends and relatives from other bands came to offer congratulations and after-fact sympathy for the dreadful experience. Each of these spent time laughing and playing with the child.

Many times, Otter Woman answered the same question.

"Why is he called Possum?"

Patiently, she explained. The reason was not so evident now. His hair had grown darker and longer. It was long enough, in fact, that it was possible to begin to plait the locks after the manner of the People. Slender strips of otter skin were braided into the plait, to lengthen and fill out the total effect. The otter strips would be worn until his own hair was long enough to complete the effect. This made Possum look even more like a wise old man. It also, however, completely destroyed the reason for his baby name. For a while, Otter Woman explained it to each questioner. Finally, she decided it was useless. One who had not seen the infant's appearance simply could not understand.

"It is only a name," she would reply now, and that seemed to suffice. For her, he would always be Possum, her baby, anyway. Besides, at his First Dance at the age of two years, he would receive a new name.

Meanwhile, she would continue to rejoice in the fact that he was *alive*. What a blessing, to have come so close to losing him. *Aiee!* She shuddered at the thought, and held him close again, as if she would never let go.

He was beginning to walk some now, which was worrisome. All the confusion and excitement of the Sun Dance, the hundreds of people milling around day and night, the horses and dogs. . . . Otter Woman was anxious lest the toddler wander off and be stepped on in the excitement. She need not have worried . . . all of the People looked after all children, their own and others'. She knew this, but this child was *hers*. People smiled at her maternal protectiveness, and understood. She had nearly lost this child.

Walking Horse was pleased at the child's reactions to the entire Sun Dance celebration. Possum seemed interested in watching, and not in the least alarmed

by all the noise and confusion. There was always a
great deal of yelling and shouting, especially around
the area where impromptu horse races were always
taking place. Many infants were frightened by this
noisy pastime, but not Possum. He watched the pro-
ceedings with the same delight that was evident in
everything he observed.

At last, the Sun Dance was over, and the bands
went their separate ways. It was necessary to do so.
The People had prospered in recent generations, and
had grown. It had been a time of relative peace, since
they had become allies with the Head Splitters, their
former enemies. That was long ago, now. The two
nations had joined against a greater foe, the Blue
Paints from the north.

With no enemies, both nations had prospered.
With no casualties in battle, population had in-
creased, and larger seasonal hunts were possible. The
Head Splitters were frequent visitors, often taking
part in the Sun Dance of the People, since they had
none of their own. But the increase in numbers at the
Sun Dance led to other problems. The grass needed
for the hundreds of horses that gathered each season
became scarce very quickly. Likewise, there was a
limit to availability of food and water. Hundreds of
people require a great quantity of food, and game
soon became scarce.

Once, it was said, the gathering for the Sun Dance
lasted nearly a full moon. Now, it was necessary to
split up and move apart to avoid a shortage of food
and grass for the horses. The first of the big lodges
came down the day after the final ceremonies were
completed. The Mountain band was the first to go.
Theirs was the longest journey. By evening, however,
the Red Rocks had headed west in their long, ragged
column, their baggage piled on pole-drags. The visiting Head Splitters accompanied them, since their ter-
ritories more closely approximated each other.

The Southern band was in no hurry to go, since the

gathering was in their own range this season. They began to pack in a leisurely fashion.

The Eastern band, too, had a shorter distance to travel, but they began preparations. They had been, for many generations, the butt of ethnic jokes. Those of the Eastern band were regarded as foolish people, bad luck people. No one knew how it had started . . . possibly because of their slightly different terrain and proximity to the woodlands. Anyone who found himself in a ridiculous situation was sure to be teased, even in the other bands. A man who had been bested in a horse trade, for instance, might overhear a conversation: "Well, you know, his grandfather was of the Eastern band."

There were ribald jokes and stories about the Eastern band. The first horses they obtained, for instance, they led around for a long time before they learned that they were to be ridden. In the other bands even now, a common remark concerning a lame, blind, or otherwise useless horse might be: "Maybe you can sell it to the Eastern band."

There had been a concerted effort on the part of Red Feather, their great leader, to live down this reputation for foolishness. He had met with some degree of success, and gained respect, but it was not complete. The band still worked hard to avoid the jibes that were so quick to come. It was good not to be the last to arrive for the Sun Dance: ("They just found their way here.") Or the last to leave: ("Are they *still* not organized?")

So, by common understanding and generations of slighting remarks, it had become custom. The Eastern band would strike their lodges not first or last, but somewhere between. They were ready to depart shortly after Sun Boy reached the top of his run.

"Where do we camp tonight?" asked Otter Woman. She lifted young Possum to the back of one of the dependable old pack mares and tied him in place.

"Medicine River," Horse answered. "So they say, anyway. It is good. There should be water and grass."

"Not at the Rock?"

"No, no."

"Good. That place bothers me."

Walking Horse laughed.

"It bothers many people. That is why people avoid it."

Medicine Rock had a big part in the tradition of the People. It was there, it was said, that Eagle, the great storyteller of long ago, had spent a winter with Old Man himself, while his broken leg had healed. Many did not believe it. The place had always had a reputation for supernatural happenings, however, even before that. There was no doubt that its spirit was strange. It had been of benefit to some, accounting for Eagle's survival in the old legend.

Then again Medicine Rock had been the site of the final defeat of the invading Blue Paints. By the combined strength of the medicines of two young holy men, one of the People and the other from the Head Splitters . . . It was unclear how it had happened, but those two caused a mighty herd of buffalo to push the enemies over the cliff to their deaths.

Since that time the People had avoided the area. The brooding appearance of the gray stone, already noted for strange spirits, added to the knowledge that many enemy spirits had departed from human bodies in that place. There were some who professed to be unafraid. But when the time came to exhibit courage, even they were hesitant. Why take chances? one asked offhandedly. There were better places to camp or to hunt.

The traveling band passed the cliff on the other side of the river, perhaps hurrying the horses a little to be far away by the time darkness fell. Three young men, goaded by the bravado of their inexperience, left the column to ride nearer the river and observe the face of the Medicine Rock cliff more closely.

They soon returned. No special reason, they insisted. A cliff is simply not very interesting. They raced forward to join the head of the column. Older and wiser people smiled at the folly of youth. They knew quite well that without the forbidding spirit of that rocky wall, those three youths would have spent all day exploring it.

They camped that night some distance to the east of the Medicine Rock. It was a beautiful camping place, downstream far enough to be free of the oppressive thoughts that clung to this stretch of Medicine River. Maybe it only seemed that the People stayed closer to the camp fires that evening, huddling near the warmth that was not really needed on this warm summer night.

Next morning they moved on toward the River of Swans, where they would camp for the summer. Otter Woman was glad to be moving away from the place. She felt somehow that its mysteries were linked to the future of her child, swaying happily on the back of the roan mare.

3

» » »

It was autumn before they began to suspect that something was wrong. The Eastern band had experienced an uneventful summer, and were in the process of deciding on a site for winter camp.

There was always a variety of opinion, and various people were quite vocal about their preferences. Some liked the edge of the woodlands to the east. Timber served to break the wind and give shelter from the full force of Cold Maker's chilling breath. Lodges erected on the south, or downwind side, of even a small area of brush and trees gained much in shelter.

The major disadvantage to the wooded area east of the River of Swans was the risk of attack by the Shaved-Heads. These were a nation of fierce and warlike people, partly grower and partly hunter. The shaved heads of the men provided the descriptive hand-sign that expressed their name. A single roach of hair was left standing from front to back, with the sides shaved. These people bitterly resented any intrusion into their woodlands. Traditionally, it had presented little trouble for the People, who were oriented to a nomadic existence on the plains anyway. But the proximity of the Eastern band, and their tendency to make foolish moves . . . *aiee*, one must not think so! This was part of the argument, especially for those opposed to such a winter site.

The location that was gaining favor in the band was to the south of their usual range. There, great areas of scrub oak bordered on open tallgrass prairie. The oaks were especially desirable as a windbreak, it was argued, because they kept their dead leaves on the twigs for most of the winter, providing better protection from the north winds. In addition, the more southern location would provide a milder winter.

"The birds know that!" declared one old woman indignantly, pointing to the long lines of migrating geese, all pointing southward.

Perhaps the best argument for some, however, was that there was less risk of attack by any who might live there. The People were not especially fearful by nature. Since the coming of the horse and their resulting expertise with its medicine, they had held their own with any nation on the plains. Discretion, however, is the better part of valor. *One does not seek trouble*, an old saying of the People observes, *for enough will seek him.*

Ultimately, a southern site among the scrub oaks was selected. It would look out on grassland, the heritage of the People, yet still furnish shelter from the wrath of Cold Maker. Otter Woman was preparing their belongings for travel, packing and arranging, while she glanced from time to time at the play of the children.

There were several of them, ranging in age from a mere toddler or two, to a spirited girl, perhaps four summers old. The girl was mothering the others, directing their play. Otter Woman smiled. It was good to see happy children, learning by their play. In a few years, this child would have a lodge and children of her own. Already she was acting out her role as the woman of her own home.

"Come on, Speaks-Not," the little girl called with a sweeping gesture of her hand.

It took a moment for Otter Woman to realize that the girl was speaking to *her* child, Possum. *How odd*, she thought.

"Why do you call him that, little sister?" she asked, puzzled.

The girl shrugged. "He never speaks," she explained as the children continued play.

"But he is only a baby," Otter Woman explained.

"True," agreed the girl cheerfully. She ran to rejoin the others.

Otter Woman was thinking rapidly. Much as she wished she could keep him a baby, he was not. But what *should* he be doing at this age? She must think about it. . . . The child had been conceived in the Moon of Falling Leaves. She smiled at the memory, a warm sunny day with the cottonwoods their brilliant yellow and the tall prairie grasses sending up their bright seed-heads. . . . But no matter. Possum had been born during the Moon of Thunder. A cooling rainstorm had swept across the prairie. It was good, because the weather had been hot and muggy for days. The storm had cooled the night and made her labor more comfortable. *Thank you, Rain Maker,* she had whispered.

Possum had been eight or nine moons old, then, when they nearly lost him with the fever. *Aiee,* how frightening! But now, he was some four moons past his first year. *Should* he be speaking? She tried to remember other children whom she had observed. When had they begun to speak? Her younger brother . . . but she had been only a child herself then, and could not remember.

She mentioned the question that was in her mind to Walking Horse, but he seemed unconcerned.

"Some speak sooner than others, I suppose. Does he not make sounds?"

"Yes, of course."

The child had made sounds before his illness, and still did, to some extent. It was difficult to remember. Many of the sounds of Possum's vocabulary were limited to grunts when he wanted something—a drink of water, another bite of food.

"Why should he speak?" Horse asked jokingly. "He has everything he could want!"

"It is not funny, Horse," scolded Otter Woman. "I am made to think that something is wrong."

"But what? He is fat and happy, and growing well!"

"Yes, but . . . *aiee*, let us watch him closely. We must talk to him often, try to teach him words."

They tried, but their efforts were disappointing. Most attempts resulted in more gutteral grunts, quite similar to all his other noises.

"Never mind," advised Otter Woman's mother. "He will talk when he is ready."

Otter Woman remained unconvinced. *Something is wrong,* she told herself as she watched him at play with the others. *I must find it.*

It was after the move to winter camp that she began to see the problem in its true light. She had become aware that a child or two in the group where Possum played were younger, but speaking more. Still, not everyone grows alike. It was puzzling to her that sometimes Possum was responsive to the others at play, sometimes not. *What is it that makes the difference?* she asked herself. *Why* does he respond only a part of the time? And why only with the grunting sounds that were becoming so worrisome to her?

Finally there came a day when she began to realize the extent of the trouble. Possum had paused in his play to look over at his mother. Otter Woman smiled and he smiled back. Just as he did so, Far Dove, the mothering-girl, called to him. The girl was quite close, but he showed no reaction at all. She spoke again, but as she did so, touched his shoulder. Instantly he nodded eagerly, and turned to join the others in some new game. What . . . how was it different when he was *touched*?

Otter Woman puzzled over this for a long time. Why should the touching make a difference? She continued to watch. When Possum was *looking* at the one who spoke, it seemed to make a difference, too. By that evening, she thought that she understood. But she must be sure. This was a very serious discovery.

She selected a choice bite of one of Possum's favorite delicacies, a confection made of pounded hackberries and dried meat, held together with tallow.

"Come, little one," she called, "here is a treat for you!"

Intentionally, she did so while he looked elsewhere. The child showed no response whatever. Again she called, now more loudly.

"Here, Possum! Come and get your favorite bite!"

Again, there was nothing. She waited now until he turned and looked at her. Without speaking, she extended the tidbit, and the child ran to her, grunting eagerly as he reached for it.

Otter Woman did not know whether to be happy or sad. She had solved the riddle of Speaks-Not, but the answer was not good.

Walking Horse returned to the lodge to find her crying.

"I have learned why Possum does not speak," she told him.

"Why?"

"He speaks not because he hears not."

"But he makes sounds!"

"Yes. But he does not hear the words of others."

They experimented at great length, speaking or even shouting, both near and far, with Possum watching them or not. To Possum this was an amusing game. Each try, however, verified the finding of Otter Woman. The child could hear nothing at all.

"Maybe it will come back," suggested Walking Horse.

"No," she said slowly, "I think not."

"But why?"

"It is a trade, a bargain," she told him.

"I do not understand."

"Nor do I. But think when he was so sick with the fever, and almost died? We prayed for him to live."

"True, and our prayers were answered," said Walking Horse.

"For his life, yes. But his hearing was taken in exchange. The spirit that wanted his life was persuaded to take only his ears."

"Aiee!" said Walking Horse softly. "Is that it?"

"I am made to think so."

"Can it be cured?"

They consulted the holy man, he who had treated the fever. The holy man examined young Possum at length and finally shook his head.

"There is nothing I can do."

"But your gift is one of great power, Uncle. You saved his life!" protested Walking Horse.

"That is true," admitted the old man, "but there is something that you must understand, my son."

He paused a moment, and then spoke to the couple very slowly and gently.

"Part of my gift, my medicine," he said, "is the knowing of when not to use it."

"And that is now?" asked Otter Woman, a little sharply. "You will not even try? You tried before, when he was dying!"

The holy man nodded, a little sadly. "Yes. Then, there was a slight chance. Now, there is none. I have seen this before, with this sickness of the children."

"But—" began Walking Horse, but the holy man waved him to silence.

"One time *never* to use my gift," he said flatly, "is when I know it will not work. I am sorry." He turned away, then paused to turn back for a moment. "Yet, as you have said, he *is* alive."

4

» » »

Speaks-Not. The name stuck. It was not intended as ridicule, or even unkindness. It was simply a way to designate an individual from others. It was soon known to all that Speaks-Not did not speak because he did not hear.

"We must use hand-signs as we talk," his mother insisted. And so it was.

In many cultures, in most, perhaps, and at any time in history, a loss of hearing would have been a great handicap. Speaks-Not was fortunate, then, to have been born at the time and place that he was. Any of the many nations that peopled the Great Plains could communicate with any other, through the universal hand-sign language. It had been a necessity for trade. Simple and effective in use, the hand-signs were understood by groups using dozens of tongues and dialects, who did not and would never understand each other's spoken words. Speaks-Not, then, had arrived in a world where communication could be carried out even if *no one* ever spoke. Everyone had the ability to speak with the signs. It remained only to encourage it.

He learned quickly. Otter Woman had been quite correct in her assumption that this was a child of high intelligence. Other children, too, learned hand-signs more quickly because they were being used. It

was like a game, and none of the children in the
Rabbit Society were even aware what was happening.
They were becoming fluent in the use of hand-sign
talk. In later years it was noted that a whole generation of the Eastern band had become exceptionally
skilled at hand-signing. Many of these became traders, storytellers, and leaders in diplomacy because of
this extra advantage.

For now, however, no one was thinking of such far-
reaching effects. It was only that one of their number,
Speaks-Not, used hand-signs exclusively. To talk
with him, it was necessary to use the signs. No one
thought much about it. It was merely a fact of life,
like coming inside the lodge if it rained.

The adults, too, found it interesting, amusing,
even, to talk with a small child in hand-signs. In the
learning system of the People, all adults felt a responsibility to any child, and to his need to learn. For this
child, it was no different. When the time came for
the Rabbit Society to learn the dance, some wondered if Speaks-Not could hear the rhythm. This
proved no problem.

"I am made to think he feels the beat of the drum,"
his mother observed.

It seemed to be true. The rhythm and cadence of
this child's steps were as true as those of any child in
the band. He seemed to sense the vibrations of the
drum by means other than his ears. Through his skin,
perhaps, the tingle of the vibrating, throbbing drum
entered his senses. In this way, Speaks-Not was able
to participate as fully as the others in the ceremonies.
He, too, could feel the primeval heartbeat of the
world, the pounding of the sea, the boom of the thunder, through the rhythmic beat of the ceremonial
drums.

When it came to instruction in weapons, Speaks-
Not was at no disadvantage at all. He became adept
at the throwing-club, hunting rabbits with the best.
When they graduated to the bow, he proved skillful
at that, also.

Without realizing it, the youngster began to depend more on observing color and motion than the others. Since he did not hear, he did not realize that the others were depending on the sounds of birdcalls, rustling leaves, or the snort of a suspicious deer, still unseen in a thicket.

There was one who did realize, an old man, well past his prime. He had held a reputation as an expert tracker in his day. His name told his story: Tracks-Well. He watched the youngster as he grew and learned. It had been many years since the tracker had helped with instruction in the Rabbit Society. His stiffening joints and aching bones made it difficult to keep up with the lively children.

But this was a special case. It was not that time yet, but some day, he knew, there would come a time when these youngsters would take part in organized hunts. It would be necessary to communicate, with shouts occasionally, but surely with birdcalls and animal sounds. No one else seemed to notice that problem ahead. This bright and capable boy would be at his biggest disadvantage yet when that time came. To face the situation in its worst light, it must be admitted that Speaks-Not would never be a reliable hunter in an organized group hunt. He would be unable to follow the signals of the others.

With this in mind, the old man resolved to help the boy compensate. He would help him develop the powers of observation that make a keen tracker. Tracks-Well had a theory that his own gift, the expertise for which he was admired and envied, was not merely a gift. Certainly not a gift like that of the holy man, a gift of the spirit. No, the gift of the tracker was that of the ability to observe and interpret. Tracks-Well had a hunch that anyone could do it, if he would pay attention. It was something that could be developed, encouraged. Maybe all "gifts" could, he sometimes thought, even those of the spirit. But no matter . . .

He approached the instruction of young Speaks-

Not very carefully. He did not want to make the boy feel different from the others. Unless, of course, he could be made to feel superior. That was not out of the question, if the youngster was as bright as he suspected.

Tracks-Well started by recruiting several of the children for a tracking lesson. At this age, both boys and girls learned the same skills. The entire session was carried out within a bow shot of the camp. He called attention to small things . . . a red-winged blackbird on a nest that he had noticed. She flew off in alarm, while her brightly colored mate loudly scolded and threatened. He was able to show them the eggs.

"There are two kinds of eggs," observed one girl.

"Yes"—Tracks-Well was careful to use both words and signs—"the white one with brown spots belongs to the redwing. The bluish egg is another."

"*Aiee!* They share a lodge, Uncle?"

"No. The other bird sneaks in to leave the egg for the redwing to hatch."

"She leaves her child for another to raise?"

"Yes, it is so."

"What bird does this, Uncle?"

"The little brown bird that follows the horses and the buffalo."

It was a matter of great wonder. The children were interested, but one boy was impatient.

"What has this to do with tracking?" he demanded.

"Ah, yes." The old man nodded. "It has everything to do. Tracking is to notice and learn."

Some were alert and impressed, but the questioner was not.

"Suppose," the tracker continued, "you come upon such a nest. The mother still sits on the eggs. You know that nothing has passed by to disturb her lodge. And see her warrior husband? He puts on a great show . . . much flying around and fluttering. That would show that an intruder is near."

"The one who leaves her young?"

"No, no. That one is stealthy. She would not disturb the owners of the lodge. I was thinking of a larger intruder. A deer, a bear, a man, maybe."

The lesson continued, with turtles on a log in the stream. The little group crept close enough to see without disturbing the creatures. There were six, of varying sizes, sunning themselves in the warm afternoon.

"See, some are dry, one is wet. What does that tell us?"

"The one has just joined them?" asked a boy.

"Yes! What more?"

"The others have been there longer. Long enough to dry!"

"And?"

"And they have not been disturbed," signed Speaks-Not, "for a long time."

"It is good!" replied the tracker.

He was delighted. As he had suspected, the boy was a keen observer, and if he continued to take instruction well, could be helped much.

At length the group began to lose interest. It was enough for the day, and they headed back toward the lodges. Some of the children hurried ahead. Speaks-Not paused by the side of the path, looking at the ground.

"What is it?" asked Tracks-Well as he approached.

"The ants. They hurry to repair their lodge where someone stepped."

It was true. An anthill, scattered by a hurrying moccasin, lay in disarray. There was a frantic scurry of excitement, with workers beginning to rebuild already. A light was dawning in the eyes of Speaks-Not, shining with excitement. He pointed and signed again.

"We can tell that someone just passed here!"

The old tracker nodded, pleased. This was going well.

"When?" he asked.

The boy looked puzzled for a moment. Only a moment, though, before he smiled.

"Just now." There was interest, almost mischief in his eyes. "If it were longer, they would have their lodge repaired."

"Right! It is good."

Now, he must encourage, but not push too hard. He continued, cautiously.

"There are some," he signed, "who look but do not see. You are one who sees. It is good!"

The boy smiled and ran off ahead among the lodges. Tracks-Well was quite pleased with the afternoon's progress. He would continue. It had been some time since he had felt so much satisfaction over anything. Even his stiff old bones felt better about the world.

There was no reason why this boy, Speaks-Not, could not become a very skilled hunter and tracker. Already, he was observant. Yes, to be sure, Tracks-Well reflected, there are many different kinds of gifts. From this one, something had been taken away, but maybe something had been given, too. The boy certainly had the gift of observation. While he did not speak or hear, he could *see*!

5

The skills of young Speaks-Not expanded rapidly. There were others, too, who took an interest. Stone Breaker, the weapons maker, taught him to work the flint. He learned to choose the best slab of blue-gray flint, how to strike flakes from the edge with a hammer-stone. Then, to press fragments from the edges with a tool made of a tine from a deer's antler, to shape and sharpen.

The boy managed to produce some quite adequate scrapers and knives, even a spear point that impressed his tutor. But his heart was not in it. He wanted to be out in active pursuits with the others. He did not yet realize that he was receiving special instruction. Various of the People, seeing that this boy would face problems not shared by the others, were attempting to help prepare him. Since he did not remember a time when he had the ability to hear, however, Speaks-Not did not miss it. He did not think of himself as being deficient in any way. And, while this was a healthy attitude, it raised another problem for him.

Like all youngsters, Speaks-Not was quite attentive to that which interested him, and bored with that which did not. He saw himself as a skilled hunter and warrior in a few years. Consequently he was eager for the instruction imparted by Tracks-

Well. The sedentary vocation of Stone Breaker, though perhaps more suited to his limitations, did not hold his attention. The weapons maker understood this, but was determined to give him at least a working knowledge of his craft. There might come a time when Speaks-Not would welcome that bit of experience.

There were others, too, who took a special interest in this boy. It was not from any sense of pity, but only that this is how things are, and they must be dealt with. And it was in this spirit that Speaks-Not accepted the extra help, not even realizing that it was out of the ordinary.

There was one, however, whose company he appreciated. Far Dove, the little girl who had mothered the others at play, seemed attached to him from the first. Though she was a season or two older, they were practically inseparable. With an uncanny instinct, she was able to foresee circumstances that would bring about potential problems. Thus she would quietly forestall them. Some children have this ability quite early, and it is apparent that they will become people who are loving and caring. Others, unfortunately, will never learn it, and remain children emotionally.

This relationship, however, was one that seemed a gift of the spirit. These two understood each other, as a couple will who have been together for many winters. Dove was not obvious about it, but quite matter-of-fact, never patronizing or belittling. She seemed to accept their relationship as a duty, but a pleasant duty that pleased her and brought a rewarding sense of accomplishment.

The People watched this relationship develop with pleased amusement. Long before the children came of age, it was assumed that they would establish their lodge together some day. For now, it was amusing to see them playing together, mimicking the occupations of adults as they prepared for adulthood.

Otter Woman, though she remained concerned for

her firstborn, gradually came to be more comfortable with his hearing loss. Walking Horse teased her about her little bit of jealousy over Far Dove, and that helped to put it in proper perspective. She was able to laugh about it and enjoy watching the young pair.

Then, she became pregnant again and a small girl-child was added to their lodge. There was less time, now, to be concerned with the special problems of Speaks-Not . . . he would always be "Possum" to her. The baby girl needed her more now than Speaks-Not did. It was actually good, she told herself, that she could rely on young Far Dove. Even so, there was a twinge of maternal guilt that she could do no more for him. Maybe it was supposed to be so, she reflected.

In due time, the children of the Rabbit Society grew old enough to learn new hunting skills. Speaks-Not was perhaps twelve summers old when those who had been instructing them decided to organize a hunt. The band had hunted well, and there was no real need that fall. This hunt would be primarily for the instruction of the young. Their quarry would be elk. A scant half-day's travel from the camp was an area frequented by a band of elk.

Their migration patterns were more predictable than those of buffalo. The great buffalo herds moved over far-flung distances, following the seasons. South in winter, then starting back to the north in the spring with the greening of the grasses. No one really knew how far these migrations might take them. It was enough that they were available to hunt each spring and fall as they passed in thousands through the grasslands of the People.

Elk, however, moved in a pattern of only a few days' travel. If not hunted intensively, they could be found in the same area again. Their movements, in fact, were much like those of the People—a few days' travel to the south for the winter, back to the north each spring.

This season the scouts, or "wolves," of the Eastern

band had watched the elk herd carefully. There were a number of young hunters who were ready for the experience of an organized hunt. A good winter's supply of buffalo meat was already drying on the racks or stored in the lodges. If the elk hunt was successful, it was good. There would be extra meat and robes to trade to the growers for corn, beans, and pumpkins. If not, it was no great loss, and the experience would be valuable. It would involve perhaps a dozen or fifteen youngsters, mostly boys, but a few girls. Many of the girls had become women, their child-bodies blooming into softly rounded curves in all the right places.

Women of the People were traditionally beautiful . . . tall, long-legged, and well formed. With these changes, many of them left the shooting and hunting skills behind, concentrating on the skills of the homemaker. There was no pressure to do so. It was a matter of choice. A woman could become a warrior if she wished. Most did *not* wish, because they were now drawing the attention of young men a few seasons older. It was exciting, flattering, and they began to pair off within a few more seasons.

In the case of Far Dove and Speaks-Not, she had begun her spurt of growth. It was apparent that she would be an attractive woman. Her young male companion, however, would not mature for another few seasons. This is the way of things. She was nearly a head taller, and much shapelier, and they made an odd-looking couple. They were amusing to watch, and some of the People wondered whether their friendship could survive this.

They need not have worried. Far Dove had long possessed the maturity to handle such situations. The two actually found amusement themselves in little personal jokes between them about the different rates of their physical changes. Meanwhile, the girl managed to fend off any serious suitors, though their efforts to impress her were sometimes quite flattering.

She continued her practice with the bow. She had

no ambition to become a warrior-woman like the legendary Running Eagle. It was merely the consequence of her ongoing relationship with Speaks-Not. For now, they would hunt together.

Therefore, as plans for the hunt developed, she was one of the girls who elected to take part. There was one other, a burly young woman whose mannishness had long been noted. No one was surprised that she chose the role of the hunter.

There was much excitement among the young hunters, much preparation of weapons, much boasting by some. Older members of the band watched all this with amusement.

"This will separate the men from the boys," observed one old man.

"Yes," agreed his friend, taking a slow puff at his pipe. "But look—there are boasters and there are doers. This will separate them, also."

The hunting party set out well before daylight. There was a special ceremony, and the holy man sang the Wolf Song, a prayer for success in the hunt.

Young Speaks-Not was fairly trembling as they left the lodges and started along the trail. The morning was chilly, but his trembling was mostly from excitement and anticipation. Very soon, however, he found that the trembling had stopped. The leaders of the hunt were setting a punishing pace, and it took all his effort to keep up. In the dim starlight, he kept his eyes on the shoulders of the youth in front of him, and struggled on.

They had traveled a great distance by the time Sun Boy thrust his torch over Earth's rim. The leaders called a rest stop, and the exhausted youngsters dropped to sitting or squatting positions.

"*Aiee,*" signed Far Dove, "they travel fast!"

She dropped to sit beside him.

"They only do it to teach," Speaks-Not answered.

"Yes, but we already know that it is possible to travel fast."

They laughed together, and began to relax as they

caught their breath. It was all too soon that the signal came back down the line. The party was moving on.

The sun was well up when they paused again. The leader gathered them around him.

"We will wait here," he said. "Our wolves will join us."

It was only a little while until one of the wolves who had been following the elk came down the ridge and approached. Everyone rose eagerly.

"Sit down," he gestured. "I will tell you of this."

They did so, and he went on to explain the hunt. Far Dove signed in turn to her companion.

"The elk are in the meadow over the ridge there," the scout explained. "Maybe thirty—"

His explanation was interrupted by a ringing call, the bugling sound of a bull elk searching for a mate.

"Ah, that is what I was about to say." The instructor smiled. "It is the rutting season, and the bulls may be dangerous, so be careful. Now, we will go around the shoulder of this hill, and spread out across the mouth of the valley. The other wolves will drive them toward us. Come."

He turned to lead the way around the hill, then paused for a moment.

"No talking, from here on," he reminded. "Now, you also see that we are moving *into* the wind? That is so the wind carries their scent to us, not ours to them."

They moved carefully into position behind rocks and clumps of brush, taking places a few paces apart. The animals would run between them.

"Try not to shoot each other," the teacher admonished in signs as they settled in.

The young hunters smiled to themselves, knowing quite well not to laugh aloud. Now came a distant shout and the sound of hoofs.

Speaks-Not glanced over at Dove, a few paces away, and she smiled.

"They have started," she signed. "The hunt begins!"

6

» » »

Speaks-Not was already beginning to realize that there were problems here. Apparently Far Dove and the others had heard distant sounds. He had not, of course, but no matter. He would watch Far Dove for signs, and he certainly could shoot at any animal that came close enough.

He looked across the little valley, its lush grass dotted with bushes here and there. There was some motion . . . yes! A yearling calf trotted into view, head high, and then retreated the other way, disappearing into the tall real-grass. He glanced over at Far Dove, but she was watching up the meadow and did not see him.

That, he realized, was to be the problem. They could not constantly maintain eye contact. Both must watch elsewhere, too. But now he was distracted . . . there was a tremor, a sensation, which he felt rising from the earth through his feet and ankles. He was kneeling, and his left knee, where it rested on the ground, also transmitted the feel of buzzing or distant rumbling. It was a vibrating sensation, like the feel of horses running. Then the truth struck him. These running animals were the quarry, the elk herd in the meadow in front of them. The wolves had started the drive, pushing the animals toward the young hunters who waited. He gripped his bow and tried to look everywhere at once. On his left, Lame Bear squatted, waiting. To his right, Far Dove glanced over and their eyes met. She smiled briefly in nervous excitement, and both turned their attention to the front again.

Dove was quite concerned over this situation. She heard the rumble of activity as the animals began to move. She also knew that her friend Speaks-Not could not hear it. How much he could feel through the earth's vibration, she was unsure. It was much like the situation of the dance, she supposed. He had told her that the throb of the drum was exciting, so he must feel it. Could he also feel the rumble of drumming hooves? They must talk of it later.

Her attention was distracted as a yearling cow dashed past. She lifted her bow, but too late. The creature was gone. Another crashed through a fringe of brush, and she loosed an arrow, but knew that she had missed. She could see other elk running, leaping aside as they chanced to encounter one of the hidden hunters. There were shouts now. Her heart beat wildly with the excitement. A cow with a calf at her side loped between Lame Bear and Speaks-Not, closely followed by a young bull. Probably, Dove thought, the cow's last year's offspring. The yearling was closer to Lame Bear, and the youth skillfully sank an arrow just behind the rib cage. For an instant, it appeared that Speaks-Not too would shoot, but he held back. Now Far Dove saw the reason for the half-joking admonition about trying not to shoot each other. The yearling had been between the two young men. The path of each arrow would have been almost directly toward the other hunter. She felt a glow of pride at the way both had handled the moment. Lame Bear had apparently been sure of his target and had successfully downed his quarry. Speaks-Not had held his shot to avoid risk.

The young bull made three spasmodic leaps and fell kicking in the grass. Lame Bear jumped up and ran to finish it off if necessary. Speaks-Not turned to

watch, distracted for a moment. It was then that Far
Dove saw the bull elk emerge from the tall grass in a
low place behind a screen of willow. It was a magnificent animal, as large as a horse, it seemed. The great
antlers must have been as wide as the span of a man's
outstretched arms as he lifted his head and swung it
threateningly. He was excited, disturbed, but certainly did not appear to feel threatened. It was more
as if the animal were looking for an adversary, expecting a fight with all the confidence of past victo-
ries.

Far Dove saw the exact moment when the animal's
searching glance fell on Speaks-Not. The bull paused
only a moment to paw the sod with one front hoof as
he lowered his head and charged. Dove saw the
gleaming tines of polished antlers pointing like so
many lance points toward Speaks-Not's unprotected
back.

"Look out!" she screamed at the top of her lungs. It
was pure reflex, because if she had taken time to
think she would have realized: It was of no use to cry
out, because her friend could not hear her anyway.

"Look out!" she screamed again. She was on her
feet now, fumbling as she fitted an arrow to her bow,
unsure whether to shoot or to run forward, and doing
neither very well.

There were little things about the scene that were
developing before her eyes that she would remember
always. The shiny white tips on the tines of the
bull's antlers. Many of them, for it was a big bull,
with many mating seasons behind him. There was
one strip of skin hanging from an antler. It was a
narrow shred, a remnant of the soft fuzzy coat that
had adorned the budding new antlers through spring
and summer. Now the bull's antlers were hardened
and mature, as hard as bone. Harder, maybe. The animal had polished his rack of weapons by rubbing off
the soft skin against trees and brush. It might have
been, even, that he had already been engaged in battle
for the favors of some of the cows in the band. At any

rate, somehow that narrow strip of unshed skin was more horrible in her memory than any other part of the scene before her. She saw the bull's eyes home in on the kneeling youth's unprotected back as he rushed. The leathery strip swung, bent backward by the wind of the bull's forward motion.

She was running forward now, still yelling her warning, knowing that it would do no good. Lame Bear was standing near his fallen quarry, about to shoot another arrow into the still-kicking body. The shouts of Far Dove finally attracted his attention, and he raised his head. Only then was he aware of the danger. Speaks-Not, in turn, saw the look of alarm in the face of Lame Bear as he looked past at something beyond. There was no time to turn, but Speaks-Not seemed to sense the rush of something behind him. The boy rolled aside, and the bull's momentum carried him past the place where Speaks-Not had knelt. There was only a slashing blow aimed at the rolling figure as the bull faced his next enemy, Lame Bear. Bear's arrow was already fitted to the string, and he raised the bow and released the arrow directly at the charging bull elk.

It was a futile gesture. No part of the forward rush of the animal's charge would be vulnerable to an arrow. The thick skull plate of the lowered head, the massive antlers, the bony shoulders and hard muscles of the forequarters—it might be that a lucky shot with an arrow would stop such a charge, but it would seem unlikely. As it happened, no one ever knew what had become of Lame Bear's arrow. It may have missed cleanly and been lost in the tall grass. . . . Or, maybe it lodged in some part of the bull's muscular frame, to remain there.

Far Dove saw and heard the tremendous impact as the great bull struck Lame Bear. He had no time even to start to run. His body was skewered, lifted, and tossed high, to descend limply back to the grass. Dove had one fleeting impression of the mighty bull, front legs braced, every hair on his back raised in anger like the hair on a dog about to fight. The massive head swung once more in a gesture of disdain, and the bull lunged forward and disappeared into the open prairie.

Dove and Speaks-Not rushed forward. Lame Bear's eyes were open, and he blinked in confusion, trying to focus as his sight dimmed. Blood trickled from several wounds in his chest and abdomen. "I . . . I . . ." He tried to speak, but the eyes were glazing and they could see that his spirit was slipping away.

"Bear, I am sorry," Speaks-Not signed.

The dying youth showed no sign of understanding. There was a rattle of the last breath in his throat, and then no more breath at all. The two friends looked at each other and back to the dead youth.

"He is dead!" signed Speaks-Not.

Far Dove nodded. It was a frightening thing, to see the lifeless form of a companion who had been with them all their lives. A short while ago he had been laughing and talking, excited over the hunt. Now he lay here, as dead as the elk that lay beside him. His first elk kill . . . and his last.

The sounds of the hunt were fading now, the rumble of hooves receding out onto the plain. There were cries of success, and people ran to look at each other's kills. Speaks-Not and Dove sat silent, taking slight comfort from their nearness.

"*Aiee!* He is dead?" said a surprised voice behind them. It was the leader of the hunt.

Far Dove lifted her eyes and turned to face him.

"Yes, Uncle. He made this kill, but another bull came. . . ."

"I see. . . ."

"It was my fault!" gestured Speaks-Not excitedly. "I should have been watching."

Dove shook her head. "No, Uncle. That is not true. The bull ran at Speaks-Not here, he rolled aside and it ran at Lame Bear, who was standing."

"You saw it all, then?"

"Of course."

The older man drew Speaks-Not aside.

"Look," he signed, "when we hunt, sometimes we are hurt. Bear knew that. He would not blame you."

"But I should have seen, and warned him, Uncle!"

"No, no. Do not think so, Speaks-Not."

But it was apparent that he would. The heart of Speaks-Not was very heavy.

7

» » »

From that time, the day of the elk hunt, there was a noticeable change in Speaks-Not. He had always been different from the others because of his hearing loss. But, he was so active and capable that no one had seemed to notice the difference. Possibly it was because he never considered *himself* different. He did not know a world of sound because he had never experienced it, beyond a few brief moons as an infant. Therefore, he did not miss it. There were few limitations on his activity as he grew up.

Now, he had encountered a real problem, and it had not come out well. The family of Lame Bear was in mourning, and the young hunters, Bear's contemporaries since their earliest days in the Rabbit Society, were numb with disbelief. The hunt had been successful, and they should have been celebrating, talking excitedly of possible invitations to apprentice themselves to the warrior societies. This hunt had been on foot, organized by men of the Bowstring Society. This was the old, conservative group who favored tradition and had a tendency to resist new ways. Many of the young men were attracted to such tradition.

Others, however, were budding horsemen, candidates for the Elk-dog Society, in whose custody rested the mystique of the horse. The elk-dog medicine itself, the silver bit worn by the First Elk-dog, was kept in the custody of a holy man of the Southern band. It was used in tribal ceremonies, of course, but more importantly, it was considered that its custodian must be a member of the Elk-dog Society.

The Blood Society, fiery young radicals by political standards, had had a large part in the history of the People. They had been, at various times, responsible for the near destruction of the Southern band, and for its salvation. There had been a time, it was said, when the Bloods were banished from the tribe for a few seasons. But that was long ago. The Bloods, though they still had a reputation as radicals, had mellowed through the years. In some respects, they were now almost as traditional as the Bowstrings themselves.

Young hunters always looked forward to their coming of age, and the invitations of the societies. This would have been the time, but a dark shadow hung over the camp, due to the tragedy of the elk hunt. It was not that such an accident was uncommon. It was a way of life. A hard, dangerous life by many standards, but not considered so by the People. It was merely the way of things. That a hunter would be gored by his quarry was one of the dangers of being a hunter. Yet this was different, somehow.

The funeral-wrapped body of Lame Bear was lifted to a tree scaffold, along with his favorite weapons and some food to see him safely to the Other Side. The mourning continued. This was very impressive to his young friends, but no less so to the older members of the band. This was a very unsettling thing, the loss of an apprentice hunter on his first hunt. An omen? And for whom? Did this signify bad luck for all the participants of that fateful hunt? The young people denied it to themselves and in their private conversations, but doubts remained. No initiation hunt could be considered a complete success that resulted in a death.

Significantly, though there was no openly stated

policy, there were also no invitations to join warrior societies. It was a time of indecision. It was generally thought by the young hunters that there must be another hunt to neutralize the misfortune of the first. But there was no announcement. No one seemed willing to make a decision.

Speaks-Not was deeply depressed, still feeling the responsibility for the tragedy. He and Far Dove talked much of it, sometimes in vigorous argument.

"It was not your fault!" she signed angrily at him.

"But I could have done something!" he protested. "I was not looking where I should have been. I could have warned him, I could have shot at the bull."

Dove calmed somewhat. It would do no good to shout at him, as she had been doing, because he could not hear her. She must be gentle and logical. She smiled at him.

"Speaks-Not," she signed, "you know that these things happen. You could not know that the bull would come up behind you. No one could. It happened. That is all."

"But because I did not see the elk, Lame Bear is dead. *You* saw it. Bear saw it. No, it is my fault. I did not see."

"You cannot see everything," she protested. "Nor can I. It happened."

"No, Dove, you do not understand. I did not know the bull was coming because I could not *hear*. You heard it, saw it. You called out to me, maybe."

Far Dove said nothing, but was remembering her frantic screams, unable to get his attention. It had been a terrible moment, and she had feared for him.

"I am made to think," Speaks-Not went on, "that I am a danger to others."

"No, no," she protested, but he waved her to silence.

"Yes, I am, Dove. I could not hear your call, I could not hear the rush of the bull, could not feel it until too late. If I had, even, I do not know if I could have warned Bear."

Far Dove was silent, for much of what he said in sign-talk was true. She hated for him to see it. She hated to admit it, herself, because she had always admired his spirit, and believed that Speaks-Not could do anything he chose. Now, it seemed that she was wrong.

"I will never hunt again," Speaks-Not signed.

He rose and left her sitting on the cottonwood log, where they often met to talk together. She started to go after him, but held back. She had no argument to offer. Maybe he would overcome this some day, but for now, there was nothing she could do. Her heart was very heavy.

But wait . . . there were those who could help, maybe. Of course! Tracks-Well, who had taken an interest in the boy. Only now was she beginning to understand the significance of that. The old tracker was feeble now, but it was not his tracking skills that she sought, but his advice. Tracks-Well could talk to Speaks-Not, show him that there is more than one way to hunt elk.

Pleased, she slid from the log and hurried to find Tracks-Well. She stopped before his home, identified by the trail of hoofprints painted across the lodge cover, and tapped on the taut skin.

"Uncle," she called, "it is Far Dove. I would speak with you. May I come in?"

There was the sound of motion inside, and a woman lifted the doorskin and beckoned inside.

Tracks-Well was seated, leaning on his willow backrest and smoking. He nodded a greeting.

"*Ah-koh*, Uncle," she said formally.

"*Ah-koh*. What is it, daughter?" he asked.

She did not know quite how to begin.

"I . . . well, you know of the hunt?"

He nodded. "Yes . . . too bad. You were there?"

"Yes, Uncle. I saw it."

He puffed his pipe a moment, and finally spoke. "What is it you wish to speak?"

"You remember a young man who is called Speaks-Not?"

"Yes, he is a son of Otter Woman and Walking Horse? Is he your friend?"

"Yes, Uncle. Since we were small."

The old tracker smiled. "I thought so. But what? . . ."

"His heart is heavy, Uncle. He thinks this was his fault. The hunt . . . Lame Bear."

Tracks-Well came straight to the point: "Was it?"

"No . . . I . . . I think not. The bull was coming . . ."

Rapidly, she blurted out her story, pouring her troubles before him. ". . . and he said he will never hunt again," she finished.

The tracker puffed two long puffs on his pipe and blew a cloud of bluish smoke that drifted lazily upward to flow out through the smoke hole of the lodge.

"So," he said at last, "maybe it *was* partly his fault?"

"No! I mean—"

She stopped short. She had been denying it, protecting Speaks-Not, but was it not true? Maybe his guilt was justified. Not intentionally, of course, but if he had heard the charge of the bull, or heard her screams of warning, it might have made a difference.

"Maybe," she agreed.

It was a hard thing to accept. How much harder, then, for Speaks-Not.

"Do you remember, when you were smaller," the tracker asked, "and I came to show your friend about the tracking?"

"Yes, Uncle. But what? . . ."

"For this day, little one. As you have learned, Speaks-Not cannot hunt with others. He cannot hear signals, or shouts of warning. But this could not be told to him. He must try it to see why. This, he did."

"But Lame Bear?"

"Yes, that is too bad. My heart, too, is heavy for his

family. But, would it really have made any difference? If someone with hearing had been where Speaks-Not was, would it not have happened the same?"

"Maybe," Dove admitted. "But how can one tell?"

"We cannot," Tracks-Well chuckled, "unless we do it again, and that cannot be. But think now . . . would it have been different if *you* had been standing in the place where Speaks-Not was?"

"I cannot tell. Maybe, maybe not."

"Yes. We can never tell."

"But, Uncle, he says he will never hunt again."

"So I have heard. But it seems unlikely. No, he will hunt again. Maybe not in a hunting party. Would he come to see me?"

"I can ask him, Uncle. May I say you wish to see him?"

"Of course, if that is needed. Do you think he would *not* come?"

"I do not know, Uncle. His heart is very heavy. I will try."

"It is good. If he does not come, we will wait. There is no need for hurry."

She started to turn away, but paused.

"I am made to think," she said slowly, "that he needs this visit soon." Then she smiled. "Or, maybe *I* do. My heart is heavy *for* him, Uncle."

The old tracker watched her go, and admired the swing of her lithe young body. *A fortunate boy, that Speaks-Not,* he thought to himself, *to have such a woman. Aiee,* any man should be proud to have the heart of Far Dove heavy for him. Tracks-Well felt good about it, though. It was too bad about the boy who had been gored. But to teach this one, Speaks-Not, what he must know had taken only one lesson. A hard lesson, yet one that was necessary to the young man. Now, Speaks-Not could settle down to learning the special skills he would require.

8

» » »

"**I**t is true. I will never hunt again!"

The boy was defiant.

"Then it is good," agreed Tracks-Well easily. "It will be as you say." He paused for a moment, as if in thought. "You will become a maker of weapons, then?"

Speaks-Not looked at the old tracker sharply. It was apparent that his thinking had not progressed this far. Tracks-Well waited, amused. He had noted that although the boy had shown talent in the working of flints, his heart was not in it. The tracker had seen the glow in the child's eyes long ago, when he watched the red-winged blackbirds or the ants beside the trail. Tracks-Well had known even then that this youth's keen powers of observation had marked him as a special person. He did not know yet precisely what form the skills would take, but they were there.

"I do not know," signed Speaks-Not. "Maybe so."

At least, he was indecisive now, Tracks-Well noted. Until now, there had been little indication that the boy was willing to think past his stubborn declaration to refrain from hunting.

"Yes," signed the tracker thoughtfully. "It is good to do something, so that one may eat."

"I can hunt for myself!" Speaks-Not gestured impatiently.

Ah, yes, thought the old man. *That is what I wanted to hear!*

"Why, of course!" he signed as if surprised. "It is good that you have thought of this! You are already better than most at watching."

"How do you mean, Uncle?"

"Ah, I remember you as a child, Speaks-Not. We watched the ants together, remember?"

The boy smiled at the memory, and it was good to see the smile.

"I must eat ants, or hunt like they do?" he asked, mischief in his eyes.

Tracks-Well chuckled. "The bear eats ants, so we could, too. But meat is better. So, there are better things to hunt. Deer . . . buffalo."

"Buffalo? That takes many hunters, and horses!"

"Sometimes. But there are many ways to do some things."

Now the boy seemed eager.

"I do not understand, Uncle. Will you tell me of these?"

The tracker seemed to consider for a little while, frowning in indecision.

"I do not know," he signed slowly. "I am old . . . my legs are stiff and slow."

"But you can teach me, Uncle."

There was more apparent indecision, and finally Tracks-Well nodded.

"Well, maybe. We will try."

"Ah, look! Horse tracks!" the old man gestured.

The two had come down to the stream at the suggestion of Tracks-Well, to begin the lessons in earnest.

"Why to the stream?" Speaks-Not had asked.

"There are more tracks. Besides, it is near. We do not have to walk very far."

"But I would learn—" Speaks-Not began. The tracker waved him down.

"Later," he signed. "First, we start here." He

pointed to horse tracks in the soft earth along the stream.

"That is easy," observed Speaks-Not. "A horse came to water."

"Of course. But tell me all you can of the horse."

"Uncle, a horse is a horse. I will not be hunting horses, anyway."

"You might. But for now, look and think. What can you tell me of this animal?"

The boy studied a little while, then began to sign.

"One horse . . . alone . . . not in a hurry."

"Good! How do you know these things?"

"Only one set of tracks . . . walking . . . dung, there . . . it stopped for that, so it was not alarmed. It stopped to crop grass there, at the water's edge."

"It is good," agreed the tracker. "Now, what did it look like?"

"Uncle, I did not *see* it—only its tracks!"

"Of course, but we can tell much." He watched while the boy studied the tracks again.

"A big horse," Speaks-Not finally indicated.

"Tall, or fat?"

"Tall."

"How do you know?"

"His feet do not sink too deeply in the mud . . . he has a long step. The feet are not very big. So, tall and thin."

"Is he fast?"

"*Aiee*, Uncle, I do not know. . . ."

"Look, then . . . the track of the hind foot, there, is on top of that of the front foot. Sometimes ahead, even. A long step, a *fast* horse. Is he surefooted?"

Speaks-Not sighed deeply and started to sign, but then knelt to study the tracks again.

"Yes," he indicated finally. "The right front foot toes out a little, and he tosses it, but it should not bother him."

Good, thought the tracker. He had seen the slight blur of sand at the outer heel of each right front track. The horse was "paddling" with that foot, but his pupil's evaluation was accurate. It would probably be no handicap.

"Now, *when* did he drink?"

Speaks-Not studied the tracks again.

"Early this morning. The sand is drying around the sharp corners of the tracks." He leaned against the trunk of a big cottonwood and smiled mischievously. "The horse was sorrel in color, with a white spot between his eyes. His left ear had a notch in the tip."

Tracks-Well stared in astonishment. The boy was either picking up information that he himself had overlooked, or was behaving in a completely foolish manner. Slightly ruffled, he became stern.

"And can you tell its owner?"

"Of course. It is the gelding of Black Squirrel."

"You are only guessing!"

"No, no, Uncle! Some, yes, but look!" Speaks-Not turned to the bole of the cottonwood and plucked three long hairs from the bark. "See? They are red . . . almost no horse has a red tail except a sorrel. How many tall, thin red horses are there? And Squirrel's gelding has a white spot on his face."

Tracks-Well was pleased, even though mildly irritated that he had not seen it himself. It was largely as his pupil said. Only the last point was a guess, that this particular tall thin red horse was that of the warrior Black Squirrel. Even that was a good guess. Most sorrel-colored horses of the People were shorter and heavyset. Only a few were tall and thin, and this narrowed the guess considerably. But maybe . . .

"How do you know," he asked, "that these red hairs came from the horse that made the tracks? They could have been left on the tree's bark long ago."

"That is true," signed Speaks-Not, "but I am made to think not. No other horse has walked here since the rain, a few suns ago." He paused to touch a leaf of the cottonwood, now yellowing with the season. "See, it is dusty now. But the horsehairs were not." He drew the hairs between thumb and forefinger, and held the hand out toward the tracker. "I did that before I picked the hairs from the tree bark. This is probably the same horse."

Tracks-Well nodded, still a bit disgruntled that the young man was noticing things that he had overlooked. But it was good, he kept reminding himself. That, after all, was the purpose of this teaching. Speaks-Not would need all the powers of observation available to him, since he lacked one, that of hearing.

"It is good," signed the tracker. "Now come, we will talk of other things. Let us sit on the hill, there." He pointed to a grassy knoll where they could overlook the valley and the river.

"It is good," he repeated some time later, when they had made their way to that point and seated themselves on a rocky outcrop. "You look well, notice things not seen by others. You did that as a child, and you must continue to do so."

Tracks-Well paused a little while. He was still a bit out of breath from climbing the knoll, and his left knee was protesting the unaccustomed activity.

"Now, watch a little while, and then we will talk of what you have seen."

That would allow him to catch his breath. There could be no conversation while they watched the valley, because to talk with the signs they must watch each other. He heard the distant cawing of a crow, and caught a flash of motion along the river, far downstream. He glanced at Speaks-Not and saw that he, too, was watching the crows. Good. The young man had spotted them without the advantage of having heard their cries. Three of them, chasing an owl and calling loudly for assistance. Even now, more birds were answering the call, sweeping upstream to help repel the threat.

He touched Speaks-Not to divert his attention.

"Tell me what you are watching."

"The crows."

"Yes. What of them?"

"Three of them . . . they found the owl, and now they chase him. Others come to help."

"It is good. Now, what can we tell from all this?"

Speaks-Not pondered a moment and then brightened. "Nothing else is happening there. No people, no hunting cat or wolf."

"Good! Now let us look at far distances. . . . The open place beyond. There are animals grazing there. What are they? Horses? Buffalo?"

Speaks-Not gave him a quick look, as if to say, *are you serious?* It was a difficult test, because the distance was great. The dark objects against the golden hues of the autumn grass were so far away that their color was lost. Not quite melting together into the blue of distant hills, but far enough to make it impossible to see color. That loss begins only a few bow-shots away, when horses of red, brown, bay, or roan, even spotted animals are indistinguishable. Size becomes more important than color. An elk, grazing with the horse herd, might be overlooked, while a deer or antelope would be smaller. A buffalo larger, of course, but their spirits do not mix well with those of horses, and they stay away.

"I cannot tell, Uncle," Speaks-Not signed now. "Is there a way to tell?"

"Maybe. Look, at great distance; if you can shut out all but what you wish to see . . ."

The tracker drew out of his shirt a scrap of raw-hide, as big as two hand-spans square. It was partly tanned, and stiff to handle, but Tracks-Well rolled it into a tube and tied it with a buckskin thong. The hole through the device was large enough to insert a finger.

"Now, look through this at some of your creatures, there."

Speaks-Not peered through the tube for a moment, and then looked back excitedly.

"How is this, Uncle? They are horses. They look bigger and closer!"

Tracks-Well smiled. "I do not know *how*, only that

it is so. But now, you can see that one cannot always carry such a thing, no?"

"That is true," the boy agreed. "One *could*, but not easily."

"Yes," agreed Tracks-Well. "So, what could be done?"

Speaks-Not pondered, but could not answer.

"What do you always have with you?" asked the tracker. "Your *hands*."

He lifted his hands with fingers spread, and then curled them, nearly closed, into a replica of the tube, one in front of the other. Speaks-Not quickly copied the act, then gestured excitedly.

"It is the same!"

"Not quite," admitted the tracker, "but much handier. Now, try it on the creatures to the left, across the river."

Speaks-Not swung his glance, and studied the far grassland for some time. Finally he turned.

"I cannot tell, Uncle. They are farther away."

"Yes. Do they move?"

"I . . . maybe. But looking through the hands . . . I can see only one thing at a time."

"Good. That is the way with that trick. It takes away something. Now how can we tell if one of those animals moves?"

Speaks-Not pondered a while. "We must see it next to something else," he signed. "A tree, maybe."

"Ah, but there are no trees there!"

The boy nodded, puzzled.

"Then we should plant one!" signed the tracker. He had been toying with a stem of sumac that he had broken from beside him. Now he ceremonially stuck it upright in the sod in front of him. "Really, we need two," he went on, "so here is another." He took a second stick, and placed it a pace closer, sighting carefully across the two toward the dark figures on the distant plain. "Now, look. They point at the animal to the left of the others."

"I see. Then we watch?"

"Or wait, and look again. Maybe we should place another stick . . . there! This one points to the two on the right."

The tracker lay back, relaxing in the autumn sunlight while his pupil sighted across the three sticks. When the young man turned back, Tracks-Well went on with his signing.

"Now, while we wait . . . about the hunt . . ."

"I do not wish to talk of it, Uncle!"

"No, no, not *that* hunt. Just . . . you said you would hunt for yourself?"

"Yes. I can do that."

His manner was defiant.

"Of course," agreed the tracker patiently. "You asked of different ways."

"Yes. Forgive me, Uncle."

Tracks-Well pushed on.

"Now, you can hunt with a horse, but usually the hunters do that with others. The problems would be as you found before. So, you hunt alone, as we are doing now."

"But we are not hunting."

"No, but we could be. If we see game, and the direction it is moving, we could go there and be waiting. It is as we have said. Look, and see, and then see yet more!"

"What if we see no game?"

"Ah, yes! Then we set traps. Snares, deadfalls."

"I have been told of these, Uncle. They are used by others, but not much by the People."

"That is true. Long ago, before the coming of the horse, our people used them. Now we hunt mostly buffalo and elk. But it is good to know the old ways. They might be important. We will talk of such things later. Now, look at your sticks."

Speaks-Not sighted across the two lines of sticks, and looked back, pleased.

"Uncle, the one at the left has not moved. It is a bush or a rock. The others are not where they were. They are animals."

The tracker smiled. "That is true."

"Did you know that already?" the boy asked.

"The bush, yes. I found it yesterday. The others, no. That was just a thing of good luck."

9

» » »

Speaks-Not lay perfectly still. If one does not move, he had learned, he is not seen. The rabbit knows this, and hides from the hawk or from the hunting owl by freezing, motionless until danger passes. Sometimes, of course, he is seen and becomes food for the hawk's young, but this is the way of things. Most of the time, rabbit's people survive by freezing. Much more often, anyway, than if they moved. Usually the rabbit who is caught is one who, in panic, tries to run.

Tracks-Well had urged him not only to learn this, but to practice the skill for future use whenever the need arose.

"See how long you can remain frozen without moving, like the rabbit," the tracker suggested. "It saves his life sometimes. It might save yours."

The main purpose of remaining invisible, however, was that of hunting.

"You can sometimes crawl, in stalking game," the tracker reminded, "but sometimes not. You will not be able to tell whether you are making noise. Dead leaves do much talking."

"They *do*?" It was hard for Speaks-Not to understand this concept. Not until he had lost his chance at a shot several times did he understand the problem. Not only must he avoid warning the quarry

with scent by placing himself *down*wind, but also
with sound. *Whatever that may be,* he thought to
himself. Tracks-Well had certainly been right. It was
more difficult for him to stalk game than for others.

This had led to the tracker's suggestion. "Let the
game come to you!" he advised. "It needs only this
skill, to remain frozen like the rabbit. It can be
learned."

This was a warm spring day, and Speaks-Not lay in
a secluded thicket, watching through an opening into
a little meadow beyond. He had already, through long
days of practice, mastered control of his muscles.
Hardly ever now, did he have the uncontrollable
twitches and spasms that had bothered him at first. It
had been difficult in the beginning to ignore the sudden muscle cramps that would seize his calf or thigh.
His natural reaction would be to grasp the offending
muscle and massage the cramp out of it. It had been
difficult for him to concentrate, to think beyond, to
realize that in a little while the hard knots would
soften and relax and the pain would go. It required
the utmost of concentration. Eventually, he had
learned, and the process of dissociating his thoughts
from the pain came almost naturally.

Even so, it had been even harder for him to tolerate
the minor annoyances that came to one who was absolutely motionless. At first it was amusing to watch
birds and other small creatures, who appeared not to
see him at all. A tiny bird, no bigger than his thumb,
lighted on a twig within an arm's reach and sang
loudly to establish its nesting site. He could not hear
the song, of course, but knew by the rippling of the
tiny throat. He smiled to himself.

Once, he almost lost his resolve in panic when a
real-snake came crawling directly toward him. He
could have gotten up, but after all, that would defeat
the purpose of the exercise. With great difficulty, he
managed to hold to his frozen position. The snake
came closer, then paused as if confused. Speaks-Not
was sprawled full-length on his belly, and the crea-

ture seemed to look directly into his eyes, only a pace or two away. The flickering tongue searched the air, questioning, trying to interpret the unfamiliar situation. This snake was large, as thick as his arm and as long. An old man of a snake, perhaps, one of many summers. He could count the dozen or so rattles at the end of its tail. They were quiet, the quiver of warning not present. The snake was merely wary, not threatened.

For a time, it seemed that they were playing the same game. The snake was utterly motionless except for the flickering black tongue. *How like a tiny flame,* thought Speaks-Not, *except for the color.* He could plainly see the forked tip of the tongue, playing in and out of the mouth, almost more quickly than the eye could see. He could almost follow the thoughts of the creature as it cautiously considered the confrontation.

Finally the snake seemed to reach a conclusion. It began to move again, sliding smoothly in a fluid motion that seemed like no motion at all. Its course was not away from him, or quite toward, but a sort of diversion from its previous course. Through the stems of dogwood in front of him, past a clump of dry last-season's grass, past his face at only an arm's length. Speaks-Not rolled his eyes to the left as far as he could to watch the snake as it passed. He dared not move, other than that. The portion of the snake's body that he could still see grew smaller, narrower, and finally the patterned colors of the creature's body were followed by the rings of the rattle, the color of untanned rawhide. Then it was gone.

Now what? he thought. How would he know when it would be safe to move? Well, he had intended to spend much more time here anyway. He would simply continue his motionless vigil, and let the real-snake continue with whatever it is that may occupy a real-snake's afternoon.

He almost jumped in spite of himself when he felt the body of the snake gliding smoothly past his leg.

Was it possible that the creature would try to crawl *under* him, as it would a rock?

He had barely time to note that distressing thought when he felt the weight of the snake's body as it lifted to crawl over his left ankle. It was all he could do to hold still. He closed his eyes and waited while the fluid-smooth path of the snake slid across the ankle, then touched the other and across it also. Though it was a warm day, his sweat was cold. *Think, now,* he reminded himself. *While it is moving like this, it is not preparing to bite.* He wondered, if he were bitten, what it would feel like. No, he must not think such thoughts.

The bulk of the snake was heavy, much heavier than he had thought it would be. It was with a great sense of relief, then, that he felt its weight lessen, first on his left ankle, then on the right. Then, it was gone. *Thank you, Uncle,* he thought silently. *A good day to you, and good hunting.*

After such an experience, almost anything became easy. He related the event to his teacher, and Tracks-Well laughed loud and long.

"*Aiee!* It is good!" he signed.

Speaks-Not was disgruntled at first by the tracker's lack of sympathy.

"It was not good at the time!"

"No, but you handled it well, and *that* is good! Your real-snake has done a good thing for you."

"Yes, he did not bite me!"

The tracker collapsed into another fit of laughter, then sobered.

"That is true," he agreed, "but more important, he has *taught* you. For this, you should be grateful."

"And I am, Uncle." He could smile about it now. "At that time, though, I was grateful only to be un-bitten."

Both laughed now.

In the long run, an even greater annoyance was from lesser creatures as he practiced his motionless ordeal. Mosquitos, gnats, flies. It required great will-power not to jump when the sharp stab of the deer-fly's bite stung into a bare ankle like a hot coal. He considered using longer leggings, taller moccasins, or wrapping his ankles with a protective piece of buck-skin. That proved the most effective protection.

But he was learning. He finally realized that though a motionless position on his belly was easi-est, it was not quite practical. When his intended quarry did make its way down the game trail, he must be ready to shoot. He could not rise and prepare his stiffened muscles to shoot before the quarry was long gone. No, he must freeze in a position that would allow him to be ready at any moment.

He tried sitting and kneeling, but it was not practi-cal. The bow seemed clumsy, getting in the way of a clear shot. Finally he decided that his best position was standing. He could lean against a tree and by locking his knees in the fully extended position he found that he could relax and allow his muscles to loosen.

"You are much like a horse that sleeps while standing," Tracks-Well teased him. "Still, it is good."

It was more difficult to decide how to hold his weapon. He could not hold it extended in a position to shoot, but it must be ready. He must be able to draw the arrow with a minimum of motion. He tried various positions for the bow, and finally decided that it would be most practical to fit an arrow to the string and hold the bow in his left hand as he would in shooting. His left forefinger would hold the arrow in position, and the tips of his right fingers would rest on the string, ready to draw. This would permit either a quick shot or a slow and deliberate one, de-pending on the circumstances.

It was some time before he had the opportunity to test his theories. When it did happen, it was totally unexpected. It was near dusk, and a chill was gather-ing. Speaks-Not was leaning against a sycamore and beginning to think of going back to the camp, when a sudden motion caught his eye. There, only a few paces away, stood three deer. All were bucks, for it was nearly time for the birthing of the fawns. The does would be together elsewhere.

There was one wary old buck, his fuzz-covered antlers just beginning to sprout well. His two smaller companions, probably yearlings, were showing their first spikes of antlers. They would be shed in the winter, and next season's growth would be more impressive.

The three were apparently unaware of his presence. They were browsing quietly. Now would come the proof of his skill. He selected one of the yearlings, the one that appeared fattest. The old buck was larger and in good condition, but his flesh would be tough and stringy.

Very slowly, Speaks-Not began to lift his weapon, beginning to draw the string as he did so. Once the old buck lifted his head to look around, and the young man stopped and froze for a moment. It was a great strain on his muscles, but just as he thought he could stand it no longer, the buck resumed his browsing. At the last moment the animals seemed to sense danger, but the arrow sprang forward and flew true to its mark. The yearling sprang forward in bucking jumps, the feathered shaft jutting from the rib cage. The others leaped away and disappeared, as Speaks-Not stepped out to watch his stricken quarry. It ran perhaps a hundred paces before collapsing in death.

It was with great feeling that Speaks-Not stopped before the still figure to perform his apology in sign-talk.

"I am sorry to kill you, my brother," he gestured, "but on your flesh our lives depend. May your people prosper and become many."

10

» » »

"**S**peaks-Not, are you angry with me?" Far Dove demanded. The girl appeared half angry herself, half sad, and quite puzzled.

"No. Why would you ask this?" he signed.

"I have not seen you. Were you avoiding me?"

"No. I have been learning from Tracks-Well."

"But I could help you. It has always been so between us."

"That is true, Dove. But this is different. This I must do alone."

The girl was quiet for a moment, and a tear glistened at the corner of her eye.

"You do not need me anymore," she accused.

"No, it is not that! This thing . . . the things I have been learning . . ." How could he explain?

Now Far Dove hurried on, hurt and anger in her every gesture.

"At first I thought that I did not see you because of the season," she ranted. "It was turning cold, and no one was outside much. But I did not even see you during the days of sitting and smoking and games in the winter. I thought you were with the young men, gambling with the plum stones. But then someone said no, you had avoided them, too. By that time the Moon of Awakening had come, and they told me you were out of the camp somewhere."

She paused, and the tears welled up again.

"There was a time," she went on, "that when you were out of the camp it was with me."

"This is different. I have been learning from Tracks-Well, and it is done alone."

"But I could help you. We have always hunted together."

He shook his head. This was not going well at all. He had been so preoccupied with all his new skills and methods, that he *had* neglected their friendship. Now Far Dove was angry, and seemed unlikely to consider any explanation.

"It is not that way," he insisted. "This is something that I must do."

He did not know that the start of his instruction from the tracker had actually been suggested by Far Dove. She, too, had apparently forgotten. That which had saved him from despair had been of her doing, and now both were unaware of it.

"It is good," she signed sarcastically. "You would rather be alone than with me. Then let it be so."

"No!" he signed. This situation was deteriorating rapidly.

He wished for her to share his success. The kill that he had made two days ago, the fat yearling, had made him confident and proud. This he had wished to share with Dove, but when he encountered her, she had been cold. Cold, but never more beautiful.

The past few moons had seen changes in Speaks-Not. He had begun to grow taller. His body had begun to sprout hair in new places. There was even a fringe of fine hair along his upper lip. By tradition, this was said to trace back to Heads-Off, the hair-faced outsider who had brought the First Horse to the People. This facial hair was a mixed blessing. There was a certain honor involved in carrying the blood of a legendary leader. Heads-Off, though an outsider, had actually become a subchief in the Southern band, it was said. On the other hand, a heavy growth of facial hair presented problems. It was much more difficult to maintain one's appearance. Much more un-comfortable, too. The plucking of each hair from the skin to produce a smooth face was not only tedious, but painful. Sometimes his fingers ached from hold-ing the clamshell tweezers.

Along with these changes in his body had come new feelings toward the women he encountered. He wanted to be near them, to notice the attractive shapes of legs, the swing of their hips as they walked, the bulge of soft curves under soft buckskin. All women were good to look at, he decided. But the one that attracted him most was Far Dove. How had he failed to notice the excitement that the changes in her body now evoked in him? Now he had begun to dream of her, to imagine the feel of her soft yet sup-ple body against his.

He had been a little embarrassed about his fanta-sies, but had finally accepted these feelings for what they were. He was becoming a man. This was some-thing that he longed to share with Dove, but he was not quite ready. First, he must prove himself as a hunter.

This he had done, and it was time to resume the friendship that had always been so important to him. It would still be a few seasons before they could marry and establish a lodge together, but they could begin to plan, to dream ahead. . . .

And now, he felt it slipping away. Far Dove turned on her heel and strode off. He followed, trying to gain her attention. Then she stopped and turned.

"You do not want me," she accused, "but there are those who do! Gray Fox has wanted to court me. Maybe I will marry him."

The weight of despair crashed down on the world of Speaks-Not. Gray Fox was older, more than twenty summers, probably. He had lost his wife to a sudden illness the past season. Since that time Fox had shown much attention to the younger women. Most wanted nothing to do with him. He was known as a poor provider, and as a gambler. He was inept at that, too.

"Gray Fox?" he signed in astonishment. "Dove, do not talk so. You cannot do that."

Now fire flashed in her eyes. "And you cannot tell me what to do!" she gestured angrily. "You wish to be alone, be so!"

She whirled and strode away. Later, he decided that he should have run after her, but he did not. He was hurt, confused, and angry himself. He watched her go, and his world coming to pieces around him, and his heart was very heavy.

He did not think that she would actually accept the advances of Gray Fox. Surely she could see the error in that. And she had always, since she became a woman, fended off all suitors. It had been an unspoken thing, but one that was there, an understanding. She would wait for him, for Speaks-Not, her friend. He was not sure how this had just happened, how that understanding had been lost, but he knew that it was gone. Maybe she *would* look to Gray Fox. The thought was intolerable to him.

He spent a sleepless night, tossing and turning in his robes, imagining Far Dove in the embrace of the ineffective gambler. The thought sickened him. By morning he was in the depths of despair.

"What is it, my son?" Otter Woman asked.

He had no answer. "It is nothing," he signed as he lifted the door-flap and went out of the lodge.

"What is the matter with him?" asked his father.

Otter Woman shrugged. "I do not know. He was happy yesterday, over his kill."

"Yes. And that is good," said Walking Horse. "But something must have happened before evening."

"I am made to think," said Otter Woman thoughtfully, "that this is a thing of love. He is becoming a man, you know."

Walking Horse smiled. "Yes, I have seen this. But, Otter, I thought that he and Far Dove? . . ."

"That is true," agreed Otter Woman. "I do not

know. They have not seen each other very much this winter. Maybe they grow apart. She is older, but that has been good, for them. *Aiee,* I hope nothing is really wrong between them."

"I, too," agreed Walking Horse. "That is a special young woman."

"Yes, I have thought so, too. We will see. It may be that something else bothers him."

Speaks-Not wandered aimlessly, uncertain in his despair. Many times that day he determined to go to Far Dove to try to set things right. But uncertainty, anger, and pride interfered. Finally he sought the comfort of Tracks-Well, who had been instrumental in helping him overcome despair after the tragedy of the elk hunt.

The tracker, skilled though he might be at his own craft, was of little help. His young pupil had been exposed to that most feared of all human experiences, the fury of a woman scorned. It had come at such an inopportune time, too. The boy had only barely regained his self-esteem by making his successful deer kill two days ago. Tracks-Well had rejoiced for that. It was exactly what the boy had needed.

And now, this. It was doubly unfortunate that it had happened to Speaks-Not at such a young age. He did not yet have the maturity to understand. Most young men, when maturing and learning the ways of women, were courting girls perhaps two or three seasons *younger* than they. In this case, the reverse was true. The girl was older, and this lent a whole new dimension not only to the relationship but to the problem at hand. A disappointment in love should happen to no one this early, Tracks-Well thought. Speaks-Not was dealing with enough problems already, more than most boys of this age.

"Surely, Speaks-Not," he suggested, "she will feel differently today. Go and see her, talk of these things. I will talk to her if you wish."

"No, Uncle, I could not ask that. And I could not go to her. I am made to think that her mind is made up."

Tracks-Well worried about the situation for the rest of the day. He wished that he had more expertise in the ways of women. He and his own wife, Fawn, had always been close. Maybe he could ask her. He did not know whether that would help. They had never had occasion to speak of such things.

Many times, later, he wished that he had gone directly to Far Dove and talked with her. Things might have gone differently. When it did occur to him to do so, it was too late.

He had slept restlessly, half-waking and uncomfortable, and it was near morning when he woke suddenly with the idea. Dove had come to *him* when Speaks-Not needed help. It would be no different for him to approach the girl for the same purpose. Good! He would approach her and explain the circumstances under which Speaks-Not had spent the time alone. She was a highly intelligent young woman, who should be interested in the welfare of her friend.

He waited until midmorning, then made his way across the encampment to the lodge of Dove's parents. The girl herself greeted him, looking up from her work. She had been fleshing a fresh hide with a scraper.

"*Ah-koh*, Uncle," she greeted. "You wish to see my father?"

Her manner was stiff and formal.

"No, it is you I come to see," he told her. "It is about our friend, Speaks-Not."

She stiffened, but said nothing.

"He is at a difficult time," the old tracker began.

"What is that to me?" the girl snapped angrily.

Tracks-Well drew back in astonishment. *Aiee*, this was worse than he thought!

"Well, I . . ." he stammered, "I thought that you and he . . . I mean . . . I only wish to help him."

The girl glared. "I, too, once. But he does not need me now, or want me."

The tracker had the strong impression that she was blaming *him* for this misunderstanding.

"No," he said gently, "I am made to think that he—"

"It is nothing to me!" she interrupted. "I am to marry Gray Fox."

11

» » »

For Speaks-Not, it was a crushing blow. Worse, perhaps than any of his life. Worse than the disappointment of the elk hunt, with guilt over having been responsible for another hunter's death. He could scarcely remember when Far Dove was not a part of his world. His earliest memories included her, at play with other children, and always ready to help.

Their quarrel alone had been a terrible thing. He wished now that he could have simply said he was sorry. Sorry that, in his preoccupation with learning the lonely skills of the tracker, he had neglected her. Probably, he realized, he had thought in the back of his mind that he *would* apologize. After both had had time to cool off and see things more rationally, he would have gone to her. Now, it was too late.

Surely he had never expected that Dove would carry through on her threat to marry Gray Fox. He had thought that she was half joking. A cruel joke, to punish him, but surely not serious . . . *aiee*, how could he have suspected?

He had learned the awful rumor from an unlikely source, his mother.

"Possum, I am told that Dove is soon to marry Gray Fox. Have you quarreled?"

He sat, numb with disbelief, unable to answer for a little while.

"Yes," he finally nodded. "I did not know . . . she did not . . ." he paused, unable to continue.

"Did she mention this plan to marry?"

"Yes . . . I thought she only said it to make me angry."

Otter Woman saw that this was no time to continue the subject, so she busied herself with the quillwork that she was embroidering on a shirt. Her son rose and left the lodge. She wanted to ask where he was going, but did not wish to intrude.

Speaks-Not wandered aimlessly. When he rose to go, he had intended to go to the lodge of Dove's parents, to confront her, apologize, and beg forgiveness. Then surely all would be well. She would laugh and tell him that she was only teasing him to get his attention after his many moons of neglect.

However, before he arrived at her lodge, he had begun to recover from the blow of his mother's news. This was simply more of Dove's subtle way, he decided. She was trying to shock him back to reality. He knew that she would never go through with such a marriage. She only wanted him to come crawling, to be able to control him at her whim and watch him suffer. The thought angered him. He realized that he must think of this at greater length before approaching her. He diverted his course and climbed to the top of the nearby hill where he and Tracks-Well had gone before.

A long time he spent there, trying to puzzle out the workings of Dove's thinking. Why would she announce such a thing? To embarrass him? Maybe. To force his attention? Almost surely. Then, when he came to apologize on his knees, she would laugh at him and reveal that she had not been serious in her threat to marry Gray Fox.

This angered him. Where at first he had been crushed, his heart heavy with grief, now he began to feel resentment. How could she treat him so? He had done nothing to deserve such torture! Finally he came to a conclusion. He would not go along with her little scheme. Even though Dove was willing to play petty games to annoy him, he would not allow her to do so. He would not apologize. Let *her* worry about him. At the last moment, he knew, she would realize that her little tricks were unsuccessful; she would announce their coming marriage, and Gray Fox would grieve.

Yes, that was the solution. He could maintain his dignity, and show her that she could not treat him so. It would be hard, but in that way he could maintain his independence. *It is good*, he thought to himself.

Now, how should he occupy his time for the next few days? Maybe he should avoid all contact with Far Dove. Yes, that would be good. Let her suffer alone, wondering about him. Suffer, as she had expected *him* to suffer. This idea began to seem better and better. He would go on a hunt, for a moon or two, to test his newly polished skills of observation. Yes, it was good. It would be like a vision-quest, though he would not seek a vision this time. There were other things that would divert his attention. He must plan just how he would ask her to establish a lodge with him, when the time came.

He watched the western sky until Sun Boy splashed it with color and neared Earth's rim with his torch. Then he hurried down the hill to the encampment. He felt much better now that he had reasoned everything out and had a plan.

"Ah, we wondered about you!" Walking Horse greeted in hand-signs.

"I was thinking, alone," he answered. "Father, I would go on a quest, alone."

"A vision-quest?"

"No . . . I need to try some of the things I have learned from Tracks-Well."

His father nodded. "How long?" he asked.

Speaks-Not shrugged. "Maybe a moon, maybe more."

Walking Horse looked very serious. He was quiet for a few moments.

"Is this about Far Dove?" he finally asked.

"No . . . well, a little, maybe. She is trying to tease me with her threat to marry Gray Fox."

"You knew of this?" Walking Horse appeared very concerned.

"Yes . . . she threatened me with Gray Fox."

"And you quarreled?"

"Yes. She is trying to force me to apologize. So, I will leave for a little while, and let *her* worry."

His father nodded, but still seemed uneasy. "My son, is it wise to go at this time? Maybe you should go to her first—"

"No!" interrupted Speaks-Not. "This is probably what she expects. I will not play her games."

Tracks-Well, too, had doubts.

"Why now, Speaks-Not?"

"Because, Uncle, she only wishes to torment me with this. To make me come crawling to her, to beg like a whipped puppy."

"I do not know, my son. She seems serious."

"Because she is angry! She knows that my heart is heavy, and it *is*. I *have* neglected her, as I spent much time alone these past few moons. Now, I will go out alone to see if I have learned. When I return, I will go to her and she will understand, and we will form our own lodge, Far Dove and I."

Tracks-Well had talked to her, though he did not want to reveal that fact, and had grave doubts. The girl was angry, yes, but he had seen no indication of repentance or forgiveness.

"Maybe you should talk of this to her before you go."

"My father said the same. I told him no, too. I will not play her games."

"Speaks-Not," the tracker began cautiously, "I am made to think that no man has understood women, ever. You and I are not likely to be the first. But this bothers me . . . ah, well, so be it. You know her better than I. Now, where will you go?"

"I have not decided, Uncle. Upstream on the River of Swans, maybe."

"That is good. Pretty country. What will you do?"

"Travel a little. Try some traps and deadfalls, maybe. Hunt as you have taught me."

"Yes. Remember, furs will not be good. They will be past prime."

"That is true. I was thinking more of snares, for rabbits, maybe. I can watch those who wear fur, think how I would set traps this winter."

"Yes. That is good. And you can snare rabbits for food."

"Unless I make a good kill or two. I can do that, you know."

"And that is good."

The tracker wished that he saw a little more maturity in his pupil. The boy had done so well . . . *aiee,* too bad that this conflict with the girl had happened just now. He knew that in spite of his confident attitude, the heart of Speaks-Not must be very heavy. Maybe it was a good idea for the boy to get away, to regain his perspective.

Ah, life seemed so complicated sometimes! Tracks-Well was glad that such worries as lovers' quarrels were far behind him. He and his wife had been together many winters now. Their children were grown and in lodges of their own. It had been good to have the company of Speaks-Not. It was like having one of their own around again, and it was good. Mostly good, anyway. There was, of course, this same worrisome thing, the uncertainty whether the young people would make the right decisions.

He watched Speaks-Not go, threading his way among the lodges. Fawn came up behind him and put an arm around his waist.

"It is like having one of our own around again," she observed.

"Yes, I was thinking of that," he agreed. "Both good and bad."

His wife chuckled, the low, throaty laugh that he still loved. "Yes . . . will he be safe?"

"Yes, I think so. He is good . . . maybe better than I was at his age."

"*That* good?" she teased, but Tracks-Well did not smile. "You are concerned about the girl?" she asked.

"Yes. I am made to think she is serious. He thinks she is just teasing him."

"Maybe both are true," Fawn observed. "But look, my husband, they must have their chance to make their mistakes, just as we did!"

"Did *you* make a mistake?" he asked, now teasing her.

"Maybe," she said flirtatiously. "Did you?"

He hugged her around the waist. "I am made to think not, woman."

12

» » »

Speaks-Not left the encampment with a certain amount of confidence. He was somewhat bitter at his childhood sweetheart, even a little vindictive. There was, however, a certain sense of satisfaction. She would worry about him, but that was as it should be. After the way she had treated him, she should be made to suffer a little. The thought of such revenge was sweet to him. He was glad that he had seen through her little games.

Of course, there was some degree of loneliness. One night in particular, with a full moon silvering the prairie, and the cool south breezes stirring the new grasses . . . *aiee*, it was beautiful! He stayed awake most of the night, sitting up and wrapped in his sleeping-robe. There was a feeling of excitement and expectation, a thought that if he closed his eyes he might miss something thrilling and important.

Only one thing was missing . . . he would have wished to share the excitement and enchantment of such a night with the one person most important to him in all the world. How perfect such a night would be, if Dove were by his side, wrapped with him in his sleeping-robe, sharing the warmth of their bodies against the night's chill. At one point, with the moon high overhead, he actually rose and began to prepare his few belongings for travel. He would go back to her, starting now. . . .

After some deliberation, he came to his senses. One does not start a journey in the middle of the night. Besides, his return now would tell Dove that she had won her childish game. No, that would never do. He spread his robe again and lay down on it, to watch the majestic trail of the Seven Hunters as they wheeled around the Real-star. It *would* be perfect, though, if she were lying here beside him.

A great hunting owl swept overhead, darkening a handful of stars in its passing. He felt a chill, an omen that he did not like. He had wondered about the owl, the hunter of the night. People told of its hollow hunting call, a sound that was eerie in the darkness, like a disembodied spirit who had lost its way. He tried to imagine what it would be like to hear such a sound. He could not remember having heard sounds of any sort.

Well, sometimes in the dim recesses of memory . . . his mother . . . He *could* remember her holding and rocking him gently as a small child. Her lips had moved comfortingly, and he could feel a humming vibration on his skin as she caressed his face with hers. She must have been singing, he now realized.

Such were his flights of fancy as he stared dreamily into the night sky. He wondered how it would feel to be held and caressed and kissed by Far Dove. He could imagine *her* lips, humming against his skin. The thought was marvelously exciting. Ah, well, that time would come.

He traveled, enjoying the freedom of his young manhood. He followed the River of Swans westward, stopping to visit villages of Growers along the way. Sometimes he made a good kill near such a village, and traded meat and the skin for supplies. Fresh corn, potatoes, once a new pair of moccasins. They fit poorly, not being of the same design as that of the People.

Far upriver, a Grower told him that the People's Northern band was in summer camp a day's travel to the west. He decided to visit them. At least, he could obtain a pair of moccasins of more familiar fit.

He stayed with the Northern band for several days, renewing acquaintances and friendships.

"Stay with us," a distant cousin urged. "We will be starting for the Sun Dance in half a moon. You can meet your people there."

He considered this possibility, but decided against it.

"No," he finally indicated, "this is a sort of quest. I hunt alone. But I will see you again at the Sun Dance."

Yes, that would be good. He would have more time to practice his skills; he would *not* return to his own Eastern band, but meet them, also, at the Sun Dance.

"How is it that you do not ride a horse, Speaks-Not?" his relative asked.

That was a complicated thing, one he had considered himself. It was hard to explain. A horse was fine for traveling long distances. It was good for hunting buffalo with either a lance or a bow. But Speaks-Not had decided that it would not work well with his style of hunting, the silent wait. There would be long times while he stood motionless, watching and waiting. What would his horse be doing? He must either tie it, which would not be very practical—the creature must eat—or turn it loose to graze, when it might easily wander away. Besides, if he ever found himself in a situation of danger from potential enemies, the horse would be a liability. His enemies could hear the call of a horse, but he could not. He would expose himself to much less danger by remaining alone.

All of this, reasoned out over a period of time, was difficult to explain to his questioner.

"It does not work well," he signed, "for one who hunts alone. For travel, maybe."

"I will lend you a horse for travel," his cousin suggested. "You can give him back at the Sun Dance next moon."

It was very tempting. It was a long way back to his own band, and his feet were sore. He could start there on horseback and travel more rapidly and comfortably. Or he could start across country, and arrive at the Sun Dance site before the others. It would give him a chance to see more country, to explore. . . . He was actually enjoying his time alone a great deal.

"It is good!" he signed. "The Dance is on Sand River, no?"

"Yes. Come, let us pick a horse for you."

They looked at several animals and finally selected a well-built roan gelding of quiet disposition. Its gaits were smooth, and it appeared to be an easy keeper. Speaks-Not rode with his cousin until he was familiar with the horse, comfortable with its spirit.

"He is not a buffalo hunter," the owner cautioned.

"That is fine," Speaks-Not answered, "for that is not my way of hunting anyway."

Even in the short time that they had been riding together, Speaks-Not had noticed one thing, however. Communication was very difficult. Most hand-signs required the use of both hands. On a horse, one hand was required much of the time to guide the animal, except at a walk. If a hand were required to hold a weapon too, conversation would be quite difficult. Yes, he concluded, for one with his style of hunting and tracking, a horse was good for travel and for little else.

He left the Northern band and made his way southwest, in no particular hurry. He stopped from time to time, hunting a bit, trying snares for a rabbit sometimes. He was never hungry, and all in all it was a thoroughly enjoyable interlude. Only one thought marred the journey sometimes. He missed Far Dove. He would see something beautiful, or interesting, and wish that she had been there to share the pleasure.

He watched a game involving a crow one afternoon. It was the crow's behavior that attracted his attention. From some distance away he saw the bird

jump from the ground into the air, nearly the height
of a man, then settle back. He paused to watch.
There was some sort of motion on the ground, but he
could not distinguish it. A snake, perhaps?

He tied the roan to a sumac stem and circled up a
little draw to come closer. It took a little while, for
he crawled the last few paces. When finally he parted
the grass and peered over the rise, he was astonished.
There, not a stone's throw away, the crow was busily
engaged in a game or contest. Its playmate was a
rabbit! The rabbit stood a few paces away, and the
two watched each other warily. Suddenly the rabbit
charged directly at the crow. This in itself was curious, because rabbits do not charge. Buffalo, buck deer
or bull elk in season, bears, wolves—all may be dangerous because of their tendency to rush at an intruder. But a *rabbit*?

The crow stood perfectly still until the rabbit was
hardly a hand's span away, then leaped into the air as
it had done before. The rabbit shot past beneath the
bird, went on a few paces, stopped, and turned to face
the bird again. The crow, meanwhile, settled back to
earth, facing the rabbit's new position.

Puzzled, Speaks-Not tried to think what this might
mean. Was the rabbit trying to defend a nest of new-
born young from the crow's predatory approach? He
watched the repetition of the charge and the leap into
the air. . . . Why did the crow not merely fly away?
The strange performance continued, the crow alight-
ing in precisely the same spot each time. Then there
was a shadow overhead, and a red-tailed hawk sailed
effortlessly past, hunting. The rabbit froze for only an
instant, then made a dash for the safety of a jumble of
nearby rocks. The crow rose and flapped away, cawing indignantly at the intrusion. Speaks-Not could
tell that by the open beak and rhythmic pulsations of
the throat as it passed over him. The hawk sailed on,
either not hungry, or realizing the futility of a hunt
in the rocky domain of this particular rabbit.

Speaks-Not hurried forward. He had marked the

spot where the crow had settled back each time, and wished to know . . . he half expected to find a rabbit's nest, possibly with tiny hairless newborns, the prey of the crow. To his surprise, there was nothing. A flat, bare patch of earth . . . not even grass. He spent some time searching in an ever-increasing circle, thinking that he would find a nest, or at least something to explain the peculiar behavior of bird and beast. Still there was nothing. Still puzzled, he went back to his horse. His only conclusion was that it had been a game of some sort. Both creatures knew that it was a game. Neither was threatened by it. Until, of course, the hawk entered the scene. *Aiee,* how strange and amusing . . . he must tell Far Dove. He wished that she could have seen it with him . . . the retelling could never be as good. Well, they would be together soon.

There was one other incident that would prove significant later . . . much later. He came to a gray cliff, facing the south. It extended along a clear swift river, stretching to the west as far as perhaps half a day's journey. He did not realize its presence until after he had crossed the river and glanced to his right. He had approached from the north, and on that side the cliff could not be seen. Level plain extended right to the edge of the bluff's face. Curious, he turned to his right and rode along the river, looking up at the rocky face. Then it occurred to him—this was Medicine Rock. He had seen it once before, at a distance, as the band passed by. He had been no more than nine or ten summers old.

The story of Medicine Rock had been told that night at the story fires. More than one story of the Rock, actually . . . what was it? Yes, a young hunter of the Southern band, was it not? Lost and injured, he had spent a winter here. Its medicine was strong. Something about the Old Man of the Shadows himself . . . but that was probably just a story.

The other, only a few generations ago . . . an invader from the north had been defeated here. The combined skills of two young medicine men, one a Head Splitter . . . Was that not when the People and the Head Splitters became allies? He thought so. There was also something about buffalo . . . yes! A stampede, caused by the combined medicines, had almost totally wiped out the enemy by pushing them over the bluff. This very bluff, he now realized. He could see the rim far above, through the tall sycamores that grew along the river. It was easy to see how it could have happened. *Aiee, what a fall!*

He paused to water his horse. Something white caught his eye on the other shore, and he waded across the riffle to investigate. It was a buffalo skull, bleached white by the sun and wind and water. There were other bones, too, moldering in the sod of the narrow strip along the bank. He could see others, too, lodged in crevices in the broken face of the cliff.

He looked up, nearly straight up the cliff's face. Dark, forbidding gray stone, pocked with crevices and holes and small caves. Its spirit could be felt. He felt drawn, however, like bees to flowers in spring. He longed to climb that rocky face, to commune with whatever spirits might dwell here.

But wait . . . was there not something else to the story? Why had the People passed at a distance instead of along the river? Thinking back, he could remember his mother's dread of the place. *I do not like its spirit,* she had said.

Apparently there were many others who shared this apprehension. He recalled, now, there had been a saying that his father had told him. *We pass this way often,* Walking Horse had said, *but at a distance.*

Standing there on the grassy bank and looking up, Speaks-Not could feel the power of the place's spirit, but little of the dread. Of the legends about this place, were not all favorable to the People? Maybe it was all in one's attitude, how one related to such spirits.

Anyway, he told himself, someday he would return and climb that forbidding rock face. He could see footholds and places to grasp, even from here. There was a great cleft, like a giant ax wound, just to the right of where he stood. The jumble of gray stone tumbling from the cleft would provide good footing. Well, not today. But someday, he would return and explore this Medicine Rock.

13

» » »

It was sometime before the Sun Dance that Far Dove realized she had made a mistake. The greatest of her life, probably. She had been furious at Speaks-Not. It had been hurtful for him to ignore her while Tracks-Well instructed him, but she understood that. She had intended only to tease him, hurt *him* a little. But then, when their confrontation came, everything seemed to fall apart.

She was still bewildered. How had that happened? She tried to recall the conversation of that fateful day when her life had been turned upside down. There was nothing really significant, no one remark or turning point. It was just that . . . *aiee!* How *had* it happened? She had suddenly found herself angry at him, and had taunted him with Gray Fox. That should have been a joke between them. Instead, Speaks-Not had become angry in turn, and had *forbidden* her. . . . He should not have done that. It still angered her to think of it. But of course, *she* had then overreacted.

After her anger cooled, she had considered going to him. But that, of course, would be to admit that he was right in forbidding her to see Gray Fox. Not that she *wanted* to, but that she would *not* be told what she must or must not do. She kept hoping, expecting that Speaks-Not would come to his senses and approach her with an apology. Nothing happened.

She saw an opportunity when Tracks-Well approached her in behalf of his apprentice. She did not know whether Speaks-Not knew of this overture or not, but it seemed an opportunity to force the reconciliation. Now she realized that it had been a mistake to say that she was about to marry. *Aiee*, what a mistake!

The story had spread through the band like real-fire. Or, she thought glumly, more like a prairie fire in a high wind. Real-fire strikes once, in a crash of thunder, and is gone. The dry grassland, though, from one tiny spark, burns like tinder, devouring everything as far as the eye can see. Sometimes, devouring the person who dropped the spark. She shuddered at the significance of that thought.

The rumor had come to Speaks-Not as she planned, but he had not come running to her to restore their friendship, as she had hoped. She had guessed wrong. Instead, he had left the band. No one seemed to know where he was going or for how long. She had been rejected once more, and her anger flared to hatred, almost.

An even more unexpected result of the fire she had thoughtlessly kindled came when word reached Gray Fox. He, of course, took the rumor for fact, and assumed that here was an invitation to come courting. She had always rebuffed him before, avoiding his advances. Now he was encouraged and pushed his courtship to a staggering intensity.

It became a great joke in the encampment. There were wagers as to its outcome.

"She will never marry him."

"But he needs a woman."

"He has needed one for a season, but he is not a good provider."

"True. And this woman is too clever to overlook that. Besides, she belongs to Speaks-Not, no?"

"They quarreled, and he is gone."

The arguments raged on, an amusing diversion for most, but a blow to the heart and soul of Far Dove.

She was spared the worst of the ribald jokes by sheer sympathy, but the pressure began to wear on her. And, Gray Fox seemed to be everywhere. She could do nothing without his following her, dogging at her heels. Her resistance began to wear thin.

"Marry him," advised an old woman, only half joking. "That will get him away from you!"

In the end, that was the sort of unreasoning logic that led to her decision. She turned on Gray Fox as he followed her on her morning chores. She was gathering firewood, and his presence was overwhelming, his person close.

"If I agree to marry you," she demanded, "will you let me alone?"

"Of course! Anything you wish is yours. You will see!" he cried, delighted.

Once the decision was made, she found herself in near panic. She wanted badly to talk with Speaks-Not. Maybe he could help her find her way out of this. Yet, he was part of the problem, not part of the answer. Her anger at him rose again, for allowing this situation to happen, though she knew that she was responsible. At least, partly.

She arrived at a compromise in her thinking. She would set a time for marriage, to stop the suffocating nearness of her suitor. A time far in the future. That would give her control of the situation. Then, when Speaks-Not returned, she would approach him, distasteful as it was to admit her mistake. That would make everything right, and she could tell Gray Fox that she had changed her mind.

"I will marry you," she told Fox, "just before we start to the Sun Dance."

She had calculated carefully. Speaks-Not, it was said by his parents and by Tracks-Well, would be gone "a moon, maybe more." The Sun Dance was fully three moons away, and he would return long before her final decision was necessary.

Her move was quite successful, at first. Gray Fox stopped dogging her steps, allowing her welcome room to breathe. The respite was good for her, and there was a certain sense of gratitude toward Gray Fox for keeping his part of the agreement. She tried to push aside the thought that she did not intend to keep her part. Actually, when she did think of it, she began to feel a strange emotion . . . pity for the inept, not-too-bright man, a compulsive gambler and somewhat inadequate hunter. She began to feel responsible for his troubles. Not for the loss of his wife, of course, though that, too, was to be pitied.

The couple had had no children, which was good. A woman marrying Gray Fox would not have another woman's children to raise. *What am I thinking!* she asked herself in panic. *I have no such intention.*

But, her maternal instincts continued to surface. Ironically, it was the same sympathetic understanding that had led her as a child to befriend a younger child who could not hear. She developed a sympathy and understanding for Gray Fox and his problems. She began to dread the time when she must tell him the truth. How would he respond?

At the end of a moon, she began to expect the return of Speaks-Not. There was no particular reason, except the vague "a moon, maybe more." She had fastened on that hope, and in her mind it had become fact. She saw his parents occasionally but was hesitant to ask if they had any word. Otter Woman was still kind and friendly. . . . If they had word of Speaks-Not, she would surely share it. For years Far Dove had been almost family.

There was, however, a change in Otter Woman's attitude at about this time. Her quiet cheerfulness gave way to a certain sadness. Dove assumed that Otter missed her son. This should have brought the two women closer, but seemed to drive them apart. Dove finally realized that the older woman resented the talk of Gray Fox that whispered through the camp. She wished that she could share her troubles with this kind woman who would someday share her son . . . *aiee,* there it was again! Otter Woman was part of the problem, not the answer. Dove could never share her resentment of Speaks-Not with his mother. And Otter Woman would surely resent the deception involving Gray Fox, if she knew. They drifted apart, and there was sadness on both sides.

It was the Moon of Growing Grass, nearly time for the Moon of Roses, when a traveling trader stopped with the Eastern band of the People. He was interesting. He told many stories, and had a variety of commodities to trade. Black obsidian arrow points, red pipestone from the north, a bitter brown cake he called *chocolatl*, from which could be made a stimulating drink with hot water.

But he carried news. His own tribe, whose hand-sign indicated the "nation of traders," lived along the eastern slope of the mountains, he said. They had frequent contact with the Mountain band of the People.

"But your Northern band, too," he added. "I have just been with them a little while. Oh, yes, I nearly forgot! A message . . . one of your young men is there. Speaks-Not, he is called."

Quickly, someone summoned Walking Horse and Otter Woman.

"You have seen our son?" Otter Woman asked excitedly.

"Yes, yes, a fine young man," said the trader expansively, for he was adept at his vocation. "He sends you a message! He will travel to the Sun Dance, instead of back here. He will meet you there."

"It is good," said Walking Horse proudly.

And it was, to know that their son was alive and well. Both parents were quite relieved, and treated the visitor with great respect and honor, giving him small gifts.

It was not so with Far Dove. She was present when the trader told his news, and her heart leaped with joy for a moment. But wait . . . this was wrong! She had been depending on his return to help her escape the dilemma into which she had become entrapped.

Now, though the thought of his well-being made her glad, the cold truth began to grip her heart. Speaks-Not would not return to assist her. A flash of anger came over her. How dare he be so inconsiderate! He did not really care at all that he had destroyed her world. Tears filled her eyes, and she turned away to be alone.

She ran, once she was out of the crowd among the lodges, along the stream past giant old cottonwoods and sycamores to a pleasant place that she had found, where no one would see her. There, she spent a long time crying silently. It was as if she mourned for a husband that had never been. Yet, Speaks-Not *had* been a part of her life, for most of it. She could hardly remember when he had not been a major part of her waking thoughts.

Now he was gone, and she felt that she was in mourning. No one else would understand, she knew, and there was no one with whom she could share her grief.

Finally, her tears exhausted, grief began to turn to anger. When someone died or was killed, it could not be helped. It was the way of things. Death comes as part of the circle, and is expected, sometimes. One has little control over such a loss. But *this* . . . Speaks-Not had *chosen* this. He had deliberately shunned her once again, had abandoned her in her time of greatest need. The more she thought on it, the more furious she became. He probably thought that she would come crawling back to him. She would show him!

Dove rose from the soft grass where she had lain crying and composed herself. She washed her face at the stream, replaited her hair, and adjusted her dress. Then, calm outwardly but burning with anger inside, she made her way back among the lodges to look for Gray Fox.

It was not difficult to find him, because he still seemed to be everywhere, though at a greater distance. He was respecting their odd bargain. She strode directly to him, stopped, and planted her feet with determination. Her heart was beating wildly, like the struggles of a trapped bird in the hand.

"Fox," she said, "I will marry you tomorrow."

14

» » »

The People began to gather on Sand River, late in the Moon of Roses, for the annual Sun Dance. It was the greatest event of the year, a mixture of joyous celebration, reunion with friends and relatives, and of course the fervor of religious ritual. It was a time of great excitement, races and contests, gambling, feasting, but also prayers of thanks for the return of the sun, the grass, and the buffalo, on which the life of the People would depend. Solemn ceremony mixed readily with the more earthly pursuits, for is it not all one, the world and the spirit?

Speaks-Not arrived in the designated area to find the Southern band already present, and their camp established. The site this year was in their customary range, so they had a shorter distance to travel. He paid his respects to their chief, according to custom.

"*Ah-koh*, my chief," he signed, "I am Speaks-Not, of the Eastern band."

The old chief nodded.

"It is good. Your people are near?"

"I do not know, Uncle. I have been traveling. I will meet them here. The Northern band is a few sleeps behind me," he signed.

"Ah! You have been with them?"

"A short while. I hunt alone."

"You are the son of Otter Woman and . . . White Horse, is it?"

"Walking Horse, Uncle."

"Ah, yes. Fine people. Your mother is a distant relative. We go back to Heads-Off, you know."

Speaks-Not nodded, thinking of the tweezers and the plucking of the facial hairs from his upper lip. He should take care of such things before the arrival of the Eastern band. He wished to appear well-groomed and confident when he met Far Dove. She would have come to her senses now, and they could resume their friendship and their lives together.

He left the lodge of the band chief and wandered around the camp area. It was a good site, with plenty of grass and the clear stream for water. He mentally noted where each band would camp. The Mountain and Red Rocks bands to the west, his own to the northeast. Due east, of course, was open, to greet the rising of Sun Boy with his torch. In the same way, the lodge doorways would all face the east, and for the same reason. In addition, there was a more practical reason. Prevailing winds would be from the south, and the smoke flaps on the lodges must be quartering downwind to draw properly.

To the southeast, there would be an open space in the camp circle of the bands. It was also left open in the corresponding circle of the Big Council. The chiefs and subchiefs of each band would take their assigned places, with the space to honor the rising sun. But there would also be an open space to the southeast. It had been so for many generations, it was said. There had once been another band, according to legend. They had been killed by enemies long ago, it was believed, when the People lived much farther to the north. It was one of the reasons for the migration southward to the Sacred Hills. There the People had found the spirits in tune with their own. Even that was so long ago that no one knew how long. Still, the extinct band was honored in memory by the empty place in the circle. It had become known as the Lost Band. There was always the possibility that some descendant of a survivor might appear, to claim his seat in the Big Council. Sometimes he wondered about the fate of the Lost Ones.

He wandered on, enjoying the sights and smells. Even though only the first band was present, there was a sense of excitement in the air, an anticipation of the festival.

It was that very evening that a young man loped into camp from the west on a horse that had been ridden too hard. He carried news. The Red Rocks were only a day away, and a delegation of Head Splitters was with them. Head Splitters, having no Sun Dance of their own, often attended that of the People. It was good to share the stories and ceremonies of others. The Red Rocks had also been in contact with the Mountain band, and they would arrive a day or two later. It was good, and excitement mounted.

Speaks-Not could hardly wait for his own Eastern band to arrive. He had never been away for this long, and found that he was missing his parents. Tracks-Well, too, of course, who had become like a grandfather to him. Mostly, he had to concede, he was anxious to begin his reconciliation with Far Dove. He thought of her constantly, and could visualize every mannerism, every motion of her body. The little crinkles at the corners of her eyes when she laughed . . . her smile. Ah, it was good.

Impatient, he rode out with a few other young men to see if the Eastern band might be approaching. He knew these youths only as acquaintances and soon tired of their company. They were interested only in racing around, showing off, and generally behaving foolishly. He parted from them and struck off on his own.

There was a high, flat hill some distance to the north. He had noticed it, coming in. From there he should see much. He loped his horse in that direction, an easy gait to let the animal release pent-up energy. The roan had become quite excited when the other horses were racing, and it would be good to tire him a little. An easy lope should do that. The roan was quite comfortable to ride, and Speaks-Not found himself enjoying the day immensely. He had no special responsibilities, the excitement of the Sun Dance was at hand, he would see his parents and young sister. . . . Best of all, he would see Dove. They could enjoy the fun of the festival together, and begin to make plans.

He drew the gelding to a stop on the flat hilltop and began to search the prairie to the east with his gaze. He had learned to sweep back and forth with his eyes constantly to compensate for his absent hearing. Then, every little while he would glance to his rear. This technique had been suggested by Tracks-Well. He had used it himself many times, the tracker said, when he had had a need for extra-careful observation.

Immediately, Speaks-Not saw a long column in the distance, easily seen by the fuzzy plume of dust that lay alongside like a rolled robe of yellow fur. His heart beat faster as he tried to calculate how long . . . They would have to stop for the night, he realized. Well, he would join them! It was well past midday, but he could reach them as they made camp, without even pushing the roan. He remounted and started east. He did not know whether his erstwhile companions had even seen the approaching travelers. Probably not, unless they had become considerably more serious since they parted. He was inclined to doubt such a possibility. No matter . . .

Shadows were growing long already when he loped into the camp of the Eastern band. They had apparently just stopped, because everything was utter confusion. No one would erect the big lodges for a one-night stay, and there was a scurry to select family campsites and erect such brush shelters as each considered appropriate. Here and there a campfire began to blossom.

A young man waved a greeting to him and Speaks-Not pulled his horse to a stop.

"My parents?" he signed.

"Yes! Over there." The young man pointed toward the thin strip of timber along the stream.

Speaks-Not turned his horse aside, moving through the crowd at a walk. His mother rose from her fire-making, saw him, and raced forward with arms spread wide. He slid from the horse to her embrace, and it was good.

"You have grown," she signed, laughing. "Look at your shoulders!" She felt his muscled arm appreciatively. "You are a man!"

"Of course he is a man!" Walking Horse signed as he approached.

For a little while everyone signed at once, and they laughed together.

"Did you have a good trip?" Speaks-Not inquired.

"Yes, good weather, no trouble. But what of you?" asked his mother.

"Good. I spent some time with the Northern band.

"They are here?"

"No. I came ahead. The Sun Dance is a day that way," he pointed. "I came to meet you."

"It is good," signed his father, touching his shoulder. "You will camp with us tonight?"

"Yes. Do you have a sleeping-robe? I did not plan to find you, and left mine behind."

"We will find something," his mother signed, laughing. "Now, sit, I will fix something to eat."

"Good. But now, I must find the camp of Dove's family. Have you seen them?"

There were blank looks on the faces of his parents.

"You do not know?" he signed. "It is nothing. I will find them."

He turned and started away.

"Wait!" called Otter Woman instinctively, though she knew he would not hear. Frantically, she turned to Walking Horse. "Go after him. It is better that we tell him."

Horse nodded and trotted after their son. He came alongside and caught at the arm of Speaks-Not.

"It is all right, Father," the young man signed. "I will find them."

"No, no, Possum. You do not understand. She is not with her parents."

A feeling of panic washed over the young man, and he felt a cold sweat.

"Something has happened to her?"

"No. Well, yes. When you left, she was very sad."

"Go on!" Speaks-Not signed angrily. *"Where is she?"*

"She is with her husband, maybe."

"Husband?"

"Yes. When you did not return, she married Gray Fox. She said she had told you."

Speaks-Not stood, staring at his father, trying to keep from bursting into tears.

"No . . ." he signed. "Yes, she said this, but she was angry. I thought she meant only to torment me."

"I fear it is more, my son. She lives in his lodge."

All of his worst dreams and fears had now come to reality. Always before, he had awakened and been relieved that it was not true. This time he could not waken. Far Dove was lost to him forever. His life, his world, was falling to pieces around him, and his heart was very heavy.

"Come, my son," his father signed, taking him gently by the arm to lead him back to Otter Woman's fire.

"No," Speaks-Not pulled away, equally as gently. "I must pay my respects to Tracks-Well, tell him how it went on the trail. I will be back."

He would, of course, go and seek out the lodge of the old tracker. That part was true. He would also return to the camp of his parents. But mostly, he had to get away, to be alone in his grief. He would return after dark.

15

» » »

They did not meet at the Sun Dance. Both were occupied with other things, but in truth, neither one wanted it. Speaks-Not spent the time with his parents for a day or two and then became restless.

"I will leave tomorrow," he told them.

"But you have just come back to us," protested Otter Woman.

She knew his problem, or at least she thought she did. He was not ready to face the daily risk of encountering Far Dove, now the wife of another. What a waste . . . they had made such a happy couple as children. Well, no matter now.

"Could you not wait until after the Sun Dance is over?" she asked.

She knew the answer. He could not, because he would surely encounter Dove. The heart of Otter Woman was heavy.

"I must go, Mother."

She nodded. "Where will you go, my son?"

"I do not know. I hunt alone."

"Yes."

It was a clumsy moment.

"You will go to see Tracks-Well?" she asked.

"Of course."

"It is good."

* * *

The interview with the old tracker was far from satisfactory. Of course, at this point in his life, Speaks-Not was made to feel that nothing in his world was satisfactory.

"*Ah-koh*, Uncle."

"*Ah-koh*." Tracks-Well returned the signed greeting. "I have not seen you." There was a slight accusation in the remark.

"That is true, Uncle. Forgive me. But, I . . ."

The tracker waved aside the apology. "I know," he signed. "Here, sit with me."

Speaks-Not sat, and there was no talk for a little while. He studied the old face, watching while the tracker took a stick from the fire to light his pipe. The pungent smoke circled the old man's head in a bluish cloud. Odd, thought Speaks-Not, that he had never noticed how old Tracks-Well had become. But that is the way of things. . . . The tracker puffed until the pipe was going well, and then offered it to the sky before he handed it to Speaks-Not.

This was a social smoke, rather than a ceremony, but is there not ceremony in all we do? Speaks-Not lifted the pipe again, then took three leisurely puffs before handing it back.

"I am leaving, Uncle," he signed.

The old man nodded. "This does not surprise me. . . . The girl?"

"No! Well, yes, maybe. But I am made to think that I should be alone."

The tracker chose to sidestep that comment. "Where will you go?" he asked.

"My mother asked that, too. I do not know. It does not matter, if I am alone anyway."

"Some places are dangerous."

"All places may be," Speaks-Not signed curtly.

The tracker saw that his heart was heavy, and did not pursue that theme, but left it with one final admonition.

"You will be careful?" It was not really a question.

"Of course."

"It is good. Now, tell me of your quest just past."

"Not really a quest, Uncle. I hunted, traded with Growers. It was good."

The tracker nodded approval. "You will do the same elsewhere now?"

"Yes . . . maybe I will see the mountains."

"It is good. You will enjoy that. They have a powerful spirit. Different, but . . . well, you will see."

Speaks-Not nodded. "Oh, yes, Uncle, I tried the snares."

The old man smiled. "Good. You caught rabbits?"

"Yes . . . I tried only rabbits."

Both were still for a little while, and finally Speaks-Not resumed, on a different subject.

"Uncle, what do you know of Medicine Rock?"

"You have been there?"

"Yes, I passed there on the way here. It is a place of powerful spirits, no?"

The old man nodded. "Our People avoid it. You know the stories."

"Yes, Uncle." He was not quite certain why he had mentioned this.

"Looks-Far, the holy man, might tell you more."

"No . . . I was only curious."

Tracks-Well nodded. It was odd, he thought, that the young man would ask about the Rock. Well, maybe not. It was a very impressive place. Speaks-Not was going through a very difficult time, and was vulnerable. His spirit was searching. . . .

"Are you going back there?" he asked.

"Medicine Rock? No. Someday, maybe."

"It is good," signed the tracker. "But be careful."

At least, the young man did not feel an urge to return there now, and Tracks-Well was glad. Things were too unsettled in the life of Speaks-Not to encounter the powerful spirits who lived there. No one was absolutely sure as to the nature of those spirits . . . good, bad, or both?

"When do you leave?" he asked, changing the subject.

"Tomorrow . . . dawn."

So, the young man was leaving without taking part in the Sun Dance. He must be deeply troubled. *Aiee*, too bad that things had happened so. Both Dove and Speaks-Not so headstrong, unable to yield. They had been so good for each other! Well, there must be some explanation, though he could not see it now. Things happen as they must. But *aiee*, how hurtful, to watch the young make their mistakes!

Now, Speaks-Not rose.

"I must go, Uncle."

"I know. You must get ready to travel."

"Yes. I will not forget your help, Uncle. You have taught me much."

"It was nothing . . . try the deadfall trap this winter!"

"I will! I will see you again, maybe next season."

But you will not, thought the old man. Then he answered in signs. "Yes. May your trails be easy!" *But they will be hard, my son*, he thought privately. *I wish that I could help you.*

He watched Speaks-Not as he walked away. Fawn came and stood by his side, resting her hand on his shoulder.

"His heart is heavy," she observed.

"Yes. And mine for him," said the tracker sadly.

"You have done what you could," she said comfortingly.

"It was not enough. We should have talked to the girl, Fawn."

"She would not have listened. But, it is too bad."

Far Dove watched him go from a distance as he left the camp at dawn the next morning. She understood, and her heart was heavy in the knowing. She longed to run to him, to try to explain. She would have, but she belonged to another.

Her husband still slept in the little brush shelter.

She had built it herself, because from the time they arrived, Gray Fox had been involved in the races, gaming, and gambling. That was all right . . . many husbands helped, but many did not. At least, when he was gambling, he was not around to bother her.

She had located their temporary lodge as far as possible from that of Otter Woman, because she did not want to see Speaks-Not. Actually, she now realized, she did want to see him, but *she* wished to remain unseen.

Gray Fox had been absent until near morning, wagering on the plum-stones with his friends, she supposed. He owned few horses, and she hoped that he was not losing too many more. When he came in, she pretended sleep, elbowed away his approach, and lay as still as possible until his snores told of sound sleep. Then she rose and made her way out of the camp. She noticed the graying of the eastern sky, preparing for the coming of Sun Boy, and stopped to watch the colors change.

There was some slight activity behind her, and she slipped into the bushes, not willing to be seen. Someone had caught a horse . . . his own, probably, since he was quite open about it. Any outsider lurking around to steal horses would be more furtive. Then she recognized a mannerism . . . Speaks-Not . . . what was he doing? She almost stood and stepped forward to greet him, but realized that she must not.

It was growing lighter now. Speaks-Not finished knotting the bridle in the horse's mouth and swung to the animal's back. She watched him ride back toward his parents' camp and tried to understand what he was doing. The only reason that she could think of to bring in a horse at this time of day was in preparation for travel. But where would he go? No one would normally leave the Sun Dance. She trotted around the encampment to approach Otter Woman's lodge from the other side. She was quite anxious not to be seen.

She peered through a screen of willows and saw

that she was right. There was Speaks-Not, tying a
bundle of supplies to his saddle while his parents
watched. He was starting a journey. But why? . . .
Then it came to her, and tears filled her eyes. She had
avoided him because of the heaviness of her heart,
and he must be doing the same.

He swung to the saddle and reined the horse
around. In the growing light he looked larger . . . he
had filled out, his shoulders seemed broader, his arms
more muscular. She longed to be near him, to talk to
him. He waved to his parents as he rode away toward
the west. The first yellow rays of the rising sun
struck his shoulders as he nudged the horse into an
easy trot.

She watched his back until his figure began to grow
smaller in the distance. *Good-bye,* she whispered.
Then she rose, circled the camp once more to come
in from the other side, and gathered an armful of buffalo chips for the fire. That would explain her absence.

Gray Fox was still asleep, but the camp was coming awake now. It would be a day of excitement. The
Sun Dance itself had not begun, but the preliminary
rituals were in progress. In the distance she heard the
singsong chant of the priest on his circuit of the encampment, calling the announcement. This ritual
would be repeated each morning until the appointed
day.

Always before, Far Dove had looked forward to the
excitement of the occasion, the joy in celebration,
the games and races, dances, prayers of thanks and of
entreaty. The buffalo effigy at the west side of the
Sun Dance lodge, an open-sided brush arbor, was being erected even now, under the direction of one of
the holy men.

Today, the usual joy was not there for Far Dove.
All of the excitement and pleasure that she saw in
others was wasted on her, for it was like ashes in her
mouth. She had watched joy leave her life, riding out

of the encampment on the back of a spotted horse. Her heart was very heavy.

It was to be even heavier, however, in the moon following the Sun Dance, when she realized that she was pregnant.

16

» » »

Far Dove dropped the armful of sticks and buffalo chips near the fire and swung the cradle board from her back. She propped it against a tree and began to prepare the fire. She had not seen her husband since they arrived. Fox had quickly joined his friends, and she would probably not see him very much for days now. She could not believe that it had been a year since the last Sun Dance. In other ways, it seemed a lifetime.

The infant, who had wakened at the sudden cease of motion, opened large dark eyes and made infant sounds.

"Ah, you are awake, Little Man," his mother called. "Be patient, and I will feed you!"

There were satisfactions to motherhood, she reflected. Almost enough to make up for the heartache of the past year. She had watched Speaks-Not go with much hurt in her heart. Her anger was beginning to leave in the realization that much of her present situation could have been avoided. Why, *why* had she not simply gone to him? Her foolish pride had resulted in a poor marriage and the loss of much that her life held dear.

She had resolved to *make* a marriage of it, especially after she discovered her pregnancy. Gray Fox had seemed delighted at that prospect. At first, that is. Then, as she became larger and clumsier, he seemed to resent the loss of her efficiency. It was no great problem, since he was seldom at home anyway. That, in a way, was the *good* part.

She had had to make do with the scant essentials provided by a poor provider. She tried to maintain their garments and the dilapidated lodge cover as best she could. But patches do show, on a dress or on a lodge cover. Usually there was enough to eat, though she occasionally resorted to a rabbit hunt herself. Gray Fox seemed not to notice.

She had been furious with him when he lost his new moccasins in a silly wagering game, on a toss of the plum-stones. She had spent many days in decorating those shoes with intricate designs in quillwork. She resolved not to do so again.

Perhaps worst of all that year had been the pitying looks of her family and friends. That hurt her pride. She was determined not to accept any help offered out of pity, but finally realized that her own pride was hurting her again.

It was in the late stages of her pregnancy that she encountered Otter Woman one morning. Both had gone to fetch water at the stream, and there was no one else around. The meeting was clumsy for a moment. They nodded a greeting, then busied themselves with filling waterskins. It was Otter Woman who finally broke the silence.

"How is it with you?" she asked.

"Fine . . . it is good," answered Dove quickly. She knew that this was more, a deeper question than a mere greeting.

"I mean, really," Otter Woman pushed.

Both women stopped at their tasks and straightened to look at each other.

"My heart is still good for you, my almost-daughter," blurted Otter Woman.

Tears welled into the eyes of Far Dove. They did that often now. It was the unsteady emotions of her pregnancy, she supposed.

"And mine for you," she answered.

Both laughed, and they embraced for a moment. Now the torrent was loosed, and they began to talk. Of woman things, of the coming child. Far Dove felt far better than she had for many moons. It was good, and they talked long.

As they prepared to part, Dove managed to ask a thing that she had been longing to know.

"Have you heard from your son?" Dove inquired, trying to be quite casual.

Otter Woman looked at her keenly for a moment, but then answered smoothly, as if it were of small importance to Far Dove.

"Why, yes," she said. "A traveler, not long ago. He spent some time with the Head Splitters, the man said, then wintered at Red Rocks."

"He is well?" asked Dove unashamedly.

"Yes. It is said that he is greatly respected as a tracker now."

Dove nodded. "He was always good at that."

"He has changed his name, too," Otter Woman went on. "We did not know that until now."

"How is he called?"

"Hunts-Alone."

Far Dove thought a moment, then smiled and nodded. "That is good!"

"Yes," agreed his mother, "but he will always be 'Possum' to me!"

"Of course," Dove laughed.

"He is coming to the Sun Dance, they said."

"Ah, that is good." Inwardly, she was not sure. "I must go, almost-Mother. It is good to talk to you again!"

"Yes," agreed Otter Woman. "Let us not be strangers, Dove."

Again, the tears came easily.

"Yes," said Dove, "let us not be."

They parted, and it was good.

* * *

The infant arrived in the last days of the Moon of Hunger. Snow and sleet pelted down on the ragged lodge cover as Cold Maker pushed one of his final forays of the season before retreating to the northern mountains. But it was good. A brief labor, common to the long-waisted women of the People, and then the indignant squall of the new man-child.

The women allowed Gray Fox back into the lodge to see his wife and son, and he was pleased. That was probably the high point of the marriage, but it was quite brief. Soon Fox was as uncaring as ever, and even more absent. And again, for Dove, that was good. She settled into a new life as a mother, and found a happiness that surprised her.

Until now, that is. Now, it was a matter of great concern that Speaks-Not, now Hunts-Alone, was expected at the celebration. She viewed the expected meeting with mixed emotion. She wished to share with him the joy of her son, yet at the same time there was still a part of her that wanted to taunt him. *This could have been yours!* She wanted to show him. And over all was the fact that it would not be considered proper for her to do more than greet him in passing. It would be a worrisome time.

She had not seen him yet. The Eastern band had been here for two days now. Dove had waved to Otter Woman as they went about the routine of the camp, but had not talked since their arrival. She was certain that Hunts-Alone was not yet staying at his parents' lodge. It was not readily apparent whether he would do so. He had been staying with the Red Rocks band and might continue to stay there. Or with the Head Splitters.

But both the Red Rocks and any Head Splitters who still might choose to attend were late. There was no concern—they had much farther to travel. He would arrive, with one group or the other, and stay either with them or his parents, she supposed. Maybe, even, he had a lodge of his own . . . *he might have a woman,* she thought, and then tried to convince herself that it was of no concern to her.

The baby was crying now, and she unwrapped it from the cradle board to lift it to her breast. She was still nursing, crooning softly to the infant, when she heard the welcome shout. Then there was thunderous greeting as the young men rushed out to meet an incoming column. The mock charge, with the horsemen of both groups voicing the deep, full-throated war cry of the People . . . *aiee,* it was exciting! She wished that she had been able to see it. To ride in the charge, even. She had always thought it would be good to do that, once, before she settled down with children. But now . . .

The riders now circled the camp, still howling the war cry, raising a dust that would soon have women shouting threats at them. She smiled and shifted the baby to the other breast.

She still wondered about Hunts-Alone and began to watch for him. The newcomers were obviously the Red Rocks, for they were the only band yet to arrive.

Then she saw him. *Aiee,* a fine-looking figure of a man! He had grown even more and had become more handsome. She was having feelings now that no wife should have. Especially, she told herself, with her husband's baby at her breast. She ducked her head to avoid recognition. She saw him inquire, presumably about his parents' camp. Then he dismounted and turned away, toward that direction. Her heart was beating wildly. Someone spoke to her, and she turned, startled.

"What?"

"I said, where is my food?" asked Gray Fox.

"Yes, in a moment," she said brightly. "Your son still needs his!"

Fox mumbled something and sat down while she busied herself, preparing meat. She handed him a bowl and a horn spoon, and he began to eat. When he finished, he belched loudly, rose, and scratched his belly.

She started to ask where he was going as he walked away, but decided against it. It did not matter much. There were new arrivals, many of them gamblers. It was like a sickness with Gray Fox, and she knew that he would have sought out other gamblers by sundown. She did not understand quite how men could spend all day or all night watching a handful of plum-stones painted red on one side skitter and bounce on a spread skin. A horse race, maybe. At least that was exciting! She hoped that he would not lose too much. She had given up hoping that he would win. He never won. . . .

The moon was high when they came looking for her. She had been asleep for a while after dark, but had been roused by the baby. She had fed him and returned to her sleeping-robe, lying there in the darkness beside her dying fire, listening to the night sounds. Sounds of nature and sounds of the encampment, she noted. There was no time, it seemed, when all was quiet and everyone slept. At any time, day or night, during the time that the entire nation was gathered for the Sun Dance, someone was awake and making noise of some sort. There were songs and dances, the rhythmic beat of distant drums. Of course, there were people who were awake merely to visit quietly, to exchange news and stories with friends and relatives they had not seen since last year's Sun Dance.

Gray Fox had not returned. She had not really expected him, of course, and did not care. She was tired anyway, and if he came home she would have two mouths to feed instead of one. She smiled to herself at the thought . . . two children to care for . . . not far wrong.

The three people approached, two men and a woman, and stood before her, tense and formal.

"Far Dove?" inquired one of the men.

"Yes. What is it?"

Now she recognized the woman . . . one of the

Warrior Sisters, a priestess of the Blood Society. Something must be wrong! Dove sat up, alarmed. Why should they be here, looking for her? Their faces were tense and serious, even in the moonlight. Thoughts raced through her mind . . . something had happened to Hunts-Alone! No, of course not. She was embarrassed to have had such a thought. Her parents? . . . No . . . *what*?

"Your husband is dead," said the Warrior Princess.

"But how? . . ." Dove stammered. It was unreal, like a dream from which one cannot wake.

One of the men spoke.

"Our hearts are heavy for you. He was gambling with us and some of the Head Splitters. He was losing and accused one of the visitors of cheating, a man called Wolf's Tail."

Far Dove sat, listening to words that seemed to have no meaning for her. The man's voice droned on.

"Fox tried to kill him with a belt-ax, but Wolf's Tail drew a knife and stabbed him in the belly. It is as I have said it."

Her thoughts were still numb, detached. She understood the delegation and their approach. There must be no mistake, no blame of anyone. If the council was asked to judge this event, these would be the witnesses. They had seen the fight, and there was no room for doubt. This had been explained.

"Wolf's Tail was only defending himself," the man finished.

"Yes, I understand," Dove said huskily. She had so many things to think of. . . .

The delegation started to turn away, but she called them back.

"Wait. Please tell me . . . was the man, this Wolf's Tail . . . *was* he cheating?"

The spokesman waited a long time before answering. "No," he said firmly. He waited again and finally blurted, "Far Dove, your husband was cheating. I am sorry."

So, she thought. She was not really surprised, only

numb, unbelieving that it had actually occurred. *I must mourn*, she thought.

"Thank you," she half whispered.

They moved on, and she lifted her voice in the Song of Mourning.

It was three days later when she looked up to see Hunts-Alone approaching. He strode straight to where she sat holding the baby. She was embarrassed that her appearance was not good. The ashes that she had placed on her head had sifted down over her neck and shoulders. Hunts-Alone should have known better than to come here at this time, anyway. Her anger rose at his lack of consideration. After all, she was in mourning.

Then she saw his face, and her anger melted. There was so much grief and hurt and sympathy. . . .

"My heart is heavy for you," he signed, "but this is enough, Dove. It is time for us to heal the hurt in our hearts. When your mourning is over, I will come for you."

She wanted to jump up, to fly into his arms, but she managed to remain outwardly calm.

"It is good," she signed.

Part II
Hunts-Alone

17

» » »

Hunts-Alone rose and stretched and walked around a little to work the night's stiffness from his joints. He had begun to realize the meaning of the old men's talk. There was no question any more. The weather was directly connected to stiffness in one's bones.

Dove was feeding the morning fire. Around them, the other families of the Eastern band were coming alive to begin the day. It had all the makings of a glorious day in early spring.

He left the cluster of lodges and went a little way outside the camp to empty his bladder, nodding greetings to other men who were occupied in the same way. Then he paused a moment to greet Sun Boy as the first rays of the torch slanted across the prairie . . . a short prayer of thanks for the day.

Life was good, he reflected. He and Far Dove had been together many winters now. *Aiee*, what heaviness of heart there had been, before they finally joined. But it was good, then. They had learned a difficult lesson, and profited by it. They laughed sometimes at the childish pride that had prevented their coming together for so long.

Now, their children were grown, and except for the youngest, Young Crow, were in their own lodges. And Crow, he thought, was showing much interest in Feeds-His-Horse, a young man of the Elk-dog Society. They would probably marry soon. Dove thought so, too. They had watched the young people together not long ago.

"Those two make a good-looking couple," Far Dove had signed.

"Yes. Our lodge will soon be empty."

She took his hand. "Is that bad?" she teased.

They had never, in all their years together, had their lodge just to themselves. Dove's son by her unfortunate marriage to Gray Fox had known no other father than Hunts-Alone. Called Bull's Horn, he was now grown, a respected hunter, and with children of his own. Then had come another son, only a year younger, Many Birds. The two had become inseparable. It was several seasons, then, before Young Crow joined their lodge. She had been a joy to her father, but was now ready to make her own way in the world. And their lodge, always blessed with children, would seem empty.

"What if we find that we do not even like each other?" Dove teased, in mock alarm.

"It is a risk we must take," he smiled. He put an arm around her. "Maybe it will be better, no?"

Now, he returned to the lodge, to find Crow chattering with her mother as she assisted in the preparation of food. The girl rose from her kneeling position by the fire to greet him.

"Good day to you, Father," she signed.

He nodded, smiling. It was good to see the face of this one, always happy, always eager to greet the joys of the world. Everyone loved Crow.

Hunts-Alone and Dove were doubly blessed. Neither of their own children had inherited the loss of hearing. Bull's Horn, though now their own, had of course been sired by another, so could not inherit the weakness of Hunts-Alone. It was his alone. He had never missed something he did not remember, though it had affected his life profoundly. His name, even, had reflected the necessity that his hearing loss had caused.

It had made him a better tracker, to be sure. Hunts-Alone had always been in demand when an extra-keen eye was needed. Many times he had given thanks for the firm yet gentle guidance of Tracks-Well. The old tracker was long gone now, but Hunts-Alone thought of him each time there was an especially demanding need for a tracker's services.

The years were passing now, and his eyes were not quite as keen. A younger man or two showed great promise, and he had helped to teach them, as his mentor had taught him. There was a slight disappointment that neither of his sons were particularly interested in his skills, but it is often so. They had grown into fine hunters, and respected men.

They were still virtually inseparable, as they had been since childhood. Bull's Horn, a year older, was usually the leader, though it was an easygoing good-natured leadership. They anticipated each other's thoughts, and were regarded as a team in the organization of the group hunts. Both had picked up more of their father's powers of observation than they realized, he thought. After all, does not any hunt depend partly on the hunter's skills in observing the world around him? He was proud of them both.

With Crow, however, he had a special relationship. This was a child born old and knowing. It could be seen in the wide-eyed look of wonder with which she greeted the new world into which she had arrived. She was the pride and joy of her father, and spent much time with him as she grew. Her childish joy and her smile of delight in all things made his heart good. He spent more time with her than he had with the boys when they were small. It was not intentional, but more time was available to him now. There were fewer demands on him as his lodge had fewer mouths to feed.

Hunts-Alone and his small daughter shared little jokes and dreams and heartaches. She was the child

of her mother, too, which made her even more en-
dearing to him. He loved to watch the two working
together, the child learning woman-skills and
woman's ways. And he was proud, his heart good.

He always knew, of course, that she would marry
some day. He wished a good husband for her, and
young Feeds-His-Horse certainly seemed to fit the re-
quirements. He was handsome, intelligent, a good
hunter, and well respected by his peers. He appeared
to be a natural leader, and would surely be a man
whose voice was respected in council. There was no
reason to think that he would not become band chief
some day. There were few serious candidates.

Young Crow and Far Dove were certain of it, and
even talked of his election to the office of Real-chief,
the most important position in the nation. True, it
was usually held by a leader from the Northern band,
but that was not a requirement.

"Maybe it is time for the Eastern band to come
into its own," insisted Far Dove. "Why not? We have
had great leaders, but have always been scorned."

"True," agreed Hunts-Alone. "But it is partly our
fault. The Eastern band sometimes deserves the foolish reputation."

"So does every band, sometimes," Dove signed.
"But, the jokes are about us, not the others."

"Some of our people like it," offered Young Crow.
"They think others will expect less of them because
they are of the Eastern band. They are lazy!"

"That may be," her father agreed. "But we have
had respected leaders. Red Feather could have been
Real-chief, but his age was wrong. The position was
not open during his best years. Maybe you are right,
and it *is* time. Feeds-His-Horse may be the one."

He was half teasing, the women knew it, and Crow
blushed becomingly.

"Oh, Father . . ." she signed.

He shrugged as if bewildered.

"You women brought it up. What does a mere man
know?"

Such teasing became increasingly common, and it was no great surprise when Crow indicated to her parents that spring that she and Feeds-His-Horse wished to wed.

"It is good," agreed Hunts-Alone. "Can he support you?"

It was almost a ritual question, which would be relayed to the young suitor. Horse, already expecting such an inquiry, would have decided what gifts he would bring to the parents. The purpose of such gifts was twofold: to impress them with his affluence, and to partially compensate them for the loss of a beloved daughter.

The choices were good ones. A beautiful robe for Dove, with a unique blue-gray color found very seldom in the buffalo herds that migrated through the Sacred Hills. It was an expensive present, and he must have given several horses for it.

For Hunts-Alone, the choice was probably harder. It would normally have been a gift of horses, a fine buffalo hunter or two, perhaps. But it was well-known that Hunts-Alone had different needs. His need for a horse was only for travel. Or, of course, for its own intrinsic value.

The young man led a mare to the lodge of his prospective father-in-law and paused before the door. Hunts-Alone stepped outside, soberly looking the animal over, as Horse untied the blue-gray robe from the mare's back and handed it to Far Dove. This was a ceremony, to be cherished and remembered. Dove was delighted.

The young man then untied a lavishly decorated bow case and handed it to Hunts-Alone.

"I know you have little use for horses, Uncle," he signed, "but maybe you can use this poor gift. It is a small thing to help your grief at the loss of such a daughter from your lodge."

Hunts-Alone nodded stiffly. The gift and the speech had been well-done. The bow was of excellent quality. But Feeds-His-Horse was not finished.

"Now, this mare," he went on, "you may find use for."

Hunts-Alone walked around the animal, admiring her beauty. A fine head; wide-set, alert eyes; ears pricked forward. Her back was long and strong, her legs straight. She was of the gray roan color admired since the People saw the First Elk-dog. At her side, a small foal nursed.

"She is young," Horse was signing. "This is her first foal. It carries both the blood of First Horse and of the Dream Horse of our ancestor, Horse-Seeker. The mare is back in foal to the same stallion. May she bring you many more fine horses, Uncle."

Again, it was a fine gift and a fine speech. The value in this mare was not in her usefulness to her new owner, but in her potential for producing horses of great value. Hunts-Alone was touched.

"It is good," he signed. "Welcome to our lodge."

It was sometimes custom for a new husband to live with the bride's parents until their own lodge was ready. This was the invitation.

"Yes, welcome," offered Far Dove in both speech and sign.

"Thank you both." Feeds-His-Horse answered. "But I . . . Crow and I . . . our lodge will be ready soon. We will wed after the Sun Dance, if that pleases you?"

"Of course. It is good."

It was later that evening when the importance of this event began to make itself felt on Hunts-Alone and Far Dove. The fire had burned low, and they were preparing to retire to the sleeping-robes by its flickering light. Young Crow was out with her intended husband, radiantly happy with the courtship and with the plans for their lodge together.

"Our lodge will seem empty," he signed. "It is as we said before."

"Yes," agreed Dove, "but it is good. This is a fine young chief, a fitting man for our daughter, my husband."

"That is true. But I will miss her."

"I, too. But here, come to bed." She lifted the edge of the robe invitingly. "Maybe I can show you that there are good things about an empty lodge, too."

18

» » »

It was little more than a year later that the lodge of Crow and Feeds-His-Horse was blessed with a small girl-child. She was so like her mother from the beginning that her grandfather was completely charmed. This was the child of their youngest, and she held special meaning for Dove and Hunts-Alone. She was called South Wind, after the fresh breezes that cross the prairie to relieve summer heat.

In addition, Young Crow had always selected a site for her lodge that was near that of her parents. Thus, they had extra opportunity to see the child develop. At any time that the situation offered, Hunts-Alone could be found amusing his tiny granddaughter.

"It is too bad that he cannot hear the sounds that she makes," said Crow to her mother as they watched the two together.

"That is true," Dove agreed, "but he has never heard. He uses her smiles, her eyes, the way she looks at him."

"I know, Mother. It was so with me when I was a child. But look at them . . . was ever a grandfather so devoted?"

The two women laughed together and turned to other things. There was some concern that summer that the weather was hot and dry. This made the hunting poor, and there was beginning to be talk that unless the fall hunt was good, it would be a difficult winter.

The council of the Eastern band considered at great length and argued about the best course of action.

"We should go out farther into the prairie for the fall hunt," insisted one. "There are more buffalo there."

"Usually, yes," came the answer. "But this season, the grassland has had drought, too. Worse than we have here. There may *be* no buffalo!"

The argument raged on. The Eastern band had always been split by argument, it seemed. They, of all the People, had been located for generations at the juncture of the grassland and the forest, the eastern border of the People's range. They had gradually adopted some of the customs of the forest people. None of the other bands of the nation was as dependent on deer as a staple food, preferring to hunt buffalo in open country.

Possibly even the leaders of the Eastern band did not understand why every council session produced argument, but it was so. They were in a state of change, in the process of shaping their culture. The Southern band had, many lifetimes ago, begun to winter among the scrub oaks in the southern part of their range. The Red Rocks and the Mountain bands had established winter sites in their western habitat, and the Northern band in the timbered bottoms along the River of the Kenzas or on the Platte. All bands hunted and camped for the summer in the grassland, but the Eastern band marginally so. They seemed indecisive, and this led to the strengthening of their reputation as foolish people. The more they were ridiculed, the more they were angered. And of course, when one is angry for whatever reason, he does not speak well in council.

For all of these reasons, not clearly understood by anyone, there was always wrangling, division, and indecision in the councils of the band. They had now lost any cohesion and political pride that had been

established a generation or two ago by their states-
man and leader, Red Feather. They seemed doomed
to argument.

"This happens too often!" shouted one man. "We
should plan ahead, *plan* to winter in the forest to the
east, not just when we are starving!"

"Of course!" another answered sarcastically. "In
the country of the Shaved-Heads! They will welcome
us into their lodges and feed us."

"Not that far," retorted the other. "Only a little
way into the forest. Establish our own territory."

"They will welcome that!" snapped his opponent.

The argument raged on. Hunts-Alone was bored
with it. He had never enjoyed councils, anyway. Not
only was he a loner by nature, but the arguments
were difficult for him to follow. Some, but not all, of
the speakers used hand-signs, and there was a disconnected result that he could follow only with difficulty. Sometimes Far Dove sat with him and
translated, but their interest had lagged through the
years. Participation seemed futile anyway. Let the
younger generation take over, make the decisions.

Crow's husband did seem interested, and his voice
was respected in council as a voice mature beyond
his years.

"He will be a leader," Dove told her husband. "It is
as I have said. Not yet, maybe, but someday! Look,
they listen to him!"

Bull's Horn and Many Birds, too, seemed to respect
the voice of their sister's husband. Often, the three
were to be found on the same side in the discussion.
They argued against some of the hotheaded young
men who wanted to invade the domain of the
Shaved-Heads.

"The People do not need another Lost Band," observed Feeds-His-Horse. "One empty spot in the circle is enough."

There was much nodding in agreement, but in the
end, those who favored wintering in the woodlands
won out.

"Our band is large," the predominant argument insisted. "We will go in openly, but peaceably, not aggressive. Our size will protect us."

Hunts-Alone, when he heard of it, was astonished
and quite concerned. "This is very foolish," he told
Dove. "The Shaved-Heads will see only a big band of
intruders. This is dangerous!"

That very night, his sons and Feeds-His-Horse approached him.

"Father," began Bull's Horn, the eldest, "our hearts
are heavy for the council's decision."

"And mine!" Hunts-Alone signed. "This is a bad
thing."

"So we think. We wish to part from the band . . .
stay near the edge of the forest, stay together."

"Who?"

"We three families. You and Mother, if you will
join us. Anyone else who wishes."

"Yes, of course! It is good!"

"To split the band?" asked Dove. "Is that not dangerous?"

"Which is more dangerous, Mother?" asked Crow.
"To stay where it is safer or go into the forest where
the Shaved-Heads hunt?"

"*Aiee*, I do not know."

The family discussion continued intermittently for
several days. It was a calm discussion, however, with
none of the bitterness and anger of the band's council. Gradually they came to a meeting of the minds.
When the time came for the band to move, they
would stay behind. They would move later to a selected spot where the band had wintered before. It
was nearer anyway, had proved safe, and game was in
fairly good supply. Many Birds and Feeds-His-Horse
made a quick journey to verify these impressions.

"It is good," they reported.

So it was decided. They announced the family decision to a few friends. One young man and his wife,
relatives of Feeds-His-Horse, elected to join them.
There was a great deal of ridicule as the story spread,

but in the end, when the Eastern band broke camp to move into winter camp deep in the woods, five lodges stayed behind. Let the others risk the wrath of the forest people, the Shaved-Heads. They would plan sensibly and cautiously, alert to the needs of their families, ready to avoid danger rather than face it. It was good.

A few days later the little group struck their lodges also and moved a few days to the south. It was a good site, to which Many Birds pointed. A clear running stream that would not freeze, a steep hillside covered with brush and trees which rose to the north, a view of open country to the southwest. The lodges would be sheltered from the howling winds of Cold Maker, and the snow would not drift badly in this isolated meadow. There would be enough grass for the horses. These young families did not yet possess large herds.

They helped each other set up the lodges, a few paces apart. A tripod of three poles tied loosely at the proper distance from the ends, spaced carefully by pacing. Then the other poles, leaned into the tripod in turn, the bases resting in a circle that would mark the size of the lodge.

All doorways faced east, for a number of reasons reaching all the way back to Creation. Does not Sun Boy approach over Earth's eastern rim? He must be welcomed by the People on his daily run. In a more practical sense, the position of the doorway also determined that of the smoke hole. Winter winds come from the north, summer breezes from south and southwest. Rarely does an east wind affect the region of the People. Since smoke flaps must be quartering downwind to draw properly, this allows proper adjustment of the flaps with the slender smoke poles.

The heaviest work in erecting the lodges was the hoisting of the lodge skin into place with the last pole, the one to the west of the circle. The men shoved the pole upright while women drew the heavy cover around the other poles and pinned the edges above the doorway.

By the time the shadows grew long and Sun Boy painted the western sky with his fall colors, the winter camp was established. There would be more work —winterizing the lodge linings with dry grass, building snow fences of brush—but that could be done later. For now, the fires were lighted, signifying their presence.

That was almost ritual, a concession to whatever spirits might inhabit a place, an announcement of the newcomers' presence. By the fire, a statement is made: *here we intend to camp*. A pinch of tobacco was offered, tossed in each fire that evening, to indicate goodwill.

With this gesture, hoping that the spirits might be appeased and feel only goodwill toward the little band, they began to prepare for their first night in this new winter home.

In his silent evening prayer to the setting sun, Hunts-Alone asked protection and peace, both for his family and for the foolish people of the main band who had invaded the country of a dangerous enemy.

19

» » »

They had made a good choice, Hunts-Alone reflected as he sat before his lodge and smoked in the warm sunshine of late autumn. This was a pleasant place, with none of the hustle and bustle of the larger camp. Hunting had been good. Even now, racks of drying venison were loaded with fresh meat. The young men hunted well together, and had harvested several deer. He would have preferred buffalo, the taste so much milder and sweeter, but no matter. All meat is good, some just better.

He watched the children at play, enjoying their enthusiasm. He glanced over at the baby, South Wind, propped near him in her cradle board. She was developing rapidly, it seemed. A very mature child. He was not surprised, of course. Her spirit was an old one, wise from the experiences of many lifetimes, perhaps.

At the rate the child was growing, she should be walking by the time they left this camp for the Sun Dance next spring. That would be good. He would feel much better when the entire Eastern band was united again. There was something about the division of a people who should be one that bothered him immensely. He could not forget the Lost Band and the empty place in the circle of the Big Council. And that chance remark by someone in the council, a few moons ago. *We do not want another Lost Band*. It *had* been a foolish thing, to weaken the band by dividing it.

Yet, he agreed with the young men of his family. The foolish ones were those who took the Eastern band into unknown territory, probably claimed by fierce Shaved-Heads. And in weakened condition, from the loss of five warriors, when the young men of his own family refused to go. Well, four, anyway. Hunts-Alone realized that his own reflexes were slowing, his strength ebbing, as the winters took their toll. But his eyes were still good, his tracking skills still sharp. At least, so he told himself.

His pipe was dead, and he decided to renew it. The afternoon was young, the sun pleasant through his buckskin shirt. In his pouch was the special mixture that he had decided was good for himself. Tobacco, of course, but a generous portion of sumac, a touch of cedar, and a bit of catnip. Sometimes when tobacco was scarce, he extended it with shavings of red willow bark. That was not necessary today, for tobacco was in good supply.

They had been visited recently by a traveler, a trader who seemed surprised to find them there. He was a jovial sort, as one must be who trades with everyone and has no enemies. His stories were good, and his visit had been welcome.

Hunts-Alone knocked the ashes from his pipe and repacked it with a pinch of the mix from his pouch. He beckoned to one of the children and signed that he needed fire. The boy jumped eagerly at the chance to assist his grandfather and brought a glowing stick from the cooking fire in front of one of the lodges. Hunts-Alone thanked him and patted the boy's head approvingly.

He settled back comfortably again, but there was still the uneasiness that he had felt earlier when he thought of the Eastern band's division. He wished again that the leaders had not quarreled, dividing the band. But it was done now. The main portion of the band, some forty lodges, were strong enough to defend themselves. This little family group was in a safe area. Both should winter well, if the larger group had found good hunting too.

Yet his mind wandered. What if the main part of the Eastern band was forced to fight the entire nation of the Shaved-Heads? It would be a bloody war . . . one that could have been avoided by common sense. But, in such an event, if many of the main Eastern band were killed, this family band—these children of his and Far Dove's—would become a powerful political force among the People. He himself had not been interested in politics because of his limitations in speaking, but he recognized the importance of leadership. Surely, this winter would be good either way. Leadership qualities in his sons would be recognized. In Feeds-His-Horse, too. He was constantly more impressed with that young man.

Ah, well, these were daydreams. Even though things looked good in all ways, he would feel better when the Eastern band was reunited. He was uncomfortable with the idea of a divided group. He tried to tell himself that it was no concern of his, that the Eastern band could take care of itself, even if there were five men absent. Well, four, anyway.

Two days' travel to the southeast, a trader stopped at a winter camp of lodges that were obviously of the prairie type. He was startled at first . . . there must be forty lodges! Then he remembered . . . yes, the family group. The Elk-dog People. This must be their parent band. Their Eastern band, was it not? Ah, yes. Good. That gave him a subject of common interest to talk about. He could bring news of relatives and friends, and would be welcomed.

He strode in, leading his two pack horses, and followed by his wife.

"Ah-koh!" he called in the People's own tongue, accompanied with the hand-sign for peaceful greeting. He had found it quite useful to use several

tongues in addition to hand-signs. His people, traders
by tradition, used many tongues. Their home territory on the eastern slope of the mountains brought
them in contact with many other nations, and they
traded with all.

These people, who had strangely split their band
and moved into new territory at the same time . . .
ah, that appeared foolish! But had he not heard? . . .
Yes, the Mountain band of this same nation was a
neighbor of his own people. They made jokes about
the foolishness of their Eastern band, did they not?
He chuckled to himself. Yes, it was all coming back
to him now. There were many jokes and stories that
were told in more than one nation. The same jokes,
told about some foolish group. The tribe across the
river, an imaginary tribe somewhere, or as in this
case, the Elk-dog People joking and teasing one of
their own bands, the Eastern band. He must be careful about foolish people jokes. Ah, well, he could still
tell such stories, but make someone else the butt of
the jokes. An imaginary tribe, maybe. Yes, that
would do.

He was welcomed warmly. These were usually
friendly people, he recalled. Proud, capable, sometimes a little haughty, even. But generous and open.
A quick glance around the camp showed him all that
he needed to know about how they fared this season.
Few new lodge covers, some meat drying on the
racks, but not an abundance. They had fared not
quite as well as their own splinter group at the prairie's edge. Well, he would trade here for a day or two
and then move on. The commodities that this band
would have for trading would be few.

"A day or two," he remarked to his wife. "Then we
will move on."

"Yes. They will have little to trade. Why did they
come here?"

"Times were poor . . . drought, so the other group
said."

"A dangerous move. Is this not the land of the Shaved-Heads?"

"Yes. And yes, it does seem foolish. But maybe they will be safe. They are many . . . see? Maybe forty lodges!"

She nodded, unconvinced. "We go on to the Shaved-Heads next? I wonder if they know of this camp?"

The trader shrugged. "Maybe. That is not our worry."

"That is true."

A trader must remain neutral. He can have no enemies, because he is vulnerable, traveling alone, and carrying valuable goods. His only real protection is his friendship with all those he meets.

They paid their respects to the band chieftain, an aging leader who seemed to have no real sense of direction. It was easy to see how one faction or another could influence a vote in this band.

There was small talk and a small gift of thanks for the band's hospitality.

"How long will you stay?" asked the chief.

"Only a day or two. We must be planning where we will winter."

"I understand. Where will that be?"

"We have not decided. South of here, someplace. Our bones do not like cold winters."

The old chief chuckled. "Nor do mine! But we will stay warm here. There is much fuel, shelter from the wind . . ."

And danger from your neighbors, thought the trader. Aloud, he said, "Oh, yes! We stopped with some of your people, two sleeps past. Five lodges . . ."

"Ah! Yes, some of our young men. Very foolish, to leave the main band, are they not?"

It was a ticklish moment. The trader knew that he must not take sides in an internal political squabble. There was no way of knowing what dissension might still smoulder here. He did have an opinion—that the foolish ones were the main band, who had penetrated deeply into the hunting lands of a very fierce adversary. He could not say this, so he only smiled and shrugged, to indicate that it was of no concern to him.

"They are well?" asked the chief.

"Yes, they too are drying venison," he said casually, "preparing for winter."

There were a few other inquiries during their brief stay. Specific inquiries about this lodge or that, and they were able to answer most of them.

"They appeared to be doing well," he told the questioners ambiguously, "as you of the main band are." *Better*, he said to himself. *They are practically in their own territory.*

They spent a pleasant two days and traded tales around the story fire. More stories were exchanged than goods, for times were hard for these Elk-dog People, and they had little to trade. The trader's wife mentioned this on the trail later.

"That was not a profitable stop."

"True. Except for goodwill. Maybe next season will be better for them, and they will have many robes, much meat, furs to trade."

"Maybe," the woman agreed. "If we come this way again."

"We will, someday. But I was thinking of finding them next season in their own country, on the plains."

"Yes," she agreed. "But I am made to wonder if we will ever see them again. Or, if *anyone* will."

20

» » »

A day's travel from that place, but in a different direction, a meeting took place that night. Light from the council fire glistened on heads that were shaved along both sides to leave a strip of hair standing erect down the center. Some men wore ceremonial paint, for important decisions were to come from this council.

The circle quieted and the council officially came to order, the elderly leader of this village presiding. There was ceremony and ritual first, befitting the serious nature of the occasion. A young man drew the symbolic pipe from its case, filled it, and handed it to the old chieftain. He in turn lifted it to the sky, lighted its fragrant contents, and puffed a cloud of bluish smoke. Then he handed the pipe to the man on his left. There was a silence of reverent meditation as this ceremony proceeded around the circle.

The pipe returned to the leader, who again offered it to the heavens, then to the four winds, and handed it to his pipe bearer.

"Now," he began, "we are gathered, my brothers, to consider matters of great importance to us and to our people."

There were nods around the circle. This was part of the ritual. The old chief recounted briefly the history of the nation, its triumphs and problems, since long-ago times. It had been heard many times by all those present, but how can one look at a problem without looking again at how it all began?

"It has been many generations," the chief droned on, "since our people came here to these woodlands. Here we have found it good. There are deer and turkey and bear, and our corn and potatoes and beans grow well."

More nods around the circle.

"But now, there is a threat to our people. Outsiders from the plains are pushing in."

There was a mutter of discontent.

"Two winter camps of the skin-tent people are known, within a sleep or two of here. There may be others."

The murmur rose, its tone more excited. Not everyone had been aware of *two* incursions. The speaker waited for the council to quiet, then continued.

"These are thought to be of the nation called Elk-dog People."

This, of course, was well-known.

"My chief," interceded an old warrior, in a formal request to be heard.

"Yes, Black Bear, speak to us in your wisdom."

Bear cleared his throat and began. "My chief, have not these Elk-dog People camped near the edge of our forest for many winters? When summer comes, they move back onto the prairie."

"That is true," agreed the chief. "But here, Mouse Track, tell us what you have seen."

Mouse Track, a much younger man, was respected for his scouting ability. His were the eyes and ears of this village. The circle gave him undivided attention.

"It is true," he stated. "There are two camps. These are an eastern band of the Elk-dogs, who often camp for the winter along a river to the west of us. The River of Swans, their name for it. Sometimes, in a dry year, they camp in the edge of our forest. It has been no problem. They have good horses we can steal, and their women are long-legged and very beautiful."

There was general laughter. It was well-known that the prairie women made good wives. Little girls were valuable for resale or trade, though this was mostly an opportunistic effort, not a customary thing. The loss of an occasional child angered the Elk-dog People, but not enough to precipitate outright warfare.

"They give up their horses more easily, I think," Mouse Track went on, producing another round of laughter. He waited for quiet.

"Now, this present situation is different," he went on more seriously.

The laughter and joking stopped abruptly. He glanced around the circle, letting the weight of his words sink in.

"Their main camp, what we believe to be the Elk-dogs' farthest eastern band, have come much deeper into our territory than ever before. They are a day's distance south of here."

"*South?*" asked someone incredulously.

"Yes. My brothers, this may become a serious matter, if these wanderers decide to settle down and stay."

There was an intense but short-lived mutter, and Mouse Track continued.

"The other camp, only a handful of lodges, is at the forest's edge, where they have camped before, the whole camp."

"What happened that time?" someone asked.

The old chief answered. "Nothing. We let them alone. Took a few horses, a girl or two. They went back to their treeless prairie in spring."

There was a chuckle.

"Will they not do the same thing again?" a man called. "It has been a dry year. Their hunting was probably poor. When the rains come, they will go home."

"It is not that small band that worries me," said Mouse Track. "It is the others, the main camp."

"Then let us kill them," someone shouted. "Take *all* the horses and women."

General laughter quieted under the serious stare of the chief, who held up his hand for silence.

"How many warriors are there, Mouse Track?" he asked.

"In the main camp, forty or fifty lodges. Probably that many warriors."

To some, the seriousness of this situation had not been apparent until now. The murmur that now went round the council circle was a sober one. The thoughts of most of those present were probably the same: They could attack such a camp and probably win, but there would be much bloodshed, much mourning.

"Maybe we could kill a lone man sometimes, keep bothering them, make them feel that it is dangerous here," an old warrior suggested. "Steal their horses . . . by spring they will be glad to go, and there is little risk."

There were derisive sneers from some of the younger warriors, not as experienced in the ways of war as the old men.

"Maybe we can attack the small camp instead," joked one. A roll of laughter relieved the growing tension for a moment.

"Wait!" cried a warrior. "Let us think on this! Maybe it is good. We can kill those at the small camp, to show the rest a lesson."

"But how would they know?" demanded another.

"We could go and tell them," suggested the jokester.

"No, be serious. Traders pass through. There is one in the area now with his wife. They carry news. Everyone will soon know."

"But winter is coming," Mouse Track pointed out. "Traders will not be moving around. This one is following the geese south, even now."

There was a moment of hesitation. Then a man spoke who had not yet been heard. He was middle-aged, quiet, known to his people as a skilled hunter and merciless in war. Respected and possibly feared even by his own people, Chops-His-Enemy had earned the name at the age of seventeen in his first taste of battle.

There are those who dread battle, those who fear it, those who glory in the songs and dances of celebration after a victory. Some love brave deeds, and the counting of honors on the fallen foe. Occasionally, though, there is one who enjoys the battle itself, for its own sake. Such a man is feared by his own people, because they do not quite understand his joy in the killing. But in time of war, he is *useful* to his people, as a leader and example. Such a man was Chops-His-Enemy.

"Let us do as someone has said," he began. "Take them a message. A head or two of their brothers from the smaller camp, as a warning. Leave them on a pole outside their camp for them to find."

There was a long pause, a moment of silence that dragged on. The time had come to stop the jokes and laughter. This was real, the decision to be made today.

The man who finally broke the silence was not one with the wisdom of years, but a young man, without experience but eager to "blood" himself and gain honor in combat.

"It is good!" he cried.

There may have been those who would have preferred a more peaceable approach. A warning, perhaps, a trading session and a demand that the outsiders move on. Their voices, if any, were not heard, or not noticed in the enthusiasm for war that now mounted. Theirs was a tradition of maintaining their rights by force, swiftly and violently. This plan would satisfy the innate lust for blood, drive out the intruders, and let some of the young men taste combat. A ground swell of enthusiasm began to rise, shouts and songs, and a few jumped to their feet to dance a step or two in their exuberance.

The old chief finally quieted the crowd long enough to resume the talk of the council.

"Chops-His-Enemy, will you lead the war party?"

The warrior's eyes glittered with pleasure. Something like a smile played over his face, and he licked his lips as if in anticipation.

"I will be honored to do so, my chief."

"It is good. When? How many?"

Chops-His-Enemy glanced at the sky as if to question the weather. The late autumn had been uncommonly warm and pleasant, but it could end at any time. The season was late, and the time of change was unpredictable.

"Tomorrow," he said. "All who wish may go. We will count many honors, steal many horses."

"And women!" shouted a young warrior.

"No!" said the war chief firmly. "That is a nuisance, and the others might come to steal them back. We kill them all. Anyone who goes will do as I say!"

This brought a moment of silence, broken by the old chief's remark of approval.

"It is good. It shall be as our brother says."

21

» » »

Hunts-Alone sat on the knoll behind the lodges, and looked across the open country to the southwest. He had discovered this place soon after they had established their little camp. It offered a view of the grassland that was his home, a place of far horizons. It was only two or three bowshots away, but it was secluded and remote from the everyday activity of the camp.

He had always felt comfortable when he was alone. It gave him a chance to relax, to meditate, to watch the creatures of the world around him. Probably his methods of hunting, from which he took his name, encouraged this habit. Far Dove understood it.

The autumn had been beautiful here in the edge of the woodlands. They had watched the colors change in the foliage of the trees. Bright crimson of sumac gave way to the gold of the cottonwoods . . . very brief, that stage. Then came the rich mixture of reds, yellows, and golden tints among the oaks and maples. Trees that were unknown on the prairie turned startling colors, contrasting with the cedars' green. There were colorful shrubs, too, largely unfamiliar to the People.

He missed the more muted hues of the tall grasses of home. They were more subtle, but as great a variety as the colors of the woodlands. There to the southwest, where he could see open vistas from his knoll, he could imagine . . . yes, surely that large patch on a distant slope would be real-grass. He could distinguish its dark reddish color as it ripened. It would be taller than a man's head now. Closer, a meadow in which heavy yellow heads of plume grass nodded above the pinkish clumps of shorter types. It was good, the sights and smells of the season mingling in the still golden sunlight.

Days were shorter now. It must be near the end of the Moon of Falling Leaves, and approaching the Moon of Madness. Days were growing perceptibly shorter. All of the leaves had not yet fallen, because the weather had been uncommonly fine. The long, still-sunny period before Cold Maker's return had been a good one. Second Summer, the People sometimes called it. It did not occur every year, but when it did, *aiee*, it was wonderful. Hunting was good, the days were warm and the nights cool . . . good for snuggling in the sleeping-robes with a warm bedfellow.

It had also given time to winterize the lodges, and this had been accomplished. Everyone, even the children, had helped cut and carry the curing grasses that were stuffed into the space behind the lodge linings for insulation. Natural brush shelter belts had been augmented with brush cut and piled in strategic rows. The dried meat was stored, in good supply. Skins were being dressed and tanned, but there was little urgency in any of the activity now. The little winter camp was ready.

And still, the Second Summer held. Warm, lazy days, sitting, visiting, smoking, playing games with the children . . .

"I am afraid we will pay for it later," observed Far Dove. "Cold Maker is watching from his ice cave and laughing at us!"

There was no argument. Everyone knew that winter would soon sweep down upon them. Yet it is hard to take such things seriously when the sky is so blue, the autumn sights and smells so pleasant. With the warm rays of Sun Boy's torch soaking through one's buckskin shirt, who can think of Cold Maker?

This long pause in the season also gave Hunts-Alone the opportunity to *be* alone. He would climb the knoll, recline at his ease, and meditate, giving thanks for all that was his. A fine family, a good life, grandchildren, a world that was good. He was ready to slow down, to let the young men take the lead, make the decisions. He did not mind the chance to sit in the sun, smoke, and meditate on past accomplishments. He lay back and watched a hawk high above him making circles in a cloudless sky. The redtail . . . not hunting, just soaring . . . too high to hunt. It, too, was enjoying the day, the weather. A good day for soaring, if one were a hawk. *Good day to you, Grandfather,* he thought at the bird. He was certain that it dipped a wing in greeting.

Such things were things that he had come to notice from his long habit of hunting alone. The actions of other creatures had taken on more meaning than they had for others. He considered this a good trade.

Today, however, he was not alone. He had carried the baby with him. The child was fussy and irritable, unusual for her usual happy disposition.

"I think her teeth bother her," Far Dove had said.

"But she has no teeth," Hunts-Alone signed.

"They are trying to come through—ah, you are teasing!" She struck at him playfully.

"Here, Father, give her this to chew," Young Crow suggested, handing him a strip of dried meat. "I have work to do."

He cradled the child in his arms and offered her the teething strip. She fought it for a moment, and then as the hard texture began to soften, she sucked at it eagerly.

"It is good!" signed Far Dove.

Hunts-Alone shifted the baby to his left arm and signed with his right. "I will take her with me to the hill."

The women nodded and returned to their tasks, and he placed South Wind in her cradle board and proceeded to his special post.

The infant had fallen asleep on the way up the hill, lulled by the swaying motion of his walking. He set the cradle board down, shading her face carefully, and now lay enjoying the day as she rested comfortably. He looked at her frequently, because he could not hear her if she chanced to awake and cry. This was not a conscious action on the part of Hunts-Alone. It was merely the way he did all things.

He glanced at her again, then rolled on his side and propped himself on an elbow to overlook the camp below. It was growing late. Still some time until sunset, and the babe still slept . . . well, he could stay a bit longer. He hated to disturb her sleep. How pretty she looked, relaxed in sleep. Long, dark lashes on rosy cheeks, so like her mother as a child.

He lay back again, looking at the sky. The hawk had circled lower now, and had been joined by another. The pair swept toward the Earth in dizzying spirals, and finally both landed on a dead snag some distance away. It was on a hillock similar to his own, beyond the camp. They were probably choosing a spot to roost for the night, he thought.

He looked at the baby again. Should he wake her? *No*, he thought, *she is comfortable now. I will wait . . . no hurry.*

It was sometime later that he realized he must have dozed. He was not certain what roused him, for the baby still slept. His experienced glance swept the area before him. The hawks . . . still there . . . he must have drowsed off for only a short while. The sun was a distance from Earth's rim yet.

Then a flash of motion caught his eye. The hawks on the distant stub suddenly rose together and flapped to gain altitude. Odd . . . one should have risen first, *then* the other. For both to fly at the same moment, they must have been disturbed. *By what?* Still he was only mildly interested, not alarmed. He knew that the men were probably out and around the camp, the women gathering wood for the fires.

Yes, he saw now, there was one of . . . yes, Feeds-His-Horse was walking toward the camp. Hunts-Alone relaxed. The young man's appearance must have alarmed the birds, caused them to fly. He glanced at the still-sleeping baby for an instant, and back at the approaching figure. Feeds-His-Horse was coming from the area of the hawks' perch. The birds were still wheeling and circling over him. Not *directly* over him, actually . . . a chill of fear swept over Hunts-Alone. Something was not right! Something *else* had alarmed the hawks on the dead tree.

That thought was not even quite complete when Feeds-His-Horse seemed to stumble in midstride. The leg that was swinging forward never reached its next step, and the young man fell heavily on his face. A feathered shaft jutted from between his shoulder blades.

A painted warrior suddenly leaped from the bushy slope and dashed past his victim, pausing only to count honors by touching the still form. Other warriors were flitting among the trees. He could see their shaved heads and roached hair . . . dozens of them.

Hunts-Alone had snatched up the cradle board and was running down the slope. He did not have the ability to shout a warning. Then he paused a moment. *What am I doing!* he thought. The attackers were nearer the camp than he. He could not warn the others. But here he was, running unarmed into a fight against stronger attackers, and carrying a baby! Had he gone mad?

He set the cradle board down and prepared to run on. But no, he could not leave the child. They would all be killed, leaving the infant to die in the woods . . . he must take her . . . no . . . The baby was awake now, catching the feel of his fear and anguish. From the open mouth and twisted face, he knew that she was screaming. She would be heard!

Instinctively he clapped a hand over the tiny

mouth to stifle her cries. She struggled, frustrated, and wriggled against the cradle's restraints, her large dark eyes alternately squinting and open wide, brimming with tears.

He looked toward the camp, unable to help as the attackers moved at will among the lodges. He could see several bodies on the ground. The lodge of Bull's Horn was blazing, black smoke from the burning lodge skins and the stored provisions rising in a greasy column into the clear blue. A warrior thrust a torch into the dry grass in another lodge lining. There was a puff or two of cottony white smoke as the grass ignited, then a change to dirty black when the lodge and the supplies began to burn.

He could see no one alive except the attackers. Surely the children . . . no, there was a small corpse against a burning lodge. Roach-maned warriors were hacking, mutilating . . .

It was good that the unused vocal cords of Hunts-Alone could not produce much sound, for he would have screamed in his agony. He sat, holding his hand over the mouth of the baby and watching everything that mattered in his world go up in greasy smoke. Everything except this tiny child.

He thought of an old story of a woman in such a situation. She had choked her own baby to keep it from crying out and revealing the whereabouts of her people to the enemy. She had saved her people by this sacrifice. He had never really believed that a woman could do so. He was certain of it, now. Especially since this small wriggling bundle was all that he had left of everything that he lived for. He must protect her, at all costs.

From his anguished throat came a croaking, gurgling cry, one that could not be heard at any distance. It was the only sound that he could muster in mourning for his loss. Tears streaming down his face, he wriggled his way into a dense clump of bushes, the cradle board held tightly to his breast.

In the western sky, the setting sun slowly changed the blue to blood-red.

Below, warriors went on with the looting until it was too dark.

"There should be one more man," someone called. "Five lodges, only four warriors."

"Let him go," answered Chops-His-Enemy. "Maybe it is good. He can tell the others what happens to invaders into the land of our people. We have what we need."

22

» » »

All night Hunts-Alone lay huddled in the bushes, shivering with the night's chill, sheltering the baby with his own body warmth. He knew that she cried sometimes, because he could feel the resonance of the tiny voice through his hands, arms, and skin. He tried to prevent it some of the time, but at other times he hardly cared. What was the use? And he cried, himself. Great, heartrending sobs, choking sounds from a little-used voice box, sounds that would have been unintelligible to any listener.

He did not know when the Shaved-Heads left, because he could not hear their shouts and cries as they methodically burned, sacked, and mutilated. Sometime before dark, probably. He ventured a look at dusk and saw no activity, but could not bring himself to go down and view the carnage yet. He knew there would be no survivors. He had watched the methodical slaughter. The very thought wrenched another great sob from his throat, and he held the baby close.

He drowsed occasionally in the night, and then would come awake in alarm, roused by the stiffness in his limbs or by the stirring of the child's body. He would recoil in horror from the thoughts that recurred with returning awareness. For a long time he could see the flickering light of the horrible greasy fires that were still devouring all that had been dear to him. He was torn between the desire to go and look and the need to protect the infant in his arms.

During that painful time, his mind went through the whole range of human emotion. Fear, frustration, grief, anger, hate, the desire for revenge, resentment . . . yes, resentment over the plans for winter camp set forth by the young men. Resentment at them, and resentment that he had listened and agreed. Resentment at the Eastern band for their decisions. *They deserve their foolish reputation*, he thought bitterly. They became responsible, in his tortured mind, for the loss of his family.

The hate and bitterness began to grow, like an evil destructive thing. He hated the Shaved-Heads for their part in his loss. But not them alone. His own people . . . the Eastern band, his sons, for their foolish decision. He had forgotten that only that afternoon he had been pleased and proud over the same choice. Everyone . . . no person in the world escaped his hate. Except Far Dove, of course, and she was dead. He was sure of that, for he had seen her fall.

The thought brought another sob. How could he go on? He was alone, horribly, completely alone, except for this helpless bundle in his arms. If it had not been for the baby, of course, he would have run down the hill, to be slaughtered with the rest. He *must* go on, for her. She had no one else, no protection. They were alone, the two of them, against the whole world. There was no one, anywhere, who could be trusted.

This very sense of isolation, this alone-ness, may have saved his sanity. There would be those, years later, who would argue that his sanity had *not* been spared. But at any rate, his alone-ness made him begin to think, to plan. Was he not called Hunts-Alone? His were the skills called upon for such a situation. The protection of this infant, he decided, had been thrust upon him, because only he could have done it. His confidence began to revive, at least a little bit.

He must wait until daylight. One major limitation was his inability to function in darkness, and he was well aware of this. The loss of a single sense is a major deficit for most people. Hunts-Alone did not miss it, but when darkness robbed him of a second mode of contact with the world, it became devastating. Those who are active in the time of darkness must depend heavily on a sense of hearing, because vision is diminished. And Hunts-Alone had no hearing. He would wait.

By morning, of course, the baby was hungry and crying. He had all but given up trying to quiet her. It was of great concern to him how her needs for food could be met. Under normal circumstances, one would look for a nursing mother who could share her milk, but this did not even occur to him. The whole world was now his enemy, and he could trust no one. He and this child would live or die together, asking no help. But he must find food. Not for himself, but for the baby. He could fast, but a child cannot.

As soon as it was light enough to see, he started down the slope, carrying the cradle board. The baby quieted somewhat, comforted by the rocking motion. He was cautious, pausing to look long and hard every few steps. He was still not certain that the Shaved-Heads had really gone. At any moment they might burst from hiding, their insatiable bloodlust ready to finish the carnage.

Nearing the shattered camp, he placed the cradle board against a tree and began to survey the destruction. With a sense of unreality he looked from one still form to another, his mind unable to really comprehend. How could he care for them? The task seemed insurmountable. The formal scaffold burial ceremony was out of the question. He could not build so many scaffolds. He suffered, wept, and finally decided on a mass grave. He found a crevice in the rocky hillside . . . yes, that would serve his purpose.

First, though, something to feed the child. He

could hardly have believed, a day earlier, that today would find him stepping past the bodies of his loved ones to rummage in the ruined camp for provisions. Most of the lodges lay in ashes, but a portion of one lodge skin was intact. He pulled it back. Ah! This would help! In the space behind the lodge lining here, there had been supplies and possessions stored. That, perhaps, had been the means by which this part had not burned. There was no dried-grass insulation to ignite here, on the south side of the lodge, and for some reason the supplies had not been plundered. Maybe the fire had been too hot to approach at the time. For whatever reason, here he found a quantity of dried meat stored in a rawhide pack. The pack was scorched, but the meat was intact. That would help. There was also a small quantity of a food that was a favorite of the People. Dried meat, pounded fine and mixed with melted tallow, nuts, and dried berries, also pounded. This was considered a proper food for children or recovering invalids. Good! He thought that this might be useful for the baby. He set the pack aside.

Perhaps a more important find was a folded buffalo robe. Apparently it had not been needed and was merely stored for future use. It appeared brand-new. The fur was badly damaged on one side, but that would not affect its warmth to any extent. He laid it beside the rawhide pack, then took some of the food and returned to the baby.

She was ravenously hungry, but was having a difficult time satisfying her needs by gnawing the hard strip with no teeth. In distress, he tried to think . . . water! Yes, she must have water. He cut a scrap of leather from the unburned lodge cover and rolled it into a cone to carry water from the stream. Patiently, little by little, he dribbled the precious fluid into her mouth. She sucked at it eagerly.

Meanwhile, he was chewing some of the meat and tallow mixture himself. He had seen women do this to provide easier food for a child. When it was soft, he transferred the contents of his own mouth to the baby's. Her eyes widened in surprise for a moment, but then she gulped at it, seeming to reach for more. He was pleased and repeated the process. Finally, the child appeared satiated and fell asleep. He spread the buffalo robe and tenderly placed her on it.

There was need to see what else he could find, but now he must return to the tragic task of taking care of the dead. One by one, he dragged or carried the mutilated bodies to the cleft and tucked them inside. He sat and cried a long time over Far Dove. He had done his best to carry out the formal funeral preparation for her, though he could not for the others. Using the unburned lodge cover, he gently wrapped and tied the precious bundle and carried her to her final resting place. He was glad that she had not been mutilated like some of the others, and that her death had been quick . . . an ax. . . . He collapsed into tears again and lay beside her a little while.

Then he prayed for the spirits of all of them, and began to carry stones to cover the cairn. It was a long and difficult task, and he paused once to feed the baby again.

The tasks of burial complete, he turned again to present needs, rummaging through the refuse to salvage what he could. Weapons would be important. Unfortunately, the attackers, too, would have considered them important.

He had been wearing a flint belt-knife, and that was good. His bow, which had been hanging at the lodge door, was ruined, one limb burned in two. He did find three arrows. One virtually intact, one broken, and one salvageable, the feathers partly burned. This gave him an idea, however. He scratched through the ashes of all the lodges again, and found several usable arrow points, some metal and some of stone.

An important discovery in this activity was a small ax head with the handle burned off. He recognized it as the weapon of Feeds-His-Horse. It was iron, one of those acquired in trade from the Spanish in Santa Fe. A valuable find! He could replace the handle at any later time when he had an opportunity.

For now, one more important find was a waterskin, overlooked, maybe. It was hanging on a small tree near one of the burned lodges, as if nothing had happened. It was important, because now he could carry water as they traveled. That brought another thought. Where would he go? He had not considered that. The burning hate for all people, which had troubled him during the night, now swept over him again.

Vengeance . . . if he could manage to kill a few of the Shaved-Heads, to avenge his loss . . . He could strike a lone warrior here and there, disappear into the forest, to return and strike somewhere else.

But he realized that he could not do that. He had the child to think of. If it were not for her, he would have become a vengeful, ghostlike figure to strike terror into the hearts of the Shaved-Heads.

No, he realized. He could not have done so. If it were not for the baby who lay here now, sleeping on the damaged robe, he would be dead. He would have rushed down the slope to join the fight, and he would have been killed with the others. Maybe his would have been one of the heads that by now must adorn poles somewhere in the country of the Shaved-Heads.

He must leave, now. It was growing late, and he could not stand another night near this place of horror. He gathered and packed his meager possessions and prepared to leave. Feed the infant again . . . one more good-bye at the grave that held all that had mattered to him. More tears . . .

He turned back to place the baby in her cradle board. He would wear this cradle on his back, freeing his hands to carry the other bundles as he traveled. Where? He had not decided. Only that it must be away from here. Back into country where he felt more comfortable. Tall-grass country, to the west. But for now, he set his goal on a thin strip of trees that he could see from the knoll. It was isolated, a little island in the distant grassland. Not too far away . . . Yes, they could reach it by dark.

He swung the cradle to his back, picked up his packs, and turned his face toward the setting sun.

23

» » »

It was another terrible night in the timbered strip. He dared not light a fire, so he wrapped himself and the baby in the fire-damaged buffalo robe for warmth. His fitful sleep was interrupted frequently by the restlessness of the child. He knew that she must be hungry and uncomfortable, but there was little that he could do to help her, except to warm her body with his own and provide a little food and water from their meager supply. *It will be better, later,* he thought at her, hoping that she would somehow grasp such an idea. Actually, he did not quite believe it himself. There were times when it seemed useless to try to go on. But he must survive, for the sake of this baby. . . .

During the times when he did manage to doze a little, he would wake in terror, tortured by the dreams. In these he relived the horror he had experienced on the knoll, watching helplessly while his family was slaughtered below. He would find himself running to help, but so slowly that he could not do so. Or, trying to strike at the attackers, unable to land a blow. Then in a panic, he would recall the baby and turn to save her, to find the cradle board nowhere . . . the slope and the knoll at its crest devoid of life. He would waken at different points in this confused dream sequence, damp with a cold sweat. He would have screamed if he had been able.

There was another dream, perhaps even more troubling, in which he seemed to hover like a hawk over the scene of the butchery. He was strangely detached, watching the horrifying events below but seeing them as of lesser importance. With some interest he watched a man carrying a child in a cradle board, and realized that it was himself. *Odd,* he thought . . . *how can one watch himself?*

He wakened from this dream, greatly concerned. He could understand the horror and grief and fear that he was experiencing, but this . . . could he be dead? He *and* the baby he had tried to save?

He shifted his position, and the stiffness and pain in his left shoulder told him he was still alive. That shoulder had never been quite the same since an encounter with a bear, long ago. It always gave him notice of a change in the weather. And the dead, as far as he knew, would not have the aches and pains of age and old injuries.

There was also the matter of hunger, the gnawing in his belly, and the way it rolled and gurgled. Yes, both he and the baby had already felt the need for food and water, so they must be alive.

By the time the gray of the dawn faded to yellow, he was certain of that fact. They *were* alive, through some miracle. As soon as the sun's rays made it possible to see the surrounding prairie, he was on his feet, searching with his skilled sense of distant vision. There was nothing important that he could see. A distant heron, graceful in flight, making his way to some distant pool . . . *The season is late, Uncle,* he thought. *You would do well to move south to whatever winter camp your people make.*

Winter camp . . . tears came to his eyes again. There *was* no winter camp for those he loved. Their bones would winter in the crevice for all time, now. He realized that his pain and grief were for himself and not for those he had lost. They would return to Earth, from which all life comes. His head told him this, but his heart was not yet ready to accept it. The anguish of his loss was too fresh.

And now, he must plan. They had escaped the danger from the Shaved-Heads, at least for now. He must continue to be watchful, but he thought that there was little chance of the war party's return. There would be no purpose in it.

But what now? Where could he go? With winter coming, he and the baby must have shelter, food, protection from the cold. . . . It seemed an insurmountable problem. He thought it unwise to even consider trying to contact the main band. They were somewhere deeper into the Shaved-Heads' territory anyway. It was quite likely that they, too, had been destroyed. The anger flared again. He should have done more to resist such foolish decisions as theirs. It had been sheer idiocy to challenge the might of the Shaved-Heads. He began to hate the leaders who had been responsible. If they were dead, they deserved it. If not, they probably would be before winter was over.

He wondered about the possibility of joining one of the other bands. The Northern band would probably be the nearest, but he did not know where they intended to winter. He felt a certain resentment toward them, anyway. They had always been so smug, so superior, in their attitude toward the Eastern band. The jokes . . .

What of the Southern band? He knew even less of their winter plans. The scrub oak country somewhere . . . He would not even know where to look. The Mountain and Red Rocks bands, of course, were far away, too far to consider.

Who would be of any help, then? Their only close allies were the Head Splitters, far away to the southwest. Farther, even, than the other bands of the People.

The Growers? There were several villages that he knew. The Growers always traded with everyone, to stay on good terms and guard against the ever-present risk of raids by more warlike hunting tribes. But he had nothing to trade. No Growers, or anyone else, would welcome the approach of an old man and a baby with winter coming on. They would be two more mouths to feed, and nothing whatever to offer in exchange.

His resentment was beginning to grow. A strange thing, resentment for people he had never met. It may have started with his hate of those who had perpetrated the wanton killing. But mixed with this was the resentment toward his own people, who must accept part of the blame. If it had not been for their decisions . . . Once more his thoughts came full circle, with yet another cycle of pain, resentment, frustration, and hate. Added to that, his lifelong tendency to alone-ness now resulted in a destructive transformation. Little by little, he was reaching the point where he felt that he could ask no one for help, could trust no one. At the same time his feelings continued to resolve themselves, and gradually focus in one direction . . . *hate*. It was no longer limited to one person, one group, but spread to include the entire world . . . every other human being except the two of them: himself and this tiny child.

But he *would* survive, he vowed. Survive to raise this baby girl, to teach her the devious ways of all people, teach her, too, to trust no one, to hate the customs that had brought them so near to death. And to survive, only for this cruel twist of fate. The tears flowed again—now not only tears of grief, but of frustration and hate.

He was a little mad, of course, though one afflicted with madness usually does not realize it. If he had, at this stage, encountered any other people, they surely would have recognized his madness. It would have furnished protection, because to all the various cultures in the area, it would be dangerous to harm a madman. To do so would release a dangerous spirit, seeking a new abode. Probably even the Shaved-

Heads, perceiving him mad, would have treated him with respect. They would not have harmed him.

Ironically, then, as his mind continued to retreat from the reality of the things he had witnessed, it pushed him farther from human contact. He was determined that he would make contact with no one. Not a single human being, friend or foe, must know of their survival. In making this decision, he wiped out all possibility of help. And this, when anyone they encountered, even an enemy, would have felt obliged to help them.

By the time the sun was well started up the eastern sky, Hunts-Alone was moving. He did not know where he was going yet, but he wanted to distance them from the scene of tragedy. Away, out onto the prairie, away from the dark foreboding forest that had been their doom. The far horizons somehow promised new life beyond.

He considered trying to steal a horse from one of the villages that dotted the streams like well-spaced beads on a string. His thoughts were clear and cunning, despite the madness. They could travel faster. . . . But what use to travel more rapidly, he reasoned, when one knows not where he is going anyway? He laughed to himself at such a joke. Then, too, he reasoned, it would be much harder to hide if they had a horse. On the open plain, a horse could be seen for nearly a half-day's travel. No, they must remain inconspicuous, let no one know they existed.

Hunts-Alone refilled their waterskin at a clear stream when Sun Boy paused overhead in his run. They rested a little. He took the baby out of the cradle board and allowed her to play on the spread robe for a little while. She seemed to respond well to the freedom from being tightly wrapped. She smiled, crawled on all fours, and sat looking around her.

"I will take care of you, little one," he signed to her, knowing that she would not understand. The signed message was for himself, not for her. She smiled.

He fed her a little, as he had before, and she gulped eagerly at the paste of chewed food, and at the water that he dribbled into her mouth. She was tired, then, and snuggled comfortably back into the cradle board when he was ready to start on.

Once he sighted some riders in the distance and hurried to hide. He did not even try to identify the riders. There was no reason to do so. He wanted to see no one, and did not want to be seen. He positioned himself and the cradled infant near the top of a rocky ridge, and watched the distant riders carefully. They seemed to be following a dim trail that would bring them near, but not too near the hiding place. Good. He would stay here.

He turned to glance at South Wind. She was crying. This bothered him, because he had not known. He was not certain how far a baby's cry might be heard. He had not had occasion to wonder such things until now. But he must take no chances. Quickly, he covered her mouth with his palm as he had done before, during the massacre. He could feel the vibration beneath his hand, and the frustrated baby struggled against it. Finally she quieted, and her dark eyes stared at him in frustration. Cautiously, he removed the hand. The infant started to pucker her face for another cry, and he quickly replaced his palm.

It was not easy, but by the end of the day the pattern seemed established. He was certain that South Wind understood his hand sign for "quiet!" She did not like it, of course, but understood it.

The distant riders had not come close enough to worry about, and had passed on, out of sight. He watched the distant prairie from a prominent hilltop that evening as the sun sank, but could see no sign of other human life in any direction. He waited until after dark and continued to watch for the glint of distant fires. Still, he saw nothing. That was good, though a bit unusual. There should be a town of Growers somewhere . . . ah, yes! As it became darker, he could see a ruddy glow in the far distance.

That would be on the river he had seen to the north. It was reassuring to know where the town was located so that he might avoid it.

He now carried everything to a little ravine below the crest of the hill and ventured to build a small campfire. It was good, and helped him to return to the reality of the world for a little while. He offered a small piece of his dried meat, placing it in the fire, and prayed silently for a little while.

When the fire died, he rose and gathered all their possessions again. Just in case someone had seen their fire, they would sleep elsewhere. He moved, then, to a previously located spot and spread the robe.

He lay there a long time, pondering tomorrow. He still did not have any definite goal, except to avoid people. *Forever!* He would find a place where people never came. But was there such a place? He tried to think whether he had heard of such places. . . . The deserts to the southwest, of course, but that was far away. And the desert was uninhabited largely because no one could live there. There was no reliable water and no game. No, it must be a place that *was* livable, but not used. This seemed an unlikely combination, though. If it had water, grass, and game, it would be worthwhile for someone to live there. Except, of course, if there was some taboo or curse on it, to frighten people away. In that case, it would . . . *Wait!* His eyes widened in the realization that there *was* such a place, and that he had been there.

Of course! he thought to himself. *Medicine Rock! No one ever goes there!*

24
» » »

He must travel rapidly, he knew. The season was late, and at any day Cold Maker would come swooping down to catch the unwary. There were times when he feared that the whole thing was an intricate scheme on the part of Cold Maker. He and the baby were being lured out into the open prairie to die of exposure in the first cruel thrust of winter.

There was a slight temptation to stop and prepare for protection, but he resisted. *You cannot tempt me!* He silently indicated his defiance with an upraised fist toward the north. No, he must not stop. The only effect that such a temptation had was to reinforce the threat that he already felt. That, in turn, made him hurry even more.

He had a few days' supply of the salvaged provisions. Enough, he thought, to sustain him and the baby until they reached their goal. They would require very little. Fasting would sharpen his senses anyway, and stretch their supplies.

Day by day the conviction grew in him that once his goal was reached, they were safe. Had he paused to think rationally, the utter folly of the whole thing would have been apparent. His goal was a place completely unknown to him, except by the legends of the People, and those were always coupled with dire warnings. In the twisted mind of Hunts-Alone, however, the warnings were for others. For him and for the small bundle in the cradle board, such warnings and threats of evil were of benefit. Dread of whatever lurked in the dark rock of the cliff would keep others away.

That was good, because he wanted no contact with other people. The bitterness that had begun with his loss had continued to grow as they traveled. He had been betrayed by people, his twisted mind continually shouted at him. There had been only a few who were loved ones, and now they were dead. Tears still came each time these thoughts recurred. Then would come again the wave of hatred and frustration. Every hurt, every thing bad in his life, he told himself, was because of association with others. The tragedy of his first hunt . . . how much better when he learned to hunt alone.

Yes, anytime that he was completely on his own, he had been able to handle whatever came. It had always been better. He tried to review his life logically and to think of exceptions. Yes, a few. His parents, dead now. Then the kindly teaching of old Tracks-Well. That had prepared him well for what faced him now. But the tracker himself was gone, long ago. Few friends . . . the others hunted together and formed friendships on the basis of those relationships.

And Far Dove. She had been the most important person in his life. She and the children that they had shared. Now they were gone. Dead, every one, some struck down before his eyes. Their grandchildren, too, except for this one that he carried. When these thoughts recurred, he was always forced to stop a little while, because tears impaired his vision, and the great choking sobs racked his throat again. And he always came to the same conclusions: Of all the people in the world, only a few had ever been an influence for good in his life. Those were dead. He wanted no others. It would be good, he thought, if he and little South Wind never encountered another person,

ever. He was not able to think of the future for her,
only that the two of them had survived. He had, partially through accident, managed to save the child.
Now, her continued survival was all that mattered.
He plodded on.

He had a general idea of the location of Medicine
Rock, and headed straight for it, within limitation of
the terrain. He did try to avoid any areas that had a
well-traveled appearance. Sometimes they traveled
by night, when there was enough moonlight. He
carefully skirted the village of Growers that they
passed, to avoid all human contact. There would be
few people traveling at this season, he knew. The
hunting tribes would have established their winter
camps. Traveling traders would have long since decided where they would winter. At home with their
own people, or as guests of some other tribe for a
season. Either way, it was likely that the decisions
had been made long ago.

Yes, no one was likely to challenge the danger of
Cold Maker's return. He would not do so himself,
except for necessity. That recalled again the urgency
of his journey and quickened his steps. He glanced to
the northwest at the thickening sky. *Not yet*, he
thought. . . .

He allowed them the luxury of a fire when he
could, and that helped. The warmth revived his old
bones, drew out the stiffness, and let him continue.
Beside such a fire one night, he fitted a new handle to
the salvaged ax head. That gave him new confidence.
Until now, he had been virtually unarmed, but escape and distance had been more important than
weapons.

Now, however, he was realizing that he could not
hunt for food of any significance with a belt-knife
and a small ax. He thought about it there by the fire,
while he finished scraping the new handle on his ax
and hefted it for balance. He was starting virtually
from nothing.

He recalled his childhood days in the Rabbit Soci-

ety. All the children, both boys and girls, had learned
to use the throwing-sticks. These were actually only
a short, stout club, used very little in serious hunting. Still, the first kill of most children as they
learned to hunt was that of a rabbit, and usually with
the thrown club. He should be able to revert to such
methods.

And snares . . . yes, that was a possibility. He
could probably snare rabbits . . . he assumed there
would be rabbits at or near Medicine Rock. But, even
so, that would not see them safely through the winter. Snaring or clubbing small game would be only a
day-to-day thing, which was a dangerous way to approach winter. People entering the season on a hand-
to-mouth basis would surely not survive the Moon of
Hunger. No, he must, in some way, make a kill. A
kill of a large animal. He would prefer a buffalo, but
an elk, maybe. Even a deer would probably see them
through the winter, if he wasted nothing. Surely,
there would be deer in the timber along the river at
the Rock.

And to make such a kill, he must have a weapon. A
bow or a lance . . . he preferred the bow. Many men
used a lance, but usually on horseback. It was a good
weapon. A bow, however, could be used at greater
distance. The lance could be thrown by a man on
foot, but he must be very close to his quarry.

On the other hand, a crude spear would be easier to
make. A bow would be quite complicated, and would
take some time. Time that he did not have . . .

He must do something, however. It gave him some
sense of security that he now had the ax. He would
begin to gather materials now, limited by his ability
to carry much more than he now had. Wood for arrow shafts, maybe. There was a dense growth of prairie dogwood where he had camped, scarcely an arm's
length away. He cut a few stems for arrow shafts and
trimmed them to length. He could fit points later,
from those in his pack, and feathers at any time.

Wood for a bow? . . . It would need some time to

cure, and would be too heavy to carry. But wait . . .
there was a straight, smooth trunk of the thorny
bow-wood tree. He had noticed it before dark. He
could cut a staff, and use it as such while he allowed
it to cure. It would serve as a crude defensive
weapon, and he could shape it later.

He could not wait, but rose and walked to the
thorny thicket, looking in the dim light for the tree
he remembered. Yes, there it was! He could not see it
clearly, but could cut it in the morning.

While he was thinking along these lines, he realized that for the arrows he would need feathers.
There would be turkeys, and this, too, could be food,
maybe. The People seldom ate turkeys, but there was
no taboo against it, as there was for bear. It was a
good possibility. This, in turn, made him wonder
what other sources of food might be useful. Beaver?
There should be beaver in the river below the Rock.
He was becoming impatient to get there and see what
there might be that could be of use. Well, first he
must get there, and quickly. The night was frosty,
and he shivered as he drew the robe around him and
lay down next to the sleeping child.

Hunts-Alone paused at the top of the ridge to orient himself. He was following the river now, in a
generally northwesterly direction. Surely, it could
not be too many days' travel to the Rock. Each range
of hills that he crossed brought him nearer. He had
half expected to see the Rock from this ridge, but it
was not so. The tallgrass prairie stretched before him,
its winter colors showing pinks and yellows on the
near hillsides. More distance added a violet, then a
bluish haze to the ridges a day's travel away. In the
far distance, the gray-blue of the most distant ridge
faded into the gray-blue of the heavy sky. Or was that
last ridge to the northwest actually a cloud bank? He
shuddered at the thought, and turned away to follow
the course of the river with his eyes.

In summer, it could have been traced by the darker

green color of the trees against the green of the
grasses. Now, most of the leaves had fallen. Stark
white skeletons of sycamores stood out in contrast to
the darker gray of the other trees. In some areas oaks
still held their dead foliage, dull brown in color now.

He traced the river's course by the slender ribbon
of timber, winding snakelike across the prairie.
Surely, he should be nearing the Rock. Could it be
possible? . . . A chill of fear gripped him, a chill that
had nothing to do with the bite of the wind, which
had shifted to the northwest this morning. Could it
be that he was following the *wrong river*? If so, he
thought, they were in deep trouble.

Hunts-Alone glanced at the dark line on the distant horizon. *Aiee*, it *was* looming larger. It *was* a
storm front, a major thrust on the part of Cold
Maker! They must not be caught in the open.

He had been following the river on the higher
ground to the north side, because travel was easier.
Now, he must seek shelter, and quickly. He scanned
the river's course to the west, hoping against hope
that he would see the stark cliffs of Medicine Rock.
There was nothing. In fact, the general course of the
river upstream seemed to have less timber than in
this area. A half-day's travel away, its direction
seemed to be almost directly east and west, and he
could see even less of the gray ribbon that suggested
trees along its course. His heart sank. He *must* be on
the wrong river. He was traveling not toward shelter,
but directly out into the treeless flatland, where
death would be a certainty with no more protection
than they had.

Well, he would fight to the end, for the child. First,
they must seek immediate shelter from the approaching snowstorm. He turned down the slope toward the river, and the scant protection that the trees
would provide. If possible, they should be on the
other, the south side of the stream. He was following
a faint game trail, and would go where it led. Deer,

for instance, might have used it to reach the shelter of a thicket.

He emerged from a rocky hillside into a small meadow, and beyond that could see white gravel. Good . . . maybe a riffle, where the river could be crossed. It was true. . . . He clattered and splashed across, and turned to follow the stream on its south bank. Already, he felt relief from the icy breath of the northwest wind. Here below the trees it was almost calm.

The baby on his back was fidgeting uncomfortably. *A short while longer, little one,* he thought. There, ahead, a thicket more dense, more protection from the wind . . . dead wood for fuel . . .

He hurried into a little clearing and dropped the packs, swinging the cradle board from his back. The baby was crying, but he must first start a fire. He took out the firesticks and began the ceremonial task. The wind, which he had feared might make it more difficult, actually seemed to help. It fanned a spark that grew on the brown powder formed at the whirling spindle's tip. Gently, he wrapped it in his cedar-bark tinder and held it aloft while he breathed life into it from beneath. As it burst into flame, he thrust it into the little pyramid of dry sticks that he had gathered quickly. It was growing rapidly colder, and his fingers were numb as he began to add larger sticks.

It had been close . . . too close. The sky was dark now, though it was still midafternoon. Cold Maker howled in the trees overhead, in his frustration at the escape of his intended victims. Hunts-Alone smiled a grim smile and shook a fist at the howling wind. He had managed to beat Cold Maker, at least this time.

As he propped sticks across some bushes and hung the robe to reflect the fire's glow, he noticed that it had begun to snow.

25

» » »

The storm was brief, as those early in the season often are. Sun Boy made his countermove by midmorning the next day. The white blanket that had been cast over the world was actually quite thin, and already was beginning to disappear. Hunts-Alone decided to wait until the traveling was easier, and settled down by the fire, somewhat impatiently.

He could not see much beyond the thicket from their campfire. The baby was sleeping. He stepped out into the open to orient himself and plan the course of his travel, when the time would come. He was on the south side of the river now, and looked upstream to the west. Should he travel on this side now, in the lee of the timbered strip, in case Cold Maker sallied forth again? It would be better protection, but the traveling might be harder.

With these thoughts idly wandering through his mind, he looked across the little meadow at the rise a bowshot away. The smooth blanket of snow was unbroken except for the tracks of early-rising rabbits. Maybe he should . . . yes, it should be possible to obtain fresh meat while he waited. He noticed tracks of deer, too. The animal had come from the dogwood thicket, there, where it had probably spent the night. It had paused to drink at the riffle, then traveled westward, casually and unalarmed. It was a good sign.

A coyote appeared on the rise to the south and stood watching him.

Good day to you, Uncle, thought Hunts-Alone. *And, good hunting!*

This, too, was a good sign.

A flash of motion caught his eye, and he turned to watch a crow sail across the meadow to land in a dead cottonwood near the river. *Aiee, a third sign!* His spirit rose within him. He began to gain an optimism that he had not had since . . . since the tragedy that had destroyed his life. Quickly, he put that thought behind him.

No, he would see if he could find a rabbit, while the snow cover still helped him. It amused him that he might be able to use Cold Maker's weapon, the snow, to their own benefit. First, he must have a club or throwing-stick. He turned back toward the river . . . had he not seen? . . . Yes, there! A beaver had been working among the branches of a cottonwood it had felled, and sticks of various sizes were left behind. He chose one as thick as his wrist and a convenient length for throwing, and turned back to the network of tracks in the meadow. The coyote watched him closely.

I do not forget you, Uncle, he thought at the creature. *The bargain between your people and mine is still good. The leavings of my kill are yours.*

It had been so since Creation, when Coyote stole fire for Man. Coyote's request, the leavings of any kill, had been honored by the People ever since. As a reminder of the ancient covenant, each of Coyote's people still bears a scorched stripe down the side of his furry coat.

Now Hunts-Alone selected a fresh-looking set of tracks and followed it. He lost the trail once where it became tangled with others, then sorted it out again. The tracks separated from the others and headed toward some clumps of dry grass well out in the open meadow. Yes, a likely place. He moved cautiously, eyeing the trail, then paused motionless to study it.

The footprints were two long marks of the hind feet, with the smaller prints of Rabbit's front feet slightly behind, for that is how Rabbit's people travel. Hunts-Alone did not even think of this, it was so basic to his skills. His observation was that the trail led to the clumps of dry grass, *but did not come out the other side.* His quarry, therefore, must be still in hiding there.

Very cautiously, he approached the grass clumps, looking, looking, his throwing-stick ready in case the rabbit should panic and run. *Ah, there!* He saw a glimpse of a shiny black eye, betraying the presence of his quarry in the almost perfect camouflage of the grassy bower. Yes, now he could see the crouching form, the ears flattened against the back. . . .

Without breaking his stride, he swung the stick as a club, and the rabbit lay kicking in the snow. He picked it up, the appropriate apology going through his mind, then placed it on the ground again, propped in a lifelike position.

I am sorry to kill you, my brother, he signed, *but I need your flesh for the lives of myself and my little one. May your people prosper and be many.*

He picked it up again, held it aloft to show to the coyote on the slope, and waved to his fellow hunter, indicating success. All the signs were good. He would dress out the animal, leaving Coyote's share.

Now, if only he could determine where he was, and whether he had made a mistake . . . was this really Medicine River? He glanced upstream, for no particular reason, and stopped in amazement. There, only a few bowshots away, the north bank of the river rose in a sheer cliff, dark-gray and foreboding. But how . . . why had he not seen this? His thoughts whirled in confusion. For a moment he considered the possibility that the power of Medicine Rock was so great that it was sometimes here, sometimes not.

Then he steadied, and began to think the situation through. He had been traveling on the grassy flat that formed the north bank of the river. The *higher* bank, so that he could see ahead with greater ease. The light had been poor as the storm came in, which had further limited visibility. He realized now that his view yesterday, which had appeared to show fewer trees along the river, was a trick of his own vision. The north bank had gradually risen, and he had been looking *across* the river's course. The impression of fewer trees was created when the bluff became so high that nothing but the tops of the tallest trees were visible. The heavier timber and the tangled thickets that snuggled and prospered in the warm shelter of the cliffs at Medicine Rock were invisible from the north.

Of course, he thought. The ancient legend of the way the People had defeated the invading Blue Paints from the north depended on this factor for surprise. The Rock was never well seen from the north side. He almost laughed at his own stupidity. He had been worried that he was lost, perhaps even on the wrong river. Now, he realized, he was not only right, but had already arrived! *This* was Medicine Rock.

The area that he sought, of course, would be some distance upstream, where the cliff was at its highest. No matter. It was a good day, and his heart was good as he finished skinning and cleaning the rabbit. He left the skin, head, and entrails where he had made the kill, and waved to the coyote again as he turned to hurry back to his camp and the helpless child.

She was awake, her bright dark eyes wide open, looking around the little clearing with curiosity. She smiled at him, and he smiled back.

Yes, many of their problems were behind them. But many more, of course, lay ahead. He began to build up the fire, choosing carefully the driest of sticks, and those from trees that would produce little smoke.

While the flames grew, he took a cottonwood stick and fashioned a spit on which to cook the rabbit. Fresh meat would provide a welcome change, and the moist juices would give strength for the days ahead.

* * *

He stood looking up at the rocky face across the river, still holding his packs and with the cradle board on his back. Time was swept away, and he remembered this experience as a young man. Yes, there, the riffle where he had crossed . . . the crevices, filled with the bones of long-dead buffalo. Once more he experienced the excitement of the place, the power of its spirit. There was, of course, the slight sense of foreboding, but that was good, Hunts-Alone told himself. It was that feeling that would keep others away.

He shifted the weight of the cradle board, and glanced at the sun, now bright in the clean blue of the autumn sky. A little past midday . . . He stepped into the icy water of the riffle, running a bit faster now from snow melt. The snow was almost gone, except for scattered patches on the shaded north side of trees and bushes.

His feet crunched in the white gravel of the riffle, sending a strange thrill of anticipation up through his ankles and lower legs. He was glad that the river was no wider, though. By the time he had reached the other shore his toes were numb, and his teeth chattering in protest.

Yes, there . . . the suggestion of a long-unused path that would enable one to climb the cliff's face. Most people, he thought, would overlook it, for the lower portion was quite poorly defined. In fact, he thought, it might require one or both hands to make the climb. This could lead to problems, for it would be necessary to carry food, water, and fuel up that path. But this, too, was good. It would discourage those who might consider trespass.

Now, how? . . . He wished to climb the rock, but hesitated to leave the child below. He considered several possibilities, and finally decided to leave everything except the cradle board at the foot of the cliff, and return for it later. It never occurred to him that he might *not* find a cave or cranny that would provide a satisfactory abode for him and the baby. Was this not the Medicine Rock that had sheltered Eagle, the legendary warrior and storyteller of the People?

He wrapped his provisions and the few small things that he carried into the robe, and tucked the bundle behind a clump of dogwood next to the cliff's base. Then he began to climb.

It was difficult going. Many times he was forced to unsling the cradle board and place it on a rocky outcrop above him while he climbed over fallen debris. Even so, he realized that the path could easily be improved for easier use. Not too easy . . . It must still appear too formidable for any merely curious passerby to attempt. He could also contrive baffles and traps to confound the unwary intruder.

In one place, the path was blocked by a dead tree that leaned its top against the wall. It was necessary to squeeze past a sizeable branch that obstructed his progress. But this, too, was good. The fallen giant would provide much fuel, easily accessible to the path. It was as if it had been provided, and his heart was good. Best of all, the dry fuel was of sycamore, which would burn well with little smoke.

When he came to the cave, it was as if he expected it, or as if he had been there before. Some insight, perhaps, given to him in compensation for his hearing loss. Perhaps only some dim racial memory, handed down through the generations of the People. Regardless, he was certain that this was the place that he sought. The strange part was that he had sought only a hiding place, a place of shelter from the evils of the outside world. *Any* place, any at all that would fulfill their needs for survival.

This was more. When he saw it, there was a familiarity that he had not expected. He *knew* this place, though he did not know how. He had a strong feeling that it was the very hole in the Rock that had sheltered the injured Eagle long ago. He stepped inside and looked around in wonder. The afternoon sun, slanting warming rays into the cavity, also illuminated it.

The ledge outside, he realized, was wide enough so that the opening could not be seen from the ground. Good. There were also signs of habitation long ago. . . . Charred remains of a long-dead fire, the blackened sticks covered with a fine powder of dust that had drifted in through many generations. There were even the remains of a willow rack at the back of the cave, which had once held supplies or possessions of a previous inhabitant.

He propped the cradle board against the cave wall so that the infant could see, but decided to leave her confined until he made the necessary trips up and down the path before night. And, he must hurry. . . .

"Little one," he signed, "we are home now. This will be our lodge."

He turned back down the ledge to retrieve their few possessions.

26

» » »

Hunts-Alone worked frantically in the remaining daylight preparing for Cold Maker's next sortie. Fuel would be important, even more so than food, perhaps. The cave was sheltered against wintry blasts from the north, and it was warmed by its southern exposure to the sun. Yet, he knew that on many days there would be no sun, and that the wind would be searching out every nook and cranny in the cold rock.

So, he carried wood, trip after trip up the steep rocky path. In places the ledge was dangerously narrow, a real barrier to one with a burden. Even as he negotiated the hard places, he rejoiced in them. These were the features that would deter intruders from approaching. He could also make the path along the cliff's face *more* difficult by placing boulders in strategic places. He even noticed one spot that would lend itself well to a deadfall. He could devise a trap, a rock slide to be started by any intruder who tried to climb the Rock.

But he would think of that later. For now, survival must depend on preparation of necessities: food, water, and shelter, though not necessarily in that order. Because of the threat of bad weather, shelter and warmth were the first consideration. Next, water. He was concerned that at times the ledge might become impassable because of snow and ice. Of course, one could *eat* snow and ice for necessary moisture. But if there happened to be only enough to make the path slippery and dangerous . . . Well, one cannot foresee every hazard that life presents. He would deal with such things as they came.

Meanwhile, he would form habits that would be helpful. At each journey to the base of the cliff, he would drink all that he could hold, and carry a full waterskin back to the cave. He would need more waterskins . . . ah, well, that too, could come later. As soon as he had collected enough firewood for a few days, he must try for a kill. Already, he was observing the habits of a band of deer that seemed to frequent a thicket a little way downstream. The vantage point of the ledge gave ample opportunity to follow the patterns of their activity, and he began to take note for the day when he would stalk them for food.

Over all the frantic activity that thrust itself upon him was one overwhelming concern: the safety of the baby. He could not be with her every moment. It was impossible to carry her on his journeys up and down the path. Yet he must face the very real danger of a fall from the ledge. South Wind was crawling already. He had, so far, managed to prevent danger by confining her to the cradle board. A small child who is familiar with such restraints accepts them easily. But soon she would walk. By custom, this would mark the end of the cradle board. By that time, a child becomes too heavy to strap on one's back anyway. It can carry its own weight.

Yet he knew that a toddler is limited both in agility and in judgment. A stumble, too near the edge of the shelf . . . *aiee*, he did not want to think of it! He must devise some method for protection.

But for now, there were more urgent needs. Shadows were growing long, and he must start the fire. . . . Their first fire in the rocky cave, and a most important one.

The first fire in a new camp was always ceremonial, a formal ritual to announce one's presence to whatever spirits might live here. In effect, *I am here, here I will camp*, a solemn request for permission to inhabit this place. It was quite important to establish good relations with the spiritual powers in a new camp site. In this case, it was essential. In the strange and somewhat twisted mind of Hunts-Alone, the entire future would depend on such a relationship. There must be not only tolerance on the part of the powerful spirit or spirits of Medicine Rock, but *help*, in the form of protection and assistance. He had no qualms about asking for such help, because there seemed no other path.

Once more, as he prepared his tinder and small sticks, he thought of the events that had brought them here. Bitterness and hate welled up again, hate against those who had butchered his loved ones, and against all whose advice and poor judgment had led to it. Against *all people*—no human being escaped his tormented thoughts. No one, except for the tiny girl who lay there in the cradle board. She was innocent of all the guilt borne by the humans of the world. The bitterness, which was like the taste of ashes and gall in his mouth, mellowed when he looked at the baby. He propped the cradle so that she could watch, and so take part in the Song for Fire.

It was a strange "song," of course, one that was completely silent. He built his tiny lodge of sticks in the fire pit. . . . *How many generations since a fire was kindled here*, he wondered, *and by whom?*

The fire-bow twirled the spindle, and the dust ignited well . . . a good sign. He blew the spark into life and thrust it into the tinder as it blazed. Then he added larger sticks . . . not too many. They had no need for more than a small fire.

Then he backed away a step and knelt in reverent prayer. In hand-signs, he followed the age-old ritual. Thanksgiving for life, for fire, for this place in which to camp. Then the ritual of supplication, the request for permission, followed by that for protection and help. It would have been a moving thing to watch, had there been any eyes to see other than those of the baby. Even she seemed impressed by the solemn ceremony, staring at the growing fire, the little curls of flame that rose and took root on larger sticks, to grow some more.

Who is to say that the heartfelt efforts of Hunts-Alone went unnoticed by the spirits of the Rock? As the cave began to warm, he felt a warming in his heart. His mouth no longer tasted like ashes, and his confidence began to grow. He spread the robe on the cave's floor and released the restraints on the cradle board. The infant rolled happily in the firelight, making soft little sounds that her grandfather could not hear. But, he could see her happy smile, and it was good. He felt safe here.

He looked around the little cave, planning, and stepped to the ledge to glance at the setting sun. Yes, there was much to be done. Some sort of curtain to hang in the opening . . . It would prevent the glow of their fire from being seen by passers-by. It was unlikely that anyone would be traveling at night anyway, but sometime . . . Well, that was for the future. A deerskin door cover—yes, he would think on it.

Maybe a willow rack to hold supplies and possessions, there at the rear of the cave. . . . Someone had done so, long ago. He smiled grimly to himself. There was certainly no need for such a rack in the foreseeable future. They had no supplies, and few possessions.

He prepared some of their precious dried food, chewing the leathery strips for the baby. She accepted it eagerly. It distressed him to see that she had lost weight. "We will eat better, little one," he promised in hand-signs. With that idea in mind, he began that very evening to shape his bow, scraping and thinning the wood by firelight. It would take many days, he knew.

As he worked, he was still thinking of one major

concern, the safety of the baby on the ledge. There could be no trial and error. South Wind must be taught the danger, for her first mistake would be her last. But how? . . .

He tried to remember some of the tricks that he had seen women use to protect small children. Children were the future of the People, and were cherished by all. Therefore, everyone looked after all children. *Everyone. But there is no one,* he thought. And that, of course, was the problem. When he was otherwise occupied, there was absolutely no one to supervise and watch this child.

He thought of a custom on the plains. A baby would often be tied on the back of a dependable old mare, which would then be turned loose to graze. This was known to be useful, since the swaying motion developed a sense of balance. The People were excellent horsemen. Some children were able to ride well almost before they could walk, as a result of this custom.

Well, no matter, he thought. Even if he had such a mare, he did not see how it would help. He could not bring the animal up here, and if he must carry the baby down, he could simply let her play on the grass or on the white gravel of the riverbank. That did not answer the potential danger of falling.

Yet, the matter continued to nag at him. There must be something that could be done . . . keep from falling . . . *Wait!* A child was tied on the mare's back to keep it from falling to the ground. Was this not a similar thing? He had been using the cradle board for such a purpose, but could the child not simply be *tied*? A rope or stout thong around the waist, perhaps, tied firmly to the rock of the wall. Yes, that might do! He glanced at the cradle board. Its lashings might provide a fetter for the purpose. And was there not a spot, halfway down the trail, that would provide a place for the baby to play? Yes, he thought, a wide strip of ledge, a shallow cavelike overhang, a large boulder . . . Well, he would look in the morning.

For now, South Wind had eaten and drunk, and had fallen asleep on the robe by the fire. She was beautiful in sleep, long dark lashes lying on smooth cheeks. Cheeks that were not quite as full and shiny as they once were, but he would remedy that with better food. But her beauty, the beauty of innocence, was there, the only beauty left in his world that had fallen to pieces in that one horrible afternoon.

He covered her gently with a corner of the robe. Later, when he prepared to retire, he would tie her in the cradle board for safety. He must, at all costs, guard against any chance of South Wind's awakening to crawl around on her own. Until, of course, he had an opportunity to think through his idea for a fetter to prevent her falling.

He picked up the staff and resumed his scraping and shaping. Bright yellow shavings curled from the blade of his ax and fell to the floor beside the fire. He began to feel a little better. Once he was armed, in possession of a bow, he could do almost anything. His confidence was returning. Or, maybe it was the spirit of the Rock entering his life.

27

» » »

He sat on the ledge and looked across the river at the prairie beyond. The trees were budding, the pale green leaf buds swelling more each day. The gray-green upper branches of the cottonwoods were visibly alive with flowing juices, and willows were yellowing with the same life-bearing fluids.

It had been a long, terrible winter, but they had survived. Sun Boy, having renewed his torch, was once more becoming the victor in his annual war with Cold Maker. The rays felt warm and good as they bathed the south face of the rocky cliff. Hunts-Alone was as close to being happy as he had been since the evil days last autumn. He would never be happy again, he constantly told himself. He was doomed to bitterness and loneliness. But he wanted no companionship, except for that of tiny South Wind.

He turned his head to look at her, sleeping in the cave, and smiled in spite of himself. She was such a joy . . . growing and developing so rapidly. He did not remember that the process had been so rapid with his own children. His and Far Dove's . . . a tear trickled down his cheek. Every thought seemed to come back to the haunting memory of his loss.

He heaved a sigh and shifted his position to bask more luxuriously in the sun. Rising currents of warm air were wafting up the face of the cliff as the warming process continued. The scent of plum blossoms mingled sweetly with another. . . . He tried to identify the fragrance. Probably the purplish-lavender flowers of the redbuds along the creek, he decided. Maybe the hawthorns beyond. It was too early to be the grapevines which clung precariously to the bushes and small trees that grew in crevices of the wall. He would be able to identify those easily anyway. The honeyed odor of the almost unnoticed grape blossoms was sweetest of all.

A flight of geese caught his eye as they came sweeping across the sky from the south, beating their way majestically toward their summer home somewhere in the northland. *There must be hundreds of them*, he thought. He started to count, but gave it up. The first leading lines in their pointed formations were already sweeping past him, up and over the cliff beyond. It was always a thrill to see their migration and wonder about their summer camping places. *They are much like the People*, he thought, *moving north and south with the seasons, only farther because they travel more easily*. Then, at the thought of the People, the bitterness returned to spoil his mellow reminiscences.

At least, he thought, *we have survived*. In spite of enemies, foolish ones of his own people, and unwise decisions on the part of his own family, they had survived. He and South Wind, none other. It had not been easy. There had been times when he almost despaired. It may have been only stubborn anger that enabled him to go on. The bitterness alone may have driven him to greater effort. The Moon of Long Nights had caused him much concern. Sometimes he had almost been convinced that this time, Sun Boy's torch *would* actually go out, leaving the world to freeze in the darkness. Even so, he was not prepared for the Moon of Snows. He had never seen such snowfall. Cold Maker had whipped the blowing, drifting white across the prairie to drop it over the rim of Medicine Rock. To drop most of it, it seemed, directly on the ledge in front of the cave's mouth. It was frightening, the morning that he drew back the hanging doorskin to see only a wall of white.

Fortunately, by that time he had made two deer kills, and they had meat. They huddled inside, carefully hoarding their firewood supply and eating the wall of snow for water. He did not know how many days . . . he should have counted, maybe.

The Moon of Hunger, despite its name, was not so bad. They did have food. Fuel was a greater problem. On any day that the trail down the cliff was open, Hunts-Alone spent all the time that daylight allowed in trips up and down the path carrying wood. He could not believe how rapidly the fire devoured his hard-won fuel supply.

In spite of the hardships, South Wind had seemed to thrive. With great pride he watched her take her first steps, in the cave. He had long since solved the problem of a possible fall from the cliff. A stout rope, braided from strips of deerskin, was fastened to her waist and tied to a solid anchor whenever he was not giving her his total attention. It had taken a little while to determine the exact length that would be appropriate. He wanted her to approach the edge but not be able to slip over, even with the safety line.

There had been one time when he misjudged, and South Wind toppled over. She did not fall far, but dangled halfway in midair for a moment, frantically clawing to regain her position. It had frightened her badly, though probably no worse than her guilt-stricken grandfather. In the long run, the accident may have been a good thing, for now she was more cautious. Seldom did she even stretch the rawhide fetter to its full length. She avoided the ledge's rim, as a burned child avoids fire.

And now, she was walking and beginning to use hand-signs, and eating well. *That* was a major triumph. Hunts-Alone had been so thrilled with her first tooth that he felt like dancing. More had quickly followed, and it was a pleasure to see her gnaw at the strips of venison in her own right, without the necessity of having them prechewed.

There was a great sense of triumph in the fact that he had been able to *do* it. Single-handedly, he had enabled the two of them to survive when their world fell apart. They had weathered that first dreadful winter. And, they had survived winter in better circumstances than they had begun it. They had weapons, food, skins, a lodge in the cave. Best of all, they now approached an easier season.

He could do more exploring up and down the river. It was possible that they could have some sort of temporary brush shelter, as the People often did in summer. Yes, they could live outside in good weather, and retreat to the cave when Rain Maker threatened. He could devote more time to their comfort, not merely survival. *That* would be good! There had been days when the chill in his bones had caused his knees to cry out in protest at the agony of the path up the cliff. Now, he could already tell that the warmth of the sun was softening stiff joints, making his knees feel younger again.

He hoped that there would be an opportunity for a buffalo kill or two this season. He was hungry for the sweet meat of the great beasts. It had been long since he had experienced the luxury of well-browned hump-ribs, cooked over a fire of buffalo dung. And South Wind had never had that pleasure. Even fresh venison could not compare.

Then, too, a buffalo robe or two would be useful. They had only the one damaged robe. It had been possible to huddle for warmth, but he must plan ahead. The girl, as she grew, must have her own bed, her own sleeping-robes. It could be no other way.

He was still not thinking logically, of course. His mind still told him that he must raise the child in the ways of the People. At the same time, he was convinced that she should be raised to trust no one, and never allowed such human contact. At this point in his life, after the tragedy of last season, he was unable to see that if one of these premises is true, the other cannot be.

He watched a pair of beavers on the river below. Next winter, maybe he could contrive traps to procure beaver. They would provide warm garments, as well as the meat of the beaver, which was said to be quite acceptable food.

Then a different odor brought him fully alert. *Smoke!* Alarmed, he rose and scanned the horizon. *Yes, there!* A dirty yellow-gray smudge to the southwest. The breeze was blowing from that quarter, toward them. His initial reaction of alarm was that of the prairie-dweller. A grass fire in the winter or spring can be a highly dangerous situation. On a windy day, it becomes a wild thing, racing across the land from one horizon to the other, faster than a horse can run, scouring the earth from river to river. Sometimes, jumping across a stream, to race on.

For the grassland, there is purpose in this devastation. It cleans the prairie of brush and trees, and results in a more pure mixture of the nutritious grasses that provide graze for the ruminants and, consequently, meat for man. It has been so for thousands of years, the cycle on which not only the religion, but the life of the People depended.

Hunts-Alone was not thinking such deeply philosophical thoughts as he watched the smoke thicken and spread across the distant prairie. He was thinking of danger. He could begin to see the flicker of orange flame now, a writhing snake sprawling across the plain. The pungent odor of smoke was stronger.

Suddenly, he smiled. They need not worry, here on the cliff. He had been thinking in terms of skin lodges in open, grassy prairie. This concern did not apply. The river would stop the fire anyway. This location had been spared from the devastation of fire for many generations, as evidenced by the huge old sycamores and oaks along the stream.

He felt South Wind come up beside him.

"Look, little one," he signed. "Fire!"

"Fire?" she signed in answer, her eyes wide with wonder. She put her hand in his, a little afraid of the vastness of the spectacle.

"It cannot reach us here," he signed. "Come, sit, we will watch."

The fire swept closer. *It is good*, he told himself. When the grass is burned, the new growth is faster, and is lush and sweet. This attracts the grass-eaters. *Maybe there will be buffalo*. This was a device, a ritual, almost, to *bring* buffalo. The People often burned the grass for this purpose.

The line of fire swept closer, and the smoke thickened. Fragments of ash began to drift down like tiny black snowflakes and settle on the watchers. When flames crossed the ridge across the river, leaping like a thing alive, they could feel the heat. South Wind crept close to him in fear, and he placed a comforting arm around her.

The fire raced through a dead stand of plume-grass, leaping high from the impetus of heavier fuel. It threaded through a clump of sumac, igniting dead stems and killing live ones. On down the slope, through the thinning grass to the stream's bed, where dry grass gave way to white gravel, brush, and trees.

Then it was over. Here and there, a smoking sumac stem or buffalo chip, a remaining flicker of orange in a heavy clump of grass. Beyond, blackened earth, as far as eye could see. In a few days, Hunts-Alone knew, the blackened earth would be green. Greener, with more and better growth than areas not burned. Surely this would bring the buffalo. Was it not always so?

"This will bring buffalo," he signed to South Wind. "Meat, robes, it is good."

The little girl looked doubtful.

"You started the fire?" she asked.

"No, I . . ." He stopped in alarm, dismayed that he had not thought of this.

Who *had* started the prairie fire? Sometimes, it was

true, they were started by real-fire, the spears of lightning thrown by Rain Maker. But there had been no storms for several days.

The likeliest occurrence, then, was that the fire had been started by *people.* It could have been an accident, a cooking fire or campfire out of control. Or, a fire started on purpose to bring the buffalo. Either way implied people.

But what people, and where? They could be several days' travel away, or just beyond the horizon. There was no way to tell. It was a matter of concern to him, because he wanted no people here. They must take great care, not to give any sign that would lead anyone to suspect that the Rock was inhabited.

28

» » »

It was much later before they actually saw any other people. Hunts-Alone never knew whether those who had started the prairie fire accomplished their purpose or not. It accomplished a good result for him, anyway.

A great herd of buffalo had arrived within a moon, eagerly following the spring growth of grasses in the burned area. They came from the south, and drifted toward the river to drink. Sometimes there were so many that they fouled the water for a little while. Then they would stand staring at the cliff, as if wondering how to pass such an obstacle. That was a matter of great wonder to him, since these herds must have been migrating on this prairie for many generations.

Finally some wise old cow would seem to remember. Possibly she had passed this way before, or maybe it was only an instinct or herd memory. She would wander up and down the river for a little while, then suddenly start downstream with a determined gait. Others would follow, and soon the entire herd was in motion, flowing like the current of the river itself.

He realized that they would cross the river and ascend the rise on the other side, through the cleft that he had used last fall. How did they know it was there? He was never certain, but he realized that their predictable pattern could be used to his advantage. During that spring migration he managed to kill two fat yearlings by concealing himself at the river and waiting with infinite patience.

Too late, he realized that he had made the first kill much too far from the cave. He spent many trips up and down the river, carrying meat to cook and to dry. The hide, too, was a problem. He could hardly lift the freshly skinned hide. Against his better judgment, he partially dressed it at the site of his kill, watching constantly for any approach of other people. There were none, however. When he had trimmed and scraped much of the flesh and fat from the skin, he was able to half carry, half drag it to a safer spot to continue the process. He had never realized how much the People depended on each other for this heavy work. He had participated, but there were always other hands to help. Now, there was no one.

A large part of that first kill was wasted. Rather, it was salvaged by the coyotes, who found it a great good fortune. Hunts-Alone was careful, when he made his next kill, that it would be nearer the cave. That made things much easier, and he was able to do a more efficient job with processing and storing the meat and skin.

He had many misgivings about this. In case any travelers chanced to pass by, it could attract attention to the fact that someone was living at the Rock. But, he decided, it was a risk that he must take, for now. Once he had managed to establish their existence here, it would be easier. The time of slim survival during that first winter was behind them. It was no longer a matter of mere survival, but of a more comfortable and worry-free life-style.

During that summer he tanned skins, using the methods of the People, with brains and mashed liver. Some of the women would have laughed at his efforts, but his skill was increasing. The second deerskin that he converted to buckskin was better than the first. Yes, he would be able to make garments for himself and for South Wind. It would be an easier winter.

The girl was growing rapidly now, and seemed to bear few scars from the events that had destroyed their lives. She was walking, using hand-signs fluently, and asking questions about everything she saw. Sometimes Hunts-Alone became so weary of her hand-sign for a question that he shook his head in despair.

"You will drive me to madness," he would sign.

In answer, he would receive yet another question, the upraised small hand, fingers spread, wrist motion rotating it slightly.

"Why?"

It was his misfortune that the same sign could also mean *where, how, when, what*—any question at all. He almost regretted that she had learned that sign. But it could not be helped, and if she questioned, he must answer. The results were good, he must admit. She learned quite rapidly. As he had expected, this was a highly intelligent child. It was a joy to watch her develop and learn.

He still took the precaution on tying the cord around her waist, anchored to a firm object, when he was not actually within arm's reach. He was concerned about this. He did not believe that the child understood the danger. Finally, with many misgivings, he intentionally tied the rope a little longer. Now it would be possible, at the farthest point of its reach, for the girl to topple over the ledge, but to be held by the rope. Then he concealed himself to watch from around the first bend in the path.

South Wind played for some time, with sticks and the pretty stones that were her toys. Finally she wandered near the edge, and it was all he could do not to rush forward. One of her toys slipped from her hand, she reached for it, toppled. . . . It was too much, and her grandfather rushed forward.

The child dangled, only partly over the rim, crying

angrily, grasping at the ledge, and badly frightened. Not so badly, perhaps, as Hunts-Alone. It had been a terrible experience for him. He gathered her in his arms, crying himself, and hugged her tightly.

"You see," he signed, "you must not go near the edge."

It was a hard lesson for both, but it had been well learned. The restraint was used for several moons more, but it was now virtually unnecessary. South Wind was always cautious about the ledge and its obvious dangers.

One afternoon, on a trip down the path, Hunts-Alone paused to look curiously at some of the bleached bones in a crevice. This was mute evidence of the great stampede that had killed the invaders long ago. These were mostly of buffalo, but he saw a skull that he thought was that of a horse. He could not see it well, packed among other bones in the dim crevice. He wondered what might have happened to its rider. He climbed down, curious, to investigate further.

Yes, it was a horse, but he could see no remains that appeared human. Idly, he picked up a bone that had once been the thigh-bone of a buffalo. The rounded end was smooth and white, and looked much like the egg of a duck. It felt good to his palm as he stroked it.

A smile came to his face as an idea struck him. He would take it to South Wind as a plaything. He had brought her pretty stones, shells, oddly shaped bits of wood that he found. He felt sorry that she had few toys. Most little girls would have a doll. . . . He looked at the polished white bone and yet another idea emerged. He smiled more broadly.

For the next day or two, when he had the time and could do so unseen by South Wind, he worked at his creation. Some scraps of fur and buckskin, a little pigment from a nearby cutbank and charcoal from the fire, mixed with fat to hold it . . . He held up the finished doll to admire it, and was somewhat disappointed. The face on the rounded bone was not quite right. There was a quizzical expression that he had not quite foreseen. The hair, tied on with a buckskin headband, looked pretty good. He had not tried to make a dress for the doll, but had wrapped it in a "robe," tied with a sash around the waist. A short stick tied across the bone formed rudimentary arms.

It left much to be desired, he realized. From a purely objective view, it was not worth the effort. Yet, he wanted to do *something* for the little girl who had become his entire life. Maybe it would amuse her.

"I have brought you a friend," he told her as he handed the doll.

He could hardly believe the joy in her eyes as she hugged the doll to her. She could know nothing of babies and motherhood, yet she *did* understand, and her maternal instincts made this her most important possession. It was always in her hand or at her side, and she slept with it at night.

He could see that she made comforting little sounds to it as she rocked it. She also talked to the doll with hand-signs. "Little Bone," she called it, and spoke of it as a person. This bothered him some, but he remembered that little girls have names for their dolls. Then he was amused that he had, himself, thought of the doll as a person, an intruder. It did not fit with his idea of no contact with other humans, ever. But such amusement was harmless, he told himself. Let her talk to her doll, as little girls do.

The Ripening Moon was nearly past when they saw the people. Actually, South Wind saw them first, and touched his arm to get his attention.

"There," she motioned. "People."

It was a column in the distance, a band on the move. There were horses pulling pole-drags, dogs running alongside, warriors riding as scouts or "wolves."

Hunts-Alone drew the child back on the ledge out

of sight, and glanced at their fire to see that it was making no smoke.

"We must be very quiet," he cautioned.

He used the sign that had become so familiar when it was essential that the baby's crying not be heard by the Shaved-Heads. A finger on the lips was a warning. If she cried anyway, the palm over the mouth . . . he had not had to use that for many moons. South Wind understood the need for quiet, if only to prevent the discomfort of the hand over her mouth. But this was a new experience, the hiding from people. She had no memory of their escape after the massacre.

"Why?" she signed.

"They must not know we are here."

"Why?"

"People are bad . . . evil. We do not want them here."

"They will hurt us?"

"Yes."

"Eat us?"

"No, no. But kill us, maybe. We must be still. Come, we will watch them."

At the rim of the ledge there was a bushy growth. The two lay prone and watched through the branches and leaves.

"We must not move," he cautioned. "Movement is easy to see."

"Lie still, Bone," the girl warned her doll. "You must not be seen."

The party, Hunts-Alone judged, was moving to winter camp. The distance was too great to identify them. Head Splitters, maybe. Possibly even the People, but he wanted none of *any* of them.

"Where do they go?" asked South Wind.

"To winter camp."

"Will we go to winter camp?" she asked.

"No. We have the cave. It is our summer *and* winter lodge."

"It is good."

"Yes."

A movement below caught his eye. A mounted warrior . . . one of the wolves of the travelers. The man was riding along the edge of the timbered strip, looking along the river and occasionally up at the cliff. Quickly, Hunts-Alone gave the girl the sign for quiet again.

The man was curious, but seemed a little nervous. He was aware of the powerful spirits of the Rock, it seemed. And the other travelers were giving the place a wide space. It was good. That was as it should be, he thought with satisfaction.

Now the man paused to water his horse, glancing nervously upward while the horse bent to drink. Hunts-Alone watched uneasily. Had they inadvertently left any sign? He could think of nothing, but he must be more careful. Yes, he would explore up and down the river to make certain there was nothing. He had become too careless.

The warrior remounted, and swung the animal's head around. A heel in the flank and the horse leaped forward at a canter. The man was eager to move on.

"He sits on an animal," South Wind signed in wonder. "An elk?"

Odd, thought Hunts-Alone. *She was too small to remember!*

"An elk? No," he answered. "But they are sometimes called elk-dogs. Those are Elk-dog People."

"They are bad?"

"All people are bad. That is why they must not find us."

South Wind nodded, satisfied for the present. Soon, the intruders had passed on out of sight.

29

» » »

It seemed no time at all until South Wind was no longer a helpless toddler, but a growing child. One has small ones in his lodge for only a short while, Hunts-Alone reflected.

Her rapid development was a mixed blessing. She required less care, and that was good. The agility of the girl was remarkable. She could dart quickly among the rocks, and skillfully negotiate the treacherous path like a deer. *No*, he told himself, *compared to her, the deer is clumsy*. She found other paths on the cliff's face, ones that her grandfather dared not even try. There were other caves and crevices in the scarred face of the rock, too. "But none as good as ours," she assured him.

"You must be careful, Wind," he cautioned. "The rocks are dangerous."

"Of course, Grandfather," she told him, laughing. "I am always careful."

So, while it was good to see her become more independent, there was worry, too. He was afraid that as she grew to need him less, she would be exposed to unforeseen dangers, and that he could not protect her. Could not warn her, even.

Despite these worries, it was a good life. Both had adapted quickly to the strange, forced existence into which they had been thrust. South Wind knew no other, of course, and Hunts-Alone was in a position to shape and teach her to his own distorted way of thinking. They were very close, because neither had any other human contact. In addition, they spent much more time together than is possible for nearly any two people under normal circumstances.

There were lazy summer afternoons and long winter evenings that were good for storytelling. Hunts-Alone had never been a storyteller, because of his major impairment, but now he found that he enjoyed it. The eager brightness in the little girl's eyes was a thing of wonder for him as he tried to remember and retell the old tales from the story fires. He found that he had retained much more than he realized.

South Wind was intrigued by the legends of the old times when the animals talked. She did not exactly understand, however.

"But how could they talk, Grandfather? Did they once have hands?"

This was a problem to explain, because there was no other human, none with a voice. And Hunts-Alone could not adequately describe something that he had never experienced. At least, not that he could remember. Talking was done with hands, and animals had none.

"You know how it felt, when you were sleepy, and I held you, when you were small?"

Small was a relative term, of course. South Wind had no more than five or six summers now. He could not remember.

"Yes, Grandfather . . . like this!"

She placed her face against his shoulder and hummed softly.

"Yes, that is it. Animals make such sounds, too."

"I have heard them, Grandfather," she replied excitedly. "The coyote does this."

She threw her head back and though he could not hear it, he was certain that the resulting sound would be much like that of the coyote to any listener.

He nodded. "Yes, that is it."

"Then they can still talk," she signed in wonder, "with these noises?"

"Yes, to each other."

"Then what do they say?"

"I do not know, little one. They talk of weather and hunting, I suppose."

There came a time when he had to at least make a try at explanation.

"They make these sounds, which you feel but I do not," he explained. "I have no ears."

She laughed and reached to playfully flip at his left ear.

"You *do*!"

"But they are not like yours," he answered. "Mine are dead, they do nothing."

The big eyes widened with wonder. She stuck her fingers in her own ears.

"Like this?"

"Yes, like that."

"Because you are big and I am little?"

Her face was puzzled.

"No, no. Most people have ears, but I do not."

"Then how is it that I *do*?"

Hunts-Alone threw up his hands in frustration.

"Because it is that way!"

She asked other troublesome questions, too. If she could use her ears to "feel" what the animals said, could she not understand their talk?

"Maybe so. You should try," he suggested.

The result was a little frightening. She would tell him what she heard.

"The coyote sings to another, over there," she explained. " 'Come here,' he says, 'the grandfather has killed a deer, and has left our share!' "

He marveled at her understanding, and was pleased. It was good to see her quickness.

One thing he was completely unable to approach in his thinking: the future. In his mind, it would always be this way. His thoughts refused to accept her as anything but a child of five or six summers. Laughing with the happiness of a child, coming to him with her small hurts and scratches, falling asleep on his lap at the end of the day. It would always be so, he told himself, rejecting any other thought that tried to surface. There would be no others in their world. Any others were not only unneeded, but unwanted and dangerous.

South Wind loved the hiding game, which was used whenever it was discovered that there were people threatening their world. There were several places that she could go if people were discovered. The selection of *which* hiding place was dependent on where they happened to be. The cave was a good place, but in the unlikely event that anyone started to climb the trail, there were other places. One, the most inaccessible, Hunts-Alone had never even seen. She had only told him of it. All of her hiding places, however, must allow her to watch, unseen. She seemed to understand this well, and he felt confident that she could avoid any intruder.

The times when they saw people were rare, of course. Usually a passing band at a distance. Each time he was pleased to see that they gave the Rock a respectful distance. No more than two or three times a summer were people seen at all. Usually, a lone scout or two would come closer, looking up at the cliff in some degree of awe and wonder at the power of its spirit.

How astonished they would be if they could see the agile flesh-and-blood nymph who scampered over the rocks and crevices. It was quite likely, he thought, that if anyone did catch a glimpse of South Wind, they would be sure they were seeing one of the legendary Little People.

In addition to her agile ability on the rocky cliff, South Wind could soon swim like a fish. The People had always had an affinity for water, and it was important to their ways. Most camp sites were chosen at least partly for the stream or lake at hand. Except in the coldest weather, a daily plunge was almost ritual.

South Wind took to the water very quickly, and was a much better swimmer than her grandfather. She could swim underwater almost as well as the beavers that lived in the deep pools of the river below the cliff. Once she followed a large beaver to its lodge.

"I found the door to his lodge, Grandfather!" she related excitedly. "I could have gone in!"

Hunts-Alone was alarmed.

"You must not do that, child! Beavers have strong teeth. You see how they cut trees!"

"But they know that I mean no harm!"

He thought frantically. How to . . .

"Look!" he signed. "We would not want someone in our lodge uninvited, would we? It is the same."

She thought about that for a little while.

"I see . . . we must be invited?"

"Well . . . yes. As we would want no one to enter our cave unless we wished it."

She quickly learned the skills of childhood, including the use of the throwing-sticks. Hunts-Alone was pleased when she brought her first rabbit to contribute to their food supply. She began to practice new skills with a small bow that he contrived for her.

He was astonished sometimes at her ingenuity, though it was frequently alarming. She had her favorite places to play, or to hide. One was a small cave, not really big enough for serious use, but wonderful for pretending. It was off the main path along the ledge, an inaccessible place that she found in her explorations. She took her grandfather there once, but it was with great effort that he made the climb. It was difficult for stiffening knee joints.

"It is good," he signed, puffing for breath. "It will be a good hiding place for you."

"A good place for me and Little Bone to live," she answered proudly.

He smiled.

"But I would be lonely," he signed.

"That is true. We will stay with you. But this will be Bone's cave, sometimes."

"It is good."

Another place was a wide spot on the ledge, partway down the cliff. A large boulder lay there, good for sitting or playfully hiding behind. It was, in fact, one of the places that he had tied her for safety while he went on his necessary trips along the river for fuel or to hunt. She had spent many days there since those times as a toddler. It was almost as much a home as the cave itself.

During good weather, Hunts-Alone could nearly always expect her to be there to greet him when he returned from a hunt. It was good, when he rounded the shoulder of the bluff, to see her sitting there on the boulder, waiting with her doll. She always greeted him with a warm smile and helped him carry whatever burden he might be bringing.

On one especially hot summer afternoon, he labored his way up the path, sweating profusely, to find her waiting on the boulder. Not quite as usual, however. She had removed her buckskin dress and piled it on the boulder with her doll.

He was mildly amused. On such a day, it was usual for them to go swimming when he returned. He assumed that, because of the heat, she had prepared for such activity already. There was an understanding that one does not swim alone.

Now she jumped from the rock and waved her greeting as he approached.

"It is good, Grandfather! Let us swim!"

He nodded agreement. He was tired, and it had been a fruitless hunt. That was no problem. They had supplies, but fresh meat was always a welcome diversion. Today they had none.

"Yes," he signed, "we swim!"

Then, to his horror, South Wind stepped to the edge and dived from the cliff. Terrified, he rushed to look over, expecting to see her broken body on the rocks below. She was nowhere in sight. Then the waters of the deep pool parted and she came thrusting up, laughing and splashing. She waved at him happily, but he was already turning to hurry down the path to the river. He was grateful for her survival, but at the same time furious with her for such an escapade.

"Come and swim, Grandfather!" she signed.

He broke into a frantic flurry of hand-signs, scolding angrily and demanding that she come ashore. Her face fell in disappointment as she waded ashore.

"But you said we would swim," she protested.

"But nothing of risking your life!" he stormed. "Wind, how could you do such a thing? You might have been killed!"

Tears were flowing now.

"I was not, Grandfather. The pool is deep, there. I know where the rocks are."

Now Hunts-Alone was confused and frustrated. What the child said was true, of course. She knew the underwater shape of the pool quite well. Better than he, and he had to admit that she was a better swimmer. He wished to bring her up strong and independent, but was unwilling to let her be so. He had not yet accepted the fact that it could not be both ways, and he was terrified of losing her. This would require much more thought. For now . . .

"That is true," he admitted, "but Wind, you must be careful. My heart would be heavy if I lost you. You will not dive from the ledge again?"

She smiled, wiping tears from her eyes as she stood in the knee-deep water.

"No," she agreed. But then her eyes twinkled in mischief. "Not unless I ask you first."

"It is good," he agreed after a long pause.

It was not, of course, but it was the best he could do.

30

» » »

South Wind did not remember how old she might have been when she began to wonder about other people. There had been several winters that she remembered, and there must have been others before that. Her grandfather, the only other person in her life, never talked of such things as how many winters. She could count, of course, because it was necessary to communicate in hand-signs how many deer in the timber or how many trips up the steep path along the ledge. But counting was never applied to time, and it did not occur to the girl to wonder about her age. She was small, Grandfather was big. It had always been so, and would continue to be so. There was no point in discussion of such things.

There was a time, however, when she began to wonder. She had always been full of questions. Sometimes that seemed to irritate her grandfather. Sometimes, in fact, she did it purposely to tease him, as children do. She had determined the signs that would indicate when she had gone too far. She always tried to stop just short of that, for her grandfather's anger was not a pleasant thing.

Most of the time he was kind and gentle, good with stories, and comforting when she hurt. It was a happy existence, overall. Grandfather was always quick to point out the beauty of the seasons, the colors of a

WORLD OF SILENCE   » 201

sunset, the pleasant feel of the cooling south breeze in summer.

Only when the conversation turned to other people did he become grim and completely unyielding. She learned not to bring up that subject, for his moodiness was quite unpleasant and lasted a long time. She became skillful in guiding the conversation away from that topic to avoid unpleasantness.

Somehow, she sensed quite early that on this one matter, Grandfather might not be completely objective. She did not reduce it to terms of logic, but in essence that is what she did. If people are bad, evil, as Grandfather always said, *what about us? We are people, too. Are we evil?* She dared not ask. Someday, maybe.

So she grew and developed, learning skills of observation from one who was a master at it. She learned to hunt, and without even realizing it, utilized the methods of Hunts-Alone, augmented by her own sense of hearing, which he did not possess.

She climbed the cliff and explored every crevice and cranny. She swam in the clear stream in warm weather, and would then lie on the soft grass to dry in the warm rays of the sun. In colder weather, she could wrap in a warm robe of buffalo or beaver . . . she liked the softness of beaver. The cave was comfortable on even the coldest nights, with a slow fire warming it against the chill outside.

Occasionally there were childhood fears, and sometimes disturbing dreams. A recurring theme was one in which she wished to cry out in terror at some vague fear, but could not. If she cried out, it would smother her, somehow. She finally realized that it was related to her grandfather's sign for complete silence, the finger on the lips. That was used in two circumstances: to avoid alarming their quarry if they were hunting, or to warn against the presence of people. Gradually, she came to connect the smothering sensation with other people, since it did not occur during the hunt. She did not understand why it was so and did not wish to ask. The sensation was offset by the excitement of the hiding game when there were people in the area. It was stimulating fun to take Little Bone and go to hide quietly until the intruders had departed. For several seasons the game was an end in itself, and South Wind did not bother to wonder about the other people at all.

There was another kind of night-vision that recurred periodically. It seemed connected somehow to a dark crevice at the back of the cave. The shadowy recess was behind the willow rack that Grandfather had made before she could remember. The rack itself, and its stored supplies, cast eerie shadows on the cave wall, dancing and flickering in the fire's light. But behind that was the crevice.

It was a vertical flaw in the stone itself, running from top to bottom of the cave's wall. It was part of the natural formation that made the smoke from their fire draw well, and that helped with ventilation in the heat of summer. Near the floor, however, it widened. At its greatest breadth, it would have been possible to thrust her arm into the crevice as far as her elbow. She shuddered at the thought, and did not understand why.

What is it, anyway, this inborn fear that repels humans from dark, cavernous places? Some primitive racial memory that instinctively warns us against unknown or unseen evil in darkness? There are obvious fears of injury from creatures that dwell in such places . . . spiders, snakes, scorpions . . . these are only normal risks in life, and we learn to avoid injury from them. But take away all such fears, there remains an ancient, ill-defined dread of something worse lurking there in the darkness, unseen. Something incredibly evil and threatening. Children know of it, and their first night-terrors relate to its unformed threat.

And it was so with South Wind. Her most fearsome dreams centered around dark evil things that might emerge from that crevice to harm her. She would awaken in terror and cling close to her grandfather, who could defend against anything. Grandfather would rock her in his arms and hum softly to her, and her security would return. Then in the light of day, the fears associated with the crevice seemed foolish.

"Those are only pictures in your head," Grandfather would explain. "They are nothing."

Sometimes she wondered why the pictures contained no real form. But, she did not question the wisdom of her grandfather, who must know all things.

There was a time, however, when she did begin to do some thinking on her own. It was late summer, and they had not yet made the large-animal kills that would provide supplies for winter. Grandfather had gone to hunt upstream, looking for rabbits or any small game that would furnish fresh meat. He had suggested that she might wish to do the same near the cave. It was a big responsibility, and she was proud.

Her hunt, however, was far from successful. She lost an arrow in a difficult shot at a rabbit and spent a long time looking for it. She never did find it, but marked in her mind the area involved so that she could return later.

Just now, she wanted badly to procure *something* to show her skill. She skirted along the stream, watching for any chance target. Another rabbit, maybe . . . a squirrel . . . even a young muskrat of this year's brood would provide a nourishing meal. There were few muskrats here, though. They must compete in this section of the river with the larger beavers.

She paused, standing perfectly still for a little while, rolling her eyes to see the semicircle in front of her. Then she caught a glistening reflection near the water's edge, the eye of some small creature, hidden among the grass and reeds. She studied it a little while, trying to define what it might be. She had been thinking in terms of some small *furry* creature. The outlines of this animal showed no fur at all. . . . Or was she looking at moss, mud, and water? Then she smiled to herself, amused at her error. It was a frog, a green monster half the size of a rabbit. Its smooth skin blended well with the grassy shadows. Yes, now that she could visualize it, the image quickly took form in her head. She could see the wide mouth, little forelegs, and giant muscular hind legs quite clearly. The frog sat, half in and half out of the water, waiting for its prey. *It is hunting, as I am*, she thought.

Then another idea began to form, perhaps suggested by the bulging muscles of the legs. Would not a frog be good to eat? Some things eat frogs . . . she had seen raccoons catch them. And are not raccoons much like small people, using their hands to wash and prepare their food? Maybe . . . even as she thought, she was fitting an arrow and drawing it to the head. The string twanged, and the frog was transfixed, pinned to the mud of the bank as it kicked its last.

She retrieved the arrow and her prize, looking at it curiously. It was easy to skin, she found, and the pale flesh of the legs looked firm and good. She hurried up the path and blew the coals of the dying fire back to life. When Grandfather returned, empty-handed, the meat was already broiling.

"A frog?" he signed.

"Yes!" she answered proudly.

"We do not eat frogs."

"Why?"

He studied a moment. "It is not done!"

"It is by the raccoon people, Grandfather. They hunt for frogs."

"Yes, but our people . . ."

There it was again. Grandfather occasionally seemed to be about to refer to customs of *his* people, "our" people. He had done it once more, but then, as always, changed the subject.

"Well, let us try it," he suggested. "Is it ready?"

The meat was good, though there was not much for two.

"Next time, I will find *two* frogs," she suggested.

It was in the autumn of that same year that she experienced one of the most terrifying encounters of her life.

It was totally unexpected. She had gradually begun to hunt a little farther from the cave, and on this day ventured into a stand of dense timber upstream. She knew that her grandfather often hunted here, especially in winter, when the deer congregated here for shelter. He had warned her to be careful, for it was nearing the Moon of Madness, the rutting season. The buck deer are searching for mates, he had told her. They are aggressive and dangerous now.

So, South Wind was being very cautious. At least, she thought so. She had stooped to look at what may have been the track of a large buck when she heard the rustle of fallen leaves, near at hand. Alarmed, she straightened, embarrassed that she could have been so unaware.

The creature stood only a few paces away, staring at her. It was not a deer at all, but something infinitely more dangerous. A *bear*! No . . . Not a bear, either, but a *man*! He looked as startled as she.

In the next few heartbeats, South Wind's keen sense of perception burned a picture into her mind. He was tall, taller than Grandfather, even. His hair was not gray, but jet-black, like her own. He was dressed in buckskins, and carried a bow. Astonishment shone in his eyes as he stared at her. Surprise, and then something else . . . *fear*! He turned and ran.

The girl barely noted that, because she, too, had turned to run. Her heart was pounding as she clattered across the riffle and nearly collided with her grandfather.

"We must hide!" he signed quickly. "There are people camping over there!" He pointed.

She nodded, trying to catch her breath.

"Yes! I saw one!"

"Yes, there are several," he answered.

"No, no, Grandfather! I saw him, as close as you!"

"*He* saw *you*, too?"

"Yes, of course."

"*Aiee*, this is bad! What did he do?"

"Well, he ran, as I did!"

"He *ran away*?"

"Yes . . . I think maybe so."

He paused for a moment, then began to sign again.

"You go and hide. I will see."

Quickly, he crossed the stream and hurried toward the woods, his bow ready.

The band was preparing to camp for the night, a respectful distance from the Rock. Women were selecting places for cooking fires and establishing camp sites for their families. They were enroute to winter camp and had paused here only for the night. No lodges would be erected, probably few brush shelters, even. The weather was warm, for it was in the days of the Second Summer.

In the midst of all the evening's preparation there came running one of the young men. He was breathless, pale, and shaken, and for a little while, could not talk. The others quickly gathered around him.

"What is it, White Bear? Tell us!"

"I . . ." he panted, still terror-stricken, "I have seen one of the Little People."

There was a murmur, a ripple of excitement.

"But that is a good omen!" said one.

"Is it?" demanded someone else. "How do you know?"

"Our Little People help us, if we respect them," retorted the other.

"*Ours*, yes! But was this one of ours?"

"What did he look like, Bear?"

"Small," panted White Bear, "about this big. He wore buckskins and carried a bow. Big eyes, mouth open . . ."

"*Aiee*," someone exclaimed with a shudder. "What did he do?"

"I do not know. I ran away."

"That is good," observed an old woman. "The Rock is a strange place, of strange spirits. Maybe this is one of someone else's Little People. Could that not be dangerous?"

There were nods of agreement.

"I do not want to stay here," stated one woman firmly.

"Nor I!" another rejoined.

In a little while, people were gathering possessions, scattering the few fires that had been started, and catching up horses that had been turned loose to graze.

It was nearly dark when South Wind and her grandfather met again at the cave.

"They are gone," he announced, somewhat puzzled.

"Yes, I saw from my hiding place."

"I do not understand, Wind. You did not do anything to him?"

"No. I ran. He ran, too."

"Yes. Well, I do not know. They left in a hurry. But please, little one, you must be more careful!"

31

» » »

South Wind was more careful after that. Several times she saw people, but mostly at a distance. The terror of the moment when she had faced one of the evil ones would haunt her dreams for a long time. Her grandfather was quite willing to use that scare to reinforce his point, of course. When he thought she was becoming careless, he would remind her of that narrow escape.

It was true, also, that the experience was told by the other party to the accidental confrontation. Told and retold, around the story fires of his band. That story grew and changed and became bigger than life, spreading to the other bands of the People. White Bear, it was now understood, had had a close encounter with the Little People.

Among some nations, the Little People are a mere humorous whimsy. For some, they are mischievous elves, helping children and functioning as keepers of lost objects. In some tribes, one must never confess to having *seen* one of the Little People, or he will die. The Little People of some of the northern tribes are fierce and dangerous, helping them fight their enemies. Still others tell of frightful gnomes who live underground or underwater and come to the surface only occasionally. These are very dangerous to all humans.

The Little People were not a big factor in the culture of Hunts-Alone's nation. Their existence was acknowledged, and tales were told around the story fires. Traditionally, these stories were whimsical and humorous. Many tales told of their helping lost or unsupervised children, though many others relied on the role of mischief-makers for the Little People.

One incident such as the confrontation at the Rock, however, could serve to change the entire attitude. A popular young man, whose bravery was without question, returning to camp with a tale of Little People . . . *aiee*, who could question it? And it was obvious that Sleeping Fox had been badly frightened by whatever he had seen. A small person with disheveled hair and carrying weapons . . . clothed in ragged furs . . . wide-eyed and staring. Sleeping Fox did not sleep well for a long time, his wife related. He would come awake in terror, reliving his experience at Medicine Rock.

So, one more legend was added to the mystic legendry of the Rock. It had always been a place where spirits dwell. Before the time of Eagle and his strange encounters there, even. And then, generations later, the great stampede of buffalo that had killed so many of the invading Blue Paints. . . . What had been the effect of releasing so many spirits from dying warriors at the Rock? It seemed hardly worth the risk of investigating its strange foreboding spirit. It was there, a place of spirits, without question. Why tempt the wrath of such spirits by asking too many questions?

Sleeping Fox had done so, being a brave and curious young man. His experience had demonstrated the folly of too much curiosity. He had, however, discovered something that had not been known before. Possibly it had not existed before, but it was now accepted as fact. Medicine Rock was the home of the Little People.

The net result of this discovery by one of their young warriors was twofold. First, his reaction to the

contact began a subtle change in the attitude of his
nation toward the Little People. They were regarded
more seriously, and with a certain amount of fear and
dread. The second result was more discernible. The
People took more care to avoid the place of so much
doubt and mystery. There was a great deal of reluc-
tance to challenge the ominous spirits of Medicine
Rock. When they camped in the area at all, it was at a
greater distance.

To the old man and the little girl who made their
home at the Rock, however, there was no noticeable
change at all. Both of them became more cautious
and observant for a while. But the seasons passed,
they slipped into a comfortable routine of hunting,
preparing meat and skins, gathering supplies of wood
for winter's use, and hiding when people were
sighted, even at a distance.

Inevitably, the active curiosity of South Wind began to reach out. She observed things, and wondered.
She still did not question her grandfather about people, because of his predictable anger. She did ask him
many things, and shared with him some of the things
she saw.

She was watching a coyote one day, a young adult
from the litter that had grown up in a den not a bowshot from the riffle below the cave. The coyote was
hunting, and was unaware of her presence. She was
lying on the ledge, partway up the path, comfortably
relaxing in the afternoon sun. She had watched a water snake hunting frogs, and heard the death cry of
the victim as it was swallowed slowly, still kicking,
by the relentless action of the snake's flexible jaws.
She would have loved to watch more closely, but to
move would disturb the process. Maybe some
day . . . Yes, she would hide there, near the reeds
where the snake made its lodge. She would be able to
see better. Some day . . . just now it was too comfortable in the warm spring sunshine to think of anything else.

It was then that she noticed the coyote. She admired its hunting ability . . . the slow stalk, the stealthy observation of a clump of dead grass that *might* conceal a mouse, or a rabbit, even. She had laughed many times at the high jump, to enable the hunter to drop from straight above on his quarry. Very seldom did Coyote miss such a catch.

Just now, she noticed, the coyote was nearing an area where she had seen a nesting killdee. Such birds build no lodge, she had noticed, but place their eggs in the open, on sandy or stony ground. She had examined the eggs, speckled and nearly invisible against a background of the same appearance.

Now the coyote was very near and seemed to become aware of the sitting bird. That would be too bad, she thought. She had hoped to watch the fuzzy chicks when they hatched. They were always amusing, tottering along to follow their mother on spindly legs as long as hers, almost. The chicks could run almost as soon as they were dry. But just now, the eggs would be defenseless. Even if the mother bird escaped, the coyote would eat her eggs. But that is the way of things.

The animal turned and took a slow, cautious step toward the thin scent that he had caught on the breeze. In a moment . . . South Wind's heard beat faster. . . . Just then, the bird seemed to notice the approach of the coyote. She sprang up and fluttered away, dragging a wing. The coyote pounced and missed his catch as the pitiful bird dodged aside. Badly crippled, she dragged herself away, crying piteously and in vain. The coyote leaped again, but again the screaming bird evaded the snap of his jaws. Three times he tried, and each time missed by the barest of margins. Surely the next try would be the last for the crippled killdee.

The coyote sprang, with even more determination. By this time the contest had moved several paces from where the eggs lay on the gravelly slope. And this time the bird dodged away and soared effortlessly into the air, no longer crippled at all! The frustrated coyote made one useless jump, missed by a long distance, and sat down to ponder his failure. Overhead, the killdee circled and stunted and screamed her own name at her would-be nemesis.

South Wind laughed and clapped her hands. It had been a clever trick by the bird to save her eggs. Killdee must have been taught such things at Creation by Old Man. Only with such tricks could Killdee's people survive Coyote's cleverness.

Now Grandfather was climbing the path, carrying a fat rabbit. He stopped and sat down, noticing her good humor.

"What is it, little one?" he signed.

She pointed to the coyote, now retreating over the ridge in disappointment.

"Coyote," she laughed. "Killdee fooled him with her broken-wing trick."

The old man smiled. "She is very good with that one. She saved her eggs?"

"Yes. They are there on the slope."

"It is good. You have seen them?"

"Yes, Grandfather." She paused a moment. "The killdee played the same trick on me, but I went back to look for her eggs."

"It is good," he answered, justifiably proud. "You see things, Wind."

The girl smiled, pleased at his praise.

"Grandfather, are her eggs good to eat?"

"Maybe. They are small . . . duck eggs are better."

"Why are duck eggs round, and the killdee's pointed on one end?"

"Why do you think?" He had learned that this was a technique to handle the incessant questions.

"Well . . . maybe the pointed end holds long legs. . . ." She paused, a hint of mischief in her eyes. "Or maybe it is so they cannot roll down the slope."

"Yes." Hunts-Alone nodded seriously. "It could be either, maybe." He paused a moment, pleased at her observation. "You have tried to roll them down the slope?"

"Yes, Grandfather. They roll in a circle!" she signed, laughing.

"That is true. Now why do the duck's eggs not do that?"

She thought a moment. "Because they are round."

"Yes, but *why*?"

South Wind thought a little longer, and an idea began to dawn. "Ah! They cannot roll . . . they are held in her nest!"

"Yes! And the killdee has no nest."

She nodded in wonder. "It is good!"

"Many things are good, little one. Among them, the fresh meat of the rabbit! Come, let us eat."

He rose and started on up the path. He was puffing a little, and his knees were reminding him that they had just experienced one more winter. It was good to see South Wind's interest, and her bright, quick manner of thought and understanding. It would stand her in good stead.

He immediately tried to change his trail of thought. He had conditioned himself not to think of the future. But he found himself inadvertently coming back to it from another side. South Wind was growing so rapidly now. A sudden spurt of growth . . . how many winters had she? Eleven? *Aiee*, he could not remember. For a number of years, he had managed to tell himself that things would always be the same. The two of them, living here in seclusion, untouched by the evils of others.

Now he was beginning to see that things *do* change, no matter how much we wish it otherwise. He was being forced to admit changes both in himself and in the child. His body was reminding him with every step that he was growing old. How would he deal with preparing South Wind for the fact that he would not always be with her?

And the changes in her . . . *aiee*, she grew taller, no longer a child. He was depending more on *her* all the time. She was a good hunter, and it pleased him greatly to see her observations about the killdee and the eggs. That was good in any case.

It bothered him some that within a few seasons, this child would become a young woman, with all the changes that would happen to her body. Once more, however, he managed to suppress such thoughts. That was far off, in the future somewhere.

He moved on up the path, his right knee creaking just a little as he climbed.

Part III
South Wind

32

» » »

South Wind sat on her boulder at the wide place on the ledge, deep in thought. There were things happening that she did not understand. She looked down at her shirt, and at the way that her swelling breasts now pressed against the confines of the buckskin. It was a strange sensation, not completely unpleasant, when her body movements caused sensitive skin to rub against the soft-tanned garment. She pulled the neck of her shirt away from her body with one hand and looked inside, down the front. The rounded shapes there were much different than a season ago.

Her legs, too, were changing in shape, the calves swelling to produce different curves. It was good, she thought. Heavier muscles there would make her stronger, make climbing and running easier. She was proud of their appearance, though it was not a thing of vanity. It was more like pride in strength and ability.

She had grown taller, too. Now, she was almost as tall as Grandfather, who had seemed so big when she was a child. Sometimes she felt that she was still a child, because there was so much that she did not understand. She had grown up watching the growing up of other creatures and the way that they became adults like their parents. The coyote pups, the eaglets in the nest at the top of the big sycamore . . . She could climb to the top of the cliff and look down directly into the nest, while the parent birds circled and screamed their protest.

"Do not worry," she signed to them. "I will not harm your children."

Some things became adults very quickly, in only a few moons. Others, like the eagles and the red-tailed hawks, seemed to require two seasons. She and Grandfather had talked of this, sometimes in great detail. All creatures require different times, he explained. Larger ones usually take longer, but not always. And trees . . . how many seasons for an acorn to become a tree like the giants just beyond the riffle?

It was several years before South Wind began to realize that she, too, was growing and changing. She inquired about it, without much success. Yes, her grandfather conceded, it is the same with people, too. They grow into adults.

"How many seasons, Grandfather?"

"Many."

She could tell by the expression on his face that the subject was closed. He was wearing the stern look of disapproval that she always found so uncomfortable. The best course of action at such times was to change the conversation to something else, or to abandon it altogether. It had become her custom to do so without really understanding why. There seemed to be one common subject that always brought disapproval, however. Critical looks and angry retorts always resulted from any inquiries about people. *People are bad, therefore we do not talk of them*, was the idea that was lifelong for her. She did not know why.

She also wondered at the fact that the animals she observed usually came in pairs, a male and a female. It was somewhat different with buffalo, but she understood how it was different. Buffalo were herd animals, rather than paired. Each small calf had only one mother, though, from which to feed. Other cows might protect, but only one was *the* mother.

Her maternal instincts told her much about this. It was like her relationship with Little Bone, in a way. She looked down at the doll, lying on the shelf beside the boulder. She had known from the first that Bone was not real, not alive. She had talked to the doll as if it were a real person, using hand-signs, of course. South Wind had no way of knowing that the sounds she could make were a way of communicating between people. But her conversations with Bone were only pretending, and she was quite aware of this. The doll's face had been repainted several times, and her garments renewed as they wore out from the rigors of play. Grandfather had been quite helpful the first time or two, but then South Wind had assumed more responsibility as she grew older. Was she not the mother of Little Bone? That relationship, that caring and protecting role, seemed fairly clear to her. It was much like that of her grandfather for her.

It was always at this point that her logic and reason began to break down. There was something missing here, information that she did not have. It was in the forbidden area that caused her grandfather to become tight-lipped and angry. She longed to know more. Once again, she tried to reason it out. . . .

Most creatures have a mother to care for them. Except, of course, for the little brown bird that sometimes leaves its egg in the nest of the redwing. The bird that comes from that egg is raised by the redwing. *Could my mother have done this?* she asked herself. *Left me for another to raise?* No, it seemed unlikely. For one thing, mothering was done by females, protection by males, in most cases. Coyote males, of course, helped with feeding. She had watched that, the regurgitating of partly digested food for the pups. Later, both coyote parents brought their kills to feed the growing family.

But buffalo . . . she could think of other species, too, in which the male was not present. At least, not to any extent. But everything, it seemed, must have a mother. *Why do I not have a mother?* The question

came back at her again. Was she like the egg in the
redwing's nest? Or like the eggs of turtles and some
snakes, deposited in sand or leafy loam and left, the
emerging young to fend for themselves? Surely not.
People must have mothers who care for them and
nurture them; *as I do for Little Bone,* she thought.

She had sometimes observed passers-by at a distance on the rare occasions when people came near
the Rock. There were clearly men and women, and
the women often carried their young tied in a cradle
board on their backs. This seemed a caring thing. But
she could remember when she was quite small, and
there had been no female. The only mothering person
in her life had been her grandfather, obviously an
adult male. An aging male, in fact. She knew that
this was not her father, because the hand-signs were
different. The "grandfather" sign was one applied to
wise or aging males among the creatures that they
observed.

So, there was no evidence of either a father or a
mother, in her case. There had been a time when she
assumed that it was so with humans, who are somewhat different than other animals. Her observation of
the humans who came close enough to watch
seemed to contradict this theory. Gradually, she had
begun to theorize that she must have had a mother,
and probably a father, too. It seemed only logical.
And once more her logic brought her back to the impossible question: *Who was my mother?* And always,
close on the heels of that was another: *Why does
Grandfather refuse to talk about this?*

There were times when Grandfather's thoughts
seemed inconsistent. He could be interesting and fun
and could explain and answer her every question.
Then at other times he would become grim and
moody and unresponsive. This mood was always
connected somehow with the mystery of her life and
of her parents. People . . . Humans. There must
have been something, some event, that had caused
her grandfather's bitterness. She tried to imagine, as

she had many times before, but with equal lack of success.

Her thoughts were distracted by a distant movement on the plain. Something that was not there before. Buffalo? . . . No, she thought not. She changed her position to see better and cupped her hands to clarify her distant vision, as Grandfather had taught her. Spring sunlight warmed her shoulder and arm from the new angle, and it was good. But this distant motion, dark across the new green of the prairie grasses . . . What sort of intrusion?

It was not long until she could see that the moving specks were people and horses. A band on the move, heading toward whatever people might do for the summer season. Their present course would bring them quite close to the Rock. South Wind watched, fascinated. It was a larger band than they sometimes saw. She suspected that there might be different kinds of people, because her grandfather seemed to react differently to some than he did to others. Their appearance was sometimes different, too. Different in the way they fixed their hair and in the cut of their garments. Grandfather had urged her not to watch the intruders but merely to hide and wait. Her natural curiosity had caused her to deviate . . . well, just a little. She had watched them quietly from safe hiding.

She paused to think for a moment about Grandfather's whereabouts, and whether he might be aware of the approach of the strangers. He was in the cave, she thought, sleeping. Grandfather seemed to fall asleep more easily than he once had. More often, too. She would go and make certain that he was aware of the danger. In a little while, that is . . .

The people were coming closer now. They were traveling parallel to the river and would come quite close to the Rock. She could see individuals and family groups, which once more stirred her curiosity. It was like watching buffalo, somewhat. There, a woman with a small baby in a packboard, with her yearling walking beside her and her previous year's calf on the other side. No, *child*, not calf, though it seemed much the same. And not a yearling . . . Grandfather had verified for her that it took many seasons for human young to mature. Ah, so many questions.

The column came closer. The young woman with the baby seemed very full in the chest, her shirt sticking far out in front. With surprise, South Wind suddenly realized the connection, and stared at her own breasts again. *This is how the young are fed!* she thought. *The milk of humans is between the front legs!* Her thoughts were spinning. *Am I to have young!* She paused, thinking more rationally. No, it could not be, without a mating ritual of some sort. And there was no male. . . . She sat, staring in wonder, lost in the enormity of her discovery. She must know more. Something like anger stirred in her. Why had Grandfather not told her of these things?

Grandfather! She had forgotten that she must warn him. She rose quickly and hurried up the path, stooping low in the places where she might be visible to the intruders.

"Where have you been?" Grandfather signed tersely. "I was worried. There are people!"

"I know, Grandfather. I came to tell you."

"They are preparing to camp here," he warned. "We must be very careful."

It was much later that South Wind's curiosity overcame her. It was fully dark, and the moon, a little past full, had not yet risen. The campfires of the intruders dotted the meadow a little way downstream. What were they doing?

Grandfather was fast asleep, snoring softly. It occurred to her to worry about that a little bit. Not too much. It would be taken for one of the sounds of the night, she thought. It was, after all, much like the cry of the little green herons that nested in the marshy shrubbery by the stream. Frogs, too, were noisy to-night. A few snores would hardly be noticed.

But she wished to get closer, to verify some of her impressions. Maybe she could actually see the big-chested woman feed her young. She rose quietly and slipped out of the cave and down the path, pausing only long enough to see that there was no interruption in the regular cycle of Grandfather's snores. If he woke, he would only think that she had gone to empty her bladder.

The fire-red rim of the moon was just beginning to appear over the horizon as she splashed across the riffle. She must be careful, because in a little while its light would allow easier visibility. She could see better, but could also be seen. That must not happen. She shuddered at the memory of her close encounter several seasons ago.

She approached the camp warily, from downwind, as she would have if she were stalking game. She could hear the murmur of voices, much like the sound of a flock of migrating birds, talking in flight. But softer, mostly. There was a good sound, a happy sound to it. Could this be something that she *remembered*? It did seem familiar, somehow. There was a tinge of irritation at her grandfather. He could tell her, if he only would! She must *demand* it, her right to know her own story.

South Wind was so preoccupied with her thoughts and with the array of campfires spread before her that she became careless. She was totally unprepared for the voice that spoke behind her. It was a voice that held a hint of anxiety and fear. A woman's voice, she realized, since it was much like her own.

"What is that noise?" asked the young woman.

South Wind froze, like a rabbit. It was an instinctive reaction, and in stopping her motion she also stopped the rustle that had caught the attention of the other. South Wind did not understand the sounds that the woman had spoken, but only the necessity to avoid discovery. There was silence for a little while, and then another voice, deeper than the first.

"It is nothing. Only a night creature."

"Yes, but what kind? A bear?"

The man chuckled, and it was a pleasant sound. What few sounds her grandfather made were similar to this, and they indicated that he was happy.

"No, no. Probably a rabbit, one as frightened as you."

Now the young woman laughed, and it was good. *I sound like that when I am happy*, Wind thought. *These are happy people. They do not seem evil.*

She had still understood nothing of the conversation.

"Come," said the young man. "Let us forget the rabbit."

"No, wait. . . . I am afraid. It is said that this is a place of the spirits."

"Yes . . . yours and mine!" he said.

She giggled nervously.

South Wind began to turn, ever so slowly, to see these people. Soon she located them, half screened behind a clump of willow. They were absorbed with each other, and it was easy for her to move into a better position to observe, while hidden from their eyes. It was good that she had accomplished this when she did, for the moon was growing brighter. It was now flooding the timbered strip with a lacy silver light that made things quite easily seen.

The two people were putting their faces together now, and their arms around each other. *It must be a mating ritual*, she thought. Then, as the moon became brighter, a strange sensation came over South Wind. It was a little bit frightening. The young man was very good to look upon in the moonlight, and as he took the woman in his arms, South Wind found her breath coming quickly, and *her* body responding. Her skin was warm, her hands sweating. For an instant, she wished that she was the woman in the arms of the handsome young man.

She took a deep breath to clear her head. *What an odd sensation!* Quietly, she slipped away, but she had learned several things.

The sounds that people made appeared to be a language, much like hand-signs.

People were happy and loving, at least sometimes. She began to wonder if they were *always* evil.

Lastly, she made a decision as she made her way back to the cave. She would demand that her grandfather answer the flood of questions that had recently been thrust upon her.

33

» » »

By the time she came to him, Hunts-Alone realized that he had made a monumental error in judgment. It was frightening to realize it now, and when he was alone he shed many tears of regret over the injustice that he had done to the child.

For several seasons he had felt his body beginning to show the ravages of many hard winters. A new ache or pain, a twinge in some previously unaffected joint or muscle. He did not have the dexterity in his fingers that he once had, nor the strength in his arms and legs. He saw this with the regret that a man does when he realizes that it is happening. The time comes when he is no longer able to do all of the things that a younger man does. The process is slow and gradual, yet it seems, somehow, that it occurs suddenly. One day, he awakens to find that he is old.

Among the People, this was accepted gracefully and with honor. Old age is greatly honored, because of the wisdom that comes with experience. At the end, of course, is death, but is that not only a part of living?

So, it was not that which concerned Hunts-Alone. It was the knowledge that South Wind would be left to fend for herself. That was something that he had failed to foresee. In the throes of his grief and bitterness, he had withdrawn. He had saved the helpless infant by his isolation, but now began to realize that he had done her an injustice. How bitter now the remorse, the wish that he could go back and relive the past ten or fifteen seasons. Again, he tasted in his mouth the regret of his mistakes, like the taste of ashes. The knowledge that he had done nothing to prepare the girl to meet the outside world hung over him constantly. It clouded his judgment and gnawed at the pit of his stomach.

The realization was gradual, and he did not quite know what to do about it. It was far easier to think of other things. Maybe tomorrow he would find a way to talk to the girl. For many moons this went on, as he suppressed his realization of the need. As long as he did not think of it, it did not exist, so he need not worry about it. Sometimes he could even think for a short while that there were only two people in their world, he and the little girl.

But it was becoming harder. He could no longer ignore the budding womanhood of his granddaughter. Sometimes he was startled by her appearance, and by the remarkable likeness to her grandmother, Far Dove. The way she moved, her smile . . . Soon, he knew, she would be a woman. He must explain to her about that, the menstrual taboos and customs. He was at a loss how to bring up the subject, because it was one usually taught by the women among the People. So that, too, was postponed, because it was easier than facing such a crisis.

Maybe he could teach her about that, the power and the hazards of the menstrual occurrence, and yet not get into telling about interpersonal customs. She could remain isolated after he had crossed over, living the self-sufficient life as the two of them had done since before she could remember.

Even as he held such thoughts, his conscience nudged him quietly. What would become of her then? Would South Wind live here alone in the Rock for the many winters of her life? Until she became old and crippled, and starved because she could no longer hunt? Or to die, perhaps, from accident or injury, to die alone, unloved, forgotten? Tears came, and he brushed them away. He rose with determination. He must right the wrong that he had done her. He would begin today, as soon as they were certain that the intruders who camped downstream had departed. He had seen the great interest that South Wind had taken in those travelers and knew that this was the time.

"Wind, I would talk with you," he began uncomfortably.

They had eaten and were comfortable, watching the sunset from the ledge outside the cave. It was good to have the intruders gone so that they could relax their vigilance a little bit, build a fire, settle back to normal routine. *Though that will no longer be,* he thought.

"Yes, Grandfather, I, too!" she signed emphatically.

"It is good. Go ahead."

The girl seemed hesitant, as if she did not know where to start. Finally she began to sign excitedly, her hands flying in the gestures, while tears pooled in her eyes.

"Who am I, Grandfather? Who are we? I have no father and mother, as other animals have. You are near and dear to me, and I have needed no other, but why is it that we *have* no others? You must tell me of these things, of people and their ways, of men and women. There are things I must know and understand!"

The tears were rolling down her cheeks now, and he blinked back his own.

"Yes," he signed. "It is good."

"It *is*?"

"Yes, little one, it is time. Long past time. I fear that I have done you great harm."

"No, Grandfather, you have not! But I want to know more."

"It shall be so. We must start back, long before you were born. To Creation."

"When all the animals could speak? I love those stories, Grandfather, but now—"

He gestured her to silence.

"No, now pay attention. There are stories of people at Creation, too."

"People?" That had been one of her questions. He had told very few stories that involved people. "Where did they come from?"

"My people . . . *our* people, came from inside the earth. It was dark and cold, and they longed for sunlight. So, First Man and First Woman crawled out through a hollow cottonwood log."

"Ah! Were you there, Grandfather?"

"No, no, it was many lifetimes ago."

It was only very slowly that he was able to unfold the story of the People, their move from a vague somewhere-else to the area of the tallgrass prairie, the Sacred Hills. That, too, was long ago. It was many tales, even, before he told of the coming of the outsider with hair on his face, who brought the first horse, which the People called an "elk-dog."

"Why, Grandfather?"

"Before that, they had only dogs to carry packs. The new animal carried packs, so it must be a dog . . . a dog as big as an elk."

She nodded, and Hunts-Alone continued.

"More important, Heads-Off—that was the outsider's name—"

"Why? Why was he called that?"

"Aiee, child, you ask too much. It was said he could take off his head."

Her eyes were big. "Was it true?"

"I do not know. Maybe so. Some say it was only a shiny hat that he removed. But his medicine *was* very powerful. It let him control the elk-dog."

"What was it?"

"A metal ornament . . . it is still among the People. The holy man of the Southern band wears it sometimes."

"Wears it?"

"Yes . . . around his neck, on a thong."

"You have *seen* it?"

"Of course. It is said that it was once placed in the horse's mouth, but now it is an ornament, a ceremonial thing."

He continued, telling of the People, their history and their legends.

"They began to hunt buffalo with the elk-dogs, which was easier than on foot."

"Then why do *we* not have elk-dogs? We do not have the power, the medicine?"

"No, that is not it. We could not hide an elk-dog in the cave."

She laughed at the thought, but understood.

"Then," he went on, "the People found that there were other hair-faced outsiders. Different kinds. Some with blue eyes came from the northeast."

"Blue?"

"Yes. We have traded more with another hair-faced tribe in a place called *Senna-Fay,* to the southwest."

"Traded?"

"Yes, the People gave them furs and robes in trade for metal knives and arrow points."

"Like your knife?"

"Yes. Some knives are stone, like our arrow points."

The process of education was not as painful as he had expected, although slower. South Wind repeatedly stopped him with questions, for her curiosity was boundless. The girl wanted to know *everything,* and he tried to oblige. Day after day they talked of customs and taboos, rituals and human interrelations. She learned of the Rabbit Society, in which the young are taught. And of marriage.

It was at this point that their communication began to break down. He could not bring himself to tell much of the tragedy that had destroyed his entire family, his life, even. Eventually, he managed to tell her that her parents, friends, all their relatives, had been killed. This, he continued, was why people are to be hated, feared, and avoided.

"But Grandfather, are all people evil? My parents? Were they so?"

"No, no," he signed impatiently, brushing tears from his eyes. "But they are dead. We can trust no one."

"Grandfather, I have crept close to some of the intruders to watch them," she admitted. "They seemed happy and loving, and not evil at all."

He was quite disturbed by her confession and became angry.

"You must not do such a thing! I have *told* you!"

That ended the discussion for several days. Only gradually was he able to resume the instruction. One thing that bothered him was that he had no clear goal in all this. He had thought to prepare her for what she would do after his death. Yet he did not know what it was. What would she *want* to do? Probably, she should make contact with the People, but his bitterness refused to let him admit to such a possibility. He could not approach a conversation that would speak of it.

It was several moons before he thought of a way to bring such things into the open. South Wind was making more of their daily decisions now, he realized, as he made fewer. It was good to share the heavy load with someone young and active. He would simply ask her opinion.

"Wind," he signed, "what will you do after I am dead?"

She stared at him a moment, startled, and then laughed.

"You are not going to die!"

"Yes, all things must."

"Of course, but not now. Not for a long time."

She left the cave and refused to discuss it further.

This, he realized, could become a problem in itself. Then another thought came to him. *She will know nothing of how to prepare a body for burial. She must let me teach her.*

34

» » »

It became a stalemate. There were things that he was unable to approach, and those that the girl was refusing to admit. In addition to this seemingly hopeless confrontation, Hunts-Alone realized that something was happening to his thinking. He was becoming forgetful.

At first, he thought that it was related to the strenuous effort to teach South Wind the culture of the People. That had been hard for him. But he also found that he was repeating himself.

"You just told me that, Grandfather," South Wind would laugh.

"What? Oh, yes, so I did, Dove."

"Dove? Who is Dove?"

He tried to conceal his panic.

"Oh . . . she was your grandmother. You look much like her."

But this worried him. Some days were better than others. Sometimes he could remember vividly the names of all his playmates in the Rabbit Society, but not those of his own children, without pausing to think and reason. On other days, he felt fine. If there had been nothing urgent about their conversation, he felt confident that he could remember anything he chose.

But there was still the urgency, a desire to finish

imparting the knowledge that would let him rid himself of guilt. Guilt that he now felt for the injustice of having deprived South Wind of any normal life.

In addition, he became increasingly concerned that the girl could not face *his* death when it came. She continued to refuse to discuss it, to deny what must eventually happen. He was beginning to feel that it would be sooner rather than later. He could see that his body, as well as his mind, was showing the wear of his many seasons. He had no idea how many . . . the years all seemed to blur together now. Of one thing he was certain. They were moving faster, flying past at an accelerated pace.

He was not concerned with dying. It mattered little what happened to his bones. He would, in some manner, return to the prairie sod that had nourished him and become part of the grassland. The grass had been replenished since Creation by the blood, flesh, and bones of his People. His would be no different.

Except for South Wind. His concern was that *she* would be distressed by not knowing, not understanding what to do with his body. In some way, he must force her to face the inevitable problem. But how, when she refused even to admit that it would ever happen?

"Wind, we must talk of this!" he would insist.

And the girl would toss her head, pretending to be casual.

"Of course, Grandfather. Later. That is a long time off. We will speak of it when the time comes. Now, I must go and hunt."

But the time is coming, he would think to himself. *"Later" may be too late.*

He did not worry so much on the days when his senses were dulled. Then, when he felt better, he would worry because he had *forgotten* to worry, and felt guilty for neglecting the problem. Still, he found no easy answer.

Day followed day, with little change except that he grew a little weaker and more forgetful. He realized that their positions were changing. He was constantly depending more and more on South Wind to provide for the two of them, to make their decisions. It was the girl who made trip after trip up the path carrying firewood as winter neared. It was she who supervised the slicing and drying of their meat supply and carried water to him when his knees were too stiff to negotiate the path because of impending weather. Their roles were reversing. South Wind was becoming the caregiver, and he the cared-for. He did not like it, but had to accept that this, too, is part of life. Each one takes his turn as caregiver on his path through life. He had taken his turn, and now South Wind was returning his efforts. Of course, she was far from the helpless infant that he had carried to the Rock so long ago. A tear came to his eye as he remembered. How bitter he had been! It seemed not to matter so much now. At least, his life had been spent well in one respect. He *had* saved the baby, and she had grown into a fine, handsome young woman. She must rejoin the People, somehow. He did not know exactly how, and it made his head tired to think of one more problem that seemed to have no answer. It was easier to set it aside.

As for South Wind, she felt much of the same urgency, but along different lines of concern. She wished to know of her people, her parents, and their customs. And, though the learning, the gathering of information, was important to her, it seemed irrelevant, somehow. She felt the pressing need to *know*, but no urgency to do anything about it, to plan ahead. The concept that she would some day lose her grandfather, the only other person in her world, was so unacceptable that she refused to consider it, much less discuss it. That, in turn, prevented consideration of any course of action beyond such a loss.

There came a time when they almost stopped communicating at all, except for routine and everyday matters. Their major concerns were too painful to discuss, and it was easier to let things go on as they had, postponing decisions and actions until some vague later time in the future. This approach was made easier by the general philosophy of all of the hunting cultures of the prairie: Let each day take care of itself . . . why worry about something that has not happened yet, and may not? Their discomfort, of course, resulted from the fact that both knew, on a deeper level, that certain things *would* happen . . . *must* happen.

They did manage to survive the onset of South Wind's puberty, though it was difficult for both. The girl resented the inconvenience of menstruation, which interfered with her active routine. Some moons she spent those few days in seclusion in her own smaller cave, where she had hidden from intruders as a child. But it was small and uncomfortable. During most menstrual episodes she was merely careful to stay on her own side of the cave. She would procure enough supplies in advance so that Grandfather could prepare his own food, and so that she would not have to touch any of her own weapons. For a bow touched by a menstruating woman will never again shoot straight.

It must have been in her sixteenth summer that the outsider came into their lives. South Wind was standing on the ledge to greet the morning sun when she heard an unfamiliar sound. The call of a horse, searching for a companion. She had observed, when outsiders camped near the Rock, that their elk-dogs behaved in this way. A single animal, separated from others, becomes concerned. It looks in all directions and gives a long, trumpeting cry that says, in effect, *Is anyone here? Where is everybody?*

It was such a cry, and South Wind was surprised because she had seen no travelers. She stepped quickly inside to sign to her grandfather, who was rolling sleepily out of his robes, yawning and stretching.

"Someone is near. I have heard a horse's cry!"

He nodded. "You have seen someone?"

"No, only heard the horse. I will go and look."

"Be careful," he cautioned.

She nodded, picked up her bow and a few arrows, and slipped out.

It would not do to hurry. It was much more important to take time to observe. She had no idea how great was the threat . . . how many, how close? Only the sound of the elk-dog's cry. There were several good observation points along the path down the Rock's face. Places where she had played as a child, peering through the fringe of bushes that clung precariously in some crevice in the rock. She had pretended often that she was hiding from the evil intruders as she peeked between the woody stems to search the meadow and the slope beyond. Now, she did so for real.

She knelt in one of her favorite places and swept the area with her eyes. There was nothing. A great blue heron, fishing in a back-eddy below the riffle . . . a noisy squirrel in the big sycamore . . . a crow making its way across the distant blue of the morning sky. All the world seemed quiet and in place. Had she imagined the horse's call? She prepared to move on, but no! There it was again! The searching cry of a lonely horse. It was closer now. Just beyond that clump of willows downstream, maybe.

The horse and rider came into view, but something was wrong. The rider sat, or rather slumped over the horse's withers, quite limply. He was doing nothing to guide or direct his mount, it seemed. The horse in turn was merely wandering, pausing to crop a few mouthfuls of grass and then moving on. It was strange . . . something must be wrong with the rider. She could not see his face, which was hidden by the horse's mane as he lay face down, his feet and arms hanging loosely.

The animal found an area of good grass and paused to graze there. It was near enough for her to begin to

observe useful bits of information. The man carried
no weapons as far as she could see. Maybe a knife at
his waist, but it could be only an empty scabbard. But
no bow or spear . . . *why?* He must have lost them.
Was he starving, then, because he could not hunt?
No, that seemed unlikely. He appeared in good physical condition. And he could have eaten the elk-dog if
necessary. What, then?

The horse turned, and for the first time she caught
a glimpse of the other side. The animal's shoulder
and foreleg were covered with blood. . . . Some of it
dried and blackened, but some bright red, shiny and
fresh against the light gray of the horse's color.
Quickly, she interpreted this new finding. The horse
was apparently healthy, so the blood must be that of
the man. He was seriously wounded, maybe near
death. She watched, fascinated.

He could have been wounded a day or two ago, she
thought, judging from the dried blood. The horse
could have come a long way. Her rider may have
been able to direct his flight well at first . . . to
travel a great distance trying to escape whatever enemy had hurt him. She could not see his wound, but
the bright crimson stain suggested that he was still
alive, or quite recently deceased.

Now, the horse lifted its head and looked around,
still searching. It gave its long *where-are-you?* cry
again. It was startlingly loud, so close, and South
Wind jumped involuntarily. Then the animal turned
and walked to the stream, its hooves clattering on
the white gravel. Now it bent to drink, and the girl
saw the rider's limp form begin to slide forward. So
slowly, it seemed, his body slipped over the high
point of the animal's withers and across the neck, to
splash heavily in the shallow water. There seemed to
be no effort on the part of the man to avoid the fall.
The sudden splash startled the horse, which shied
away, dragging the limp form for a few steps. *He
must have been tied to it, somehow,* she thought.
The horse quieted, started to move on, and then

stopped at the tug of its burden, now dragging from a saddle that had been pulled askew. The animal gave a long sigh and stood quietly, waiting.

South Wind stared, wide-eyed. What to do? This man might be pursued by others. He was probably dead now, but would the horse just *stand* there? How long? And how long until any pursuers would come? This whole thing was far beyond the realm of her experience.

Grandfather! Of course! He would know what to do. She rose and scampered back up the path to the cave.

35

» » »

Hunts-Alone was instantly alert.

"Where is he? Did you see any others?"

He practically leaped to his feet, more alert than she had seen him in many moons.

"Come. We must take care of this," he signed as he turned to start down the path.

Soon, however, the old man was forced to slow down. He was breathing hard and paused to rest a moment, leaning against the wall of rock. Even as he did so, his eyes were seeking the far horizon.

"Which way did he come?" he asked.

"From that way."

"And you saw no one else?"

"No, but somebody hurt him."

"Yes . . . what sort of wound?"

"I do not know, Grandfather. I was afraid."

"Yes, it is good. You should be. But, any riders in the distance?"

"I saw none."

"Good. But we must watch. He may be followed. And he is still alive, no?"

"Yes . . . I think so. Some of the blood is still red . . . but, nearly dead."

"Ah . . . we may have to help him cross over."

"Kill him?" South Wind was astonished at this suggestion from her gentle grandfather.

"Maybe not." He moderated his statement. "But if he lives, he could tell others that we are here."

She nodded, numb at the thought. They had never killed, except to eat. The thought flitted through her head that maybe Grandfather thought they should *eat* the hapless warrior. No, surely not.

They reached the bottom of the path, splashed across the riffle, and carefully approached the still form on the ground. He lay unconscious, still tied to his horse by one leg. The animal had quieted now, and stood, still peering nervously at its erstwhile rider. The animal was a bit frightening to South Wind, who had never seen a horse up close before. She jumped when the animal gave a curious snort at their approach.

"Will it bite?" she questioned.

"No. But we must cut it loose so it will not drag him again."

Very slowly and carefully, Grandfather approached the taut rawhide cord and severed it, nearer the body of the rider. Now free of the unaccustomed pull on the twisted saddle, the horse relaxed somewhat and began to graze. South Wind stared at it in amazement.

"Come," motioned Grandfather. "We will care for that later. Let us look at the man."

They rolled the man over onto his back. He was of an age somewhere between that of South Wind and that of her grandfather, rather younger than older. *In his prime*, thought Hunts-Alone, a little sadly. He cut away the buckskin hunting shirt to expose the wound. *Ah*, a stab wound between the ribs . . . A knife, or maybe an arrow . . . A feeble, pulsing hemorrhage came from the wound. *A strong man*, thought Hunts-Alone, *or he would be already dead*.

But what to do with him? Simplest, and probably safest, would be to smother him, or cut his throat, load him back on his horse, and drive it away. This, however, was not in the heart of Hunts-Alone. Even the years of bitterness could not destroy the basic kindness that had governed the lifetime of Hunts-Alone. He must try to help this stranger, even though it might put them at risk.

South Wind touched his arm.

"His wound . . ." she asked, "a knife?"

"Maybe. An arrow . . . there may be an arrow point inside."

"Then he will die." It was a statement, not a question.

"Yes. We will try to make him comfortable."

South Wind looked up at the path along the bluff to their cave. Could they possibly take him there?

"No, not there." Hunts-Alone anticipated her question. "We could not carry him. We will keep him here. Now, go to the top of the rise and see that no one comes."

She was off in an instant, trotting up the slope. The old man turned his attention to the wounded warrior. Carefully, he palpated the wound, finally inserting a finger. He could feel no foreign object, but it might be deeper. No matter . . . The exploration started a little fresh bleeding, and he cut a piece of the man's shirt to place over the wound. Then with more strips he tied the bandage tightly around the chest. At least it would look better. *I should have let South Wind help with this*, he thought. *She could have learned.* But his efforts would not result in much success anyway. Maybe it was as well this way.

During the procedure, the wounded man had shown no signs of life. There had not even been a response to the probing finger in the wound. Hunts-Alone lifted an eyelid and found the victim's pupil wide and dark. . . . *Not good*, he thought. He felt for a pulse in the throat. *Fast and fluttering*, very faint.

Wind returned from the slope to report no sign of anyone in pursuit.

"He may have traveled far, Grandfather."

"Yes, it is true."

"Who is he? Is he of your people?"

Hunts-Alone paused for a moment. How deeply did

he want to delve into this with the girl? *Well,* he finally decided, *why not*? It could be a learning time for her. Patiently, he began to explain his thinking to her.

"He is not of the People," he began. "His hair is not right, and his moccasins. . . . The cut is a little different, the thong at the heel. . . . No, this is a Head Splitter."

"You have told me of them. Once our enemies?"

"Yes, that is the one. Now they are allies of the People. They are hunters, like us."

"Where are his weapons?" she asked.

He had not thought of that. . . . A knife at the waist, but no bow or lance.

"He must have lost them in the fight."

The horse whinnied and South Wind looked up.

"What of the elk-dog, Grandfather?"

He had forgotten that in giving his attention to the man.

"The horse cried out?" he asked.

"Yes. I will go and see if it calls to others." She trotted away.

It pleased him to see her making such observations. She soon returned.

"No. It only asks," she reported.

"Good. Now, help me drag this man over by the tree there. And we must take care of the horse."

"Do what with it?"

"We must take off the saddle and the thongs in its mouth."

Her eyes grew wide.

"Is it safe?"

"Of course. Now help me here, and then you can go and bring the horse."

"I? . . ."

"Yes!" He signed impatiently. "Now come here!"

They dragged the limp warrior to the grass beneath the tree, and Hunts-Alone sat down to rest. Ah, how frustrating to have no strength even for such simple things!

"Now," he signed when he was rested a little, "bring the horse."

"But, Grandfather, I . . . *how?* It is large!"

"You do not *carry* it, child! It will walk!"

Finally he realized that she had never seen a horse at close range before. He must be patient.

"Look," he began, "see the dragging thongs at its mouth?"

She nodded.

"Good. That is the elk-dog medicine. There is a circle of rawhide around its jaw, that gives us power over it. Now, walk slowly over to it and take one of the thongs. It will follow you then."

"Are you sure?"

"Of course! It *must.*"

Very cautiously, she approached the creature. It raised its head curiously, soft brown eyes looking into hers.

"I will not harm you," she signed.

The horse took a step or two, then stepped on one of the dangling reins and came to a stop. She gingerly reached for the rein, and to her surprise the horse turned to follow her. It was a little frightening to have a big creature so close, but she tried not to show her concern.

"Good!" Hunts-Alone greeted as she came near.

"Now what?" she asked.

"Now I can help you. We must first take off everything except the medicine-thong, then remove that and set the horse free."

"Where will it go?"

"Anywhere it wants. Find some other horses and join them, maybe. Here, help me with these knots."

They slid the saddle from the animal's back.

"What do we do with this?" the girl asked.

"Leave it here for now," he signed. "We will dispose of it later, after . . ." He did not finish.

"He is dying?" she asked.

"Yes," he assured her.

Then a thought came to him.

"Wait," he signed. "Do not remove the medicine-thong yet."

South Wind had not even considered such a thing, but now asked, "Why?"

"We may need to use it."

He did not take the conversation any further, but he was starting to plan ahead. When the man died, they would have the body to dispose of, preferably far away. The horse could be used for carrying it. . . . The two of them could certainly not carry such a burden for any distance. Yes . . . He was pleased with himself for having thought of this.

"Here," he showed her. "We will tie the reins up over its neck, like this. Now, let it graze."

36

» » »

The wounded warrior never really regained consciousness. Once or twice he moaned, but even that was not certain. It may have been only the sound of a slightly different pattern of breathing, his hard-won breath fluttering past limp vocal cords. Once the man opened his eyes for a moment. They were blank, unseeing, as if the spirit had already departed and the body was empty.

"There is no one inside," the girl signed to her grandfather.

"Yes, the spirit still lingers, but only just barely," he answered. "He is dying."

They sat by the still form all night, keeping a little fire going for light and warmth. Several times, Hunts-Alone sent the girl to watch for the possible approach of this man's enemies, but there were none.

"Should we try to feed him?" asked South Wind.

"No, he cannot swallow. He would choke," her grandfather explained.

Along toward morning, the victim's breathing changed. There would be a long pause, when it seemed that another breath would not come. Then a tiny, shallow effort, increasing slowly with each short breath that passed his lips, longer and deeper until one or two seemed almost normal. Then another stop, as suddenly as it had happened before, and no effort at all for a time.

"This is not good," Hunts-Alone explained. "These are the breaths of one who is dying." He had seen this before and knew that the end was near.

Still, the sun was peeping over Earth's rim before the spirit left.

"It is good," Hunts-Alone explained. "For his people, it is bad to die in the darkness. The spirit cannot find its way and will wander forever."

"Is that really true, Grandfather?"

He shrugged. "For him, yes. Our people do not fear such a death."

"Then it is different for different tribes?"

"Yes, of course. That is their custom, that of the Head Splitters, but not ours. I am made to think that the spirit of this one waited until daylight to try to cross over. He was a strong man, and very brave."

"Now what do we do with him?"

"We prepare him for burial. The ceremony of his people is much like ours."

This will do well, thought Hunts-Alone. He had had the long night to think on it, and this circumstance seemed to him to be perfect for the teaching of South Wind. He could show her the necessary preparations, the ritual, and they could care for this unfortunate warrior's last needs. Then, when his own time came to cross over, South Wind would understand what to do. Yes, it was good.

"We must find a place for him," he told her.

"What sort of place?"

"A scaffold . . . like a rack with a platform."

"But people will see it!"

"Yes, that is why we will not put it here. Downriver, a long way."

"We will *carry* him?"

"Ah, that is why we have kept his horse! Now, first, we must position his arms and legs. He will stiffen soon."

He straightened the legs and crossed the hands over the chest. The dead man's mouth had fallen open, and he tied the jaw shut temporarily.

"Now, we need some poles for a drag. Then we will use more to make the platform. But first, let us wrap the body."

"Wrap it?"

"Yes, in a robe. Go and get a robe. . . . Wait! Was there not a robe tied to his saddle?"

"Yes."

"Good! We will use that. Then we go to cut poles."

The tasks of caring for the body of the unfortunate warrior occupied the entire day. They wrapped the corpse after washing the face and hands and cleaning the dried blood away.

It was a challenge for South Wind to utilize the advantage of the horse, because she still feared it. But, with her grandfather's encouragement, and the absence of malice in the soft brown eyes, she managed. Hunts-Alone questioned whether he had the strength to walk far enough downstream. He climbed on a rock and mounted the horse, while South Wind walked alongside. She had no desire to come into such close contact with the animal.

A long way they traveled, it seemed. It was mid-morning when Hunts-Alone pulled the horse to a stop.

"Here," he signed, sliding stiffly from the horse.

It was an area where a giant old ash tree was breaking down, its limbs broken, some hollow, others fallen to the ground under their own weight. But for many paces in all directions there grew a myriad of the old tree's offspring, tall and straight and as thick as a man's arm.

"Our poles," he signed. "And our scaffold."

He shuffled around, selecting four of the saplings for uprights on which to build the platform. Finally he nodded, pleased.

"These will be our corners. Cut that tree and that one, and the three over there."

The platform took shape quickly. They had brought lashings to tie the poles to the uprights, and the construction was simple. The platform need be only long enough for the supine corpse, and no wider than his shoulders. South Wind did most of the heavy work, but Hunts-Alone was still adept with the lashings.

"This is a good place," he observed. "The trees will grow, and this grove will be thicker and darker. Maybe no one will ever find him."

"Is it always so, the platform?" Wind asked.

"Usually more in the open," he admitted. "It could be somewhere on the cliff. . . ." He was trying to plant an idea. Some day, South Wind would be forced to make such a decision, and he wished it easy for her.

They finished the burial scaffold, then fashioned a pole-drag to pull behind the horse.

"I will ride on it," he told her. "You lead the horse."

South Wind wanted to protest, but she could see that her grandfather was tiring rapidly. He rolled onto the small platform of the drag and heaved a deep sigh of exhaustion. They had been working hard all morning, and it was now past noon.

The old man slept part of the way, but was wide awake when they reached the burial-wrapped corpse. He slid from the drag and stood stiffly.

"Now, we must put *him* on the drag, and everything that is his. Saddle, the small saddle-robe, his medicine bag . . . everything."

"Will you? . . ." she started to ask.

"I will ride the horse."

It had been a long time since her grandfather had had so strenuous a day, and she worried for him. But, he seemed to keep going, drawing on hidden strengths. He showed her how to pull the stiffened corpse up to the platform with the aid of the horse and a rope over a limb of the big tree.

"Now," he signed to her, "straighten him on the platform. Put all his things on there with him . . . except the saddle. Leave it on the ground."

It was nearly dark, now, as she swung to the ground.

"Is there a ceremony?" she asked.

"Yes, a song of mourning. They sing it for three days. But we cannot do that." He stepped over to face the silent figure on the scaffold. "*Ah-koh*, my brother," he signed. "There are those who will miss you, and will mourn for you. We have done what we can. May your journey to the Other Side be an easy one! May those of your people who stay behind prosper."

He turned away, and his face was tired and drawn.

"Are you all right, Grandfather?"

"Yes. Let us go home."

"How? . . ."

He paused to consider a moment.

"We should leave the horse and walk home, but. . . ."

"You ride the pole-drag, Grandfather. I will bring the horse back here."

He seemed indecisive, but nodded weakly. "It is good," he signed.

He slept most of the way back, wakening only when they reached the stream near their cave. He rolled from the drag and lay there.

"I cannot climb the Rock tonight," he told her. "Bring me a robe?"

"Of course, Grandfather. What shall I do with the horse? Take it back?"

"Not tonight. Take the pole-drag off. We can use the poles for fires. In the morning, take the horse somewhere and take the thong out of its mouth. Let it run free."

No sooner had he finished signing than he was asleep. She covered him gently with a robe from the cave, then cared for the horse. Then she wrapped herself in her own robe and sat down beside him. She was tired, but it had been a day that required much thought. She must ponder its events for a while before she slept.

* * *

As it happened, it would be several seasons before a hunting party of Head Splitters chanced upon the rotting burial platform in the ash grove. One side had given way, and a few bones were scattered among scraps of the burial robe.

"Look," said one man, "this is much like our burials."

"Those of the Elk-dog People are much the same," answered another.

"But when we lost Calling Bull . . . look, is this not his knife under the platform?"

They examined the weapon, and most agreed.

"It would seem so. How did he get here?"

Their tracker, who had been examining the area, spoke.

"We will never know. This scaffold was built maybe five summers past . . . the trees have grown. That was when Calling Bull disappeared after the battle.

The rest nodded.

"This was done well," one observed. "Whoever cared for him did well for our brother. He crossed over with honor."

"Yes. It is good," said the tracker.

The leader of the party spoke.

"Well, let us bury his remaining bones and move on. I do not want to spend the night in this area. Is not Medicine Rock near?"

"Yes," answered an older man. "Let us move."

37

» » »

For South Wind, the coming of the wounded stranger had been a major event. His death, the events surrounding his burial on the platform in the ash grove had given her an insight into her own heritage in a way that she had not experienced before. She had actually had the opportunity to see another human being at close range, to *touch* him. She had been saddened when he died, and felt a loss.

It was like the loss of the pets that she had occasionally encountered during her childhood. A caterpillar, a baby rabbit, a frog. These usually died because there was something wrong from the first, which had enabled her to catch the wild creature. Sometimes, though, it was a temporary matter, and the wild thing recovered, or matured, and was gone. Like the young crow with an injured wing. A narrow escape, perhaps, from the great hunting owl, *Kookooskoos*, who relishes young crows snatched from their roosting place in the darkness. She had cared for the crippled bird, feeding it and nurturing it back to health. It would ride on her shoulder or perch near her as she sat on her boulder at the ledge. The crow was her companion for many days . . . several moons, even. Then one day it flew to join some other crows who were passing by, and was gone.

She had been heartbroken, feeling abandoned and alone.

"But she has only joined her own people," Grandfather explained.

That did not help very much. She had mourned the loss for many days. Now, the loss of this human who had come, at no threat, was a similar sadness. She would have liked to talk with him, to learn more of *his* world. He had not seemed dangerous at all as he lay helpless and dying. Surely he was not completely evil. She wished that they could have helped him somehow.

She did understand the danger that he presented to them, and the concern that her grandfather felt. If he had recovered, this man would know all about them and their secret lodge at Medicine Rock. So it was as well that he had not recovered. Still, she felt a loss.

One thing *had* pleased her about the incident. She had seen her grandfather change remarkably. For one day, there, he had become alert and efficient. He was weak and unsteady, but his mind seemed clear and effective. He was more like the strong and dominant figure that he had been during her childhood, and the feeling was good.

She wished that it could continue, but it was not to be. The effort required to accomplish what they had done for the dead man had taken a great toll on Hunts-Alone. He slept for most of the next day, replenishing his strength. He never quite came back, though, to the point where he had been before the incident. It had apparently taken much out of him. He moved slowly and stiffly. This was logical for a day or two after such unaccustomed physical activity. South Wind felt it, too, the soreness in the muscles of her back, arms, and legs. But her stiffness was better in a day, while her grandfather continued to move as if he were crippled. This was a matter of great concern to her. It was as if he had called on a last reserve of strength and had used it up. She waited for it to be renewed, but it seemed that it was not to be. True, his day of extra sleep did seem to allow him to return to more mental alertness, but that was all.

He seemed to have no interest in becoming more active, but only sat, rocking gently, lost in his own thoughts.

Sometimes, on his good days, he was communicative. The old urgency was there, the need to tell her all he could of the ways of their people. She listened avidly, and asked many questions, and that was good. But in a completely unpredictable fashion, Grandfather might be quite irrational. Sometimes he thought he was a small boy again. This was frightening, because she knew nothing of small boys or how to deal with them. At such times he greeted her with the hand-sign for "mother." That was frightening. At first she thought that he was teasing her.

"I am not your mother!" she chided.

"What? Oh, yes . . . who? . . ."

It was with a great deal of dread that she finally realized the depth of his confusion. She was his caregiver, and at the times when he thought himself a child again, the caregiver would be his mother.

At other times he called her by names that she did not know. "Far Dove," who had been his wife. Others who may have been relatives, maybe daughters. Possibly one of these was her own mother. She tried to inquire, but was never certain whether the answers she received were accurate. She thought not, because they were not always the same. Sometimes he seemed to regard Far Dove as his mother-figure, but he also mentioned such names as Otter Woman and Crow.

"Was she my mother?" South Wind would ask.

"Oh, yes," her grandfather would sign.

When she realized that he did so only to please her, and that he answered yes to any such questions, she was very discouraged.

"Was my mother's name 'South Wind'?" she asked as a test.

"Yes! That is right!"

After that disappointment, South Wind stopped asking. Along with the realization that her grandfather's mind was slipping came the sense of responsibility. She must care for him, protect him. Her maternal instincts came to the fore, and she began to mother him. Little Bone was forgotten, gathering dust in the cave. Grandfather was her child.

She called him Possum sometimes. He had used that name for himself, and it seemed to be a pet name from his childhood. He was pleased when she used it, and smiled happily, and it was good.

The thing that was not so good was her increasing feeling of being alone. It was like it had been when she was a child and Grandfather would leave her to go and hunt. She would cling tightly to her bone doll and wait for his return. The thought had sometimes crossed her mind: *What if he does not come back?* But he always did, and it was a joy to see him, to feel protected and unafraid.

It was like that now, the loneliness part. Little Bone had been set aside, and her comfort, yet the one she must protect, was Grandfather himself. Her presence was both a comfort and a responsibility. But there was a difference. As a child, she could hand-sign to her doll and assure Little Bone that Grandfather would return to care for them. Now, what could she tell *him*? There was no end to her uncertainty, no point at which she could tell herself, *Yes, when that happens, we will all be happy again.* She was completely unable to consider that the end point of the present situation was the death of her grandfather. And there were times, she reassured herself, when he was fairly lucid. On a good day, he knew who *he* was, South Wind's name, and all about their home here in the Rock. Unfortunately, the good days were becoming fewer and farther between.

South Wind's insecurity was manifesting itself in more frequent dreams now. The gnawing fear was returning, the dread of the dark corner of the cave, where she had envisioned the evil thing that lived there.

Her childhood dread of being alone crept back, and

she relived the waits for the return of her grandfather, her protector. Asleep or awake, there was the smouldering dread, the suspicion that there really *might* be something that lived in the crevice, a dreadful thing of darkness. And now, there was no one to reassure her that it was only the imaginings of a child. The dread of the dark crevice was growing stronger.

What is it, this fear of dark places, this primal instinct? Does this dread go back to the caves and dens of a million generations ago, before the use of fire drove the shadows back and furnished early man with some protection from the hunters of the night?

South Wind might have been astonished, had she known that her grandfather, too, was experiencing such fears. As he relived *his* childhood in the deterioration of his mind, there was coming back to him the dread of things that lurk in dark places. He was glad that he had his mother . . . Far Dove . . . Crow. No, not those, either. If he could pause and think carefully enough, he could reassure himself. Usually, that is. This was South Wind, the child that he had raised. His daughter . . . no, granddaughter. Sometimes he could not be sure. There had been the massacre, when everyone was killed. He cried when he thought of that. It seemed to upset South Wind when he cried, so he tried not to do it, not to think of that.

He knew that he had some days that were far better than others. He tried hard, on those days, to tell his granddaughter (yes, *that's* who this is!) all that he could think of about the People. Those things were easier to remember, anyway. Some days he rather enjoyed telling her about it. The annual Sun Dance, the warrior societies, the holy men and women of the tribe. There was the vision-quest, on which young people fast and pray for guidance. The Rabbit Society, for the teaching of children. That made him think of Far Dove again, the childhood friend who had become his wife. That in turn made the tears flow, and he would hurry on to another subject.

But he felt that he was doing some good. South Wind *was* absorbing much of the culture of the People.

On his bad days, he could remember virtually nothing. It did not disturb him greatly, because he did not remember enough to cause him concern. If he had something to eat, a little water, and was neither too hot nor too cold, what was the worry? He could retreat into the happiness of childlike simplicity, where others do the worrying and the caregiving.

Even there, however, there are fears. The fear of the things in the dark. He could recall the many times he had held South Wind in his arms and rocked her gently, and reassured her that there was nothing there to harm her. But on the days when he became a child again, the fears of childhood returned. In reliving his childhood, he forgot the times when *he* was the strong protector, giving comfort against doubts. The doubts returned to him, too, bringing fears that evil things lurked in dark places. More specifically, he began to fear the dark crevice at the back of the cave. He did not want to look at it, because he might see some evil thing that lurked there. It appeared in his dreams, too, a formless wisp of dirty brown fog with some sort of evil intent.

In his more rational moments, he remembered that South Wind had feared that corner as a child. Odd, now that their places were being reversed, it would become a thing of fear for him. He said nothing, but when his fear began to come forward in his more confused moments, he knew that it helped to be held in her arms and be comforted, as he had once done for her.

In this odd manner, both were becoming aware of their dread of whatever the crevice might hold. It may have been only Fear itself, brought on by the insecurity of the future and the threat of being alone.

Neither was able to share such doubts and fears with the other, for completely different reasons. And the dark thing that dwelt in the crevice continued to grow, as it did in their minds.

38

» » »

Sometimes it seemed that the short and emotionally exhausting episode of the dying stranger had been a major turning point for Hunts-Alone. South Wind noticed, looking back, that his attitude had changed. It was as if something had been lacking, had wanted completion, and now it had occurred.

Almost from the day of their hard work at preparing the funeral for the unfortunate man, her grandfather seemed different. It was something that she could not define, but it was there. It was as if he had finished that task, the preparation of the body for the scaffold, and thus finished all other tasks, too. He still talked to her, told her things of the People. But it became increasingly clear that he considered his duties finished. It was not in a spirit of failure, although there was a sense of sadness for past mistakes. At times she had the impression that the thing which had seemed incomplete was his life. Now that he had participated with her in the ceremony of death and crossing over, it was finished.

She did not quite understand the mourning that he mentioned, celebrated with songs of grief and loss. There were songs, he had told her, to celebrate many things . . . fire, the morning sun, the return of the grass in the spring. It was quite difficult to understand the concept of a "song," when explained by a person who could not hear the song, nor sing it.

"We do not need it," her grandfather always explained. Instead, he performed ceremonies such as he had done for the dead man. A short statement, a prayer of thanks or of apology to the kill, or a statement to the spirits of a place . . . he had told her of that. A new camp must be symbolized by a new fire, and the simple statement, "Here I will be, here I camp tonight." She had seen her grandfather do these things, make these signs, many times. She thought that she understood . . . these were what he did instead of the songs of the People. She was not quite certain about what the "songs" might be, but she understood their purpose.

Now, the information that he gave her was in bits and pieces, disconnected scraps. Sometimes it was very confusing. Especially now, when she asked a question. The likeliest answer was "yes, that is it." Sometimes she knew that it was *not* correct, and this worried her greatly. What of the times that she asked and received wrong answers that she would never discover?

Even with all of that confusion, her main concern was for her grandfather. He had always been so strong, so sure, but now he had become hesitant, uncertain, and insecure. Weak, almost helpless. She realized with some alarm one day that he had not even been down the path to the river since they had carried the body of the stranger away. That had been more than a moon ago. She was now assisting him to walk the few steps outside and along the ledge to take care of his body functions. As she realized this, it also became apparent to her that he was not only weaker, but thinner. He was losing weight.

With this in mind, she began to watch him more closely. He picked at his food, seeming not to relish it as he once had. He would take a bite, chew slowly, swallow, and then just sit there, staring blankly at nothing. His spirit seemed far away. She would speak to him, and he would rouse, sometimes appearing surprised to find food before him.

"Grandfather, you must eat!"

He would turn and look at her, mildly irritated at her concern.

"Of course!"

But he continued to show little interest, and he became thinner and more frail. He seemed to lose control of bowels and bladder, and sometimes soiled himself. South Wind patiently cleaned him. On his worst days this seemed to mean nothing to him. He was a child again, and she the mother. It was then that he called her Mother, or sometimes Otter Woman. *Was that his mother's name?* She wondered.

On better days, at times when he knew her name, he was apologetic.

"Wind, you should not have to do this for me," he signed sadly as she washed the loose bowel excrement from his legs.

She smiled. She had thought of the distasteful task as merely a duty.

"You have done so for me, many times, no?"

"Yes," he nodded, smiling weakly. "But I am a burden to you."

"The burden is light. I was a greater burden to you!"

Still, she could tell that he worried about being a problem to her. On his more lucid days, that is. On some, he worried about nothing, or was cross and irritable. She was not certain which was harder, to have him understand nothing and not know her or to watch his sadness and remorse over the care she must give him. Her heart was heavy for him.

She hated to leave him, because of his intermittent confusion. On one occasion, she left him while he slept, to replenish their waterskins. She was gone only a short while, but she returned to find him outside on the ledge, tottering precariously. She dropped the waterskins and raced forward, at the same time trying not to alarm him. He seemed unaware of the sheer drop to the rocks below. He looked up and saw her as she drew near.

"Grandfather," she signed, trying to hide her alarm, "let us go inside now. Will you tell me of the People?"

"What? Oh, yes, Crow, it is good."

She had come to ignore his mistakes when he called her by the name of another. There seemed to be no point in belaboring it. She helped him inside, where he quickly fell asleep again, exhausted from his exertion.

She considered some sort of tether to prevent his falling off the ledge. Had he not once told her that as she learned to walk he had used a plaited length of rawhide around her waist to protect her from falling? She hesitated to initiate such a thing. She was not sure how he would react. Maybe he would be better . . . and on some days, it would be true.

There came a time, however, when the question of the rawhide tether solved itself. Her grandfather simply became too weak to stand. It was a mixed blessing. She could go for water, or fuel, or to hunt, with some confidence that he would not try to leave the cave. But her heart was heavy over the reason.

Autumn was drawing near, and as the days grew shorter and she laid up supplies for the coming winter, she was faced each day with a thought that she could not escape: It was highly unlikely that her grandfather could survive the harsh Moon of Long Nights, followed by the Moon of Snows. It was frightening to consider. She had denied this eventuality for so long, and now she could no longer ignore it. She had come face to face with the fact that soon she would be alone.

There were two parts to this. One, of course, the concern for her grandfather. But in her world, the death of any creature is only a part of life. She had seen the stranger cross over, and it had been a quiet thing. Grandfather had not seemed to fear death, except for leaving her. Sometimes, too, she felt that the frail form in the cave was no longer the same anyway. She had already lost him, the strong, dominant parent and teacher who had nurtured and taught her. That one held little resemblance to the failing, sometimes mindless person who now needed her care. *Maybe*, she thought, *his spirit has already crossed over, and only the body is left behind*. They had not talked of this, and she did not know whether it could happen.

In any case, she could see that the body could not continue as it was, losing weight and strength each day. That brought her to her second concern, which was not for Grandfather, but for herself. When he had finished crossing over, she would be alone. He was the only other person in her world, and when he was gone, what then? He had explained to her that when the spirit crosses over, it is still here, but is merely on the Other Side. That was a comforting thing, but how could she talk to him then? Without hands, how can a spirit sign? The thought of being alone, once a childhood fear that she had outgrown, now came creeping back. With something like panic, she thought of it . . . no one to talk to, to laugh with, to share stories, to protect. . . .

What about the dark thing in the crevice! Grandfather had been able to hold and comfort her as a child, and to make the bad thing go away. Now, in his childish moments, he seemed to fear it, and she had been able to help him suppress it. Together, they had repulsed the danger that lurked there. But, after he was gone, what would happen? Could she, alone, keep it in its place, away from any harm? Sometimes she felt like a helpless child again as she thought of it.

As it happened, the end came rather sooner than later. It was not in the throes of Cold Maker's winter sorties from the northern mountains. It was in the warmth of Second Summer. The season was late. A delayed frost had turned the sumac its bright crimson, the cottonwoods golden yellow, and the prairie grasses their assorted hues of pink and gold and deep red. The seed-heads of the tall real-grass nodded higher than her head, and the warm smells of autumn filled the clear blue of the sky. But the nights were growing long. Soon Cold Maker would come.

This had always been a favorite time for Hunts-Alone, and he seemed to rally for the occasion.

"Wind," he signed, "will you help me outside? I would sit in the sun."

She was startled. It had been several days since he even knew her.

"Of course, Grandfather."

It was easier than it once would have been. The thin frame was so frail that she could have lifted him now. Carefully, she assisted him to the ledge and helped position him comfortably, seated on a robe in the sun. He breathed deeply and smiled.

"It is good!"

All afternoon he sat there, watching the eagles soar and a distant band of buffalo graze their way across the valley. A long line of geese honked their way south. He could not hear their song, but he loved to watch them on their way.

Shadows grew long, and South Wind, returning with firewood, asked if he wished to go inside.

"A little longer," he signed. "Sun Boy uses wonderful paints tonight."

It was true. On the tallgrass prairie, the sunsets are the world's finest at any time because of the vastness of the sky. But there are none finer than those of autumn. The haze of Second Summer, lying over hills a day's travel away, lets Sun Boy paint the world and the sky with golds and reds and purples, and it is good.

"Yes," South Wind agreed. "It is good."

He insisted on staying until the first stars began to show against the gray-purple of the sky and the breeze became chill.

"Now," he signed, "help me inside."

He ate well, of fresh buffalo that she had killed, then rolled in his robe and fell asleep.

Sometime during the night, his spirit crossed over, quietly and without trouble. South Wind discovered this at daylight. He appeared calm and comfortable, and there was a faint smile on his lips. His long and troubled journey was over.

South Wind knelt beside him, touching the cold skin, knowing that it was over for him, and that it was good. This made it no easier for her.

She rose, blinded now by the tears that came in a flood, and retreated to the ledge. There, she greeted the rising sun with a long, keening wail of sorrow, which echoed along the face of the Rock and across the valley. She did not even think that someone might hear. She did not care.

In her grief, she now understood the Song of Mourning.

39

» » »

South Wind, after her initial grief reaction, began to undertake the tasks that she knew must be done. The body of Hunts-Alone already lay in a position that appeared comfortable, supine at full length. She folded his arms across his chest, weeping openly as she did so. His eyes were closed as if in sleep, and she straightened his head to face forward.

"There," she signed to the still form. She would do for him as they had done together for the stranger.

She sat a little while and thought about that, trying to remember. She had been preoccupied with the experience of touching and being near another human being. But, she recalled how insistent her grandfather had been that she observe and learn. She had thought it strange at the time that Grandfather had actually seemed pleased at the opportunity to care for the body of the departed one. Now, it began to make more sense. At that time, she had been denying to herself the possibility that she would ever be faced with this duty. Grandfather had seemed immortal. Now, she had seen him fail, had suffered the heartbreak of watching his mind go and his strength weaken. He had been so strong, in spirit and in body. The tears flowed again.

But now she must plan . . . where would his resting place be? In her mind, she thought of the scaffold

in the ash grove. It seemed appropriate, the place of
the only funeral she had ever seen. She was strong
enough to take him there; frail as he had now become, she could carry him. The other man had been
heavy, and it had been good that they had the horse
to assist. Yet, she wondered whether it would be appropriate for Grandfather to rest with a stranger. She
worried about this, even as she cleaned the body and
wrapped the robe around him and secured it.

She covered his face last, pausing to shed more
tears and once more to release her grief in a long wail.

"I will miss you, Grandfather. . . . I am already
lonely for you," she signed. Then she tied the flap of
the robe firmly around his thin shoulders and tucked
in the edges.

She still had not decided where to put him. Not in
the ash grove. There seemed no purpose in that, except that there was a corpse already there. The corpse
of a stranger. Grandfather had chosen that place,
but . . . yes, he had mentioned that it was a hidden
place, one that would not lead passers-by to find their
home in the Rock. But he had also told her something else. . . . It should be a high place . . . the
cliff! Yes, had he not said something of that? It could
be on a high ledge. . . . Not too near the cave.

She spent the rest of the day scrambling around the
face of the Rock, searching for the right spot. One
place was ideal, up near the nest of the hawks. The
nest was abandoned now, but she knew that the birds
would return to rebuild it and use it again next season. Grandfather would have liked that, high on the
cliff, overlooking the tallgrass prairie, and near the
soaring feathered creatures that he loved to watch.

But wait . . . the short and narrow ledge was
ideal, but how could she bring him here? She had
climbed here many times over the years. Not until
now had it become plain to her that it could not be
done without the use of both hands. She had never
made the climb with a burden of any sort. Even her
weapons and yes, her doll, had been laid aside when

she came here. No, it was impossible. There was no way that she could bring him here. She sat there heavy of heart, listening to the murmur of the wind through bare cottonwood branches. Well, she must find another place.

She climbed down to sit on the boulder in her favorite play spot. It had always been a place of comfort, halfway between the river and the cave above. It was near the point where the dim path on up the cliff branched away. Her eyes misted again as she thought of the many days when she and Grandfather had sat together on this boulder, and he had held her, rocked her to sleep, or told her stories. She would miss his company here. . . .

Her eyes widened. Yes, why not? Why not *here*? She stood, took a step or two along the ledge, and looked back. Yes, there was a space, partly behind the boulder, a space of the right size and shape for a robe-wrapped body. The overhang would hide it against observation from above, and the ledge from beneath. In addition, he would be near, and would be in a place where she could visit him each time she passed up or down the path. She hurried back to the cave.

"Grandfather," she signed, "I have found your resting place! The boulder where we sit."

She felt that he knew and understood, and her heart was good.

It was a long and arduous task to bring him there. At some places where the ledge was narrow and the overhang steep, she could not carry the clumsy burden. She must place it on the ledge and drag it forward as she carefully backed along the path. The task was too great to begin now. Shadows were already lengthening. She would wait until morning.

Through the long night she sat and watched over the body, keeping the fire burning. From time to time she cried and tried to think of the good times, the way her grandfather's eyes crinkled at the corners when he was pleased. Though he had been a bitter old man, there were rare times when he had seemed happy and his heart filled with laughter. She had treasured those times, and would still do so.

She thought further of the things that she would leave with him. His bow and arrows, his knife. She was not sure what one would need on the Other Side, but they had sent the weapons of the stranger with him. Food, maybe . . . she spent a little while preparing small bundles of dried meat and some of his favorite mixture of pounded meat, dried plums, and melted tallow. These things she wrapped and tied and laid aside with his weapons.

Water? She thought not. Her impression was that the Other Side had plentiful streams of clear water, and that game would be plentiful. Had they not sent with the stranger only enough food for a day or two? Grandfather would surely make a kill soon after his arrival. A fat buffalo, probably, she thought. That was his favorite. Preferably a yearling cow, fat and tender. She smiled, remembering his delight at such a kill.

Daylight came at last, and she began her task. It took longer than it would have under usual conditions. She wished to handle her burden of sorrow gently and with great care. Frequently she stopped to rest, and when she did, she talked to him in signs.

"A little farther, Grandfather. We must rest a little while. Wait until you see the place I have for you. It is good, the place by the boulder, where we have sat for stories and to watch the valley. . . . Well, let us move on."

It was quite tricky to maneuver around some of the rocky twists in the trail. She had never realized before what a difference the shape of a burden can make. One as tall as a man, even though not heavy . . . even more so because this burden must be handled gently and with love.

It was past noon before Grandfather was settled into his final resting place. She positioned him so that she was facing the bundle when she sat sideways on her boulder. Also, she was pleased that from his position, the spirit of her grandfather could look out over the rolling prairie.

"See, Grandfather, is it not as I said?"

She did not know whether or how long the spirit might stay around. He had once said something about three days, but beyond that? . . . Maybe the spirit would come back sometimes to visit her. Yes, that must be it. Spirits must travel with great speed, so her grandfather would probably come back anytime that she wished to visit him.

Another trip up the path to the cave, and she placed his weapons and supplies at his side. She cried again, then stood to address the still shape in a formal manner.

"I will miss and mourn you, Grandfather. May your journey to the Other Side be easy. I have brought your favorite pemmican to nourish you on the journey."

She paused, uncertain.

"Will you come back to help me sometimes?" she pleaded. "I am alone, now, you know."

She stopped again and took a deep breath. Was such a request proper? She was unsure.

"But I will be fine," she assured him. "Have I not been taught well?"

She sat on the boulder, lost in thought, until it began to grow dark. When the night became chilled, she rose and went to the cave to bring her robe. She could not bear to stay in the cave tonight, alone. She built a small fire. She knew that it was not a good idea, but it did not seem to matter. It would help her to watch over Grandfather, and she somehow felt that responsibility. Anyway, she told herself defensively, there had been no sign of trespassers for some time. The People, he had told her, were somewhere else at this season, preparing their winter camps.

She, too, must do that now. There was much work, carrying firewood and drying meat to store against the onslaught of Cold Maker.

40

» » »

It was a bad winter. Not weatherwise, especially, but a time of deep emotional loss for South Wind. Her moods fluctuated, from confidence to loneliness to sadness and yes, to *anger* at her grandfather for leaving her.

With her lack of experience in the world of other humans, she had nothing for comparison. Her anger, therefore, was not over the injustice forced on her by Grandfather's strange hatreds. It was merely that he would leave her alone and unprotected. Of course, if she paused to think about it, she knew that he had had no choice. His time had come, and he died, not unpleasantly. His last day had been good, and she was glad for that. And for the fact that his troubles were over for this world. He was safely on the Other Side.

However, she saw all this with mixed feelings. Her own world had become infinitely more complex now. She had thought at first that it might be simpler. She would be able to come and go, to hunt without worrying whether Grandfather was safe. Whether he might have tried to get up and had fallen from the ledge, or gotten into some other danger.

Then such thoughts would bring guilt. She should not feel *good* that he was no longer here. She would think of the times when she was irritated with him

271

or impatient over his inability to move and think and function in their little world. Many times she wished that she had been kinder and gentler to him in his last days. Almost forgotten was the fact that most of the time she *had* been kind and gentle. The things she now remembered with remorse were the exceptions.

She would also think of things she meant to ask him, and would realize that now it was too late. Or she would see something new. . . . A beaver lodge downstream that had not been there before. A doe with twin fawns, who had joined the herd that always wintered in the timber above the riffle. This animal was of a very strange color, more gray than reddish. There was always a variety of color in the deer herd, from red to gray to yellow, but this was unique and striking. She would enjoy sharing the information with Grandfather when she returned to the cave.

But then the truth would come to her. Grandfather would not be at the cave, waiting for her. He lay on the ledge, ritually wrapped in the custom of his people. At least, his body was there. His spirit had crossed over. She believed so, because that was what he had taught her. Then the loneliness would descend, and her heart was heavy.

Maybe this was one of the things that caused her to begin to talk to her grandfather. She passed the still form on the ledge many times a day as she tried to lay in a supply of firewood. One afternoon, already tired from a day that had been busy and hard, she paused at the boulder to rest. The armful of wood was somewhat heavier than usual, and she set it down for a moment, breathing heavily.

Despite the coolness of the late fall day, she could feel the dampness of perspiration inside her tunic. A rivulet tickled its way down her back between the shoulder blades, and her arms were sticky with sweat. Exhausted, she sat on the boulder and looked across the river at the distant grassland. Then she turned to look at the still form beside her. How many such trips up and down the Rock he had made through the years! And he had been old, his joints creaking in protest. Here she was, in the prime of her youth, exhausted and panting from the effort. She smiled wryly.

"Grandfather," she signed to the still figure, "you were quite a man!"

She wondered whether he would approve of her efforts to prepare for the winter. She knew how much fuel would be required through the long Moon of Snows. Actually, she had done much of the planning and providing for the past two winters. But it was different now. Last season she had been able to ask advice: "Is this right, Grandfather?" And he had nodded approval. Probably, she now realized, there were times when he had not even understood the question. He only nodded to end the annoyance of further conversation.

Now her breathing was easier. She rose.

"I must go, Grandfather," she signed. "The night will be cold. Cold Maker comes tonight, maybe."

It seemed logical, easy, to slip into the habit of conversation with him. He did not answer, but there had been many times that he had not when he was alive. There was little difference. Some would have thought her a little crazy, perhaps, but she had nothing with which to compare. It was comforting to her to talk with him. And was his spirit not here, only unseen because it had crossed to the Other Side?

It became perfectly logical to pause each time she passed the boulder. She would boast of her success in the hunt or tell him of her failure. A sudden shift in the breeze, bringing a warning to her quarry, a misstep that spoiled her silent stalk. She would laugh as she related the antics of a pair of coyote pups, hunting on their own now for the first time. She told him of the weather, the thickness of the ice on the pool below and the blossoms of frost crystals that adorned each grass blade and twig on some mornings. It was good.

Sometime later, she began to realize that she was spending time here instead of at the cave, and the reason puzzled her at first. Finally she admitted to herself that it was for companionship. Here, her grandfather dwelt. In the cave, there was no one.

Except, maybe, the dark thing in the crevice. And that, she knew, was something she must think about. During the first few days after her bereavement, it had been quiet. Now, it seemed to be coming to life again, more vigorously. She would have attempted without hesitation to fight a bear or a wolf, and would have felt confident in the outcome. But this . . . she had feared the imagined creature of darkness as early as she could remember. Grandfather had told her that it did not exist, and it gradually went away. Then, when *his* power began to fail, it grew again. Even *he* had seemed to fear it at the last.

She was confused. Of all the dangers that she might encounter in their world, Grandfather had given quite specific advice. How to avoid the bite of the real-snake, how to deal with a disturbed winter bear, roused by accident from her sleep. But in this one area she had no example to follow. She had received conflicting information: It is not there, it is nothing, yet it is something that must be feared. She wondered if it was something that had been held in check by the power of Grandfather's spirit. When he began to fail, the thing in the crevice became stronger. Now he was gone, and she felt a chill of fear. . . . Would it become stronger now? She tried to tell herself that *she* was strong and could control the fearful thing. Most of the time she was successful, but there were times when doubts overcame her. The dreams, when she was pursued by a vague and shapeless form and could not run. The times when she sat in the cave, alone, afraid to look at the dark corner because she might see something there.

She developed the theory that it feared the light.

During the light of day she was never even concerned about the dark thing. She was stronger than anything that could lurk there in the crevice. Besides, was it not likely that Grandfather could help her, even from the Other Side? Was this not a thing of the spirit, and was not *he* a spirit now?

This worked quite well during the daytime, but with darkness came doubt. True, she had actually seen nothing, except in dreams, but fears came crowding in. For a few nights, she kept a fire burning brightly in the cave. Then she realized that this using too much of her fuel supply. It would not do.

A few nights were spent elsewhere when weather permitted. On the ledge outside . . . In a smaller cave where she had played as a child. That was not a good idea. The play-cave was smaller than she remembered, and she woke after a restless sleep, cramped and aching.

Finally another idea struck her. She would stay in the cave during daylight, sleeping when the creature in the crevice was inactive. Then she would go out at night. South Wind became one of the hunters of the night, a seminocturnal creature herself. This helped some, but there was also another problem, related indirectly to the first: What would she do now? Sometimes it seemed reasonable to merely go on as they had been doing, enjoying the fruits of the hunt and the solitude. But not *complete* solitude. There was the loneliness.

"What am I to do, Grandfather?" she asked.

There was no answer. At least not one that was apparent to her, and it was discouraging. Sometimes she considered leaving the Rock, but quickly rejected such thoughts. She would know nothing of what to do. So day followed day, and the winter nights likewise, and she went on. It came to be that her most comforting times were those spent with her grandfather. She would sit on the boulder, weather permitting, and tell him of all that she saw and did.

"The ice is breaking up on the river, Grandfather.

It is almost the Moon of Awakening. The beavers were out today."

She even spoke to him of the thing in the crevice.

"I do not quite understand about that," she told him. "In the daylight, it seems powerless. At night, I am afraid, except if the fire gives light. So, I sleep mostly in the daytime. At night, I go out, and this is good. You know I like the outside night anyway. . . . The moon on the snow was beautiful last night."

She paused a little while.

"I wish you could tell me about the dark thing. I do not know how to fight it. Well, I will avoid it as I have told you. Only . . . sometimes I dream of it. It chases me and I cannot run."

She waited again, as if for an answer, but there was none.

"I wish that you could help me. You told me that there is nothing there, that it cannot hurt me. But I am made to think that it *is* there, and . . . I *am* afraid, Grandfather. I hope you can help me. I will go on as I have said."

She rose and started down the path toward the river. Then she paused and turned back.

"Grandfather, is it that it takes two of us to control the dark thing, to keep it in the crevice? Does one person have enough power to do it alone?"

She waited, still thinking about that idea. Grandfather had been virtually alone when he came there, with her as a tiny infant. And he had kept the evil thing in check. *So,* she told herself, *I can, too!*

"Yes, I can do it," she signed confidently as she turned away.

She wished that she *felt* that confident.

41

It was better when spring came. It was hard to be sad or morose when everything was bursting with new life. Even the Dark Thing seemed less ominous now.

Cold Maker withdrew to the north against the increasing power of Sun Boy's medicine. South Wind wondered if perhaps the Dark Thing and Cold Maker were allies. There were certainly longer nights during Cold Maker's season. Nights in which the thing in the crevice seemed more powerful. Or did she only imagine that? It was hard to take it seriously as she sat here in the warm sun and looked across the familiar landscape.

"It is good, Grandfather," she signed. "The geese are traveling north, many of them."

She wondered sometimes if her grandfather might be up there, traveling with them. She had seen him watch the long lines of geese until they were out of sight. There seemed to be a certain longing, a wish to go with them. Now, maybe he could do so. Except that she felt strongly that he was still here, still watching over her, somehow. She could not explain that, but she was certain of it.

She was a little more comfortable now with her loss and the loneliness that it brought. She had worried for a long time, had been bothered by the little things that she could not tell him. There were questions that she had always intended to ask but never did. And the guilt feelings . . . *did I treat him as well as I should have?*

Those doubts, fears, and annoyances had mostly been laid to rest by a strange experience. It had been in the Moon of Hunger, though she really had no hunger. The cave was well provisioned, thanks to the teachings of her grandfather. All her life he had insisted that they store adequate supplies, and it was now second nature to her. Starvation was not to be one of her worries. But she was restless and fearful for herself and for Grandfather. She was sleeping poorly, and found herself uncertain and indecisive.

Then came the dream . . . or vision, maybe. She was asleep, but is not a dream only a vision that takes place during sleep? She and Grandfather were seated on the boulder beside the path, watching the beavers in the pool below. Strange, she thought, is he not dead? She even looked beside the boulder to see the robe-wrapped form, but it was not there. Still, there was the strong feeling that this dream-vision was not of a time long ago. It was as if she recognized that it was all part of her dream.

She studied her grandfather's face. It looked younger, healthier. But she herself, her body and her dress, were plainly in the present. He saw her watching him and smiled.

"What is it?" he signed.

She was embarrassed and fumbled for an answer.

"I was only thinking," she answered clumsily. "You are looking well."

"Of course!" came his signed answer. "This being dead is no problem. Do not worry about it."

So she was right! He *was* dead, but was reassuring her. A feeling of calm, a warm comfortable feeling came over her, and she smiled. The worries, the unasked questions, the loneliness, all seemed unimportant now.

"It is good," she signed.

But there remained unanswered the question of the Thing in the cave. She hesitated, wondering if she should ask of it, or if that would be inappropriate. He seemed to sense her concern and smiled again.

"Do not worry," he signed. "Help will come."

She awoke, startled. But the sense of reassurance and calm was still with her. She was in the cave, and it was late afternoon. She rose and hurried down the trail to the boulder. The still funeral bundle was there, unchanged.

"Thank you, Grandfather," she signed.

From that day, she felt better, more cheerful. She did not know how it might occur, but only that somehow, all her questions and problems would be answered. Her worry was much less, her fears reduced. Even the dark crevice seemed less threatening. Maybe it was only that the nights were shorter now, but she thought not. Grandfather's reassurance had helped her immensely.

In turn, she was now talking to him more. Today, in the Moon of Greening, she sat and described in signs all the things before her.

"A redbird, Grandfather. He makes his nesting song."

She was not certain whether, in his present spirit-state, Grandfather could hear such things. That was something she had never fully understood anyway. When he was alive, she knew that he had not been able to hear the coyote's cry or the warning slap of the beaver's tail on the water. She knew that at least some of the people she had seen made sounds to each other. Did many people make such sounds, or were they the exception? It did not occur to her that her grandfather might be the exception. But maybe he could hear now.

Since she was not sure, she described to him the sounds as well as the sights and smells.

"I can smell the plum thicket from here, Grandfather. It is covered with bloom, and the smell rises up the Rock when the sun warms it. The grapevine on the cliff below the ledge is not blooming yet, but there are many buds. That will smell even better, no?"

She described the colors of the violets that were beginning to bloom, the sounds of the calling geese, and the hollow cry of the rain-bird, "though it does not look like rain . . . maybe he is mistaken. The night-singer is back, the gray and white bird who sings others' songs. I do not know if you can hear him."

And so it went. It was a great comfort to her, to have these one-sided conversations. Her comments were not answered, yet in a sense they were. Her answer came in the calm confidence that was now hers. Only a thing or two now troubled her: the question of what she would do in the future, seasons ahead. This was only a passing thought sometimes, when she was not feeling as confident as usual. There was no easy answer, and she was always able to repress the question. She could worry about that when the proper time came. A more worrisome thing was that of the fearful dark crevice in the cave. Despite the suggestion that it was weaker with the return of the sun, it *was* there.

On a dark and rainy day, when the only really comfortable place to be was the cave, she could *feel* its presence. On such days, she burned more firewood than she really should have and sat facing the dreaded corner, her back against the other wall in a defensive position. She would doze, and come awake with a start, almost certain that she had seen a Something move in the dusky corner. Or had she dreamed it?

This was disconcerting enough that she discussed it with Grandfather. At least, she told him of it, on more than one occasion. She received no concrete answer, but on each of these occasions she recalled her dream-vision. She had the assurance that Grandfather would be here and that help of some sort would be available when needed.

* * *

It was now late in the Moon of Roses. They had bloomed in all their glory, in reds and pinks and whites . . . even one clump that was pale yellow. The scent had been everywhere. The blooms were past their prime now, and the fruits beginning to swell on their thorny stems. She must gather some, but not yet. Later.

South Wind was watching the weather carefully. It would soon be the Moon of Thunder, with its towering cloudbanks reaching into the hot blue sky, growing until they gave birth to storms. Rain Maker was in his glory at this time, marching across the prairie, wrapped in his dark robes of driven rain, his drums rolling as he moved. He hurled spears of real-fire at random to strike lone trees or even people who were caught in the open. She had once seen him split a giant old cottonwood tree. The fiery spears of Rain Maker, Grandfather had told her, are drawn to this tree. That is why one should never take shelter under a cottonwood.

The river might rise if heavy rains came. It often did. But so far this year, the fine weather had continued. The clarity of the air was so accentuated that it was possible to see objects at great distances with greater clarity. Only in the warmth of the afternoon was there some distortion by the shimmering heat waves.

It was on one of these fine days that she first noticed the figure in the distance. At first she was not even certain that it was moving. Maybe it was a lone tree or bush, newly in leaf and grown larger than last season. She continued to look at it from time to time, and finally decided to use the sticks to determine whether it moved. She placed her twigs, sighted across them, waited, and then returned to look again. Yes, the distant object had moved. She was not particularly concerned, but curious. A lone buffalo, or perhaps a horse? She had seen scattered bands of both recently, but a lone individual . . . there was some-

thing different here. Carefully, she continued to observe the direction of movement by placing new
twigs, until she could recognize the pattern of this
progress. It appeared quite deliberate. The direction
wavered with the terrain, the moving object sometimes even disappearing for a little while as it crossed
some small watercourse or swale. But one thing was
becoming certain: This was an intentional, deliberate
course, and it was heading straight for Medicine
Rock.

This was most unusual. South Wind was still not
particularly concerned, though there was a hint of a
distant warning in her mind. Why would a lone rider
be approaching the Rock, usually avoided by people?

It was not long after this that she was able to distinguish that this was not a horseman, but a lone
individual on foot. Much later, she determined that it
was a man carrying a light pack. As he drew nearer,
she continued to watch, gleaning new information
bit by bit. The man carried a bow, but his demeanor
did not seem aggressive.

Why would a man be traveling on foot, alone? Her
grandfather had told her of the necessity for a horse
on long journeys. Yet this man had none. Had his
horse been lost or injured, killed, perhaps? No, there
was none of the attitude of a defeated survivor in this
man. He moved with confidence and purpose.

It was late in the day when he finally stood on the
slope across the river, looking up at the cliff. He
seemed to be studying the face of the Rock with interest and with purpose. He appeared young, not
much older than she, maybe. He was not unpleasant
to look upon, even though he represented a threat.
Well, she could watch him. She was ready to play the
hiding game if necessary, but felt compelled to
watch.

The stranger shifted his pack and stepped toward
the river. He paused to wash his face and fill a waterskin, and then, to her surprise, splashed across the

riffle. He paused again to drain the water from his
moccasins and looked up at the cliff.

He is coming up! She felt the grip of panic. What
would she do? Such a thing had never happened before. She wished for the advice of Grandfather. Was
she supposed to merely hide while the stranger
climbed the path to invade the privacy of their lodge?
Anger rose in her. Maybe she should kill him. But
what then? Prepare *him* for burial, too? It seemed
offensive to her, to share the Rock with the corpse of
an invader.

Now he was starting to climb the path, with great
determination, as if he had a purpose. She retreated
upward, beyond the boulder and Grandfather's resting place, to an area from which she could see part of
his ascent. There was a place where the path divided,
one branch leading on upward, the other along the
ledge to her boulder and on to the cave.

The young man climbed, pausing to study a crevice
which she knew was filled with bones. That was a
reasonable curiosity, but she still had no clue as to
his purpose here. He moved on.

At the place where the path divided, he did not
even pause, but climbed on, straight upward. South
Wind breathed easier. She had hoped he would do
that. The branch that led to the cave was not well
seen from below, but this stranger was behaving so
unpredictably. . . . He climbed on, out of sight, and
she moved to a vantage point from which she could
follow his progress. Why would he want to climb the
Rock, for what purpose? Her anger rose, resentment
against him for desecrating her world.

The stranger climbed all the way to the top, drew
himself up and over the edge, and disappeared. She
knew the place well, an open flat shelf of stone where
the level prairie above came to an abrupt end at the
rim of the cliff. It was near the hawk's nest.

But now what? Had he kept going? She thought for
a moment. The day was late, and a traveler should be
looking for a place to camp. This one obviously did

not *fear* the Rock, but why did he climb to the top? The best camping place was below, on the south side of the river. There was more fuel, water was more convenient. He had filled his waterskin, so he must not intend to come back down.

South Wind slipped along the ledge and across a narrow place that she had discovered long ago. She had used it seldom. It was another path to the top of the cliff. She could go up there to locate the intruder and make certain that he had moved on.

She had not yet reached the top when a stray breeze brought a familiar scent to her nostrils. Smoke . . . the intruder had kindled a fire. Anger washed over her, making her face flush and her skin tingle. A *fire* . . . a declaration that he was camping here! The girl waited a moment, wrestling with her anger, and then continued climbing.

Before she reached the top, she heard the voice of the stranger, rising and falling in a sort of chant. This must be a "song." . . . There was an exciting quality about it, and even through her anger at the intrusion, she was curious. She would wait, for now. After dark, she would go up and look more closely at this stranger.

42

South Wind squatted, watching the sleeping man. It was a risky thing, because the full moon was silvering the world and she could be easily seen if he awoke. However, this danger only added to her excitement. She felt a strange mixture of anger and curiosity. She must know more about him. He was young, as she had noted. He was also attractive, and she felt strangely drawn to him. There was an excitement stirring in her body that had nothing to do with the risk or the threat of an intruder. The risk did not bother her. She could kill him if she needed to. But this other feeling. . . . It felt, somehow, like she had felt that time when she watched the young couple with their arms around each other and putting their mouths together. It was a strange excitement.

But this young man . . . What was he doing here? She tried to puzzle it out. He had come carrying few supplies. She could see virtually none. His sleeping-robe, his waterskin, his bow and a few arrows seemed to comprise all of his possessions. He could not travel far so poorly equipped.

Yet again, it did not appear that he had been the victim of any misfortune. His attitude said plainly that his present activity was *planned* that way. For what purpose? It was very puzzling. A traveler, yet poorly equipped to travel. He had approached the

Rock with confidence, though most feared it. His campfire was at a poorly selected place, away from water, but he had carried water with him as he climbed the bluff. And he had gathered a great quantity of firewood, though it was scarce at the top of the Rock.

She thought about it for a long time and finally came to a tentative conclusion. *This* was his goal. Here, at the cliff's rim. He had built his fire with deliberate ritual and had even chanted a song to mark the occasion. At least, that appeared to be its purpose. The fire was not needed for warmth, he had nothing to cook, and was not hunting. The fire was symbolic, then, the statement, "Here, I camp."

But for how long, and for what purpose? He could not last very long without food. . . . Wait! Her grandfather had mentioned such a thing! A young person would go out alone and fast for a period of time while he sought a vision. *The vision-quest!* Yes, that must be the explanation. And how long? *Three, four days, maybe more,* Grandfather had said.

South Wind had been fascinated by this idea, but it had been put aside for all the more important things of her grandfather's last few moons of life. Well, this might be a good opportunity to watch, unseen, while this stranger established his contact with the spirit world. She wondered if her presence would interfere. The vision-seeker was supposed to be alone. Well, she could not help that. This was *her* home, the stranger was the intruder. She would remain unseen, and if his quest proved unsuccessful, so be it. It was his fault, not hers.

It was threatening, though, to have the stranger present. She slept poorly, and her dreams involved danger and fear, and the unknown horror in the dark crevice. During her waking hours she was curious, and she tried to watch the intruder at every opportunity. She felt drawn to him in spite of the danger, as a moth is to the flame.

She discussed the situation with the still form on the ledge.

"There is a stranger here, Grandfather. I did not know what to do. I thought of killing him, but I think he means no harm."

She waited a little while, trying to decide how she might explain. She could not share with Grandfather the strange attraction that she felt toward the intruder.

"I am made to think," she went on, signing carefully, "that this is a young man on his vision-quest. So, he will finish his fast and then go away, no? No harm will have been done, if he does not see us."

She was not quite certain that her grandfather would approve of this interpretation, but she wanted badly for it to be right. She realized that in this case, silence did not necessarily mean assent, but chose to interpret it so because she wished it so.

"It is good," she signed, rising. "I will watch him closely and tell you all that he does."

As nearly as she could tell, the intruder had not eaten since he first climbed the cliff. She had eaten hardly anything, either. She could not build a fire without risking discovery, and she was unwilling to do that. It would be only a few days anyway, she reminded herself.

Probably not only the stranger on his vision-quest, but both of them, therefore, were feeling some of the effects of fasting. They were much closer in spirit than either realized. Of course the young man was not aware of South Wind's presence. Even had he known, it is likely that both would have been surprised at the similarity of their thoughts and feelings. The vision-seeker was feeling South Wind's dread of the threatening evil thing in the cliff, while she in turn was experiencing part of his vision-quest. Each was receiving part of the spirit-feeling of the other without realizing it.

As a result, the puzzled young man was experiencing the interference of the dark fear in South Wind's

mind. She in turn felt *his* confusion. She also felt his
vision-experience, the sensation of being inside the
head of the animals he watched. She, too, knew the
lift of the rising air currents against the wings of the
red-tailed hawk, and the dull, sullen thoughts of the
massive old herd bulls across the river. South Wind
could not have told *how*, but she knew precisely
when he found his animal spirit-guide, though she
could not have told its identity.

Good! she thought. *Now his quest is over and he
will go away.*

This did appear to be correct. She watched as he
prepared to leave, extinguished his fire, and rolled his
robe to carry. His waterskin was almost empty, she
noted. No matter, he would fill it at the stream before he started to travel.

South Wind slipped away, down one of her own
secret routes on the cliff's face. She would hide on
the ledge around the shoulder of the rock from
Grandfather's resting place. There was a bush there,
and she could watch most of the young man's descent through its branches, unseen. She paused a moment at her boulder to sign to her grandfather's
wrapped form.

"He is leaving now, Grandfather. I will watch him
on his way. It is good."

She hurried on, to reach her place of concealment
before the intruder's descent began. She had barely
reached her selected observation point when she saw
him, carefully picking his way down the cliff. He was
doing well, she thought, for one unfamiliar with the
rocky precipice. At one point or two, there would
have been an easier foothold, but she knew that only
from years of experience.

He arrived at the main path from the top. Good. It
would be easier going now. She had not paused to
think why his safety in this descent was important to
her. If she had been asked, she would have answered
that she wished him safely gone. If he fell, she would
have to care for his body. Worse yet, if he were only

injured in a fall, she would be faced with a decision. Should she help him or kill him?

Such tensions helped her to conceal even from herself the concern that she really felt for this stranger. She entirely overlooked the fact that in truth, she would miss the companionship of the spirit that she had felt for the past few days. For a moment, there even flickered through her mind the thought that she might follow him when he left, to learn of his ways.

Such thoughts vanished abruptly as he neared the place where the path branched. If a person ascended from the river, the path seemed to climb on and up. The branch that led to the cave was not well seen from below. But from above . . .

The young man paused and stared at the ledge for a moment while South Wind held her breath. He had noticed something. She, too, stared at that portion of the ledge. She had never before noticed how well-worn it looked. How could he *not* suspect something amiss? *Go on,* she wished silently, *there is nothing here for you.*

As if he had heard her unvoiced suggestion, the youth turned and started on down. South Wind was able to breathe again. But wait! He turned to look back up the path. He had only been testing his impression. Nodding in apparent satisfaction, he started back. Wind stared helplessly as he carefully studied the rocky path. She wondered if he was seeing footprints that she might have left there only moments ago. He seemed undecided.

She could tell when he made the decision. He seemed to nod to himself in satisfaction, and then to her horror, he stepped boldly onto the ledge that led to the cave. *I should have killed him!* she thought. She was unable to move as she watched him come toward her. Now he was approaching her boulder and the funeral-wrapped form behind it. She heard him gasp in surprise, and saw him jump back as he recoiled at the unexpected appearance of a corpse beside the path. He recovered quickly, then stepped back to examine his find more closely.

All the pent-up frustration and tension in South Wind's heart exploded in a wave of rage. She sprinted forward, her knife in her hand. The man turned to defend himself barely before she struck. He managed to deflect her knife thrust and grasped her wrist as the two fell heavily and rolled together on the ledge. He was strong, and South Wind felt that she was fighting for her life. But her anger at the desecration of her grandfather's resting place drove her to superhuman effort. Her opponent had not been able to draw his own weapon. She clawed at him with her free hand but was unable to reach his knife.

She *must* do something, and quickly! An idea came to her, a memory from her childhood . . . her grandfather had been very angry. . . . This same spot . . . With a sudden lunge, she rolled over, pulling her opponent with her and on top of her. She felt his weight, but at the same time her left shoulder reached past the rim of the ledge and out into empty space. The weight of the young man's body carried them on, their momentum toppling the pair over the edge.

He gasped and tried to kick free but she held tightly as they fell. He would have no way to know that below this point lay the deep pool, and he would be expecting death on the rocks below.

With a frantic cry he released her knife hand just before they struck the water. She slashed at him and missed. Both plunged deep, and she turned to see him swimming toward the surface. A stroke toward him, another knife thrust, just as they surfaced. She felt the flint blade rip into something, and the water began to turn red with his blood.

She was certain that the wound was not mortal. It had been a blind, slashing stroke. He was wearing buckskins, which would absorb much of the force of such a blow. He was still dangerous.

He dived again, and she hesitated. There had been

time for him to draw his own knife, so she must be cautious now. She submerged and moved toward him. There . . . he was swimming underwater, heading deeper to escape her. The man was an expert swimmer. She lost sight of him for a moment, then saw a flash of motion off to her right. She turned to defend herself. No . . . a beaver! Then where? . . .

She surfaced, and looked quickly around to locate her opponent, but he was nowhere to be seen. Where had he gone? Surely if he had left the river she would see him.

A slight disturbance in the water at the other shore caught her attention and she focused on that. A giant sycamore grew there, and a tangle of its roots reached into the water like knobby knees. The splash had come from that tangle. There was a loud slap from the same area, the alarm signal . . . *beaver*, she thought.

Then where was the wounded man? She swam to shore on the cliff's side and explored up and down the narrow strip of land. There were no tracks or any sign that he had left the water here. She found one of his arrows, lost from above when he dropped his weapons at her attack. It floated, point down.

She crossed the riffle and searched the other shore. Nothing. *Strange*, she thought. Had he been wounded more seriously than she realized? Had he dived more deeply than he intended, and in his weakened condition lost consciousness and drowned? She was not certain.

She climbed the path and stopped at her boulder, exhausted. There on the ledge lay the stranger's bow and scattered arrows. It had been a narrow escape.

"Grandfather," she signed, still breathing heavily, "the man is gone. I tried to kill him. My heart is heavy that he disturbed you."

She rested a little more.

"He may be dead," she went on. "He was wounded. I cannot find where he left the water."

She was not certain that her grandfather would approve of the way she had handled this. She knew that he totally frowned on the escape of a wounded animal in the hunt. She wondered if the same thing applied to wounded enemies.

That had all happened so fast. She had been feeling kindly, even, toward the stranger, who after all, *had* been leaving. Then, his discovery and her subsequent rage. Her attack had been a mistake, probably. He might have been only curious, and would most likely have departed, out of respect for the dead. He may not even have suspected the presence of any living person there. Yes, that attack had probably been stupid.

"I am sorry, Grandfather."

She was also sorry, now that her anger had subsided, because the attack might have been unjust. She had rather enjoyed the presence of the vision-seeker. She had found him good to look upon, and she had watched him for long periods while he slept.

There was another curious thing, one which she could not share with Grandfather. She was not certain, even, that she wanted to think of it herself. There had been a brief moment, when she and the stranger rolled together in combat on the ledge. She had experienced a strange sensation, like no other that had been hers. As they had rolled, the closeness of his body, the pressure of his weight against her chest, just before they fell . . . It had been almost pleasant.

43

» » »

It was the next day that she found the place where he left the river. Partially screened by a clump of willows, the stranger had pulled himself up the bank and into the grass. She could follow his trail a little way, and it led directly away from the Rock.

She was a bit embarrassed that she had not seen him leave, and she tried to determine why. He had been an excellent swimmer. She had discovered that when they plunged into the river. Apparently he swam downstream underwater, emerging behind the screen of willows. But when? While she looked for him along the river? Or did he wait in hiding to emerge later?

And why did it matter? Only that it irritated her immensely to realize that it had been a situation over which she had lost control. She had a sense of failure, an anger at herself, that she found hard to forgive.

"He is gone, Grandfather. He has escaped, not dead as I thought, maybe. I have tracked him straight away from the Rock."

It was as if she asked approval from her grandfather for the way she had handled the matter. Approval was important, because she was unsure, herself. She did not totally approve of the way things had gone. There was no sign from the silent figure on the ledge, of course. She had expected none.

"I will watch closely," she went on. "If he comes back, I will be ready. He may die, though. He *was* wounded."

She was a little bit deceptive on that point. It was apparent that the man had been able to swim powerfully underwater. There was also no sign of blood where he left the river. His wound must have been slight.

South Wind was actually glad that he was alive. He had been good to look upon, and she did not like to think of his attractive body in some deep hole in the riverbed, food for fish and turtles. Even though he was an enemy, she told herself. But *was* he an enemy? She was quite confused. Alive, he presented a threat, because he knew that she lived here in the Rock. Yet she was glad that he was alive.

Looking back, she had to admit that she had enjoyed his presence here. It was exciting, challenging, and a diversion from the loneliness that she had felt since the passing of Grandfather. There was something else, too. The fearful dread of the Thing in the crevice had lessened during his stay here. She had not realized it until now. It had been a diversion to have him here, and she had not been so preoccupied with the Thing . . . no, it was more than that.

She recalled her feeling that she and Grandfather had been able, together, to control the evil, to keep it confined in its crevice. Then, when Grandfather's mind began to fail, the Thing became stronger, more threatening. She was sure that it had grown since his passing.

But during the last few days, while the vision-seeker had been here, it had not seemed so powerful. True, she had had a dream or two, unpleasant fears. . . . Not the dream of being pursued, though. Had the spirit of the stranger helped to control the evil? He probably did not even know about the dark Thing. Maybe he would not *need* to know. Maybe just the presence of his spirit . . . She was certain that it was a powerful thing, because she had felt his thoughts reaching out. He must have a gift of spirit, a holy man.

And she had tried to kill him. A sense of guilt and a certain fear swept over her. It must be a bad thing to kill a holy man. She was glad that she had failed, and she found herself wishing that he would come back.

What am I thinking? With a feeling almost like panic she rejected such an idea. She hurried to her boulder on the ledge.

"Grandfather, you must help me," she signed. "I am made to think that the man, the one I told you of, was a holy man. I have done great harm by trying to kill him. And now the Thing in the crevice grows stronger."

It was the first time that she had admitted her fears of the crevice to Grandfather. She had not wanted to worry him. *Do spirits worry* she thought to herself? Yes, surely there is concern for a loved one left behind. Did not Grandfather come to her in a dream, to reassure her? What had he said? *Help will come when you need it?* Something like that.

She felt better. It was a strange experience. It was almost as if her grandfather had reassured her, here in broad daylight, while she was fully awake.

"Thank you, Grandfather," she signed happily. So that was it. He could still supply help, support for her spirit when it was needed. And if the intruder returned, she could handle him, too. She would be more alert, more resourceful, less trusting. Yes, now she understood.

Why, then, in the next few days, did she become more fearful? Her dreams became more frightful, the chase more real before she awoke, the seeming reality of the dream longer after she was fully awake.

Once, when she took shelter in the cave against a sudden rain squall, she dozed off to dream that the Thing came out before her very eyes. Dark and dirty brown, a creeping, formless mist, it started like a wisp of smoke, curling from the crack to materialize in the cave. This time, the light of the fire did not seem to deter it. It grew larger, more threatening. There was an odor about it, a damp animal smell like the nest of a mouse, or maybe . . . yes, like a bear's winter den, heavy with body scent. And the Thing made a hissing noise as it oozed along the wall.

She awoke in a panic to find the cave empty. The hissing sound was now identified as the steady patter of the rain outside. She shrugged off her fears and got up to move to the cave door and watch the rain.

She could see the sheets of water move across the slope as a heavier shower passed. The river below seemed to be boiling as rain pelted its surface. She was cold, she realized, and at about the same time a few white pellets fell, mixed with rain, and bounced along the ledge. The sound changed, too, as larger hailstones began to crash through the treetops below her. Tattered leaves, torn from their branches, fluttered toward the earth.

Then suddenly the rain, hail, and wind stopped. A bird sounded its song, tentatively at first, and then in full volume as the sun began to strike through the overcast. The storm was passing.

South Wind turned to toss a stick on the fire, pleased that it was over. Sunlight could always be counted on to make a person feel better. She even smiled at the thought of her dream a little while ago. Boldly, she looked directly at the crevice, and there was nothing. *I do not fear you,* she thought silently.

It was unfortunate, perhaps, that at that moment a chance shift in the cave's air currents brought a smell to her nostrils. It was a damp animal smell, mixed with odors that were like rotting vegetation, a musty scent that she had smelled before. . . . *In her dream.* The hairs prickled on the back of her neck. *What an odd thought.* It was like a threat.

Startled, she stepped outside. The rain had stopped, and the day was brightening. The dream seemed far away. Well, she would go and visit Grandfather. That always made her feel better.

* * *

It was that night that the vision-seeker returned. South Wind became aware of his approach largely by chance as he crossed the slope in dim starlight. She was not even certain at first that it was a man. The form that cautiously descended to the fringe of sumac could have been an antelope . . . a coyote, even. The light was poor. By the time he had reached the sumac thicket, however, she had discerned that it was a man.

As skillfully as the other creatures of the night, she moved to a better vantage point. Yes, she identified him as the one who had been here before. Her anger rose, and she forgot that at one time she had actually wished for his return.

Before, he had come openly, honestly. Now, he came skulking in the night. Why would he do this, unless he meant her harm?

She spent the rest of the night watching, moving cautiously to try to ferret out his intentions. He had hidden himself in the sumac thicket and seemed to make it his intention to stay there. This was a new sort of hunt, in which she was the hunted. She tried to imagine what he, the hunter, would do.

He knew she was here, of course. His actions seemed to indicate that he wished to watch her, discover her daily routine. He had made no move to leave the thicket as day approached, so he must have chosen that as his watching place. It was a good place, giving a view of the cliff's face and the river. Well chosen . . .

What might be his purpose here? She did not think he intended to kill her, though that must be considered. At any rate, he first intended to observe. Now, what should *she* do? It would be easy to merely kill him and be done with it, of course. That was one option. But she still found him fascinating, and wished to know more. Regardless of his intention, she could watch his actions for a while. Watch him watching me! She smiled at the thought. She had a major advantage. She could watch him, unseen.

But wait. His purpose seemed to be to watch her, so to avoid suspicion, she must allow him to do so. At least, until she discovered his motives. Then she could kill him if need be, or could hide until he left. Another idea began to form. Maybe she could *capture* him! It would be dangerous, but it might be possible to question him, *ask* his motives.

First, she must avoid the appearance of suspicion. He must not know that she was aware of his presence. He wished to watch her, of course. As any good hunter would study the movements of his quarry, this one would probably spend the day observing her movements. So be it. But she must hurry, now. The gray smudge of the false dawn was already showing in the east.

She slipped across the river, avoiding the places where loose gravel would clatter, and started up the path. She must contrive a daily routine that would appear reasonable to the stranger, yet allow *her* to observe *him*, too.

She paused for a moment at Grandfather's resting place.

"He is back, the vision-seeker," she told him. "I cannot tell what he wants, but he is hiding to watch us. I will be ready for him!"

She hurried on, to gain a good vantage point before daylight. She rested a little, actually dozing for a moment or two before the sun crept over Earth's rim. Coming awake, her first task was to make certain that the man was still in the thicket.

Yes . . . a worried small bird with a nest in the sumac scolded indignantly. Soon she could make out a moccasin and part of a legging through the flickering shade of the sumacs. South Wind smiled. She knew how hot, damp, and mosquito-infested that thicket would be by afternoon. Well, he had chosen it.

Now she rose and moved around on the face of the cliff, trying to appear furtive yet to make certain that she was seen. Then she took her bow and descended to the river, pausing only a moment.

"He is there, Grandfather. I will let him watch me. And, I will be careful."

Boldly, she stripped and bathed in the deep pool, in plain sight of the watcher. He was out of bowshot, and there was no way that he could leave his mosquito-ridden concealment without showing himself.

She dressed, squeezed the water from her hair, and picked up her weapons. The watcher would probably expect her to hunt, so she would oblige. She was fortunate enough to shoot a fat rabbit very quickly, and then found a comfortable place where she could observe the discomfort of her adversary. All in all, this was rather enjoyable.

Finally she tired of the game and moved into the open with her rabbit, trying not to look at the sumac thicket. She crossed the riffle, clattering a little, and started up the path.

"He is there, Grandfather. It goes well," she signed as she passed.

She built a fire, using just enough damp fuel to make sure that the watcher saw a puff or two of smoke. She cooked and ate her rabbit in a leisurely way, one eye on the thicket. There was still no way to tell what the man might intend. Since he had not moved all day, she reasoned, he must make some sort of move tonight, probably after dark. She would be ready.

Now, where to conceal herself? Near the foot of the path grew a thicket of prairie dogwood. It dominated the narrow strip of land against the cliff's base, where the path started to climb. It was the ideal place for an ambush.

She timed her move at twilight, when vision is poor, and flitted down the path to settle in the dogwoods. Then she waited while the darkness deepened and the stars began to appear overhead.

Her timing was good, and she did not think she had been seen. It was only a short wait now, until a figure rose stiffly from the sumac across the river and came straight toward the riffle. Excitement rose in her. Her scheme was working. Now if the capture worked as well . . .

44

» » »

Ah, thought South Wind, *I was right!* He had
waited until just after dark, and now would change
his position, to ambush her as she passed. She had
done well to hide here. It was amusing to see that he
had actually selected the same thicket. . . . He
crossed the riffle and approached the dogwood
thicket, completely unsuspecting. She readied herself
for the rush.

She had thought about it for a long time, of how
she would attack. The easiest and safest way would
be a single arrow, shot from concealment. Then it
would be over. A knife thrust, almost as good. Or the
ax . . . Her mind rejected all of these things. She
had to admit, she did not wish to kill him outright.
She *had* enjoyed his company for the few days of his
vision-quest, and she had been pleased to see that he
returned. It was a mixed emotion, of course, because
there was danger. Maybe that in itself led to a thrill
of excitement in his return. Then, too, there was a
burning curiosity, a wish to know more about him.
She *must* capture him, keep him alive at least long
enough to learn something of the ways of people. He
was the only human she had ever touched, except for
her grandfather. And, of course, the wounded warrior
who had come here already dying. He did not count.
Now, how to capture this young man with the

least danger? She knew from the encounter on the ledge that he was strong. She did not want to become involved in a test of endurance. She must disable him temporarily somehow, handicap or confuse him until she could tie him.

This was a new problem. Any creature that she had ever wanted to capture, she had also wished to kill. Now, that was not the case. She thought of traps and deadfalls and snares. A snare seemed a likely possibility for a time, but she rejected it. It would be too easy to accidently strangle her quarry.

She finally decided. A simple blow to the head, not too hard. Then, during the next few moments, while he was weakened and confused, she would tie him. With this plan in mind, she had spent part of the day making preparations. Soft buckskin thongs, prepared with loops that could be slipped over a wrist and pulled tight. More, for his feet. She chose a stout throwing-stick with good balance for her initial blow. And, since she did not want to *break* his head, she decided to pad her club. She realized it was dangerous. If the first blow was not effective, it would only anger him and make him more dangerous. She could not account for her compassion toward this stranger. She simply did not relish the thought of the appearance that he would have if she killed him. She had, after all, watched him sleep, and had admired his fine features. It was not good, to envision this man dying with his head crushed, bleeding from the nose and mouth and perhaps his ears. . . .

She shook her head. She was having a hard time with this. Anyway, she told herself fiercely, if it should go wrong, she could revert to the knife.

So now she lay in wait, watching him approach her hiding place. Sweat moistened her palms, and her heart beat so strongly that she was afraid he would hear. He paused at the edge of the water, indistinct in the dim starlight, listening, cautious. Then he came quickly across the grassy strip to enter the thicket. *He does not even suspect*, she thought triumphantly.

She readied her club, timed her steps, and swung. The young man was barely aware of the attack, she thought, before the *thunk* of the padded club. He dropped to the ground, and she was astride him in the space of a heartbeat, taking the thongs from her teeth and jerking the loops tight on his wrists and ankles. She bound his hands behind him.

During all of this, her victim did not move. He was completely limp. South Wind rose, trembling from emotion and from the sudden brief burst of activity. She was still breathing heavily.

Now what? she thought. She had not planned beyond this point. The man still did not stir, and anxiety rose in her. Had she killed him, after all? She knelt and felt the throb of the heartbeat in his throat. It was strong and regular, and his breathing, too, was good. She had seen two men die, and it was not like this.

Somewhat reassured, she dragged her prisoner into the open and stretched him out on the grass. She found the lump where her club had struck, behind his ear, and there was no blood. His left forearm was tightly wrapped. . . . That must be where her knife had struck before as they struggled in the water.

Now, what to do with him? The easiest thing was to leave him here until daylight, or until he recovered, whatever might be first. But she had doubts about that. What if someone came looking for him? No, she must hide him, and before daylight came. But where? She could drag him deeper into the thicket, but that would be cramped and uncomfortable at best. And, when the day warmed, it would be hot, damp, and mosquito-infested. She needed a concealed place where she need not worry about any passer-by seeing him, and where she could learn more about him. Some place as secure as the cave. *The cave!* She thought about it. Could she take him there? Why not? She had many times carried heavy burdens of firewood or meat or hides up that path.

Her prisoner was heavier, but she need not carry, she could drag him.

Slowly, resting often, she began the task of transporting her prisoner. Before the waning moon rose, she had reached Grandfather's resting place. Here, she paused for a long rest. She checked the prisoner's pulse and breathing again.

"This is the man I told you of, Grandfather," she signed. "I will take him to the cave and learn more of him and his people."

She completed her task, settled him in the cave, and went back to bathe herself in the stream. She was hot and dirty from the night's activity. Returning to the cave, she found that she was exhausted. She was asleep almost before she stretched out on the robes.

She was up and out at dawn. Her prisoner was asleep, but showed signs of rousing. She would go and try to find something for food. Fresh meat would be better than dried strips from her supply. Besides, she wished to make certain that all traces of the man's presence here were eliminated, in case someone came searching.

Her hunt was not too successful, and she cut it short because she did not wish to leave her prisoner alone for very long. She had managed to catch one large frog . . . well, that would do for now. She hurried up the path, pausing hardly at all at her grandfather's resting place.

"Good day, Grandfather. I will be back later," she signed hastily.

The captive awoke, slowly and with much discomfort, as she built the fire and started to cook the frog. She thought that he had moved from his previous position, so he may have been awake before. She caught his eye and signed to him.

"You are awake!"

He answered with a series of sounds that had no meaning to her. She had heard others make such sounds, but not this close. These noises must be used

to communicate. He tried again, different sounds, but
she shook her head, not understanding. She tried a
grunt or two, which seemed to mean nothing to him.

The meat was ready, and she signed to him. "Sit
up. You eat, now."

He struggled to a sitting position, and she repeated,
"Eat!"

Then she realized that he could not with his hands
tied behind him. She released his ties and watched as
he rubbed his numbed hands. She handed him the
frog legs, and he began to eat, slowly.

"It is good," he signed. "How are you called?"

She was startled, but tried to recover her composure.

"No," she signed, "how are *you* called?"

"I am White Fox, of the Elk-dog People."

"What are you doing here?"

"I came on my vision-quest. I did not know anyone's lodge was here."

"But you came back."

"Yes. I came to help you."

She curled her lip to show disbelief.

"No!" she signed. "You lie! You hid and watched
me!"

"But you tried to kill me, before!" he signed.

"Yes! You disturbed the bones of my grandfather!"

"I disturbed no one. I . . ."

Her anger flared, and he seemed to recognize that
there was danger here.

"I did not know anyone was here," he signed more
slowly and calmly. "I would not disturb anyone's
burial. I was surprised, and stopped to see."

She pondered this, unsure.

"What is your tribe?" he asked.

"I have no tribe," she indicated.

"Is there no one?"

"Only my grandfather. He died in the Moon of
Long Nights."

"I am sorry," he gestured. "No one else?"

"I need no one," she gestured defiantly.

He nodded.

"You and your grandfather," Fox signed. "Have you been here long?"

"We have been here always."

"You have never seen others? Other people?"

Cautiously, she answered.

"Sometimes they come here. We hide; they go away."

"Your grandfather," he asked, "talked with his mouth?"

"What do you mean?"

"People make sounds to talk."

He spoke the sentence as he signed it, and she was startled. Then she regained her composure.

"You spoke with sounds before," she signed. "I have heard others do this."

"But you?"

"Yes, but I do not need to."

She threw back her head and gave a little barking cry that sounded like a coyote calling to her pups. Then she shrugged as if to indicate that there was no purpose, and smiled, a little embarrassed.

"Your grandfather . . . did he make such sounds?"

"No, no," the girl signed. "He made no sound at all. He heard no sound."

"But you hear sounds. You could make sounds, too."

"Why?"

"It is easier. Look, I am called 'White Fox.' "

He used the words as well as the signs.

"Now, how are you called?" he asked.

She hesitated, then gave a shy smile.

"Grandfather called me South Wind," she gestured.

"It is good," Fox signed back. "South Wind."

He used the words as well as the hand-signs.

"White Fox," he said, pointing to his chest, "South Wind," pointing to her.

"South Wind," she said hesitantly, pointing to herself. She smiled again. "White Fox."

He nodded, pleased, and then reverted to handsigns again.

"Did your grandfather tell you why he left his people?"

Her face darkened as the old suspicions rose.

"Because people are bad! There is danger!" she signed heatedly.

"But, your grandfather was not bad. You are not bad. I am not bad!"

South Wind hesitated for a moment of confusion. Then she came to a decision.

"It is time to tie you again," she signed.

She picked up a rawhide cord and stepped toward him. Fox was not pleased at the unpleasant prospect of being tied again.

"Wait! If my hands are tied, we cannot talk!" he gestured frantically.

The girl paused.

"No," she signed. "You are a danger to me!"

"No, no! I want to help you!"

"You came back. You hid and wanted to catch me," she accused.

"Yes, but only to talk to you. You would run if I came to you. And, you tried to kill me before."

She hesitated. She wanted to trust him, but was unsure. It was also tempting to share her fears of the Thing in the crevice. With him here, she was somehow more secure. How could she explain this?

"I thought you would disturb my grandfather," South Wind signed. "And, I was afraid you might be with the Evil One."

White Fox appeared startled. She knew somehow that he, too, had felt something. Perhaps only *her* fear. There had been a time when she felt the progress of his vision-quest, his spirit probing, contacting that of other creatures. And . . . and *her* spirit. Such thoughts brought back her insecurity. He had no right to invade her spirit! She became defensive.

"South Wind," he gestured and used words together, remembering that it had seemed to please her, "I am not with the Evil One. I learned of your fears, and that is why I came back. I wanted to help you."

It was too much, too fast-moving for her. She was not ready to trust.

"You lie!" she gestured angrily.

She seized his wrists and tied him expertly, despite his protests. Then she stood and faced him for a moment.

"Maybe you speak truth," she gestured, "but I do not know, so I must keep you tied. I go now."

She picked up her bow and left the cave.

45

» » »

Now, South Wind found herself with a problem she had not foreseen. She had managed to capture the young man . . . White Fox, he called himself. Now, what? He lay tied in the cave while she went to hunt.

It had not occurred to her to plan ahead beyond his capture. All her life there had been very little planning, except for preparation and storage of food supplies for winter. She must think of that soon, too. It struck her that she was to hunt today for two, again. Not since the death of her grandfather had it been so. Her hunting had been to supply her own needs only. It was good, to have someone else. Her spirit lifted.

She recalled a time long ago when she had captured the coyote pup. Grandfather had allowed her to keep it, and she had been pleased with the responsibility. It was a living thing, dependent on her, not like her doll. Little Bone . . . she smiled at the memory. Bone had been real to her, but did not require care or food in the way her coyote pup did. The pup responded to her, and they played together. It was also slightly dangerous. It could inflict a painful bite, even in play.

She had had the pup for most of a season. When it matured, it ranged farther away in its hunting, returning only occasionally. Then in the Moon of Madness, when all animals (and people as well,

Grandfather said) behave somewhat irrationally, it did not return at all. What is it about late autumn, she wondered? A final urge to migrate or to prepare for the coming of the Long Nights Moon ahead?

Strange that she should be thinking of this. It was several moons away. But she found that she was thinking of the similarities in her capture of the young man, White Fox. He was dangerous, like the coyote. Yet, like the pup, he was fascinating. She found herself hoping that, when the Moon of Madness came, he too would not leave her like the coyote.

Or the crow. It, too, had abandoned her. Grandfather had explained that it is so with wild things. They become wild again and leave. *Or die*, she thought. She had not realized until now that she had unconsciously resented the fact that Grandfather, too, had left her. Then came the twinge of guilt, again, that she would feel so. *I am sorry, Grandfather*, she thought.

She forcibly turned her thoughts back to her prisoner in the cave. She was fascinated by him. It had been an exciting experience to talk with him, to find that some sounds have meanings, as hand-signs do. *Names*. She smiled as she thought of the way he spoke . . . aloud, *and* with signs. "South Wind," she said to herself, quietly. *"I am South Wind."*

She could not make the sounds exactly like he did. She loved to hear his voice as he said her name. It was deep and full and resonant. She could hardly wait to learn more of the talk-sounds. It was as if she had been waiting all her life for White Fox to come. She thought of other things, too, like the odd feeling that she had when she remembered how it felt to wrestle with him on the ledge.

She was glad that he had returned. It was good to feel the presence of another person, another spirit. She regretted that she must tie him again when she left to hunt, but she could not trust him. Not yet. Not until she knew more about *why* he had returned.

She must talk more to him about that. And about her other, her great fear that seemed to return in her sleep. The Thing in the dark, the Evil One. She had accused him of being allied with it, and he had denied it. He had, in fact, claimed that his return was to assist her in defending against it.

But *he knew of it.* That meant that she could no longer tell herself that it did not exist. It *must* be real, if this outsider knew. Again, she thought of her theory that *two* spirits were able to keep the Thing at bay, force it to remain in the crevice. One alone could accomplish this most of the time, but not entirely. This allowed it to grow and threaten. She must ask White Fox about this. If she was right, then the two of them could control it together. That was a nice thought, that they could do something together. She smiled.

She realized that she was already assuming that he spoke truth. She hated to do so without proof of some sort, but she was beginning to trust. The two of them . . . yes, her heart was good at the thought.

South Wind brought herself back to reality. Two of them meant that once more she was *hunting* for two. She must feed them both, at least until she and White Fox established what would happen next. How could she approach that subject? She had two fears if she released him from his fetters. One that he would become a danger to her . . . that fear was lessening rapidly. The other was that he would leave and that she would be alone again.

But she must stop the idle dreaming and concentrate on her hunting. It was good to hunt for two again. She must find something today, though. The frog had been primarily a symbolic thing, a sort of peace offering. She needed something more solid. The ideal kill would be a deer or a buffalo. That was unlikely, but a rabbit, maybe. She saw a movement in the clearing ahead and froze to identify it. A rabbit . . . yes, three of them, engaged in the mating dance of their kind. They would be preoccupied, and she should be able to secure one.

Carefully, she waited for the right target. *There, now!* She drew the arrow to its head and released smoothly. The feel was good, the knowledge before the arrow reaches its mark that its flight is true. She stepped forward to retrieve her quarry while the others scampered away.

She paused for a little while on the way back to the cave.

"I wish I could talk to you, Grandfather. I mean, that you could talk to me. There are many questions." She held up the rabbit. "I hunt to feed two, now. The man, White Fox, he is called . . . I have him tied in the cave. I learn much from him. Did you know, Grandfather, that people can talk with sound from their mouths? You probably knew. He knows of the Evil Thing, too. It is back. He says that he returned to help me with *it*! I do not know . . . I still have him tied. I will talk to him again."

She rose and held up her rabbit. "Now, I must go and cook this. I will come back later."

She hurried to the cave.

Her captive lay with a look of anguish on his face and motioned with his bound hands.

"What is it?" she signed anxiously as she untied him.

He motioned toward his hips and to his bound ankles and she finally understood. He had not had a chance to empty his bladder since last night.

"I am sorry," she signed. "But you will not run?"

He shook his head. As he stood, it was apparent that her question was unnecessary. He could hardly stand, on feet that were numb from lack of circulation.

"I am sorry," she signed again as he hobbled to the ledge outside. "I did not think!"

"It is nothing," he signed back, but she knew it was not true.

She turned to skinning and dressing the rabbit. He

moved back into the cave and looked around. She saw his eyes light on his own pack and weapons by the supply racks. She touched his shoulder.

"If you try, I will tie you again."

He nodded agreement.

"I will cook meat," she signed.

In a short while the rabbit was sizzling over the fire, and she turned to him again.

"Now! Tell me more of the talk-sounds."

He began to teach her common sounds for everyday objects, and she reacted with delight.

"Did your grandfather ever mention your tribe . . . its name?" he asked in signs after she began to tire.

"No, I do not think so. Grandfather always said we had no tribe."

"But you were with other people. Some were killed, and the others ran away. You told it."

"Yes, that is true. I do not know."

"Let me show you signs for names of tribes," he suggested. "See if any look right."

He began to sign. . . . Growers? Forest People, Pawnee, Mandan, Head Splitters? She shook her head.

"Maybe the Forest People are the ones who killed us," she considered.

One last possibility occurred to him.

"This?" he asked, making the sign for a man on a horse.

The girl's eyes widened.

"Yes!" she signed eagerly. "Yes, that is the one!"

White Fox was astonished.

"Really? Elk-dog People?"

"Yes," she nodded. "Grandfather used the sign, a man on a horse."

"That is my own tribe!" Fox signed. "We call ourselves 'the People,' but others use the elk-dog sign, because the People used the horse long ago."

He paused, lost in thought.

"There was a story about an incident," he indicated, "a family or two of the Eastern band, camped apart from the rest. They were killed by Forest People."

"Then I am of *your* people?" South Wind was asking in hand-talk.

"Yes," he nodded. "I think so. My grandmother, who died long ago, was of your band, and her father was a chief."

The girl clapped her hands, delighted.

"It is good!"

White Fox smiled. He sat massaging his sore wrists and ankles. She saw the reddened and chafed stripes on his wrists.

"I am sorry," she signed.

"It is nothing," he answered again.

When the rabbit had finished cooking, South Wind divided it in half, and handed him a portion. Then she came and sat beside him. There was a new and strange closeness, a communication without words. It seemed that the discovery of who she was, where she had come from, was important to the girl. She was now more relaxed and cheerful. There seemed to be a trust not previously found here.

They finished eating, and she made no effort to re-tie him. Suddenly she jumped to her feet.

"Let us swim!" she signed, starting for the entrance.

White Fox rose to follow her. Even though she paused a moment to speak in signs to her grandfather, she reached the shore well ahead of him. Quickly, she stripped the shirtlike dress over her head and dived headfirst into the pool. Fox followed, quite self-consciously at first. They swam, splashed, and cavorted like otters in the clear water, laughing like delighted children, and it was good. White Fox's cares were cleansed away, like the sweat and accumulated grime from his skin. He completely forgot, for a little while, the ominous reason for his presence here, and he was a child again, enjoying the swim, the day, and a pleasant companion.

Even as they played, she was asking and learning. A small green heron croaked its raucous cry, and she lifted a right hand in the question sign.

"Heron," he answered aloud. "Little green heron."

"Green?" she asked.

"Yes. A color. Like trees, grass."

"Green!"

She laughed, and it was good to see his reaction. She waded from the stream to lie on the sandy strip of beach in the sun. Her companion followed, taking obvious care not to come too close. She realized that he was a bit afraid of her. Well, maybe that was good. After all, she had nearly killed him a few days ago, and he was still her prisoner.

The shadows were lengthening when she rose and picked up her tunic. Fox watched as she gracefully tossed it up and slipped it over her head, settling the garment over her shoulders and hips. She walked upstream a few steps to the riffle and knelt to drink, then started toward the path.

"Come," she gestured.

They returned to the cave, and she made no effort to retie him. There was a new bond between them, though they had not even begun to discuss why he was here. They prepared for sleep. South Wind indicated to him where to spread his robe on the opposite side of the chamber, and they settled for the night.

46

» » »

When South Wind fell asleep that night, she was happier and more confident than at any time since her grandfather's passing. The sheer emotional strength of another person's presence was reassuring. It was like the protective feeling that she had felt when she was small and would take her tears to Grandfather for comfort. Now, it was not the tears of bumps and scrapes and minor disappointments. She had outgrown all that. No, she thought, this was more like the reassurance that Grandfather's presence had provided when her night-terrors had wakened her as a child. Or, maybe, her irrational fear of the dark crevice at the back of the cave.

In the clear light of day, she had always been able to reason that there was nothing there, and she was not afraid, even when she was small. It was only after dark, by the flickering light of the fire, that she would begin to wonder. She would cast quick glances at some half-seen movement in the shadows, and there would be nothing. But the uneasy suspicion would remain. Or she would dream, and waken in terror, to run to Grandfather's bed for safety and comfort. He would hold her and rock gently, and lay a few sticks on the fire. The blaze would bring light to the cave, and everything would be safe and happy again.

In time, she had outgrown the fears, and they had

not returned until Grandfather's mind started to fail. Then it was as if the Dark Thing in the rock had been there all along, held at bay by the two spirits of South Wind and the old man. As Grandfather's spirit weakened, the Dark Thing seemed to grow stronger. Yes, that must be it. It required the force of two spirits to hold the Evil One at bay. The loss of Grandfather had so weakened her defense that it had become a danger. She had been able to avoid it by leaving the cave when the dark presence became too overpowering.

Tonight, though, there would be no need. She had a companion. She had enjoyed, even reveled in, the excitement of learning the word-sounds, and he had enjoyed it, too. She had seen that in the expression of his face, the light in his eyes. He was happy when he was with her.

She began to fantasize. They would stay here, sharing the cave together. They would be happy, and they would never need anyone else. White Fox would be her husband. She was not completely certain what that involved, but her grandfather's stories had implied that usually, a man and a woman live together. Her heart told her that would be good. Maybe White Fox would know more about it. She already had a feeling that it would feel good to be held in the arms of White Fox, as her grandfather used to hold her. No, it would be different. The feeling she perceived when she thought of White Fox was warm and tender and protective, and . . . well, it was *different*. Maybe she could ask him about it.

The fire was dying, and she lay there in the darkness, listening to the deep, regular breathing of the young man. She was too excited to sleep. She longed to waken him to talk some more, but felt it would be inappropriate. At least, she told herself with satisfaction, she would not need to leave the cave tonight to escape the influence of the Thing in the crevice. The combined strength of the two of them could deny it entry, could bar it from the cave.

There had been no thought of tying him tonight.

After the day they had spent together, she could not find it in herself to distrust him. Besides, he had shown no sign that he would be dangerous. None, even, that he wished to leave. That helped with her fantasy about living here forever together. Maybe she should mention that tomorrow.

She regretted, now that she knew him better, that she had left him tied in the cave that first night. That had been a bad thing to do, to leave him helpless with the Thing while she went prowling. It could have been dangerous to him, and she was glad that he was safe. She would not do anything like that again. She only hoped that he would forgive her, and he seemed to have done so. At least, if he held resentment, he probably would not have been so pleasant to talk to.

She finally fell asleep, with a warm comfortable feeling that all was well. There was a companion only an arm's length away, who could be of help in an emergency. It was the most secure that she had felt for many moons. It felt almost as good as sleep-time had when she was a child.

It was perhaps not surprising, then, that after a period of deep sleep, she began to dream, and saw herself as a child. She and Grandfather walked along the stream, and he taught her to hunt and to shoot, and to swim like the beavers. Days were long and happy. She played again on the rocky ledges with her coyote pup, and felt the twinge of sadness when it ran away. She relived the long nights in the Moon of Snows when they stayed in the cave. They wrapped themselves warmly against the onslaught of Cold Maker, and huddled over the tiny fire that must not be allowed to go out. That was a time for Grandfather's stories, and she learned of other people.

She dreamed of the games they played when others came to the Rock, and how she must remain hidden and quiet until they left. All of these were happy dreams.

Then came the one with the old fear. She was still a child in this dream, but alone in the cave. Her grandfather would be back soon, but night was falling. Carefully, she placed a little stick on the coals of the fire, and it blazed up to throw a flickering light around the rough walls. The little girl looked apprehensively toward the dark crevice and shuddered. There had never been anything there when she looked, and there was not now. She looked away, resolved not to look again. But the flicker of the fire made little shadowy movements, which she saw out of the corner of her eye. She would look quickly, and the movement was gone. There was nothing there but the dark crevice.

She looked anxiously to the doorway, hoping to see the tall form of her grandfather against the dull smoke-gray of the twilight sky. There was no indication of his return. What if he *never* returned?

She whimpered softly in her sleep, like a child, and the dream continued. There came a time when her glance at the dark corner *almost* revealed something. A flickering, slithering Thing that moved briefly and was gone, a part of the rough rock of the crevice and the flicker of firelight.

Fascinated, she stared at the crack, like the bird who is stalked by the snake. Horrified, she watched a formless shadow vaporize, spewing from the crevice, like smoke or mist, but dark, dirty brown-black. There was an odor, too, of slime and decay, and a sense of evil that grew, threatening to fill the cave.

The little girl screamed out in terror and scrambled toward the entrance to escape. She ran headlong into the arms of Grandfather as he entered. He rocked and held her tenderly, and she felt secure again. Her sobs began to subside, and Grandfather reached to place a stick on the fire. Flames produced more light, and the cave brightened.

Then she was awake and no longer a child. The man who had placed the stick on the coals, into whose arms she had fled, was not Grandfather, but White Fox. He held her in his arms and rocked back and forth, crooning soft words of comfort. It did not seem to matter. She clung to him as her terror slowly subsided, holding her arms tightly around him, fearing to let go. She felt that if she did, he might disappear, and she would be defenseless again.

She could look over his shoulder and see the back of the cave in the flickering light of the fire. The crevice was once more only a crack in the rock, and there was no horribly evil brown mist from her dream of the past to threaten the little girl. It had been only a dream, as had her night-terrors of childhood. And, as her grandfather had dispelled her fears then, the man in her arms had done so now.

She released him from her embrace, and he did so, too, a little reluctantly it seemed.

"I am sorry," she signed. "A dream . . ."

He nodded sleepily.

"It is over now," he assured her.

Yes, she thought, it is over. Only a false vision in the night. A little embarrassed, she turned to pick up the robe she had flung aside, and spread it to return to sleep.

47

» » »

White Fox awoke next morning with such a mixture of emotions that he doubted he could grasp them all. He had come here on his vision-quest with no suspicion of all that he had now encountered.

Since the first time he saw Medicine Rock as a child and from a distance, he had been intrigued by the place and its legends. The tale of Eagle, who had spent a winter there while a broken leg healed after an accident. Eagle had been thought dead, but was discovered alive and well the following spring. The remarkable part of that story, to young Fox, was the change in Eagle's life. He had become a skilled storyteller and a seer of things of the spirit. It was said that no other could make quite so real the stories of Creation and of the Old Man of the Shadows. "It was as if Eagle had been there," it was always said.

Fox was also deeply impressed with the reputation of Medicine Rock as a place of the spirits. Everyone was a bit afraid of it, and the People took care not to camp too near. There was the additional impact of the incident in which the invading Blue Paints from the north were ambushed and killed in a buffalo stampede. That had taken powerful medicine. It was a cooperative effort by two holy men. One was Wolf's Head, of the Head Splitters, and the other a young man of the People. Looks-Far was his name. He was still alive, though many winters had whitened his hair and slowed his step. He was now the most respected of holy men.

White Fox had grown up in awe of this holy man, a distant relative. He had been a teacher to the youngster and had encouraged him to take his vision-quest to Medicine Rock when Fox inquired about it.

"It is a place of great spirit-power," the old man advised. "Some think it evil, but both good and evil are everywhere. It is how you approach such things. It is a good place to find your spirit-guide."

White Fox had already decided in his own mind, but had a few questions. "What of the spirits of the Blue Paints who died there, Uncle?"

Looks-Far nodded. "They crossed over. I am made to think that the problems we face here are often insignificant when we cross over. People once enemies may be allies, as we and the Head Splitters now are."

"Then you do not think the *place* is evil? The Rock?"

Looks-Far was silent for a moment, and finally spoke.

"My son, you are a deep thinker. Some day . . . but never mind. Now think on this: It is known that the Rock is a place of the spirit, a holy place, no?" He went on without pausing for agreement. "Now, look at the experiences of the People there. There may have been many, but those of which we have the best knowledge are two: that of Eagle, whose spirit was touched long ago, and the thing of the Blue Paints, in which I had a small part. But think on these. Both led to great *good* for the People, did they not?"

White Fox nodded.

"Now," continued the holy man, "what you have really asked is whether some places are evil and some good. This, I do not know. But I am made to think that what happens depends much on the spirits of those who approach such a place."

He paused, a puzzled look on his leathery old face, as if pondering how to explain.

"Some men and women," he said carefully, "are offered a gift of the spirit. Maybe you are one. Now, with this gift, you can do different things. You can refuse it, or merely not use it, which is really the same thing. That is no disgrace, but no blessing either. It is as if it was never offered. But if you accept it, use it, you accept a great responsibility. If you are offered the Gift, and use it for evil, it is very dangerous. If I misused the power of my medicine, it would kill me."

"*Aiee*," murmured White Fox. "How will I know, Uncle?"

"I do not know how, my son. Many are offered the Gift much later than others. I am made to think that Eagle's spirit-gift came later, *after* his accident at the Rock. But, no matter . . . *you will know!*"

So White Fox had set forth in all his innocence to seek his vision. In retrospect, it had worked well. He had found his spirit-guide, though he had been aware of interference and the terror of evil dreams. He did not know yet whether, as Looks-Far seemed to suspect, he would be a recipient of the spirit-gift. He did feel that he had been given a powerful guide.

Some of the confusion of his vision had been accounted for when he discovered the presence of the girl. Now he realized that as his spirit had searched in its quest, it had encountered hers. That, of course, is why one seeks solitude for the quest, to avoid such chance contact. But he now understood, at least a little bit. The spirit he had encountered had been a troubled one, full of fears of evil, a lonely spirit.

At first, after the girl tried to kill him, he was happy to escape with his life, with the help of his guide. Unarmed and without supplies, he had hurried back to the summer camp of the Southern band, thankful for survival.

It was not until after he had broken his fast and

talked with Looks-Far that he began to realize the situation. The young woman at the Rock might be in grave danger. In some strange way he felt a responsibility to her. There was no one at all to help her. The fear in her would grow, the terror of some unseen evil Thing. If it was not real, now, it would become real, for her.

But why should he risk his life to help her, he argued with himself. It should have been no concern of his. Yet it was. He had been greatly impressed, not only by the girl's beauty, but by her strength, her self-reliance, her skills of survival.

He went back to confer with the holy man again, telling him of his thoughts. Looks-Far had questioned him at length and finally nodded.

"What you are called to do, you must do," he agreed. "Listen to your guide, use all your skills, and be careful. Now, before you go, let me teach you some things that may be useful. Chants, some herbs that will help your spirit-contact, increase its power."

He had spent most of a day trying to cram that instruction into his brain, and had set off for the Rock again with many misgivings. He had no illusions. The girl might try to kill him again. . . .

Now, he had experienced an even more remarkable series of events. Instead of the way that he had planned things, he had been captured by the girl. There were times when he had feared for his life. But gradually, they had established communication. He was impressed with her abilities, with her quick mind, and her absorbing interest in learning all that he could tell her.

And, with her beauty. He had never seen a woman nearly so attractive. They were relating to each other so well. . . . It was no surprise, now, that their spirits had made the accidental contact. It was meant to be. His purpose, it now seemed, was to assist her in dealing with the evil Thing in her life. It had affected him profoundly to learn of her fears of the Evil One when she accused him of being associated with it. Not so much the accusation, but the realization that in his spirit-quest, he *had* encountered *her* terror.

Then, the incident in the night, when in the terror of her night-vision she had flown into his arms. She had mistaken him for her grandfather, who was apparently the only other person she had ever known. His heart went out to her. Without him, she would be helpless, he realized. There was no question in his mind that the evil Thing which she perceived to be in the dark crevice at the back of the cave could have grown stronger until it destroyed her. It could, and *would* have, without help. He was glad that he had been called to furnish that help.

There were some problems ahead, to be sure. South Wind had expressed the idea that one person alone could not keep the Evil One at bay in the crevice. It required the spirit-power of two to control it. Well, so be it. There are things impossible to explain. He kept thinking of the statement of Looks-Far. "It does not matter . . . if it is real to *her*, it is real, and dangerous."

He looked across the cave at the sleeping form of South Wind. She looked so innocent, so like a child, her long lashes lying on cheeks that were as smooth as the petals of the roses that still bloomed here and there on the prairie.

His heart went out to her, and he experienced a sense of gratitude that he could help her.

It would not be easy. There would be some danger. He already knew that, from the way he had been affected by his own contact with the terror in the crevice.

But he was confident. He would remain flexible. . . . "Nothing ever happens exactly like you thought it would," Looks-Far had said. Now, if he could remember all the other things that the holy man had taught him. And his biggest task, of course, would be to convince the girl that the two of them could handle anything, together. Only then would she be able to leave the Rock and return to the People.

48

» » »

South Wind sat looking across the valley, as she had done since childhood. Just downstream, the leaves of a giant old cottonwood whispered their soft song of the summer. She could see the deep pool straight below, where the beavers frolicked, and where she had so angered her grandfather long ago with her dive from the ledge.

That had been good, though. It had allowed her to use that same fall in her fight with the intruder. She smiled to herself, that she had once thought of White Fox as an intruder. She had actually tried to kill him!

"Grandfather," she signed to the still form beside her boulder, "there is much to tell you. I wish that you could answer, but . . . maybe you have. There is the young man I told you of, White Fox."

She paused, trying to think how she could explain. There was a tendency to lose her concentration when she thought of Fox. She wondered what he was doing now, back at the cave. He had remained there . . . he seemed to understand that she needed to be alone to talk to Grandfather. She would go back later, and maybe they would swim again, and he would teach her more of the talk-sounds. . . . She shook her head to clear it and returned to her monologue.

"Grandfather, you have taught me that people are bad, and I am sure that is true. But not *all* people.

You and I . . . And, I am made to think that this man, White Fox, is not bad. He came here on a vision-quest, but came back to help me."

She paused again, pondering how to explain.

"Remember, Grandfather, when I was small, how I feared the dark, and the evil Thing in the crevice? You helped me hold it back, so I did not fear it? And then, when you were no longer able, it came back stronger, and it grew. But still we held it back, you and I."

She took a deep breath and continued.

"I hope you will understand how alone I was after you crossed over. The Thing grew, and is still growing, and I had no help to control its evil. Then White Fox came, and I was afraid of him at first. But he knew of my fears and of the evil Thing. I am made to think that he and I can control it. No, can *kill* it. You would like him, Grandfather."

Again she paused.

"I do not care any less for *you*, Grandfather. My heart was heavy when you left, and it is still heavy. I have mourned, but you were part of my life, the only person I ever knew. Now, I am made to feel that here is another who understands. You told me that help would come when I need it."

She was taking much longer with this than she intended, so she hurried on.

"My heart is good for this man, Grandfather, and I wish for yours to be, too. You need not worry for me, now. This is good."

She knew that she would not receive an answer, yet she felt that she may have, in the whisper of the cottonwoods and the call of the quail across the river. She rose, brushed aside a tear, and turned up the path to the cave. She was made to feel that, finally, Grandfather could rest in peace.

Look for the new Don Coldsmith novel, WALKS IN THE SUN, a specially priced Bantam Books Hardcover, in April 1992.

The Spanish Bit Saga continues with WALKS IN THE SUN, the story of an epic journey by a band of the People far to the south—to the Gulf coast of Mexico—where they encounter strange and wonderful spirit animals and a savage tribe of cannibals!

Turn the page for a preview of the new hardcover novel by Spur Award winner Don Coldsmith,

Walks in the Sun

Ask your local bookseller to reserve a copy for you today.

At first, there was nothing out of the ordinary. We were in familiar country, grassland spotted with areas of oak thickets. Good country in which to winter. Blue Jay led us south and a little west. We did not want to go too far west, because winter in the short-grass country is hard, and an early snow could surprise us.

But the weather was good, a fine Second Summer. It was enjoyable, and I thought that it was good, a good way for young men to make their feelings known about the winter camp, yet do no harm, and have some fun, besides.

After about five sleeps, Snake-Road called us to notice that it seemed no later in the season than when we left the band. It was as if time stood still, though the sun had risen and set several times. We talked of this around the fire that night. Someone noted that the moon showed that time *was* going on. It was rising later each night. When we left the band, the moon was just past full. Now, it was only half there, and did not rise until far into the night. So, we asked each other, why does the moon change, but not the sun? It was a great question.

Partly, I knew the answer because I had been watching the plants. Some are the same, of course, as they are here. I was interested because of the plants that are used for my medicine. Those and others. I was noticing that the ripening of some seeds, the falling of some leaves, were just happening in that area, but had done so here before we left the band.

We know, of course, that the winter is milder to the south. That is why we winter there. Why the buffalo migrate, and the geese, and . . . but never mind, you know of these things.

But as we talked around the fire, we began to wonder. We were traveling, it seemed, about as fast as the season. A little faster, maybe. What would happen, someone asked, if one continued to ride south? Would he reach a spot where the season turned to meet him, and started back north? Maybe the buffalo know this, and turn around to start back each season, in midwinter.

"When?" asked another. "In the Moon of Long Nights? The Moon of Snows? That would be stupid."

"But think!" Blue Jay answered him. "In such a place, there would *be* no Moon of Snows." He then turned to me. "What do you think, holy man?"

"I do not know," I told him honestly. "I am made to think that there is a limit somewhere. Of its nature, I cannot say. We have never been sure how far the buffalo go to winter."

"Some winter at home," another man said.

"That is true," said Blue Jay, "but only a few."

"Look," pondered Snake Road, "we know that Cold Maker's lodge is an ice cave far to the north, no?"

"So it is said."

"Then there, it is *always* winter?"

We nodded, wondering what he was getting at.

"Well," he went on, "if there is a place of Never-summer, should there not be another, of *Never-winter*?"

We all looked at each other, and no one had an answer. Cold Maker, of course, is probably only a legend, but is a handy way to think of the far north. I was startled over this. The People have spent so many lifetimes fighting for survival against "Cold Maker" . . . have we made him more than he is? What if we could merely move *where he cannot go*? To the *south*.

True, it would mean leaving the Sacred Hills, but . . . Forgive me, friends . . . the tears try to fill my eyes. You must realize that as we talked so, times were good, we were comfortable, and well fed. A place of Never-winter sounded good to us. We could go back north to *summer* in our Sacred Hills. As someone said, we follow the buffalo, let us follow them farther.

I was uneasy about it. If this was a good thing, surely since Creation somebody would have discovered it. But, at the time, I have to admit, it sounded good, even to me. So good, I am afraid, that I was not listening to my spirit-guide. He would have warned me. . . .

Maybe the thing that was the greatest evil just then was that we encountered a hunting party of Head Splitters. They are our allies, of course, and as soon as we recognized each other it was a day of joy.

"Greetings, our brothers," said their leader, using hand signs as well as our tongue. Some Head Splitters speak our language quite well, you know, but this one was only fair at it.

We camped together, about the same number in our party as in theirs. They had meat, and we all feasted well. We talked of many things. The weather, the hunting, where our Sun Dance would be next year. The Head Splitters sometimes like to attend, you know, because they have no such ceremony of their own. And, that is good.

Then Blue Jay began to ask many questions about their customs. I did not quite understand why for a little while, but then I saw. The Head Splitters range farther to the south and west than we do, and Jay was asking of the southern extent of their area.

"Do you know how far the buffalo go to winter?" he finally asked.

"No," the Head Splitter replied. "Everyone winters somewhere . . . why?"

Blue Jay then explained to him of our observations about the seasons, and that we wondered about a Never-winter place. They nodded.

"It is said that there is such a place," they told us.

"*Aiee*! Where?"

They were vague about that, pointing southward.

"Do your people go there?" asked Blue Jay.

"No, there seems no good reason. It is far, my friends, and there are dangers. . . .

"Enemies?"

"No . . . well, maybe. Caddoes . . . Spanish. We trade with them, sometimes. But the country is hard."

"Harder than the prairie winter?" asked Blue Jay. Everyone laughed.

Now, I was wearing the Elk-dog bit, which was used in the mouth of the First Horse by Heads Off. As you all know, it is one of the most powerful of the medicines of the People. It has been handed down since White Buffalo learned that its circle enables control of the horse. I was made its keeper when I finished my apprenticeship . . . a great honor.

I had had a worrisome choice to make, when I decided to go with Blue Jay. My purpose would be to offer advice and counsel, and to try to foretell trouble or good. I did not really want to risk harm to so powerful an emblem. But it might be that I would need its power. Also, if I left it behind, who would care for it?

In the end, I decided to carry it, to use its power if we needed it. The easiest and safest way is to wear it, so that is what I was doing that night. Suddenly, the leader of the Head Splitters seemed to realize its significance.

"Holy man," he said, "you wear an amulet. Is that the Elk-dog medicine of your people?"

I nodded that it was, and there was a gasp from the Head Splitters. They moved to see better as I held it to let the firelight sparkle from its silver dangles. It is very impressive, of course.

One of the Head Splitters, a thoughtful man who had not said much, now spoke.

"Then this is a *medicine quest*?"

There was another gasp from the Head Splitters, and some of our men swaggered a little, pretending that this was our purpose all along. The Head Splitters began to treat us with even more honor and respect, and it felt good. No one bothered to deny that this was our purpose, even I—I am sorry to say. Maybe this unearned pride was to cause . . . but never mind.

By the end of the evening when we sought our robes, I think most of us had convinced ourselves that it *was* a medicine quest. Surely Blue Jay believed it. From that time on, he seemed to believe that he had been called to lead this important quest. And I must confess, I thought so too, at that time. I was proud to be the advisor to the leader who was chosen for such a quest. I should have cast the bones, or consulted some of my other gifts, but I did not. Pride causes blindness sometimes. . . . Forgive me, my friends. Tears come easily tonight. A moment . . .

Well . . . After we had convinced ourselves that it *was* a medicine quest, and that we were a chosen group, we asked the Head Splitters for more detail about the land to the south. They were happy to tell us. It was grassland, they said, for many sleeps south. All the way, in fact, to a great salty body of water, an ocean. There we would find many strange things to see.

"Is it always summer at this salty water?" I asked.

"Pretty much. So the Caddoes say. They live in grass lodges."

"Aiee! In the winter?" asked someone.

Blue Jay was skeptical. "Have you been there?" he asked. "Any of you?"

The Head Splitters looked from one to the other, and it seemed that no one had been. We all laughed. They had been telling us of things which they did not really know, either. But some things they *did* know.

"Should we go straight south, or southwest?" asked Blue Jay.

They conferred a little in their own tongue, and then gave what we took to be good advice. Head Splitters do know some of that southwest country.

"If you go straight south, you stay mostly in grassland. Southwest, you would get into Spanish territory. A little more south than west takes you to the great canyon, the place of Hard Trees, which the Spanish call Palo Duro."

"Yes. Our people call it the Hole-in-the-Ground. Our holy man found the White Bull there."

"Yes, that is true. You know it, then."

"We know of it," answered Blue Jay. None of us have been there."

"You wish to go? We can tell you the way."

"No," said Blue Jay. "That is not the purpose of our quest."

You see, he had already convinced himself that this was an important medicine quest.

"I am made to think," Jay went on, "that we should go on straight south, to the Salt Water."

Even his followers were surprised, but excited at this prospect. I was, too, I admit it.

"How far? How many sleeps?" we asked the Head Splitters.

They did not really know, but told us anyway, because they wanted to help us.

"Maybe a moon . . . maybe more."

"It is good!" announced Blue Jay, as if it was all he needed. "We can be back with our families by the Moon of Long Nights.

Somehow, that seemed to make sense. It could not really be done that quickly, but we did not know that, then. It is hard to be realistic about the unknown when you are warm and comfortable and your bellies are full and there are pleasant companions. I hope you will understand how it was, my friends, how all of us could be so wrong. *Aiee*, the tears come again. . . .

Next morning, we parted from the pleasant company of our Head Splitter friends. One of them, a very good man named Bear's Head, offered to go with us. He knew the tongue of the Caddoes, and could be of help to us. They used some hand-signs, he said, but not as fluently as those of us from the tallgrass prairie.

Some of our men were a little concerned over

how his name came to be. Bear's Head . . . for a Head Splitter to kill a bear, or eat it, or cut off its head, is good. They eat bears, though the People do not. That is their way, and of no concern to us. But, some disliked the use of the Bear's Head name, so we called him "Caddo-Talker."

No matter . . . We were now twelve as we moved on to the south that day. All of us were convinced that we were taking part in a great quest that would affect the People for many generations.

When we left the Head Splitters and moved on, it was with a great sense of purpose. We had all convinced ourselves that this was a great, important thing that we were doing. As big for the People, perhaps, as the coming of the horse. I have to admit, my friends, that I should have seen the dangers ahead. That was my purpose in being there. But I, too, was caught up in the excitement of the thing. I, too, believed in our quest. It is always easy to look back and say "I should have known" but we did not. In our defense, I would only say that the back trail is always plainer than the one ahead.

Then, too, I was possibly confused as I looked for signs. On the morning that we parted from the Head Splitters, I saw three crows fly to alight on a little ridge to the south of us. *Ah*, I thought, *what better sign.?* The crow's power to assist in listening for the guidance of the spirit is well known. And *three*. It seemed very good. I have wondered much of the meaning of this. Did I somehow misinterpret the sign? It seemed plain enough.

As I look back, I see a possibility or two. One, we were entering strange country. Maybe the signs are different in different places. Maybe in that country the three crows meant something else. In light of later events, this seems very likely. Or, maybe they were just crows, who happened there at that time.

Yet another thing comes to my mind, one that is a constant threat to any holy man. Was I, maybe, seeing in the signs what I *wished* to see? If so, I am guilty of misuse of my gift. But I was swayed by the lofty purpose of the quest. I *was* allowed to survive, so maybe . . . but enough. If we ever think we can understand all the things of the spirit, we have already missed the point. Some things are not meant to be understood.

So, we moved on southward, we twelve, counting Bear's Head, or Caddo-Talker, as our men were now calling him. He was a pleasant companion, and told us much about the land we were crossing.

I had noticed plants of many sorts not known here, and we talked of those as we rode. There were grasses which seemed unlike ours. Where ours are tall and upright in the Sacred Hills, many of these seemed to creep upon the ground like our short buffalo grass, but heavier. Well, you would have to see it to understand. And, though most were now dry for the winter, it was plain that there were more hot-season grasses. The bushes, too, in brushy areas, were of types I had never seen. Many wore thorns. There has long been a saying among the People that in the desert, everything that grows carries a weapon. This was not desert, but a kind of dry grassland unfamiliar to us. More cactus, of several sorts. The fruit of one which Caddo-Talker pointed out, he said was used as food. We did not know whether to believe him. There were times later when we would have welcomed a chance to try it.

In low places, where there may have been more moisture in the ground, there were heavy thickets of a sort of reed or giant stemmy grass, which grew maybe twice as tall as a man on a horse. Caddo-Talker said we should avoid these places, because giant real-snakes make their lodges there. He was right, too. We saw one sleeping in the sun that must have been longer than a man is tall. I rode nearer to get a better look. It was fatter in the middle than my arm here above the elbow, and carried eleven or twelve rattles at its tail. My horse was alarmed, and I decided that she was right. I moved away. That real-snake seemed very dangerous at the time, but later we would have been happy to be faced with problems no greater. Real-snakes, we could understand.

We saw another creature at about that time . . . forgive me for telling in such detail. This is my function, my gift, to know the plants and animals. And it *is* important to the story.

This one was about the size of a possum. It looked like a possum, in fact, and acted like one. It was digging in an ant-lodge just at dusk, near our camp. It let us come quite near, though we were cautious. Now hear this: this creature wore a bony shell, like a turtle. Not exactly . . . well, you know how the turtle's lower shell is jointed, so that he can go inside and close the door? Yes, this little animal's shell was jointed all over. When it became alarmed, it pulled in head, tail, and feet, and rolled itself into a hard round ball. Yes, it is true! We rolled it around a little to examine it.

Caddo-Talker said that some of the people eat these animals, but we let it go. He also said that the Spanish with whom they sometimes trade have a name for it, *armadillo,* which means a little armored one. It is a good name . . . it is much like a possum wearing Spanish armor. I see smiles . . . no, it is *true!*

Now, why do I tell you of this? Because later, I wondered if this was a sign that I had overlooked. I do not know, but surely there was a hint there that we should keep our defenses ready. We interpreted it so.

By this time we had encountered villages of Caddoes, and other people who were growers. These people live in grass lodges, made of poles with grass tied on them. Yes, in winter, too. They are not round like the lodges of the Wichitas, which we have seen. These are square. Sometimes there is a big long meeting-lodge . . . well, like the Mandans' meeting lodge, but grass. We wondered about the danger of fire, and they said yes, sometimes it happens. This seems not to worry them much.

We were fortunate enough to find a small band of

buffalo near one of these towns, and we killed a couple of them for fresh meat. What we did not need, we gave to the growers, which pleased them greatly. That was a fortunate thing all around, because they treated us well, and gave us beans and corn to carry with us. More importantly, word went ahead of us that we were friendly and could hunt buffalo well. All through the country of the Caddoes, we were welcomed. This helped us to trade for supplies, and was so successful that it seemed that the sun was shining on our quest.

We pushed on, going almost straight south, a little west. Each time we needed it, there was game. Each time we were in an area where water seemed scarce, it would rain a little. These rains seemed to come from the northwest, as they do at home during this season. But at home, as someone noted, these would be bringing sleet or snow by this time. This made us feel that our quest was good.

One night we were camped in oak thicket, a pleasant place not near a village, and our watchers heard and saw a small band of animals approaching in the moonlight. They made strange snorting noises, but were the size of dogs or maybe small deer. The horses seemed alarmed at the strange scent, and one of the scouts smelled them, too. He was afraid, because he thought maybe these creatures acted and smelled like bears.

They woke Caddo-Talker, who knew quickly what they were. Not bears, and good to eat, he said. They were probably coming to eat the acorns under the trees where we were. Quietly, they woke the rest.

These were strange creatures . . . we killed two with arrows and the rest ran away. I must tell a little more of them, though. They were animals with legs and hooves like a deer, but short-necked like bears. Instead of fur they were covered with short bristles. On the back of each one, above the tail, was a musk-smelling opening like a navel on the wrong side. We laughed. The creatures were dangerous though. As they scattered when we began to shoot, Dog's Leg had the misfortune to get in front of one. It gashed the calf of his leg deeply with its tusks as it passed him.

Caddo-Talker called them *pecari*, which is a name that some of the local tribes use for this creature. And, as he said, the meat was very good. He said that the *pecari* seemed much like an animal that the Spanish raise for food.

We took all this to be a good sign, in spite of Dog-Leg's injury. It was clean, and healed well. It seemed no more than the accidents of any hunt.

Not quite so easy to dismiss was a thing that happened a few days later. We had come to a river, which had low and swampy areas along its banks at some places. Even so, it was pleasant. There were groves of fine nut trees along its course, the day was sunny, and our hearts were good about our quest. We had noticed that many trees . . . some were oaks of kinds unknown to us . . . many had leaves that were still green. At home, it must by now be nearing the Moon of Long Nights. So, we thought that this was all favorable.

There was a village near by, of a hunter nation who used hand-signs well. They often wintered here, they said. The river was filled with clams, of an excellent size and type for eating, and they use them in part for their winter food. We tried some of the clams, and found them good. Many times later we would have welcomed such food.

These people, who used the hand-sign for "snake" to describe themselves, were friendly enough. We did not mention our quest for a Never-Winter-Place to them. We thought that they would fear our entry into their territory. So, we assured them that we were only passing through.

But the trouble, there. . . . Lean Antelope was wading in the stream when a snake struck him. He had seen it, he said, but thought nothing of it. It was black, and had no rattles, and he ignored it, thinking that it was of the harmless sort we see at home. Even when it struck him, a glancing blow with one fang, he was not concerned. But the pain was unexpectedly severe, and he looked down at his leg. There was the wound, a hole oozing purplish blood. The skin around it was turning blue and swelling. Antelope staggered up the bank and fell.

It was fortunate that we were with the snake-people, because they knew what to do. Their holy man quickly made a gash across the wound and sucked it clean, much as some do for the bite of the real-snake. And, the bite *is* much the same, their holy man told me. He bandaged it with a poultice. Even so, Antelope hovered near death for three days, while the swelling crept up his leg. It nearly reached his groin, which I thought would be fatal, but then the poultice and the chants and dances, my own and those of the other holy man, suddenly worked, and the swelling began to go down.

Maybe this should have been a warning, too, but we saw it only as a sign for caution. And, we had learned to fear and respect this snake that was new to us, as dangerous as the real-snake. More, maybe, because he gives no warning.

Our friends who helped Antelope called this snake the "cotton-mouth" because of his white jaws.

MAGNIFICENT FRONTIER ADVENTURES
FROM KERRY NEWCOMB

IN THE SEASON OF THE SUN

❏ 28332-4 $4.50/$5.50 in Canada.

Brothers Jacob and Tom Milam were separated when outlaws ambushed their wagon and murdered their parents. Jacob would become a warrior of great courage among the Blackfeet people. Tom was tricked into riding with the outlaws, growing up bad and wild. But the season was coming when the two would find each other again and the days of battle and vengeance would begin.

SCALPDANCERS

❏ 28560-2 $4.50/$5.50 in Canada

Drawn together by destiny, a courageous shaman-warrior and a boisterous sea captain battle side-by-side against a ruthless pirate and his crew. But only Lone Walker's magic—and Morgan Penmerry's bravado—stand between the evil shaman White Buffalo and the destruction of Lone Walker's people.

SACRED IS THE WIND

❏ 25183-X $4.99/$5.99 in Canada

Feared by his enemies, betrayed by his brothers, Panther Burn sct off on an epic journey to save his people and to shape a new future. His name, his deeds, and his courage would become a legend in the sacred songs...and whispered in the wind.

MORNING STAR

❏ 24149-4 $4.99/$5.99 in Canada

A magnificent saga of a white man in a Cheyenne world, forging a place of courage, honor, and blood. Joel Ryan was driven from his Kentucky farm and rode west in search of a new home and a new life. After finding peace and love among the Cheyenne, an old enemy brings betrayal and tragedy, sending Joel on a 12-year quest in search of justice.

Available at your local bookstore or use this page to order.

Send to: Bantam Books, Dept. DO 24
    2451 S. Wolf Road
    Des Plaines, IL 60018

Please send me the items I have checked above. I am enclosing $_____ (please add $2.50 to cover postage and handling). Send check or money order, no cash or C.O.D.'s, please.

Mr./Ms._____

Address_____

City/State_____Zip_____

Please allow four to six weeks for delivery.

Prices and availability subject to change without notice.   DO 24 10/92